ONE. NEVER ABANDON THE PLANET WE WERE BLESSED WITH, NO MATTER HOW MUCH OUR DISREGARD FOR MOTHER NATURE HAS LED TO HER PUNISHING US. WE DESERVE TO BE PUNISHED, GIVEN HOW WE HAVE TORTURED HER. NOW IT'S TIME WE GAVE BACK, NOURISHED THE HOME THAT WE HAVE RUINED. FIND NEW WAYS, REAL WAYS, TO LIVE ON PLANET EARTH. TWO. NEVER GIVE IN TO TECHNOLOGY, NO MATTER HOW MUCH EASIER IT MAY MAKE THINGS, NO MATTER HOW MUCH BETTER LIFE MAY SEEM "LOGGED IN". LOG IN AND YOU LOSE EVERYTHING. YOU LOSE WHAT EVERY HUMAN BEING IN THE HISTORY OF THIS PLANET HAS EVER FOUGHT FOR, OR CARED ABOUT. THREE. BE RESOURCEFUL, BE CREATIVE, BE IMAGINATIVE. KEEP THE HUMAN SPIRIT THRIVING.

KID

PICCADILLY CIRCUS DEPOT

LIBRARY OF THE CELL
Offliner headquarters

Date Due	Borrower's name
18/03/2021	Sebastian de Souza

SHARE THIS BOOK AND HELP SAVE THE WORLD

#OFFLINER

FROM FUTURE,
NEED HELP...

KID

A HISTORY OF THE FUTURE

SEBASTIAN DE SOUZA

Offliner Press Publishing, London

First published in Great Britain in January 2020 by Offliner LLP

This paperback first edition published in March 2021

www.offlinerpress.com

Offliner Universe is a registered trademark of Offliner LLP

Text © Offliner LLP 2021

Editing and additional story development by John Garth

Design by Hugo Alexander Riley & Beige

Typeset by Hugo Alexander Riley

Illustrations by Bannister

ISBN 978-1-8383894-0-6

Printed and bound in Great Britain by Clays Ltd, Elcograf S.p.A

To be kept up to date about our authors and books, please visit www.offlinerpress.com and sign up for our newsletter

For Mum and Dad

and

For Milica Kastner, whose astonishing bravery and unstoppable
sense of humour in the face of seemingly insurmountable obstacles
inspires me every single day

CENTRAL LONDON
2078

TO HAB-BELT (15km)

KENTISH TOWN

68 REGENT'S PARK Rd

PRIMROSE HILL

THE LOCK

MAP AREA   BURBS

HAB BELT

SPECTA COUNTRY

OLD ZOO

REGENT'S PARK

SPECTA COUNTRY

TO HAB-BELT (22km)

EUSTON Rd

TO THE CITY (Old financial district)

MARYLEBONE Rd

SPECTA COUNTRY

BRITISH MUSEUM (ruins)

SPECTA COUNTRY

THE SOHO GHETTO

COVENT GARDEN

HYDE PARK

SPECTA COUNTRY

THE CIRCUS

GREEN PARK

St JAMES'S PARK

TRAFALGAR SQUARE

SOUTH BANK

\\\ MARSHES

OFFLINER CELL

TOASTER (FLOOD BARRIER)

PODD WAY

PODD STATIONS

BUCKINGHAM PALACE (ruins)

WESTMINSTER INTERNATIONAL INSTITUTE OF TECHNOLOGY

THAMES

0   ½   1   1½   2

KM

SPECTA COUNTRY

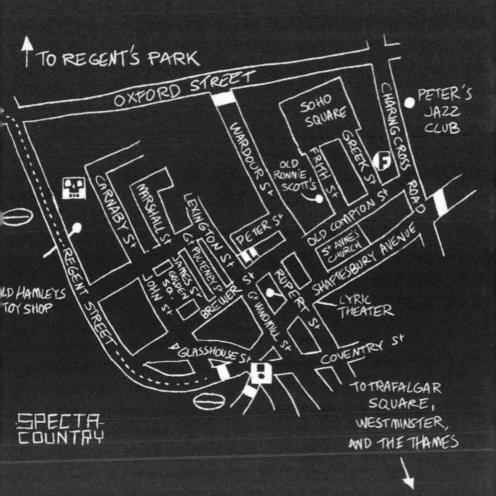

SOHO 2078

OFFLINER TERRITORY

↑ TO REGENT'S PARK

OXFORD STREET

SOHO SQUARE

PETER'S JAZZ CLUB

CHARING CROSS ROAD

WARDOUR St

GREEK St

OLD RONNIE SCOTT'S

FRITH St

F

CARNABY St

MARSHALL St

LEXINGTON St

OLD COMPTON St

PETER St

G* PULTENEY St

JAMES St

GOLDEN SQ.

St ANNE'S CHURCH

SHAFTESBURY AVENUE

REGENT STREET

JOHN St

BREWER St

G* WINDMILL St

RUPERT St

LYRIC THEATER

OLD HAMLEY'S TOY SHOP

GLASSHOUSE St

COVENTRY St

SPECTA COUNTRY

TO TRAFALGAR SQUARE, WESTMINSTER, AND THE THAMES

↓

----- PODD WAY

⬭ DOCKING STATIONS (PODD)

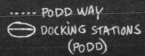 PICCADILLY CIRCUS OFFLINER CELL

Ⅱ THE BUS WALL

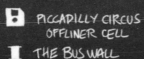 LUCIEN LOFFABOND'S

SKULL'S MISCELLANY

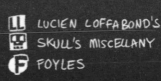 F FOYLES

PROLOGUE

It was the weirdest, scariest feeling I've ever had, it was like time was stuck and nothing was moving. We just stared at each other. Like we . . . I dunno, it sounds stupid

Say it

It felt like I could see inside his head, and he knew it.

This is ridiculous. I mean, it's amazing, after everything but I'm just kinda mind blown. How could it feel like . . . that?

All I could see was him staring at me, but at the same time I could see this whole mess of things swirling about, you know, like a collider scope.

LOL! You mean a kaleidoscope? Thought I was bad at spelling!

Haha, fair enough. But do you wanna hear or not?

Sorry.

I saw these images swirling like they were in my own head but I could tell they weren't. And they were obviously things he'd seen, like himself in the mirror. I could even see me standing there as he saw me right then.

OMG

And he wasn't saying anything but I could hear him wanting to know who I was and how I could read his mind without a Plug. He was intense, like I had something he'd wanted all his life. And there was something else, too, that's been bugging me more and more since . . . I mean we don't, can't, know each other, but there was some kind of unspoken recognition. I saw it, so clearly. I don't know how to explain it, not properly. He terrified me, of course, but it was like he was just, I dunno, so familiar for some reason. I mean beyond the obvious reason that he's insanely famous. Does that sound stupid?

Completely insane TBH. Soz.

To be honest, I didn't have any time to think about any of it. Next it was just this nightmare of guns and explosions, and I guess it's only luck that I didn't end up dead.

Dead on the floor of the Houses of Parliament!

What USED to be Parliament before Gnosys took over. At least it's still standing, I suppose. I can't get it out of my head

wot?

all the devastation we saw when we flew away along the Thames. It actually felt worse than the fact that we were being chased and shot at. Looked like half of south London was under water. Ruined buildings sticking up out of a big black swamp. And the river looked terrifying. Just foaming churning angry water. Like it would only take another spring flood for it to swallow up the rest.

You there?

ye, ye. I'm here. Jus hard to reli imagine things will ever get so bad, TBH, when you talk about London. Predictions about the future don't bring it home like actually hearing from the future. I'm reli sorry. I mean, it's my generation – I guess we could have done more.

Anyway, I got away. Good luck and good friends.

Ha! That bunch of juvenile delinquents!

They're great. And they said they'd be there for me if I ever needed them again. It's completely crazy, you know, that they turned up like they did. Would've been toast without them. As soon as they vanished into the Wall I felt like falling over, TBH, it was all so heavy.

Not surprised . . . You saw all that destruction AND you nearly got killed! In one night you met Rosie and Hamilton and had the Teeth chasing you. AND GOT AWAY WITH IT . . .

Wait? Actually, did you get away with it?

PART

ONE

CHAPTER 1

CHAMPAGNE SUPERNOVA

I'm definitely coming up. They must be too. The CD in my Walkman skips a little before finding itself again. Liam Gallagher singing about a champagne supernova and being caught beneath a landslide . . . The Roxi hits just in time for the chorus. Timed to perfection. I look to the others on either side of me, our jackets tagged up with badges and other miscellaneous tat we've found in the Ghetto over the years; each of our pairs of jeans more shredded than the next; me with my red scarf flying. Walking all in a line, bopping our heads, jamming to Oasis. I'd love to know how many people listen to Oasis these days, let alone Britpop, let alone music. The smile leaves my face.

We're out of place. Weird. Just how we like it. Well, we would look weird, if there was anyone else around to see us.

Everything's changing colour, my legs are getting lighter. It's what happens when you take more Roxi than you're supposed to. More than one pellet of this stuff will get you high as a kite. I do a 360; the Circus is empty this morning, from the Wall to the desolate streets running away south and east. Not unusual, but always disappointing.

Eliza's eyes have gone from their usual bright green to a kind of metallic grey and her pupils are dilated. Pascale just won't stop smiling and, yeah, there it is again – his famous bear hug.

Jeeeeeeeeesus. I'm high as a kite. It never fails to amaze me how, if you take a tiny bit more than you should and pair it with a great song, you can totally change the way things look. Change the world. If only it was that simple, I think.

It's a bright day, not sunny, but that's no surprise as it's hardly ever been blue in my lifetime. It's an ugly shade of brown, but a bright brown, an aching kind of brown that hurts your eyes if you look up for too long. I guess the sun is throbbing away somewhere behind the soot and the ash and the mud, but I can't see it. That's where the Roxi comes in. Take just a pinch more than you should and the seemingly impossible happens – it makes the rubble and dust turn back into the jostling crowds of buildings they once were, and all the ghosts of the Ghetto suddenly seem to come alive once more. It's like going back in time, especially with the music blaring in your ears. The statue, holding its bow and jauntily standing on one foot with its wings spread, must be just about the only thing in Piccadilly Circus that looks the same as it did before the Flood. But right now I feel like I'm walking through London during the Golden Dusk, the time when people walked these streets freely, when people lived in the real world. Before the Upload when everyone cocooned themselves in haptic rigs, logged in, and the world went silent.

Scavving like this – the Walkmans, the uniform, the squad – means we can turn a totally lousy situation into a kind of game. Everyone in the Cell knows when Eliza, Pas and I are on duty – when it's our turn to bring home the bacon – because we make an event of it. The others must think we're such arseholes as we snake round the statue of Anteros, on our way up into Soho, Pascale dancing like an idiot, Eliza tripping like she's a fairy.

It's been like this since the first time we were sent out into the Circus on scavenger duty. Aged twelve. Six years on, we're still a unit, a squad, the Scav Squad. It's the name of our band too. Pas on drums, Eliza on guitar, me on keys and vocals. I love music, we all love music. I write the songs and the three of us jam together in my dorm room. My mum left me some manuscript paper to write the songs down. I've got an upright acoustic piano, a Kawai, which I scavved years ago from Ronnie Scott's, an old jazz club on Frith Street. My prized possession. It's suffered a lot – cigarette burns on the keys, pale circles bitten in the polish by the bottoms of whisky glasses, a few bashes from when we hauled it down here. I often wonder how long it had been there at the club, and who used to play it, back in the Dusk. Sitting at those keys and singing my songs with my best friends, I'm happy. I can forget.

Scavving is a dangerous job and scavvers come and go. We don't. We started earlier than most and we're the only ones who've stuck with it more than a couple of years. I suppose not having any parents is part of it – no one to cry when you run out of Roxi and end up dead in soWme alley.

We pretty much wear the same clothes every day. I don't own a second pair of jeans and I've never gone a day without wearing my Harrington jacket, blue canvas with tartan lining. It belonged to my mum when she was my age – luckily she was tall and I'm pretty skinny. She was wearing it when she met my dad; at least I think that's how the story goes.

All us youngers are expected to scav – running errands, finding food and other supplies. We congregate in my dorm beforehand with our Walkmans and our Roxi disps, just before Mungo comes doing rounds, so we have some time to prepare. First we pick a song from my record collection. I say 'record' but really what I mean is CD. I've searched and searched for vinyl but I'm pretty sure actual LPs were considered prehistoric in the early 2000s, so by the time the Flood came around and the Upload happened, they must have all gone. Disappeared into thin air, along with the rest of everything that was beautiful about the Golden Dusk.

I mean, I know CDs were pretty much over by the end of the Dusk, and everyone just streamed music on their phones, but now Streeming is strictly for Spectas.

Actually we're not supposed to have anything digital in the Cell – we'd be evicted as soon as you could say iPhone. But we begged and begged and the elders said CDs were just about okay. No link with the Gnosys world, see? So we jam with CDs, and I kind of dig it. I like holding the music in my hand, having an actual, real thing in my hand. That's rare these days – experiencing something real. We scav all our discs from what was once Foyle's on Charing Cross Road, where a few racks of CDs gather dust among the shelves of rotting books.

Once the three of us have agreed on a song – never an easy task – we load the CDs into our Walkies. Then it's time to get our Roxi disps out and do the deed.

Roxi – Retinal Oxygenating Xanthic Isopentyl if you want to be a geek about it – is a gas. Inhale it and it helps you breathe when you're up above. It temporarily coats your lungs and throat in this protective chemical film that stops them getting clogged up with all the shit that's in the air. It comes in black pellets which you load into blue plastic dispensers. We're told that London is one of the most polluted cities in the world, and it definitely feels like it when you get back down into the Cell after scavving too long. One pellet equals roughly one hour. Any longer and your spit looks like liquid tar and you nearly cough your lungs out of your chest. Nobody gives a shit about pollution now though. Why would they, when most of the world lives in hermetically sealed boxes?

We're between the devil and the deep blue sea, I always think to myself. Log in and live forever without any freedom whilst your brain turns to mush, or become one of us and almost certainly die from breathing in the poisonous atmosphere, but live out your days in the real world.

It's how my mum died – from the bad air – when I was eight years old. When we first started living in the Cell she went back to her old job as a singer in an underground music hall in Soho. It was all she could get. Even back then, in the early days of the Upload, no one was employing Offliners.

Everyone told her not to – that she was asking for trouble – but I guess coming from where we came from, from the life we had before, she couldn't bear it without some money to buy nice things now and again. When she managed to get peppermint tea, her own special treat, she'd hoard it in a tin and have about one cup a month. By 'nice' I'm talking like bread and pasta, or cocoa to make chocolate water, which is still, to this day, the sweetest thing that's ever passed my lips. Those are our luxuries today.

When they found the tumour it was the size of a tennis ball and getting worse every day. Yottam Yellowfinch, our doctor in the Cell, gave her two weeks to live. She saw the month out – it was May – but was gone by the summer, which was her favourite season like it is mine. After she died, I asked Yottam whether anything could have been done to save her.

'She loved you enough to kill herself for you to be happy. That's what counts.' I think it was kind of a harsh thing to say to an eight-year-old. I thought it was my fault. But once I started leaving the Cell on scav, I figured it all out pretty quick.

The production and supply of Roxi is controlled and

rationed by the UN, in conjunction with Gnosys, the megacorp that provides Perspecta, the virtual reality in which most people now exist. We Offliners are only entitled to two Roxi pellets per week, maximum. I'm sure they'd much sooner give us no Roxi whatsoever and just let us suffocate. But the UN couldn't be seen to publically condone genocide, could they?

There is a black market in Roxi, of course, but it's a murderous business. Roxi runners are notoriously untrustworthy, and notoriously prone to ending up dead in some old dumpster. Gnosys hates them and everyone else envies them. So we can never be sure of our supply.

After my mum died, Ursula Stillspeare brought me a huge box full of pellets. She said Mum had never used them and so now they belonged to me. That's when I got it; that's when I understood what she had done.

Every time she had left the Cell, whether on scav or to go and earn a bit of spare cash at Peter's, she had gone out naked, unprotected. Instead of taking the meds, she'd been saving them up for me. She always said she wanted me to see more of the world, to go up above and experience it. I suppose she thought she'd just take the chance – *Hey, what's the worst that could happen?* Well, Mum, what happened was I lost you but gained a lifetime's supply of . . . perspective.

I use the drug just as she intended – to allow me (and my two best friends) the freedom to be up in the world as much as possible . . . having as much fun as possible.

Here's to you, Mum. Here's to the Champagne Supernova.

CHAPTER 2

COMMERCIAL BREAK

'Go On Baby, Dream Baby, All You Gotta Do is STREEM Baaaaaaby!' A holo-pop materializes out of nowhere as we get to the corner of Shaftesbury Avenue. Its bright colours and smooth lines look amazingly out of place against the backdrop of crumbling, abandoned Victorian theatres.

Streem is Gnosys's content service. Just another way they kill your brain: millions and millions of hours of on-demand 'entertainment' spoon-fed directly to you, wherever you are, whatever you're doing. As long as you're logged into Perspecta.

The pop scares the living bejesus out of all of us. I jump to get out of its way and immediately feel like an idiot.

'Ahahaha! All good baby! Smoke and mirrors!' Pascale clocks my surprise and runs straight through the midriff of the holographic human being. They're sent by Gnosys to bug the hell out of us, to taunt us. I mean, who do they think they're advertising to? No one in Soho's logging into Perspecta. That's the whole point of the Ghetto. That's why we're called Offliners. That's the whole reason we're here.

No, they're not selling at all. It's a control thing. A domination thing. A *we're here and we're in charge and you better not forget it* thing. Honestly, except for the pops and the billboards and the occasional Tooth patrol, it would be easy to forget there ever was an Upload. Well, except for that and the interminable poverty, hunger and desolation.

'Thanks mate, but you make me want to SCREEEEEEM!' Eliza takes it the worst out of all of us. She would. She whips her headphones off and shrieks in the face of the hologram. The pop must have read her vitals first and targeted her. 'Seriously?' She looks from Pas and I to the perfectly chiseled, blue-eyed, blond-haired hunk that some idiotic algorithm has decided is her type. 'This is my guy? This is who they think I am? Give me a break!' She spits in the face of the pop, unimpressed. The gob flies straight through it, just missing Pas's feet.

'You know it's not real, right?' I taunt Eliza.

'Oh shit, no way, it's not real? I had no idea. Thanks

man.' She walks on. 'Wait.' She spins back around. 'Did you just move to get out of the way of a hologram? Pas, I'm not dreaming, right?' Kid just moved out its way! Hahaha! Kid's scared of the holo-pop!' A sarcastic grin replaces her usual furrowed brow.

The holographic Aryan follows us up the street gormlessly for a few hundred metres, until we walk out of range of its sensor and it disappears.

'Shame you two didn't get along.' I put my arm around my best friend. 'I reckon you were a perfect match.' She searches for a comeback. She doesn't have to look far for ammunition.

Up ahead, floating in mid-air and the size of a giantess, is another hologram. Rosie Rogers.

'Psssst! Psssssst! Pas!' Eliza says in a loud whisper. 'Don't tell Kid, but look. It's . . .'

'Ah shit. C'mon Lizy, don't!' Pas joins in. 'Look at the guy . . . He's dying inside.'

They look over at me, pouting like idiots. They're a double act.

'She's a beauty. That's for sure!' says Eliza.

They look up at the girl for a moment – just hanging there, smiling down at us. Then they run off down Great Windmill Street giggling.

'Catch you later, Romeo!' As she scampers off, Eliza makes an 'L' with her finger and thumb on her forehead and sticks out her tongue.

'We'll be at Lucien's when you're done jerking off!' says Pascale.

Fine. I don't care. I turn around, stand there and stare – it's the same every time she appears.

Some things are better said in song than in conversation. Put even the simplest words to music and they always seem to mean something more than they did without a tune. But when it comes to describing this girl, I'm lost for words.

Rosie Rogers isn't beautiful; she's bewitching. Her eyes don't glow; they're incandescent. I can't remember a time I wasn't in love with her. It's in my stomach. Butterflies. Passion. Adrenaline . . . Love, right?

'I believe in my future. I believe my future lives in Perspecta. I believe in its possibilities and its adventures; in its wonders and excitements,' she says, her voice somewhere between husky and honeyed.

Here we go . . . Once the algorithm's worked out who I am – age, height, gender, heartbeat, *heartache* – Rosie's hologram begins selling me Gnosys's next product.

'I'd rather you just kissed me,' I whisper back.

'But there will always be people who wish for you to fail; who are jealous of your future; who would rather see you come to nothing. Like all those who claim our incredible innovations have reached a dead end. And like all those outside of our perfect Perspecta Universe.

'My father is all too aware of this. He wants to protect my Perspecta future. He wants to make sure that, after he's gone, I continue to thrive and so does every other young person in our Universe. That's why Gnosys Technologies has spent so many years perfecting Perspecta Three, the most revolutionary hardware ever. With Perspecta Three, you will never need to leave the Perspecta Universe again. With Perspecta Three, your future will be in safe hands –

wherever you are, whatever you're doing. So do it. Pre-order the new Perspecta – protect the future. I know I will.'

PERSPECTA 3.0®
GNOSYS TECHNOLOGIES INC.

The most revolutionary hardware in history
COMING SOON

Butterflies. Passion. Adrenaline . . . Love. And then she had to go and open her mouth.

Even if she wasn't the most famous girl in the world and even if it wasn't the most unlikely thing ever that we would meet, and even if she wasn't completely and utterly out of my league, Rosie Rogers also happens to be the daughter of Hamilton Rogers.

To call him Offliners' Enemy No. 1 is putting it nicely. He's the CEO of Gnosys, responsible for a virtual reality that is now virtually the only reality. Except for us: the people not logged in, living in the real world, underground, off the grid, in abject squalor.

In fact there's a whole dynasty: Rosie, Hamilton, and Hamilton's mother, Sylvia – the founder of Gnosys itself, without whom none of this could have happened. Gnosys would have you believe she was a saint, a visionary. *When civilization was going down the pan, my grandmother Sylvia Rogers pioneered the path to a better tomorrow.* That's the official line, the line I hear from Rosie's hologram lips. It's always followed by *God rest her soul,* because Sylvia is long gone, presumed dead. Offliners don't miss her. If Offliners had an official pantheon of the damned, Sylvia, Hamilton and Rosie would be its unholy trinity.

They say bad luck always comes in threes. In 2060, it went a bit like this . . .

One. Worldwide environmental disasters, like the Flood which made the centre of London unsalvageable and uninhabitable, combined in a toxic brew with soaring cyberterrorism.

Two. The Pittsburgh Pact, when the UN agreed to pay Gnosys to log billions of people in all 193 member states into Perspecta. The British and American Governments, the European Union and the Asian Federation enacted a law decreeing that all banking, communication, voting and other such essential parts of being a citizen could only be done via Perspecta.

Three. Last, but by no means least, the start of the Upload, which went on during the first four years of my life, when I was too young to know it. People swarmed out of the major cities into suburbs, into the interlinked Hab-Belts built by Gnosys, each tiny home not much more than a box. There, in their haptic rigs they now exist constantly in the Perspecta Universe, vacuum-packed away from viruses, safe from the killer air outside. They dress in white shell suits, and we call them Spectas.

And that monumental mess was, in large part, down to one man. Hamilton Rogers. The Pact is what triggered the Upload, which is what gave rise to the Offliner Movement. So this doesn't exactly make Rosie the ideal prospect for a young Offliner like me.

Problem is, she's become the face of the whole company. Rosie is Perspecta's golden girl. She's impossible for mere mortals like me to ignore. I watch her promoting the latest incarnation of Perspecta. *The most revolutionary hardware ever?* I think. *How often have we heard that one before?!* Her blonde hair shimmers in the artificial sunlight, her piercing eyes make mine water, her smile seems to give me a minor cardiac arrest. Every single time you see her you feel like your body temperature's rising by a thousand degrees, like you could run five marathons just to hear her say your name.

CHAPTER 3

THE MOGUL

As if, you loser. The rational side of my brain takes over. I snap out of my romantic daydream, turn my back on Rosie and cut a left up Great Windmill Street. I start running, conscious of the time. The others will have already got to Lucien's by now. *Sorry Rosie, love, you're just going to have to wait.*

On the corner of Lexington Street and Brewer Street, Lucien has his showroom – a huge, disused multistorey car park. I see a group of men and women huddled around an open fire. As I pass by, my head down, they turn their thin, haunting faces away from the flames and watch me suspiciously. Because of the perpetual pall there's so little light that even during the day, the amber glow of the fire casts dancing shadows across their faces. It gives me the creeps.

We call these people Seekers. I guess it's the fact they're always looking for somewhere to call home, or a group of people they can call their own, without ever really finding either. When the Upload happened they either weren't registered as taxpaying citizens with addresses and birth certificates and all that stuff, or they just couldn't care less. They're the only people in the Ghetto that have always been here, since before the Upload. The invisible people. In the Golden Dusk people called them tramps. Funny thing is, a lot of the time it's the invisible people that are the most useful to know. But what's even more useful is to know someone who knows everyone, whether they're invisible or not – like Lucien Loffabond.

Soho's king, queen and court jester all rolled into one, he runs the last bar in London, maybe the last bar in the world – Muriel's. Climbing the car park stairs to get to Lucien's showroom, you always pass the entrance to Muriel's. The soundproofing must be something else, because even though you can't hear the music at all, sometimes you can feel the bass throbbing underfoot. On my way up, I always stop and press my hands to the wall, craving the feeling of the vibration running up my arms, making my heart thump with longing. Today's no different.

There's no one around these days called Muriel; it's

named after the woman who ran Soho's most notorious drinking hole back in the Dusk. How Lucien got the place is a tale worth telling – and also how he twisted Hecate Horrocks's arm to keep Gnosys off his back. But that's for another day.

We reckon there are three kinds of people that frequent Muriel's: rogue Spectas looking to make a black buck; Seekers who've somehow struck it lucky and come to waste their winnings and themselves; and finally the rarer oddballs. From all the hidden corners of the Ghetto, every secret cellar or attic or lift-shaft apartment, these people come to Muriel's – if they've got the readies and are ripe for danger, that is. They're exhibitionists who need a crowd to wow, or loners who want a crowd to hide in. So many stories are told about the place that some of the regulars – people we've never actually seen – have the aura of legend: Quentin the Scribbler; Porcupine Pete, so prickly that no one's ever spoken to him twice and lived; the mysterious Bus Conductor . . . Even Alberto the barman is the stuff of Ghetto myth – said to knock back more booze daily than all the punters put together. But no Offliner is supposed to go through that red iron doorway, and for us youngers Muriel's is strictly *verboten*.

What matters for the Scav Squad is that Lucien is the biggest black-market trader in the Ghetto. The Mogul of Marshall Street, he calls himself, or a string of other names that trip off his tongue when he's got the verbals. Whatever you want, he can get. Rather than scouring the whole Ghetto for scraps of food, or materials for building and making things, we go to Lucien. For a price or a favour, he hooks us up.

The Walkmans were given to us 'for services rendered'. We ran errands all over town for the slimy, carrot-haired wheeler-dealer. Sometimes he'd make us head into the dreary, dangerous borderlands beyond the Ghetto – even into the ruin-filled North Circular scrublands – to deliver or pick something up from rogue Spectas with rackets of their own. Drugs, meds, food, alcohol, you name it.

I can't really believe we did that. Pas and Eliza say it made us streetwise; I say we were just young and dumb. I wouldn't leave Soho now if you paid me. I don't have a death wish.

Nowadays the arrangement is a lot more equal. Lucien doesn't think so, but he's easy to manipulate, if you know what he wants.

'Kid!' He snarls in his thick cockney accent. 'Thought you'd never come!' Of course he did. We scheduled this trip last time by randomly picking a street in Lucien's dog-eared old *London A–Z* street atlas.

We only ever talk about the street, never the day and time when we'll come. Back at the Cell, we find the street in the index of our identical *A–Z*, and next to it there's a grid reference with a number and a letter. The number, one to seven, tells us when to come back two weeks later, Monday to Sunday. The letter, A to K, tells us the hour from eight in the morning to five in the evening. It's like our own little Enigma code. 'Meet you in Whitechapel Road,' we'll say, or 'Catch you in Park Lane'; but it means a day and time, not a place. The point is to make sure Gnosys patrols never know when we'll next cross the Ghetto. But Lucien knows.

When I walk into the showroom he's sitting at his

desk – a big, old oak thing piled high with bric-a-brac. He's surrounded by some of his most prized possessions. On his left, a grand old oil painting of Winston Churchill hangs on chains above a ragged mannequin, to which clings a little black dress. He's always maintained the dress was the first ever to be made by Coco Chanel. Both painting and dress were stolen – or, as he puts it, repatriated – from the home of the 7th Duke of Westminster somewhere between '63 and '64. On his right, he's flanked by a stuffed giraffe ridden by a wax model of King William V, which he took from Madame Tussauds.

Got a thing for aristos, I think.

All this stands in a large open space, one of the levels of the car park, filled to bursting with junk. From a Routemaster bus to a non-stick frying pan – you name it, he's got it. Thick sheets of old tarpaulin keep out the weather, but he must have the Roxi habit from hell to survive in the poisoned air.

I walk towards him, pulling my scarf clear of my mouth.

'Where are the twins?' I say bluntly, once he's within earshot. It's always important to get to the point with people like Lucien, otherwise they try and fleece you.

'Went upstairs love; fancied taking in the view.' He chews a wad of ersatz tobacco – actually small, pea-sized balls of ground ants held together with sawdust. Real tobacco is impossible to obtain these days.

'They give you the list?'

'It's nice to see you too, my boy,' he says sardonically.

We read *Oliver Twist* in Counsel once, a long time ago. Lucien Loffabond reminds me of Fagin.

'Always a pleasure, L. Goes without saying.'

His lips curl. He addresses the shopping list Mungo gave us.

'Six pigeons. Dead. The inner tubing of two bicycle wheels. A transistor radio. Working. And *Rubber Soul* by The Beatles, compact disc.' He looks up at me; his bushy red eyebrows flex inwards and join in the middle. 'I presume the last item on this list is not a request of Field-Marshal Moore.'

'Think Mungo's always been more of a Rolling Stones man.' I grin. I've got all the other Beatles albums, but I've never been able to find *Rubber Soul*.

Lucien sits back in his gigantic leather chair, raises one eyebrow so his monobrow looks like a lightning bolt, and spits out his wad of ant-baccy.

'What's in it for me, son?'

'Didn't the twins give you the battery packs?'

We generate our own electricity in the Cell using sewage water to power hydroelectric generators, which Rory Still-speare engineered. It's also what we use to trade. Even if we had any money, it would be useless. No one's interested in money any more – for most people, the only currency worth having is Gnotes, and we definitely don't have any of those. Electricity is extremely hard to come by in the Ghetto and we're just about the only people resourceful enough to produce it.

'They gave me the packs all right.' He flashes his lemon-curd teeth at me, the two at the front so rotten they're hardly there. 'But they were from Mungo. And Mungo's always been more of a Rolling Stones man, my boy.'

Touché.

'Oh come on, mate, do me a solid,' I say, adopting Lucien's cockney lingo. 'I've been looking for that record all over town.'

'Don't do solids. No point. Nothing solid about nobody nowadays.' He slams the list down on the table angrily with his big, hairy hand, opens one of the drawers in his desk and sticks his head inside, searching for more baccy, as if to say *Now shove off.*

'Three pellets.' I chuck a paper bag on the desk. He looks at it immediately.

'Five and you've got yourself a deal.' *You old addict. I can read you like a book.*

'Three.'

'Three and you bring me a pot of Ursula's finest on stew day.' The most delicious meal he'll have this week is half a burnt rat. And Ursula's ring-necked parakeet hotpot is famous all over Soho.

'Done.' I offer my hand. He shakes it. Lucien tells me it'll take his 'chappies' a bit of time to gather everything on the list and it would be best if I wait with the others. We'll get the *A–Z* out just before we leave.

When I get to the roof Pascale and Eliza are sitting with their legs over the brink discussing whether any argument can be made for Coldplay, a pop band from the early 2000s, being as musically significant as the Red Hot Chilli Peppers, another band with a funkier groove. Their sibling banter ranges freely from the Clash to Rage Against the Machine, from Post Malone to Adele.

'Dunno why you're laughing, bruv, you're Coldplay's biggest fan.' Pas punches me in the arm.

'All I ever said was *A Rush of Blood to the Head* is a good album, which it is. But I never said it was Stevie Wonder!'

'It's all right, Curls, we won't tell anyone that deep down you're actually a soppy little flower,' Eliza laughs. 'But if you ever want some Stormzy, you know where I am.'

We all fall silent for a moment, taking in the sprawling city. We're looking north, across the crumbling old rooftops of our abandoned centre, towards the suburbs and beyond, where a Zep glides ponderously beneath one of the serpentine arcs of the Hab-Belt.

The enormous structure winds its way around the perimeter of the city like intertwined snakes or a kind of helical shackle. From a few storeys up, you can't avoid seeing its alternating waves of steel and concrete, each rising from ground level to crest several kilometres into the murky air. A bracelet a hundred and ninety kilometres long and blindingly lit, where the rich, foolish and weak have gone to live out their days in brainwashed bliss.

What would we look like to them, if they ever logged out and looked out of the window? I wonder. *What must Soho look like from there, all razed to the ground and dilapidated?* The thought makes me sad. But then this is where so much of it began – in the Ghetto. So much of the music and art and culture that came out of the Golden Dusk. And it's still here.

In our own small way we're allowing the music to play on. In Soho: a beautiful tumour in the heart of Gnosys's gleaming London. Surrounded by machines. Besieged by the future.

CHAPTER 4

MUNGO

We're in total darkness. It's probably only just turned six – I don't know, I don't wear a watch – but it's only March; the days are still short and the long, stifling days of summer seem a thing of the prehistoric past. The proud old streetlights that once lit Piccadilly Circus are all dead. There's no electricity to power them.

'Something kind of eerie about an unlit lamp when the sun's gone down, don't you think?'

Suddenly – like someone heard what I said – the entire Circus fills with bright white light. The three of us wheel around, even though we all know very well what it is. An enormous illuminated billboard, clinging precariously onto the side of a building, fifteen metres up, rusty, and looking like it could fall at any moment, fills the big circle with light. It's like someone sloshing milk into a cat's bowl.

I once scavved a book from Foyle's, *London Through the Years, from Pepys to Punk,* with hundreds and hundreds of drawings, paintings, photos showing what London used to be like during the Dusk, and even before. Back in the day this billboard advertised companies like Coke, Samsung and McDonald's. It screamed London like the Empire State Building screamed New York and the Eiffel Tower screamed Paris. I can only imagine what it was like living when what they advertised was more than just a teasing, quivering reminder of all that's been lost; all that came before; all the colour that we never knew and never will.

The billboard flickers and sparks. Then it cuts out, goes black, and the Circus is plunged back into darkness.

'Just a surge.' Pascale says, deflated.

Eliza puts her arm around her twin brother. 'C'mon. We're gonna be late for Counsel.'

She and I turn around and walk towards the entrance of the Cell. I look back at Pascale, who is still looking north to where the lights were just moments ago. He rarely thinks too hard about much. He'd rather let the drudgery of life wash over him like the ocean over driftwood, sure he'll be wet for a short while but eventually he'll float to shore and dry off. Me, I think too much. Eliza just gets angry. But when Pas stops to think, he feels; and when he feels, he feels deeply.

He knows as well as anyone the Lights are never coming on again.

'Pas. It's time to go, dude.'

He waits a beat, turns and jogs over

We rush down the steps towards the gates of the Cell, which used to be Piccadilly Circus Tube station. All these years later, the London Underground logo – a red circle crossed by a horizontal blue bar – still sits above the locked yellow security gate. Powered by the Cell's generator, the logo is like a glowing bull's-eye, inviting you down into the depths.

Behind the original yellow security gate, which is now drawn closed nearly all the time, there is another line of defence – a steel door, sixty centimetres thick. It would seem more appropriate as the door to a vault than the entrance to an Underground station. It's a barrier against all unwelcome visitors – especially the poisonous air. There is a symbol carved into the metal door that's been engraved by hand, the grooves deep and jagged. It's the old symbol for a floppy disk. The floppy disk – the first portable computer storage, used a long time back in the Dusk – is our mark.

Just above the mark, HIC MANEBIMUS OPTIME is scrawled in blue, child-like script. No one knows who did it. Whoever it was, though, it's become our motto. In Latin it means, 'Here we will stay, most excellently.'

'Mungo! Let us in! It's gross out here!' Eliza rattles the railings.

Nothing. We all stand there shivering in silence, waiting for something to happen.

Suddenly a peephole appears in the door – in the centre of the floppy disk. It slides open revealing a pair of dark brown eyes, set below the bushiest grey eyebrows anyone's ever seen and above a bright, red, bulbous nose. The old brown eyes stare back at us, sizing us up as if they're struggling to decide whether to let us in or keep us out.

The porthole slams shut.

'Drama queen,' Pas huffs. Eliza and I giggle.

'Password?' Mungo barks, like he's ordering a platoon of men into battle. He wasn't always a lowly gatekeeper; Mungo was field-marshal of the British army in the Thirties and he can't help himself.

'Ceccarelli!' the three of us reply in happy unison.

Behind the door, chains are pulled and cogs turn. The yellow railings open as if by magic. Then a smaller door set into the big steel one, its outline at first invisible, opens slowly. The three of us step inside as the railings behind us are pulled shut and the steel door locks to secure the Cell once more.

Standing there in his old racing-green, army-issue jumpsuit (which as far as I can tell he sleeps in and has never washed), smoking a Sherlock Holmes pipe and beaming at us from below his yellowing moustache, is Mungo Moore, the Cell's first line of defence.

'Lovely day for it, *mon brave*, what what!' Mungo grins gruffly at Eliza, who gives him nothing.

'I've told you a million times Mungo – I'm not your bruv!'

'*Mon brave*, Miss Lovethorne! *Mon brave* as in brave. Valiant, mettlesome, stouthearted, spunky, galla—' The old boy falters as she storms past, disappearing down the steps into the Cell. He looks at Pas and me, a little bit squashed.

'Girls, Mungo. Girls. Can't live with 'em, can't live without 'em,' Pas says with a big smile on his face. 'Don't worry, she loves you really.'

'Indeed, indeed!' Mungo rallies. 'Nothing so equally brilliant and confusing as a young lady, Lovethorne! And your sister is the most brilliant, and confusing, of the bunch, what!'

Pas pats Mungo on the shoulder lovingly and follows Eliza into the Cell, carrying half a dozen dead pigeons over his shoulder and what is supposed to be a working transistor radio under his arm. It looks pretty broken to me. The aerial is bent and there are wires hanging out at one end. *For God's sake, Lucien.*

'See you in Counsel, mate.' Pas shouts back to me, before vanishing from sight.

'Out on scav were we, Jonesy?' Mungo says to me, blowing a stream of ersatz tobacco smoke that smells faintly of formic acid. 'Or was it a covert mission this time, eh?' He gives me a knowing wink and taps his wrinkled forefinger against his wine-red nose.

'Nothing too exciting I'm afraid, Mungo. Business as usual for the most part.' I hike the inner tubes over my shoulder and stuff the Beatles CD in my jeans, trying hard to hide it from him.

He's been the gatekeeper since the Cell was founded. Sure, he's old and nosey and a bit rough around the edges, but he's got our backs. And he wouldn't hurt a fly, or that's how it seems to us. How he ever managed to do what a soldier's supposed to do is a bit of a mystery. He was high up in the army during the Dusk – real establishment, friends in government, patriotic, Queen and Country . . . Then the Upload happened and everything he'd ever believed about his country and about his fellow Englishman turned out to be a load of old horseshit. The world lost its way in the latter part of the Dusk. Reality TV stars began running countries. Wars became games between powerful men and the human cost meant nothing. No one had morals any more. No one expected to have to try any more – all they expected was to be given everything they desired. No one was prepared to do their time, to serve others. All anyone wanted was fame and power, and if they couldn't get that, they'd settle for the easiest, laziest, least accountable life they could find – a virtual life.

It wasn't the world Mungo had grown up in. And he wouldn't stand for it. He tried hard to protest against the deal the Government was cutting with Gnosys during the Upload, taking it as high up as he could.

He was stripped of his rank and told to go quietly into early retirement. So I guess he joined us, the resistance, and never looked back.

Well, I say he never looked back, but . . .

'Speaking of covert operations. Helmand, 2010. Remember it like it was yesterday. Our mission was to . . .' I feel bad doing it, but I've been stuck way too many times reminiscing about his time in Afghanistan, his campaigns in Iraq, and the Indus Valley disaster. At eighty-six – just about a miracle for an Offliner – he has endless war stories, but I haven't got three hours to spare. I quietly leave him behind, knowing that once he's actually noticed I've gone he'll simply take up whatever enormous history book he's currently reading, sit back in his armchair and sip his glass of claret. A few years ago, whilst out on scav, a group of youngers happened upon the abandoned cellars of Berry Bros & Rudd, long forgotten and thought to have been emptied. The youngers had inadvertently stumbled across some of the best and most famous wines produced during the Dusk. Needless to say, when the booty was brought back to the Cell, Mungo confiscated the lot.

CHAPTER 5

THE CELL

The hallway leading to the main communal area of the Cell is a staircase with a low vaulted ceiling and candles in wall alcoves. I guess the elders want to conserve energy wherever possible. The flames flicker in the filtered air that blows from ducts here and there, and the shadows dart as I pass by.

At the bottom of the steps the roof suddenly opens out and I'm in the Ticket – once the station ticket hall, now the main area of the Cell.

The Ticket has been rebuilt a few times over the decades, and the last makeover made the space much higher and airier than before. Just in time for the Podd Way to make it all redundant by dealing Tube travel its death blow. But the new Ticket might as well have been specially commissioned for us. A lot of the time it's easy to forget you're underground at all. Even after all these years, it hits me like a Roxi rush.

Far beneath my feet there are connecting tunnels which were formerly platforms and are now our dorms, store-rooms, Galley, Sanatorium and more. But the Ticket is the only common area in the Cell; the heart of our world, the hive of everything.

The floor is on two concentric levels. The upper level is the perimeter, with doors opening off it to various impor-tant rooms. From this outer circle you can walk down one of two curving ramps to the lower circle. And that surrounds the Chute, a huge shaft leading diagonally down to the deep levels where trains once ran. The escalators, which ferried people up and down, used to eat up a ton of electricity and so Rory Stillspeare replaced them with slides and pulleys. Partly straddling the Chute is another of his designs from the early days of the Cell – the Spider, like a gigantic climbing frame.

But what makes the Ticket feel most like a world in its own right is the domed ceiling above the whole temple-like space. It's covered by multicoloured stars and planets – an exact replica of the galaxy hidden from us by the smog. It was Rory's way of giving us our own night sky. Before, life and colour and culture were up above. Now, after the Upload, they're down here.

If they're not just messing around, the youngers – Offliners under the age of twenty-five – rush about the Ticket completing chores like scrubbing and building.

Meanwhile elders discuss points of philosophy – or whatever it is that people over twenty-five like to talk about – while complaining bitterly about the bothersome 'teenagers'.

There are about five hundred Offliners in the Piccadilly Cell, the biggest of all the cells dotted around the old London Underground network. I suppose you could call it Offliner HQ. It wasn't just the first settlement in London; it was one of the first in the world, after Rome. Two or three hundred Offliners are in front of me right now, going about their daily business; working, learning, singing, dancing, reading, relaxing.

In one corner a group of eight assorted older men and women – one wearing a moth-bitten cardigan, another dressed in a green velvet ball gown – sit around a table playing cards. They're listening to *Ziggy Stardust* and I catch one of them saying, 'Bowie – if he wasn't a prophet, I don't know who was!' Another shakes her head: 'Nah, man, he said when things turned upside-down we'd have five years, but we've nearly had twenty-five already and we're still going strong!'

Two little kids run past me towards the Chute, carrying a big bag of flour they're taking down to Ursula's Galley. One of them sticks his tongue out at me. 'Careful you don't drop it, you little jerk,' I chuckle to myself. Things seem busier than usual tonight and I can't work out why. Youngers carrying benches on their shoulders laugh with each other as they set them down beneath the Spider.

My eye drifts up above their heads to the Spider and, as always, a million memories come back to me. Pas, Eliza and I grew up competing over who could climb fastest and furthest on the webs of netting hung about the enormous steel 'Spider legs', or on the ropes and ladders and narrow walkways hung beneath. We'd race to the top and the winner would whoop and whistle as he rode down the zip wire back to the Ticket floor. I say *he* because Pas always won. These days, the Spider strikes me as a pretty random design for a climbing frame – if that's what it was meant to be – but it certainly gives Offliners the opportunity to exercise without having to go up above and risk their health.

The huge, gold station clock – just about the only original thing in here – brings me suddenly back to the present as it chimes six times.

Bugger! I'm late for Counsel.

There's no time to go back to my dorm and drop off today's booty. *Rubber Soul* will have to stay down my trousers for now.

I quickly make my way around the outside perimeter of the immense space, passing each of the Offliner Seats as I go: the Office of Defence; the Office of Intelligence; the Office of Sustainability; the Office of Identity; the Office of Education.

These Seats – formerly ticket booths – are offices in which the Chief Offliner Officers work and govern the daily lives of every Offliner in London. They are the closest things we have to government ministries. Most of the offices have windows, so that the COOs can see out into the Ticket.

Every room is decorated differently, according to the strange and varying tastes of the COOs. So Defence, Mungo's department, is plastered with old propaganda posters from each of the two world wars. Its bookshelves are lined with biographies of Napoleon and Churchill, interspersed with accounts of battles all the way from Agincourt to the Bulge. There's also an array of serious-looking, if rather antique, military hardware ranging from binoculars to something with a plunger on top, which I think is an old detonator. Standing against one wall is a huge, sausage-shaped object that Mungo has lovingly restored from when it was found rusting in a derelict cellar – a World War Two bomb. We're assured it's been safely defused.

Intelligence is the most sober-looking of all the Seats. Really it's just a big filing cabinet, dedicated to gathering as much information on the world outside the Cell as possible: politics, environmental catastrophes, Gnosys. With its beige wallpaper matching the beige carpet, it'll send you to sleep if you look in for too long. Intelligence COO Suzannah Key reminds me of a Tube tunnel mouse, almost inhumanly unobtrusive but with eyes that seem to be constantly darting about for some morsel or another; though if we've actually learned anything through her years of work, I'm not sure what it is.

Sustainability is responsible for coming up with new and innovative ways to work with the planet instead of against it. But it's run by Yottam, the Cell doctor, so it has a split personality.

One corner of the small room is like a shrine to Yottam's hero – the man he says did more to promote the study of zoology and the preservation of the environment than anyone before or after him. Yottam has a truly impressive collection of the guy's books and DVDs stacked all round. Saving endangered species is a keen focus of Yottam's, but I reckon he wrote that part into the job description himself.

It's thanks to him that we're only five hundred and can still fit into the Cell, can still find enough food to feed ourselves. 'We're an endangered species too,' he says. 'But we can't just breed until we burst.' Years ago he persuaded the Offliners that no one under twenty-five should be getting hitched and having kids. That's how we got split into youngers and elders.

For any Offliner child, a fixture of growing up in the Cell is to be settled down crosslegged in Counsel in front of a life-size Sir David and watch the cardboard cut-out's face, so kind and wise, suddenly spring into motion. It's an old display scavved years ago from the Natural History Museum a couple of miles west of the Ghetto. The cut-out stands on a base with wheels which conceals a hidden projector powered by a bottle of Cell-generated electricity. For a few seconds, a piece of video makes it look like the old man is right there in the room talking to you. For us this is hi-tech; in fact Yottam's only been allowed to keep it because its message is so important.

'The human race,' our cardboard Sir David intones in an unforgettable voice, 'has brought our planet to the brink of one of its most terrible mass extinctions. The geological clock is ticking. We have only seconds to live. What will you do to stop the clock ticking?' This ought to be terrifying. Problem is, it's voice-activated. When the thing's switched on, you only have to say 'Attenborough' and it launches into its spiel. We always just found this hilarious – that, and the fact that there are two cardboard sloths hanging from the old naturalist's arms.

In another corner of Sustainability, rusty old medical implements are piled haphazardly, reflecting Yottam's other job as Cell doctor. When he's working away in the Sanatorium far below, his Office is occupied only by Sir David and his sloths.

But tonight all the Seats seem to be empty.

That's bizarre, I think. *Where the hell is everyone?*

Whatever. Right now, I need to take the Chute down to the southbound Bakerloo Line tunnel for Counsel. I head around the upper circle of the Ticket towards one of the down ramps.

'Oi!' someone calls. The voice is muffled. *Are they yelling at me?* The sound seemed to come from the last and smallest of all the Seats – the Office of Education.

I scan the Office.

'Kid, mate!'

I look again. Nothing. Then, suddenly, Pokes pops her head up above her desk.

The person in charge of educating Offliners isn't some wizened old philosopher, nor indeed the former headmaster of Eton (now a Perspecta VEA – 'Virtual Education Academy' – or, as we joke, 'Virtually Everyone's an Arsehole'). No, we've got Poppy Elizabeth Arabella Pokeman instead.

'Pokes' for short. And she calls me Kid instead of Josh, just like my mates. Unlike the other COOs, Pokes isn't an elder. She's a twenty-four-year-old. The elders decided that the only way they could inspire the youngers to keep learning about the Golden Dusk would be for them to be taught by one of their own.

Right now she has a half-eaten hunk of bread in her mouth and a big book in her hand. Once up on her feet again, flustered, her multicoloured bob falling all over her face, she gestures *come here!*

I stick my head around the door to the office, a warm, cosy space crammed to bursting with books and knick-knacks.

'All right mate?' She is unshakably positive.

'I'm good thanks. How about you, Pokes?'

'Ah, you know how it is, the old grind!' She rolls her eyes.

'Lose something?' I ask.

'What?!' A big, confused grin. 'Oh!' She realizes what I mean. 'When I was on the floor like an idiot! Dropped this on the floor.' She waves the book she's reading. 'It's about flamenco dancing, right? Bloody fascinating. By this guy Joaquín Cortés, who was this gypsy boy that became like the most famous flamenco dancer in the world.' Then there's that grin. 'And I'm trying, really hard, to get through this book. But I just can't!'

'Why?'

She leans in cheekily, like she's going to tell me a secret. 'I just can't stop going to the back page and staring at his photo. He was so fit, babe, like seriously! So fit!' She winks at me and laughs hysterically.

Don't be fooled. There's *nothing*, and I mean nothing about the Golden Dusk, that Pokes doesn't know at least *something* about. She's read every book and seen every film and watched every single TV show anyone's ever heard of. It's what she does. She learns stuff. She's the best teacher I've ever had and, on top of that, she's kind and caring and loves to laugh.

'See you in Counsel tomorrow, yeah?! I'm gonna take

all you wronguns down the Galley, teach you how to make potato vodka like they did in Russia in the old days! Be there or be square, mate!'

'Tomorrow? Counsel's tonight, Pokes.'

'What?' She swivels around to look at me, her nose sticking out above the spine of her book. 'Oh! Don't you remember? Special assembly tonight. Twenty-fifth anniversary of the Cell, dummy, everyone's going to be there!' She scoots her chair over to me and lowers her voice. 'Mungo says a few of the elders scavved a crate of Dom Perignon from the old Ritz the other day. God knows how they made it that far West. Anyways . . . They're gonna crack it open after Ruth's speech! Woo!' Pokes likes a drink.

Counsel cancelled! I decide to go back to my dorm before special assembly starts. *Might even manage a minute of shut-eye,* I think, suddenly feeling drained. Coming down off too much Roxi will do that to you.

CHAPTER 6

TEETH IN THE TICKET

It's not meant to be. As soon as I get to the other side of the busy Ticket, which is filling up fast for the assembly, a clear voice echoes through the hall. I turn around begrudgingly. *Where the hell are Eliza and Pas*, I wonder jealously. *I bet they're napping!*

'Good evening everyone!' It's a calm voice, in control of every syllable, with a gravitas beyond its years. It's the voice of Ruth Stillspeare, the COO of Identity and Chief Elder. Kind of like a president, the Chief Elder of the Piccadilly Circus Cell is also responsible for the welfare of the Offliners in every one of the other fourteen Cells in the London network.

When I turn around, Ruth has already wheeled herself up a ramp and positioned herself on a kind of stage or podium at the feet of the Spider, where she can be seen by all the Offliners ranged around the upper and lower circles and on the ramps. Ruth is in a wheelchair, though I always forget it. She is easily the strongest, wisest person I've ever met.

In salute, she crosses her forearms in front of her face, so that her arm tattoos align with each other to make the floppy-disk insignia. Everybody reciprocates, including me, holding their arms crossed in front of their faces to show a sea of inky floppy disks. Don't think I've ever seen so many of us in the Ticket all at the same time. Let alone so many new faces from the other fourteen Cells! I wonder how so many people managed to get here from the Lock or the Bec, from Banksy Cell on the other side of ruined St Paul's Cathedral, or from the Dogs even further out east. It's a difficult and dangerous business, travelling between the ghettos.

'Today is a momentous day!'

She's so young for the job – she must be in her late thirties – but never seems to lose her sense of duty, or, indeed, her sense of self. Both are always there, in her eyes. 'Today we celebrate twenty-five years of the Offliner Movement! *Hic manebimus optime!*'

Everyone is shouting and screaming, '*Optime! Optime! Optime!*' Some elders are already in tears, hugging each other and saying, 'We did it! We're here to stay!' It is an amazing thing, and against all odds.

'Today we celebrate twenty-five years of freedom!'

Again people yelp and whoop, but she raises her hand.

'Whatever we feel about the Spectas—' Ruth pauses to let the Offliners vent their feelings '—we should also feel pity for them. For these twenty-five years, they've been waiting for their new dawn, for the next version of Perspecta which – if the holo-pops can be believed – is set to whisk them away into perpetual ecstasy. What they don't realize is that if the claims are true, they're probably better off now than they will be then. Because now they still have a toehold on reality. We, meanwhile, have spent a quarter-century with our feet firmly on the ground and our heads held high.'

Elders clap, youngers punch the air.

'We've spent twenty-five years trying to preserve our environment, protect our neighbours of other species, learning ways of continuing to live in our world rather than just abandoning it altogether.'

A deep murmur of approval runs through the crowd.

'When my mother and father started this Cell, there were only three Offliners.' We all laugh knowingly. Ruth's father Rory was the first Chief Elder and Head of the Cell. He ran it from its foundation in the Sixties to his death two years ago, when Ruth took over. She inherited his piercing green eyes and eerily calm voice. Her mother, Ursula, is still alive and runs the Galley, our communal kitchen. I've always wondered whether she's really Ruth's mother: Ursula's the bounciest, clumsiest, friendliest, roundest, silliest, mumsiest old girl you'll ever meet, where Ruth is as serious and measured and steely as they come.

'I thank God for my parents every day. Not just for giving me life, but also for giving hope to so many others who believe in the same thing. That the human race and all of the wonderful things this real world has to offer ought to be fought for, continued, promoted.'

She stops and looks around. 'Speaking of which, where is my mother?' Ruth quickly locates Ursula when a group of youngers begin chanting 'Ursula! Ursula! Ursula!' The Spectas may almost worship their dynasty – Sylvia, Hamilton and Rosie Rogers. But that's not how we feel about the Stillspeares – to us, they're just part of the family.

'There you are! Come on, Mum . . . Come up here. I want you by my side for this!'

Sure enough Ursula – after a good deal of *oh, no, don't be silly Ruthie! You don't need me up there,* and *oh do stop it everyone* – is persuaded onto the podium. Ruth holds her mother's hand and takes an envelope from her lap. People crane to see.

'Boo!' Someone jabs me in the ribs. 'Could've reminded us, dick!' It's Eliza and Pas.

'We fell asleep, you arsehole,' hisses Pas.

'Reminded you?! You could've reminded *me*, idiots!'

An elder sternly shushes our giggling.

'Keep your hair on, granddad!' Eliza squawks. The elder can't be much above thirty. Pascale and I dissolve again until Ruth resumes.

'I received a letter today from Stefano Ceccarelli, the father of this movement, congratulating us and thanking us for our support. I would like to read it to all of you.'

Stefano Ceccarelli? Sent a letter? To us?

'As everybody in this room knows, Stefano founded the Offliner movement and established the very first Cell in Rome exactly twenty-five years ago this month. He started the Offliner initiative with three core values. Because he saw that, as the Dusk was coming to an end, the world had lost sight of every single one of them.

'One. Never abandon the planet we were blessed with, no matter how much our disregard for Mother Nature has led to her punishing us. We deserve to be punished, given how we've tortured her. Now it's time we gave back, nourished the home that we've ruined. Find new ways, *real* ways, to live on Planet Earth.

'Two. Never give in to technology, no matter how much easier it may make things, no matter how much better life may seem "logged in". Log in and you lose everything.' The bitterness in Ruth's voice is palpable. 'You lose what every human being in the history of this planet has ever fought for, or cared about. Log in, and you spit on the blood, sweat and tears of billions of people over tens of thousands of years striving to better themselves.

'And finally, three. Be resourceful, be creative, be imaginative. Keep the human spirit thriving!'

She pauses.

'*Hic manebimus optime!*' she shouts, and everyone echoes her call.

'Here we will stay, most excellently!'

We all cheer, and I feel a huge smile erupting across my face. I'm proud to be here, proud to be an Offliner.

'We, here in London were the second Cell to be founded, by my mother and my father.' Ruth looks up at Ursula, who has tears in her eyes. 'Now, around the world, there are more than one hundred Offliner Cells with a membership of over ten thousand people.' Deafening cheers abound. Life is hard and this statistic is heartening. *Maybe there is hope*, I think, for a second.

Ruth pulls something from her pocket. 'Now, to this letter—'

The thought is interrupted by a flurry of activity and sudden hum of consternation near the Ticket entrance.

'Silence!' Ruth's voice booms, drowning out the remaining cheers. The hairs on the back of my neck stand on end.

'Mungo. What is it?' Ruth says. I turn and see the old man, his face full of fear, beads of sweat hanging from his eyebrows. 'What on earth's the matter?' Now the entire crowd turns around to look at Mungo, standing at the bottom of the stairs leading out of the Cell. Everybody goes completely silent.

'Wh–Whi–White Teeth, Ma'am, at the gate.' My heart begins beating at a million miles an hour. I hear Pascale's breath get louder and louder. Eliza grabs both our hands. Her palms are hot and sweaty. Loud whisperings run through the crowd, becoming murmurs and then shouts.

'I said silence!' Ruth booms again. The crowd goes quiet once more, but it won't last long. The fear is palpable.

'How many and what do they want, Mungo? Speak very slowly. And everybody stay calm.' But before Mungo can answer, footsteps can be heard coming down the stairs.

Boots. Heavy-duty military boots. The boots get closer and closer. In the hall you might hear a pin drop.

Then, they're here.

'I am MIG90B7234. This is 90B8912, 90B5789 and 90B9001.' Dressed in sleek black all-in-one bullet-proof suits, their plastic masks moulded to their faces, four Mobile Intelligence General Service personnel – Gnosys private security – stand at the bottom of the steps, e-cannons primed. Matte black visors cover their eyes. The hope in my heart is extinguished.

This isn't the first time I've seen a Tooth. Not by any stretch of the imagination. Mostly it feels like Gnosys would prefer to forget the Ghetto exists, but it does send in small random patrols often enough to make you jumpy. This is, however, the first time I've ever seen a Tooth in the Cell, let alone four. Somehow, down here, in the safety and security of the place we call home, they are more ghoulish and petrifying than ever. Their smooth oil-black visors mirror only darkness. It's a hypnotic, all-encompassing darkness that makes you forget there ever was a world before this one, a world full of colour and light and freedom. The White Teeth are the walking, talking, murderous representation of all that has gone wrong and all that's been lost.

I can feel my heart beating like it's going to fly out of my chest. I hear a child crying and look around to see a mother cover her little boy's eyes as he sobs, terrified of what he sees. She cries too – silent tears – staying strong for him. She reminds me of my own mother and how she was with me. *What would you make of this, Mum?* I wonder. *What would you do if you were here?*

'I am here to speak to the leader of your organization. I have a message from Gnosys.' The Tooth looks at Ruth on the raised platform; his Plug will have identified her as the person to address. Like a single entity, the other three simultaneously look up at Ruth, their movements matched inch by inch. Beneath their visors, the light from a thousand flickering candles dances across each identical plastic breathing apparatus, their shimmering white teeth. It's like watching hyenas bare their glinting fangs at the scent of blood.

CHAPTER 7

A LONDONER'S DIARY

DATE: Sunday 14th February, 2021

I feel terrible. I just found this in my bottom drawer. You know, that drawer where you put all the things you can't throw away but know you'll never use – like a diary. I'd totally forgotten about it.

I feel terrible, I do, but you know what I mean! It's so annoying when people give you diaries as presents. I mean WTF are you supposed to do with a diary? It's such a classic 'i-forgot-to-get-you-something-so-this-is-the-best-i-could-come-up-with-sorry' present. An 'I'm-extended-family-and-don't-care-but-have-to-give-you-a-present-cos-it's-christmas' type present. That's why it annoyed me! Why it ended up in the bottom drawer! Cos I got it from Nana! And we were super tight! I shouldn't be saying this. No. Definitely shouldn't be saying it. Nana died last year. She got coronavirus, not long after she gave me this diary.

She was the only person in my family that I actually liked. In truth that's probably not an enormous compliment. I have a pretty small family. But she was the only member of my, like, extended family that I ever had much contact with. I mean, I see my dad's cousins and their kids, but only like every other Christmas. And honestly, without wanting to sound like a complete a-hole, they're all a little weird. As far as I can tell the three boys are mute. Seriously. They just sit there, in silence, demolishing my mum's canapés, saying absolutely nothing. Mum always does that super-annoying 'mum' thing and says 'Sean, you've just started Year 11 haven't you?' and Sean will nod, embarrassed, like a spotty, blotchy, pubescent idiot. Then Mum will hand me the olives or carrots for the hummus, which she's been trying to hand around the room to everyone for hours, because she's really shy and hates talking and prefers busying herself with the food, and say 'Isabel's just started Year 12 and she's doing marvellously. You two must have a lot to talk about! Oh – here – have an olive! They're stuffed with feta cheese!'

No Mum. Not at all. We don't have ANYTHING to talk about. Please take the stuffed olives back and leave teenagers to do what teenagers do best – not talk.

At least this Christmas we had a good excuse not to have the cousins over. Anti-coronavirus lockdown and all that.

Mum and Dad are another story entirely. Let's just say living with them feels more like living in a flatshare with people who are both complete strangers, but also work for the police force: strict would be an understatement. There is no hugging in my family. We are not an 'I-love-you-Mum-oh-love-you-too-Dad-love-you-wooooh-go-us!' kind of a family. No, sir. On top of the fact that we have little to no understanding of one another, my parents are just about the most conservative people I have ever met.

My dad was brought up a devout Catholic in a tiny village in Cornwall where the only other people were very devout members of the Church of England, or dairy cows, who weren't much use for broadening the mind. And BOY did Dad buy a ticket to the Roman Catholic roadshow. He was all set to become a priest himself when he met my mum.

Mum was never religious, not before she met my dad. She grew up in Islington, the daughter of journalists who were – as far as I can glean from the one or two times my mother and I have ever had an open discussion about the past – atheist champagne socialists ('champagne' being the operative word), largely absent from her childhood because they were busy either chasing news deadlines or bouncing from one drinks party to the next. Mum was quiet, bookish, and left as soon as she could to go to Bristol University. She hated it there because her fellow students – with their loud voices, progressive ideals and material tastes – just reminded her of her parents and the home she had been so eager to leave. Dad, who was also at Bristol (taking theology, of course), was her saving grace; her conservative, God-fearing, straightforward saving grace. She became a Catholic, got married to him and the rest, as they say, is history. A twisted kind of history.

Dad always regretted deciding to marry. Called it his 'fall', and blamed her for it – like they were Adam and Eve. And Mum just took it, heard him, agreed. And so, the only way she felt she could prove that he'd made the right decision – that SHE was the right decision – was to out-Catholic him. Makes me feel sick, the idea of Mum, of any girl, feeling that she needs to persuade any man that they've made the right decision loving them.

I'm guessing I don't need to go on or elaborate? Yes-i-have-a-curfew-of-nine-thirty-no-they've-never-let-me-go-out-on-weeknights-no-I'm-not-allowed-boys-in-my-room-and-yes-they-think-I'm-a-virgin-and-that-the-only-alcohol-that's-ever-passed-my-lips-is-in-church-on-a-Sunday.

Eurgh. As if.

So, yeah, Nana was pretty awesome. A breath of fresh air. She was wise and cool but most of all she was kind and generous. She 'renounced her faith' a long time ago. That made it much easier not to hate her! 'Wasn't going to have some old bearded man in the sky telling me what to do!' she'd say. 'When've I ever looked up there shouting "now don't you go kissing any of those angels up there, Jesus, don't you go doing this or that or the other!" Live and let live, I say!'

I always felt able to tell her things I would never – in a million years – tell my parents. She was family, but it's like she was separate somehow. Removed. The most amazing thing about my grandmother was her brain. She was the most intelligent person I ever met. She knew things – fact after fact after fact – and was never shy about letting you know. Which is why, when she got me this 'Londoner's Diary', I got so annoyed! I was like 'boring-mundane-blurgh-a-diary-Nana-really'.

But I should have known better, spoilt brat. She wouldn't have given it to me if she didn't have good reason to.

It's one of those diaries that has the Tube map on the cover and every section is another station somewhere in London. Hence 'Londoner's Diary', which is actually kinda funny because The Londoner's Diary is the only bit of the Evening Standard newspaper that I read. It's the celebrity-gossip section. I usually read it on the way home from school, to numb my brain after double physics or biology, my two favourite subjects. I find it kinda hard to come down off a science binge – it gets me going. The idea that everything in the universe is made up of subatomic particles, atoms, and molecules; the notion that we are all connected, whoever we are and wherever we're from, just because we're made of the same shit. Science, I mean, the space-time continuum, $E=mc^2$! I love it all, and when I study it it's like I'm running a sprint as fast as I can, never getting tired.

Some people drink to stabilise themselves. Others take drugs. I read celebrity gossip and science magazines. I know right? I'm a real rock star!

I did think about using this diary to scribble down some of my more out-of-nowhere thoughts – the kind of stuff that gets stirred up inside me when I start reading about what's going on at the cutting edge in physics. For a while it was a toss-up: dedicating each page to a summary of a Love Island episode or to the elementary particles – electron, muon, gluon, up, down, charm, strange, and the rest – all coloured-in and with references to how the particle behaved and what it was made up of . . . God I'm weird . . . !

'There you go sweetheart, that'll make for wonderful reading on the train when you're my age.' That's what she said when she gave it to me. Then she mentioned Oscar Wilde, who she remembered had said the same thing but she'd forgotten the exact quote.

Then I got thinking about who I would be when I got to her age and what it would feel like being that close to my mortality, when everything starts slowing down and life is coming to an end. I began feeling like life was short and I was lucky – beyond lucky – to be young and have even more future than I have past. My future self – I thought – would want to know that my life had been an adventure and that I'd achieved amazing things and that I'd made the most of it all.

CHAPTER 8

FUTURE ME

'Future me wants to read about a Somebody, not a Body', I thought.

Bodies and Somebodies: a distinction, dear diary, that it's crucial you grasp. Let's take ME, shall we? See, I'm just a Body. Nothing special, interesting or extraordinary. A 'Body' not a 'Somebody'. There's a difference. Not Kendall, not Kylie, not a model or a singer, not Billie Eilish. They're

Somebodies. The Somebodies can be who they want to be because they made themselves a Somebody. Or someone else decided they were worthy of being a Somebody. Maybe it was decided by millions of followers on Insta, or maybe by a stupid, fat, balding white man in a shiny office somewhere. Maybe they're talented at like a zillion different things, or they're just really hot TBH. Yeah, mostly it's just that they're all really hot. FFS! But Somebodies don't seem to care if anyone criticises them. They have an army of other people telling them they're amazing. And anyway, they believe in themselves: they're just it – Somebody – and they know it.

Conversely, Bodies are part of a bigger anonymous body – the great unwashed masses, the general public. It's worse than being a nobody, even. If you're a nobody, you have achieved something in being completely invisible! As a body you are visible, but people choose not to look your way or even consider you. Take me, for example. It doesn't matter what I think, or how pretty or intelligent my mum and dad or my nan thinks I am. It's what THEY think: the people who give the jobs, my future boss, the examiner marking my exam paper, the people at school. A Body is only as good as what some other person thinks it is. There's no army of followers to leap to your defence, to make you feel you count. Being a Body sucks.

You spend your whole life changing how you look, or trying to. You wake up and tip-toe past the mirror, but you can't help looking at yourself to see if swapping your toast for muesli made any difference. Then you sit there, for an hour, sometimes longer, just staring at yourself in that stupid mirror wondering what you did wrong in your previous life to get no lashes and absolutely no boobs. And cankles, yeah, cankles!

Then you wait for the bus knowing that your stop is after Pearl's and Jazz's and Frankie's stops, and you're just praying that their mums took them to school today and that they didn't catch the bus. Then you get on the bus and, yeah, you guessed it, they're there, sitting at the back pretending to eat prawn cocktail crisps so the boys think they're cool and eat, even though everyone knows they eat like one grape every three days. They tell each other plain-ass, bold-faced lies about the boys they made out with over the weekend, and you just keep your head down and you hate yourself for being so lame. But you don't know what to do except bury your head in Carl Sagan's Cosmos or in Cosmo. They laugh at Carl Sagan, and Cosmo just makes them stare even harder because nerds aren't supposed to be into what everyone else is, right?

Then there's what everyone else is going to think of you when you step into class in the morning and the floor goes from being that really nice-to-walk-on plastic flooring they have in the corridor to being horrible soft, squidgy, bristly carpet, which is really hard to walk on in heels and you can just feel the boys at the back staring at you as you walk to your desk. You sit and it's really, weirdly hot and you feel all sweaty in your school blazer and then Frankie shouts out (in that stupid, fake low-but-high, wannabe Miley Cyrus voice 'cool' girls do) 'Miss, can Isabel please be allowed to take off her blazer, Miss, she's feeling really hot!', and everyone in the class laughs which makes you feel so shit.

And all you want to be is back in your bedroom, in your

bed, with the covers pulled over your head, forgetting it all by reading about Ada Lovelace. Who's my latest science crush, by the way. Her dad Lord Byron was a famous poet. But she imagined something completely new which she called poetical science. She was the first to realise a machine could do more than maths, and she invented the first computer algorithm. She even imagined that machines could create music.

I guess that besides Ada, who's actually been dead for 170 years and so isn't really much use to me, I've also got Stephen, who is very much alive. Beautiful, kind, loving Stephen, with whom I am romantically engaged . . . Is that how you say it? I was trying to be poetic. We're not ACTUALLY engaged. We're just going out. He's the year above me at school, which isn't just nice because it's kinda cool to be dating someone in the year above but also because we don't have to share any classes. Like, I literally couldn't bear that. It's not that I don't love him. I do, I think . . . It's just that I like having some space; it's nice to be able to separate the different parts of your life. And there are places I can boldly go where I know he can't follow, like inside the atom. Guess that's why I'm sitting here at home writing this diary on Valentine's Day, right? (Actually to be fair he had to work tonight – mock A-level geography tomoz – so we're going out on our date on Friday instead. Or staying in for it, I suppose, depending on the latest Covid rules. And also TBH this morning he did pop by secretly and leave a heartachingly cute brown teddy bear sitting on the doorstep looking like a little waif and stray.)

Stephen – 'Lanky Steve' to his friends – is six foot four. I hate his nickname. To me it makes him sound stupid and goofy, which he is, but in a cute way.

Stephen and I have been going out for half a year now, or thereabouts. We got together at Abi Fergusson's 16th. We had sex the first night we met. He took my virginity. I guess I just wanted to get it over and done with. Everyone else had. I was bored feeling like the odd one out. And no. It wasn't beautiful. Not at all. In fact, it was a perfect storm. First he couldn't work out how to put the condom on, then asked me to put it on with my teeth because he'd seen it on PornHub, which led to me ripping and wasting almost an entire pack. This, in turn, led me to temporarily despising him for having such demeaning and unrealistic sexual fantasies and expectations. When he did eventually, you know, do it, it hurt like nothing I'd ever felt before and then – being a virgin himself – he lasted a grand total of 27 and a half seconds and immediately wanted to do it again and again for the rest of the night. Feeling sorer than I'd ever felt before and not just a little bit bored of being treated like a slot machine, I politely declined after our second go.

To his credit, he did ask me out on a date the next day. The sex got a lot better and he's about as obsessed with me as it's possible to be. I feel bad saying it, but he is and it's nice. I feel like I'm owed a bit of obsession: I've only got two hundred and eighty followers on Insta. (Tragic, I know. I guess those are the only 280 people in the world who fit in the Venn diagram where particle physics intersects with the Kardashians.) Seriously though, Stephen is my rock. He's always there for me, come rain or shine, and he's never let me down, apart from that first time in bed together. Problem is . . . I don't know . . . I must have had butterflies for three straight months. But then, like the rest of my life, it became the same old, same old thing. People started calling us a couple and treating us like a couple and he wanted to be a couple on Facebook and he gets really mad if I don't like his photos on Insta or he's not in one of my Stories. I MEAN COME ON!

I'm kinda done, tbh. I'm done with the girls at school and I'm done with the stupidity of it all. I'm done with giving a shit whether I'm a Body or a Somebody. I'm done feeling unhappy being me. I'm done with Snap and TikTok and Insta. I'm done with being addicted to social media and living in a total fantasy land, populated by pics and stories and posts that aren't real and depress the shit out of you. I mean, come on! This time last year the whole world stopped and now there must be four million dead because of a virus nobody had even heard of the year before. At least four million so far, I reckon, when they come to count them all properly. My Nana was one of them. When you look at it like that, like when you think of how fickle it all is and how short life can be, none of the trivial stuff matters.

So, dear diary, I've made a decision. I – Isabel Jane Parry, sixteen years old, from Kentish Town, North London – have decided that this year I am going to keep a diary. BUT! This isn't just going to be any old diary. It's going to be the diary of an adventurer, a kick-ass Somebody, a bad-ass mofo.

I'm gonna make my Londoner's Diary a good read. A different read. I'm gonna write an awesome story that my future self can devour on the train.

All I have to do now is figure out the plot.

CHAPTER 9

INSOMNIA

I can't sleep. I haven't, all night.

I stare up at the worn red brick of my dorm's arched ceiling. I've been staring for several hours now. I needed to process what happened last night but I can't seem to close my eyes and focus on the thoughts.

I began the night gazing vacantly at the old Persian rug on the floor, but the threaded patterns made me think of the Dusk and how good things must have been before the Upload. Then the patterns gave me a headache, and the threads of my thoughts seemed to knot themselves into a scrambled ball.

I tried the old clock over there on the wall, but clocks don't stay still for very long, and ticking makes you think of time, running down and out, second by second, towards oblivion. After that, I focused on my CD collection – no unhappy stimuli there – but every time my eyes settled on a specific album my head filled up with music so loud it drowned out everything else.

Each of the dorms is tiny, a mere two by two metres; maybe less. Mine feels smaller than most because it's full of all the spoils I've liberated from the Ghetto over the years. One side of the room is plastered with old posters advertising concerts, plays, exhibitions. Some are flyers from the old Soho sex shops, promulgating more carnal pursuits. My battered piano from the jazz club, on which I write all my songs, takes up almost all the space on the other wall. My bed – a small camping mattress – dominates the floor space. Whatever's left is filled with books, CDs and trinkets. The Persian rug was once on the floor of the King's Suite at the old Covent Garden Hotel – only the dressing room, mind you: the rug in the big room was too heavy to drag back to the Cell. For such an amazingly small space, my dorm is full of memories and stories, happy and sad. I find it hard to relax in here. It's hard to focus on anything specific.

Eventually I gave into the insomnia and took solace in the blandness of the brick ceiling, unornamented by any decoration, untethered to any memory.

I've stared and stared and stared. I'm still staring. I must have studied every crevice and crack by now.

That's it. I can't stand it. I get up, out of bed. It's freezing, but it always is down here. I feel the hairs stand up on the back of my legs like guards at attention. It isn't just the cold. I'm in a panic but at the same time everything feels like it's going in slow motion. *I have to get out of here, I have to get up above. Why do I feel like I'm suffocating?* I pull on my jeans and my jacket and slide into my boots. My muscles haven't woken up yet and I'm tender everywhere. Taking my disp, I load a pellet, put the mouthpiece to my mouth, and push the pellet in so its seal is broken. Breathing in hard, I feel the cold gas coat my lungs. I go to grab some extra pellets, just in case, but get a brain freeze. This always happens. Once the freeze has passed, I stuff the extra pellets in my pocket and wrap my scarf around me. I'm ready to go up above.

It's always like a fridge down here at this time of the morning, I say to myself rationally. *You're always cold and stiff and aching right now; this is normal.* I try to ignore the heaviness in the pit of my stomach, the dread I've been trying to shake all night. Passing other dorms along the corridor on my way to the Chute, I take care to be as quiet as I can in my heavy boots.

I look in at Eliza's for a second. I guess I feel protective; we have to look after each other at times like this. She sleeps soundly, in the moonglow glimmer of her wind-up night light. In the cold air, her quiet breath billows from her mouth like steam from a kettle.

'I love you, girl,' I whisper.

Immediately next door to Eliza's dorm is Pascale's. With

no night light, it's pitch black inside. He's the only person I feel up to talking to right now. But I resist the temptation to wake him up.

Just get out. You need to get up and out, I tell myself. Or at least, I try to think of this as me telling myself. But really it's as if someone, something, somewhere inside me is willing me up and out of the Cell. It's been that way for years, ever since I hit my teens, ever since I first started getting stressed about the world and what I'm doing in it. Since then, I've always had voices in my head. Well, one voice. It's a man's voice, at least I think it is. It's too faint and distant to identify – it's somehow there and not there at the same time, like a thought – my internal friend.

I creep past Pas's room as quietly as I can. But as I move to go, a whisper in the darkness makes me jump.

'Can't sleep? Me neither, bro.' Pascale strikes a match, illuminating his dark features and black eyes. He lights the candle above his head and sits up, his feet straddling the camp bed. 'Sorry I startled you.'

'I didn't sleep all night, man. Couldn't.'

'Same here.' I can always rely on Pas. 'Couldn't get what happened out of my head.' He grabs a Roxi disp to take the edge off and inserts a pellet from our Scav Squad stash, the same supply left to me by my mum. He takes a hit, sucking on the dispenser aggressively, dragging as much out of it as possible. His lips turn blue for a moment and his eyes cycle through a series of different colors, before returning to their natural chestnut brown. *The freeeeeeze.*

He offers it to me.

'One step ahead of you.'

'Suit yourself.' He gets nonchalant when he's on edge; he retreats into himself.

'I have to know what they said.'

'The Teeth?' He lies back on his bed as I lean up against the arched doorway.

'Ruth shouldn't have sent us all to bed—'

'She had no choice,' he interrupts. 'What, was she gonna have like Tommy and Rita and Sammy and all the other kids running around the Cell with White Teeth on parade in the Ticket? It was the only thing she could have done. It's her job.'

'We all have a right to know what happened.'

'You know what happened, Kid. We all know what they wanted.'

I stand there for a moment, avoiding his intense gaze, imagining the conversation between Ruth and the White Teeth. After the Migs had marched into the Cell and said their piece, she ordered all the youngers to their dorms and led the four White Teeth down into her chambers. Her Office of Identity is the only one of the five Seats with no window onto the Ticket. Instead there's just a locked door with a small lift behind it that leads, apparently, to a grand labyrinthine office and living quarters. I've never been inside. Not many people have.

With others, Eliza and I protested that we weren't going to leave another Offliner alone with White Teeth – that we didn't want them here at all. One look from Ruth shut us up. So we all shuffled off to bed, with one eye in the back of our heads, feeling scared and confused and sick to our stomachs. Most of the elders left too. As far as I know, only the COOs remained in the Ticket, but I don't know if any of them attended the meeting between Ruth and the Teeth. Picturing Ruth sitting across the table from the four Migs, I feel my whole body fill up with anger. In this picture, she's the victim, the weaker party. I've never thought of her that way. She's not a victim, she's not weak.

'It's been a long time coming, bro,' Pas continues. 'We're lucky we lasted this long.'

'I'm going for a walk,' I say a bit too sharply as I stalk away. He's right, of course. It's amazing we've lasted this long down here relatively undisturbed, but the way he put it makes it sound as if we brought this on ourselves: that it's our fault we're forced to live in the sewers like animals. We're not lucky. There's nothing lucky here.

'Kid!' He gets out of bed and comes to his door. I look back at him, just before jumping into the swing to pull myself up the Chute.

'I'm sorry dude, just need time to think,' I say. It's not his fault; he's being realistic.

'Nah man, I'm sorry,' Pas says. He has such an open face, so full of empathy and sensitivity. 'I love how much fight you and Eliza have in you. Like I respect it, you know, so much. And I'll get there, to that same level, of course. I'm with you and her and everyone. Of course I am. None of this is fair. We all just process things in different ways is all.'

'I know, man,' I say, offering a conciliatory smile. 'Wish I could be a bit more like you and, like, just let it be.'

He screws up his face in scowl. 'Why you gotta mention Paul McCartney at a time like this? You trying to depress me even more?!' I can always rely on Pascale to lighten the mood.

'You go get yourself some beauty sleep, Pas!' I say as I hoist myself into the harness, strap in and pull. The tune to 'Let It Be' echoes through the Chute as I whistle it on my way up to the Ticket.

When I get up into the hall, chills run down my spine. It's eerily calm. Still, you never know who's around, and I'm careful to tread as softly as I can as I emerge from the Chute below the Spider. The pendulum beneath the enormous station clock swings back and forth above me, like a giant wagging his finger at me. The painted stars twinkle in the shadows over my head.

As I go up the candlelit stairs, approaching the entrance, I hear loud, furious snores coming from around the corner. Dammit. Mungo's decided not to go to his quarters. Really doesn't want to let any more Teeth in after yesterday, I guess. *Good idea mate*, I think, *if you hadn't fallen asleep.*

Very quietly, I peep my head around the corner and, sure enough, there's Mungo, asleep in his armchair, an empty bottle of burgundy clutched precariously in his right hand. *Great. How on earth am I supposed to get past this?* He'll never let me out before daybreak, especially after last night. *Whatever.* I take a breath. *Nothing to lose.*

I begin walking towards the door on my tiptoes. Miraculously, he doesn't even stir. Once I get to his left-hand side – and the lever that operates the door – I realize why. On the floor by the armchair there are another two empty bottles of red wine and a half-empty bottle of Scotch to boot. I pull the lever with abandon. It clanks and clinks, cogs turn and whir, making an awful racket, but I'm not worried. 'Glad you've got this one covered, old boy,' I whisper to the sleeping

general as the giant, vault-like door swings open. I run up
the stairs and off into London at first light.

CHAPTER 10

CHICKEN-WIRE NECKLACE

You've got to be kidding me! I find myself in the middle of a morning storm. Morning storms happen when the air pressure drops, typically at dusk. The clouds sink like a fog and a strong wind whips down the dust and soot of our polluted atmosphere. I can't see a thing. It's like the Wild West up here.

I pull my jacket across my face to protect my mouth and nose and temporarily shield my eyes from the rolling dust clouds. Even coated in Roxi, my lungs aren't standing up to this shit. The canvas of the jacket smells old and musty; it comforts me. I run as fast as I can to get out of the Circus, an amphitheatre that amplifies the effects of the storm. The wind wails around my head and the air burns my throat. There's a penetrating damp, the kind that finds its way into any nook or cranny and feels like it will rot you from the inside out.

I pass underneath the Lights and into the relative safety of the narrow streets of Soho, just to the north. Though the buildings are mostly hollow shells, they provide a little shelter from the squall. I go up Glasshouse Street and pass what was once Zedel's Brasserie, where, during the Dusk, all the actors and artists and performers in Soho would congregate after hours to eat steak and mussels and gorge on other French delicacies. It's empty now; its once beautiful gilded glass facade is smashed to pieces; the wind howls through the grand old entrance hall. Eliza says it's home to a group of squatting Seekers who frequented the Brasserie before the Upload.

Soho has four sides, bordered by Oxford Street in the North, Charing Cross Road in the East, Shaftesbury Avenue in the south and Regent Street in the west. The Circus is the most southerly point of that square, connecting Shaftesbury Avenue with Regent Street. London is broken up into ghettos like this – though naturally we call ours *the* Ghetto – and there's an Offliner cell in each one. Anywhere outside is Specta country: a place Offliners have no business going, unless they want to be beaten up by White Teeth constantly patrolling on foot or up above in their MantaRay Chariots; kidnapped by crooked Spectas and used as slaves; or run over by a Podd on the Gnosys transport system. That's the network used by Spectas to get around – in the unlikely event that they ever leave the safety of the Hab-Belt.

So Soho is like an island, and to avoid any of these hazards I decide to stay inland, as close to the centre of the Ghetto as possible.

How can you be so sure you're safe here? I ask myself. After what happened last night, I'm not certain of anything any more. Several times I think I see a black-suited figure in the shadows, and expect a head to turn revealing a white plastic grin; but it's just my imagination.

When I get to Carnaby Street the storm has calmed and I stop running. Things are brighter now; the sun must be coming up; the occasional pigeon flutters from window to window. It's livelier up here in the north of the Ghetto. The Flood made most of the south uninhabitable, and most of those left behind by the Upload migrated here. Seekers emerge from alleyways, crevices, doorways and windows as I make my way up what was, in the 1960s, the most famous street in London.

A little girl runs up to me. She carries two or three necklaces made out of chicken wire and bits of broken brick. When she comes close, I stop and kneel down so I am on her level. I'm careful not to get too close – I've already clocked her mother standing in the shadows of an old shop door a little way up the street, watching carefully. The mother's lips tremble in anticipation. They're blue and cracked, like the rest of her face. *I know what this is*, I think to myself, keeping a vigilant calm.

'Hello,' I say softly, with a reassuring smile. 'What have you got there?' The little girl is emaciated, her pale cheeks are concave and her skin is more cracked than her mother's. She wears denim dungarees that are far too big for her, stolen from Levi's, Replay or one of the other jeans shops that this street was famous for in the Dusk. She starts coughing – the air – and can't stop. I take out my flask of water – distilled and purified from the sewers, as all our water is – and she drinks from it. She gives me back the flask, black phlegm on its rim. I hand it back to her. 'Have it. It's yours.'

She stretches out her arm and offers me a necklace. As I reach out to take a closer look, out of the corner of my eye I see the mother step from the doorway. The little girl looks back at her. Her mother nods quickly, bidding her on, then retreats back into the darkness; she doesn't want me to notice her.

'It's all right.' In clear view of her mother, I reach into my inside pocket, pull out a Roxi pellet and give it to the little girl. In return she puts one of the necklaces in my hand. 'It's beautiful. Thank you.' She turns around to go.

'Wait!' I grab her arm, gently because she's still very scared. 'It's okay. There's nothing to be frightened of.' I draw her in even closer to me, so that the mother can't read my lips. She's walking towards us now, at a pace. *You'd pimp out your own daughter.* The little girl is trembling. I reach into my pocket, pull out the three spare pellets I took from my dorm, and give them to her. 'Put them in your pocket and don't tell your mother. They're yours, not hers. Only yours. Understand?' I smile a big smile. 'It can be our secret.' She looks at me, with wide eyes. I wonder if she understands what I say. There's a chance she's deaf or doesn't speak English. Just before her mother reaches us, the little girl whispers in my ear.

'Kindness,' she says. 'Good. Thank you.'

The mother – her suddenly looming face covered in boils and scabs – grabs her arm and pulls her away, snatching the Roxi from her hand.

I get to my feet and watch the girl being pulled back into the shadows, back to her almost certain death. I can't bear it. Her life is over before it's even begun. Suddenly I feel it welling up inside: the panic, the anguish, the pain that rises from the base of my neck to fill my skull.

It's not your fault. It's the voice again. *Not everything's your responsibility. All you can do is hope. That she'll get away, get a second chance. Like your mother gave you.*

I stand in the middle of the street for a second, in a daze. What the hell is wrong with the world? I feel sick with sadness at the state of things. The voice seems to be butting in more and more these days, but this time it's right: it isn't my fault. And it's not the mother's fault she's on the street and addicted to Roxi. The scars on her face, the boils and burns, aren't self-inflicted. She's where she is because of what happened to the world, to all of us. Because of what they did to us.

I turn around and look back in the direction of the little girl and her mother, hoping to catch one more glimpse, maybe even hoping to find them again, to help, but they're nowhere to be seen.

Get to Liberty's, to Leo. She'll set you straight.

Leonora Skull is my godmother, though I didn't know it until after I lost both my parents: my dad walked out when I was very little – I never knew him – and Mum died four years later. I was eight years old. A few months later, Mungo came to my dorm with a letter. No one receives letters in the Cell – that's one of the reasons we were all ears when Ruth got one from Rome by who knows what secretive smuggling routes. No one gets letters outside the Cell either, for that matter: they use Gnosys Messenger, or Gnome as the Spectas call it, which is instant. And yet here in Mungo's hand was a letter, addressed to me in beautiful joined-up handwriting and with a crisp red stamp.

'Found it lying outside the gate. Most peculiar, most peculiar. Royal Mail closed down long before you were born, *mon brave*. Haven't seen a stamp in what feels like a thousand years. Where in the devil's name would one get a stamp from in this day and age? Most peculiar, I say!' I remember Mungo frantically recounting the strange series of events to me, as I ripped open the letter and read it, totally bewildered.

Liberty's
Regent Street
London W1B 5AH

Dear Joshua,
    We have never met.
    I am your Godmother.
    Your mother El and I were friends from before you were born and before the world became what it is today. They

were strange and uncertain times, and I always felt protective towards her.

She remained – and remains to this day – my greatest friend.

Subsequent to your mother's passing, I gladly accept the position of 'legal guardian' to you and any siblings you may have procured unbeknownst to me.

Do please come and visit me soon. I relish the opportunity of meeting you.

Return address above.

Yours, ever,
Leonora Skull

I couldn't believe it. After months and months of thinking I had no family – that I was totally alone in the world except for Pas and Eliza – suddenly there was someone else. Not only that, but it was someone I'd never even heard of, let alone met.

A week later I snuck out of the Cell and paid Leo my first of many visits.

'Not at all like how it was in the good old days, my dear,' I remember her saying with a kind of aggrieved indifference as she tapped three teaspoonfuls of powdered milk into her tea. 'You'll forgive me. The traditional fare is no longer available,' she continued, impaling two tinned sardines on her fork and smushing them onto an oatcake. 'In the old days there would have been something sweet, a Victoria spongecake, and cucumber sandwiches for sardines,' she said without making eye contact, as if she was embarrassed. 'Alas, things are only edible these days if they are grey, or brown. And they must absolutely always be stale.' She poured half a bottle of out-of-date Worcestershire sauce onto another oatcake, drenching it but failing to penetrate its concrete density. 'Nowadays the only people who see fresh, green food are Spectas locked in virtual reality, people who choose to live a lie, people who fatten themselves on illusions. No, no, Joshua, the only real stuff left is what comes out of a tin. Anything that looks unpreserved . . . well, that's poison.' She paused there, deep in thought and, despite her protestations to the contrary, I remember being utterly amazed as Michel produced an approximation to full afternoon tea, all stacked on top of an ostentatious Edwardian cake stand. Then he stood there and passed me titbits from the stand as I wolfed them down. I'd never tasted anything like it. Leo ordered him to pour a shot of brandy in my tea, which made me feel a little foggy. 'I'd sooner starve,' she proceeded, breaking the pensive silence, 'than live a lie.' I really felt that looking into her eyes, I could see her soul and, within it, all the pain and heartbreak and terrible misery the Upload had caused.

During the Dusk Leo had been a famous costume designer, travelling all over the world, designing clothes for movies and plays. Then, in the Thirties and Forties, she saw that virtual reality was consuming her business and every other art or craft; it was chewing them up and spitting them out. So she returned to London to enjoy an early retirement.

Liberty's of London, a famous department store that sold beautiful things to the rich and fashionable, had closed a few years before and the beautiful wooden Tudor structure had been left to rot. She bought the building, restored it to its former glory and reopened it as 'Skull's Costumes and Miscellany' – a veritable warren of an emporium selling strange and exotic goods from fine silks to couture dresses, fur hats to feather boas.

In addition to hawking her peculiar inventory to an eclectic collection of punters at the shop, Leo enjoyed free-lancing elsewhere. She'd take her pieces to all the music halls of old Soho and the West End and offer to dress the girls. She did it for free. By then she was already a rich woman and wanted nothing more or less than to enrich the soul. She loved the work. It reminded her of the early days of her career as a dresser in the theatre.

That's how she met my mother. Leo dressed her at Peter's for years, before Mum moved forward from being nightclub star El Kellis: gave it all up to be with my dad. Peter's was really on its last legs when Mum returned to the stage after we'd moved to the Cell. And maybe her death was the death-blow for the club as well. From what Leo has told me, hardly anyone came any more. Peter pulled down the shutters for the last time a year or so later and has not been seen since.

CHAPTER 11

SKULL'S,
EST. 2048

I'm standing at ornate, glazed double doors with the half-timbered Tudor-style facade of Liberty's towering overhead. Pokes once told me those oak timbers were originally reclaimed from warships in the age of sail. It makes me think of a huge ship at anchor, proudly weathering the changing times.

Knock, knock, knock, ring. 'Kid.' Three knocks, pull on the bell, then say your middle name. That's how you get in to Skull's.

The old oak doors swing open by themselves. I walk inside. Just as it was in the Dusk, a grand, old, wooden staircase dominates the lobby; like something you might find in a country manor, it spirals down into the depths and up towards the stained-glass roof, eight floors above me. Coming into this magical old atrium, full of drapery and candles and flickers and flashes, always makes me feel like I've stepped out from behind a curtain, onto the stage at the old Royal Opera House in Covent Garden – derelict and abandoned now, but not at all far from here.

It's the smell of the place. The musky, moth-bitten, sourish mould of its wood: I can't get enough of it. This building, its atmosphere, does something to me that should be impossible: it takes me far beyond Covent Garden even, and back to somewhere I've never been. Somewhere that existed long before the Upload, right in the middle of the golden age of human creativity, invention and imagination. Was it the 1920s or '30s? Perhaps before, perhaps after; it's all such a long time ago now. A time when people cared about how things looked. A time when people cared about how buildings made you feel. A time when people cared about bricks and mortar. A time when people cared, full stop.

Once, in Counsel, Pokes told us the story of Beauty and the Beast. This place feels like what I imagine the Beast's castle must've looked like, built and painted and constructed on a stage somewhere here in Soho. Its purpose?

Nothing but to enchant and beguile an audience willing to believe the unbelievable.

I take the stairs down to the basement of the building where Leo has her stores. Behind me the giant oak doors slam shut of their own accord.

Dancing candlelight only dimly lights the bottom of the stairwell, where I pause, hardly able to see where I'm going. Here is a large, square atrium, its walls panelled with wood. Each of the four walls has a door; all the doors are ordinary looking and identical.

I hear a sudden flurry of voices before one of the doors opens and what appears to be a massive, multicoloured ball of fabric flies out and lands with a thud in a heap on the bottom step.

'Merde!' a high-pitched male voice cries out from beneath the pile of cloth as its owner struggles to extricate himself. *'Pourquoi a-t-elle besoin de tellement de tissu?! Elle n'en vend pas de toute façon!'*

I stand smiling at the ball of fabric writhing around at my feet. 'Michel?'

The fabric stops moving.

'C'est moi.' He clears his throat and drops an octave. *'Qui est là?'* He's obviously embarrassed. The wriggling starts again and, after a moment, a small, moustachioed Frenchman emerges from in amongst the material. Before he even looks up he tries, feverishly, to remove all the dust and smut from his crisp white shirt and tight black tailored trousers. Michel d'Achon, an angry Frenchman and Leo's long-suffering assistant. When I say long-suffering, I mean really long: I think he's been at Skull's since the beginning, nearly thirty years

ago, and I reckon he wasn't a young man even then. But he gives no sense of being slowed down. A small, dapper man, absolutely bald, his face a masterpiece of sags and wrinkles, he springs about in his polished black brogues like he's in the prime of life.

'Kid?' He looks up at me as if amazed, even elated, to see me. 'Is it really you?!' Daintily stepping over the mess of fabric at our feet, he embraces me tightly.

'How are you, Michel?' I say, as he kisses me twice on each cheek.

'*Mon ami!* Overworked, underpaid and apparently without any coordination whatsoever!' He gestures to the heap on the floor. 'Forgive me. How embarrassing.'

'Don't be silly. No need to be embarrassed. May I—' I point to the mound. He cuts me off.

'*Es-tu stupide?! Absolument pas!*' He tuts at me as only a Frenchman could, then chivvies me through the door. 'She's in there. Mad, crazy, beautiful woman.' He seems to drift off into a reverie. 'You know the way. *A tout, mon cher!*' He sings, not looking at me; remembering the good old days, no doubt. I leave him and go through the open door.

The room is very wide and very long. The walls and ceiling are painted in blinding white; the room itself is filled with racks of clothes, of every different style and colour and pattern. The miles and miles of dresses are accompanied by hundreds of mannequins, some clothed, some unclothed. Evidently this is not a showroom but a workshop. It is like being in an old factory or mill.

I walk through the middle of the workshop, where an aisle is railed off from the drapery, to another door.

Click. I close it behind me gently and find myself in a small but enormously tall room. It must once have been an elevator shaft or perhaps even a garbage chute. All the way up to the ceiling, on all sides – floors and floors above my head – are bookshelves full of old books. Behind a huge schoolmaster's desk, messy with fabrics and books and papers, sits a diminutive old lady, elfin in build and features. Despite her size and age, she is remarkable to behold. She wears a chain-mail coif over her head, like a medieval warrior, and black heart-shaped sunglasses. Her face is painted with pale make-up; her cheeks are rosy red; her lipstick, thick and smudged, is the colour of fresh blood. Her dress is long and black and made of feathers.

My godmother stands here in her office, arms outstretched to welcome me as ever – though, as ever, when I do come towards her, she waves me away with her hand. 'There's this dreadful lurgy going round,' she says, then quickly sits down, her dress swooshing around her petite frame like a spiralling double helix. She's done it ever since I can remember. I've always found this kind of 'carrot and stick' affection really peculiar.

She raises an eyebrow. 'I've been worried sick! Why didn't you come sooner?' Her voice is deep and old and croaky, how I always imagine trees would sound if trees could talk. She pushes the chain mail back from her face and sits. 'Cigarette?'

'No thanks, Leo.'

She removes one from a gold case and inserts it into an old-fashioned cigarette holder that looks just like the ones made famous by actresses such as Audrey Hepburn during the Dusk. Lighting it, she inhales and exhales a prodigious plume of rose-coloured smoke.

When I first saw her doing this I remember thinking, *Why doesn't this smell like Mungo's ant-tobacco?* As a matter of fact it doesn't smell like anything – not even like the stuff that Audrey used to smoke. Later, after I'd plucked up the courage to ask Michel about it, he explained that the cigarette holder isn't a cigarette holder at all; it's a modified disp that enables Leo to maintain the right level of Roxi to survive up above. Like a good number of extremely wealthy people, when the Upload came Leo had the foresight to stockpile enough of the drug to last her a lifetime – just before Gnosys bought the patent and took over control of its supply.

Ironic, I think to myself as she puffs away. *You've got to kill yourself to keep yourself alive.*

'Is everyone safe?' she asks. 'What did they say?'

I look at her in disbelief. 'How the *hell* do you already know about the White Teeth coming to the Cell?'

'Don't ask stupid questions. There isn't time. Was anybody hurt?' Concern is etched on her face.

I continue to sit in silence and smile, the corners of my mouth wrinkling. It's fun to wind her up.

'Oh Joshua, I wish you wouldn't. I have my sources; that ought to be enough. Really!'

Word travels fast in the Ghetto. She raises her eyebrows and her eyes twinkle. It's almost as if she can hear me think.

'You do know why they were there?'

'Yes, but I don't want to believe it.'

'Why?' She leans forward, seeming half terrified for me, half relishing the quiz.

'They want us to log in, of course.'

The light seems to leave her eyes.

'What is it, Leo?'

She pulls hard on her Roxi cigarette before responding. 'They want you gone.'

'What do you mean *gone*?'

'They have no interest in acquiring new users. They have no reason to.' Her eyes darken. 'What they need is real estate.'

What she means dawns slowly. 'They want the Cell?'

'The Cell, and more. And they'll get it. Unless—' She pauses.

'Unless what? Leo!'

'Unless someone stops them. And it's not going to be Ruth Stillspeare, I can assure you.' She sucks hard on her cigarette. 'Nor any COO or elder for that matter. No, not at all. Their attention is on the moment – today and tomorrow, and not much beyond. But the only way to fix the future is by revisiting the past.'

'I don't understand. Why would Gnosys want to take over the Offliner Cell?'

'Take yourself out of the equation, Joshua. Take all the Offliners out of the equation. When you say *take over* it sounds as if you're implying that they mean to be your over-lords, that they mean for you to be their unhappy subjects.' She leans across her desk. 'Gnosys only has eyes for the Circus, and beyond that, the other cells; they mean to take back the Ghetto – all the ghettos – regardless of the Offliners, of you.' Flecks of spit fly as she speaks – her enunciation is marked; there is genuine concern in her voice. 'It's only a matter of time until they do. You can't fight it – none of you can – you don't have the resources.' Her voice cracks a little when she says this; she seems oddly and uncharacteristically desperate. Like she, too, is in danger.

'You're saying they're going to force us out? What if we won't go? What if we refuse to move?'

She looks at me for what seems like an eternity.

'Joshua, I am not a visionary, and there are many, many things I do not know. But I do know this. The only way to fix the future is by revisiting the past. And you, Joshua, are the only Offliner that can. You can't stop the juggernaut of Perspecta in the here and now – you have to go back, to where it all began. Understand it, change it.'

'Change it? Change what? The past?' I don't understand a word she is saying. She always talks in riddles, but this is different. She's too sincere, her expression too grave, to be playing a game. 'That's impossible.'

'For most, yes, but not for you. I've always known it. And it is written in the book of your life, even if you cannot read it.' She breathes out another colossal cloud of smoke. 'Go back. Re-examine your past. Only then will you be able to stand up to what's coming.'

CHAPTER 12

CADBURY'S AND DROSTE

I'm trying to remember.

But sometimes it's hard to determine whether my early childhood recollections are really memories at all. Did they actually happen as I remember them in my own head? Or has my brain filled bits in and taken bits out, editing them almost? Or maybe I've altered them entirely to make remembering them less painful?

But I can't remember what I'm trying to remember.

I study the feeble glow of the light hanging above my bed in my dorm. Squinting, I try my hardest to focus only on the bulb; I stare so hard that I think I can make out the filament. It looks like a silver thread, or a glow worm, or a dancing fairy. *If the bulb's the Earth, then the filament's the Earth's core. If you get to the core – to the centre of the Earth – then everything makes sense, then you have the answers.* Another poetic but completely nonsensical thought crosses my mind. This is my brain's way of saying stop, close your eyes, go to sleep. I'm deliriously tired now. I realize I've been staring at the thing for hours, ever since I got back from Leo's. Her words are bending and twisting and looping themselves into indecipherable algebra inside my mind. The more I try to make sense of what she said to me, the further away I get from her words, from the answers to my questions.

I give up. I close my eyes, but it's still there. The black hole of my blindness is filled with a yellow spot, right in the middle of everything – a hangover from staring at the light for too long. Moving my eyeballs around their sockets makes the one big spot move around the black hole, then break up into other, smaller spots of light, little moons. *Must be what cells look like multiplying under a microscope*, I think.

Cells, I think, *we're made up of cells.* I stop trying to control my thoughts and give in to the intoxicating fatigue. *Where do my cells come from?* I continue. *From other cells*, the thought tumbles on into the endlessly dark expanse, *which come from other cells, which came from my genes, my genetic code. My DNA.* The thought carries on, growing in size and gathering pace. *Mum and Dad: my cells, my code – my DNA*

— all came from them. Is that the book of my life? Suddenly the thought-dustball stops and rocks back and forth slowly, in the nothingness. Then, very quickly, all the little spots of light are drawn to it like moths to a flame. They seem to fly into it, lighting it up and making its impenetrable, tangled form shine from within so that once again there is just one big yellow spot in the middle of the darkness.

I can do this. I can remember. I WILL remember.

'Go back. Re-examine your past.' Leo's words thunder through the vast darkness. All at once, an unusual moment of clarity. *'Re-examine your past? Yes,* I reason, *but where is my past? It's in my memories. Okay, but how do I know I can trust my memories? How do I know they haven't been tampered with?* The same thought I had in the beginning returns to the forefront of my mind: *how do I know my brain hasn't messed with them to make them less painful?* The light in the dustball begins to flicker and fade; the clarity of the previous moment's thought fades with it. I open my eyes as stinging tears begin to well up and my forehead thumps with pain.

'How can I remember,' I scream out, ripping myself from the murky world of my memory, 'when I don't even know what it is I'm trying to find?' Seething with frustration, I throw off my blanket and jump up to stand on my bed. My head hits the lamp above. Beside myself, I stand still. *Stop*, I say to myself. *Enough now.*

Eeek. Awwk. Eeek. Awwk. The bulb swings back and forth on its frayed rubber wire as I stand on the bed, bent double like a madman bereft. I feel sure of nothing but my next breath – watching the light swing and swing, hypnotizing me as tears stream down my face.

After a while I begin to calm down, my breathing becomes more metered and my headache starts to subside. *No point going to sleep now*, I think. *Only one thing for it.* I jump off the camp bed and kneel down beside it. The floor is freezing and it hurts my knees as I crane to look under the bed, scrabbling around for the tarpaulin bag where I keep a lot of my precious or perishable stuff to protect it from the damp. I sit back up on the side of my bed and open the bag, retrieving my disp and a fresh pellet.

'I wanna be sedated,' I say smiling, quoting the title of the Ramones album. They're one of Pokes's favourite bands, and now they're one of mine too.

Blowing out my cheeks and going to put everything back underneath the bed, I notice the small tin at the bottom of the bag. My mum gave it to me as a Christmas present when I was four years old; my first Christmas in the Cell. I never pay it much attention these days, but now something compels me to pull it out. I suppose I feel nostalgic, given what's been on my mind tonight: memories. I put the disp and pellet down beside me and put the box on my lap.

The tin is covered with purple paper, faded and frayed. On the lid, in a big, traditional, gold font it says *Cadbury's Roses*, with a big red flower in the middle and an elaborate red floral border around the text. The flowers look like roses, I think, but I've never seen one in real life so I can't be sure. I never tasted a Cadbury's Rose and, considering how dilapidated the box was when she gave it to me fourteen years ago, I'm not sure that Mum did either.

It's not that I've never looked inside it, or taken things out, but I feel that what's inside belongs there. The scruffy old toy dog, for example, which I named Lilly, after the real dog we brought with us when we first came to the Cell. My comforter, torn to shreds by Lilly when I was a baby, is scrunched up in tatters in one corner. It happens less and less nowadays – growing up I guess, growing up and away from my old life – but if I ever feel the need to hold it and smell it, if ever I'm scared or lonely, I always put it back in the box as soon as I feel better.

Underneath the comfort blanket are a couple of old books. One is a children's retelling of myths and legends, Greek, Norse, Indian, Irish – a whole mixture. I think it was actually my dad's when he was little. The other is a book of music manuscript paper. It was blank when Mum put it in here. Since then, it's played host to the beginnings of all the Scav Squad's greatest hits, and not an inch of it is unfilled with melodies and harmonies and poetry. As I take it out and flick through the yellowing pages full of chords and lyrics, a thousand images are conjured up in my mind, like a movie of our lives together, from the moment I was born – the moment we met – right up to now, all set to music, our music.

Something slips out of the back of the book and onto my lap. *There you are*, I think. *Was wondering where you'd got to*. A photograph of my mum and dad, me and Lilly, all together, a year before he left us. In the picture I'm three years old and sitting on my dad's lap. He must have been bobbing me up and down on his knee when it was taken because I'm laughing uproariously, ecstatic and excited, my arms flailing in the air. He's smiling too. It's a completely unaffected smile, the kind of smile you have on your face when something wonderful is happening to you and everything is going right and you're bouncing down the road, listening to your favourite song on repeat. His healthy young face is full of pride. He is hugging Mum with his other arm and drawing her close to him, her head resting on his shoulder. She seems happy too, but then she always was. Happiness and warmth radiated from her, and they radiate from her even now, through a photograph taken almost two decades ago. She is indescribably beautiful in this picture. She could have been a famous actress if life had been different for her, I'm sure of it. Her long chestnut-brown hair falls across her face and frames her high cheekbones and gorgeous green eyes. Lilly sits between her knees, as she always did. That was her happy place. *These are my memories*, I think, *this is it. This is all of it.*

I'm about to put the picture away again when something in the box catches my eye. I pull it out from beneath my comfort blanket. In my left hand, I now clutch a shiny black object as wide as a pack of cards; on the back of it an apple with a bite taken out of it and the letters *iP*. The iPhone. How did I forget about it?

It was a kind of mobile smartphone that was very popular during the Dusk. My dad gave it to me when I was really little. It had belonged, I think, to his mum before him and he had inherited it from her and kept it, but as with all my powers of recall, I can't be sure of anything. He was fascinated by digital things and worked as a software engineer; at least that's what mum told me. When she and I came to the Cell she was sure to tell me not to take it out of the box in front of people: now that we were Offliners the others might not understand that it was just a harmless toy. So only very occasionally, when I thought nobody was around, I'd take it out and look at it at night-time. But it never switched on and I didn't understand how to work it. It was as if my dad needed to be there for it to function. As time has passed, I've stopped taking it out of the box.

I stare at the iPhone lying there, inanimate, a relic of another time, and at first I'm as blank as the dark screen. *How do I switch you on, damn it?* I look at it from every angle. *That looks like a lens, and that tiny slot is definitely for a jack of some kind.* As I try to imagine what could fit in the little letterbox-shaped slot at one end, I remember once removing a loose cable from the tin and tucking it in my box of small scavved oddments. A moment later I have the white cable and a chunky old electrical plug – the kind we still use in the Cell – and I've got the phone attached to a bottle of juice. *Woah!* Immediately a little icon appears on the screen – a battery, barely charged. *Oh!* Just as quickly, it's gone . . .

I come to with a start as the phone buzzes and vibrates in my hands. I've nodded off and the candle's burned itself all the way down, but now the iPhone has switched itself on. The bright white glow of its screen is blinding as it swallows up the darkness of the dorm.

The screen shows another photo of me. There I am again, still about three. My little eyes explosively wide, I'm thrusting the phone towards the camera to show what's on the screen – and it's the same photo of me holding out the phone. Smaller and smaller versions of the same image recede to vanishing point.

Cool trick! I think. How it's done is beyond me. But as I gaze wonderingly at this – me holding up the image of me holding up the image of me holding up the image – Leo's words play back in my head like they're on a loop of their own: *the only way to fix the future is by revisiting the past.*

CHAPTER 13

FROM FUTURE, NEED HELP

DATE:
Thursday 11th March 2021

I think I've found it! The plot for this thing! For my diary, remember? (Of course you remember – you ARE the diary). At least I feel like it's the beginning of a plot. It's not exactly what I thought I was going to write in this diary and I don't have a clue if it's going to amount to anything, but I think it's a start. It's a mystery, of sorts, and I'm going to solve it. Right here. In my diary.

I went to bed really late last night. Stephen snuck round after Mum and Dad went to bed (he managed to creep up the staircase – the creakiest in the world – without waking them up, which, being six foot four and extremely clumsy, was a total miracle). I never sleep that well when he comes over; he snores and does this weird thing with his feet where he gets them all tangled up in the duvet cover and tugs at them over and over. Weirdo. No, actually, it was a really nice night. He's such a sweetie really. He Deliverooed a Nando's – which was special enough anyway during lockdown and all that. Not only that, he paid for everything! EVERYTHING!

He ate a chicken burger and I had wings. They were amazing. Then again, Nando's is always amazing.

He even managed to get us some alcohol from the corner shop. Wahey! (Stephen has been growing a beard lately to look more his age, but ATM it's more bum fluff than stubble.)

He had two beers and I had a glass of white wine. TBH, I've never really liked the taste of alcohol – wine especially. I mean, I really, really don't get the attraction. It's sweet but it's also acidic (what I imagine wee tastes like). As wine goes, however, this one wasn't bad. LOL. Think they said it was called a Sauvignon Blanc. #Connoisseur.

By the time we got home it was kind of late. Stephen dropped me off, then waited outside my house at the bus stop until Mum and Dad had finished watching TV (yes, he's an actual real-life angel). They went to bed, he crept in and we just 'Netflix and Chilled'. KIDDING! No sex. At all. Nada. Very much on my period RN.

We talked for a bit in bed and kissed and cuddled and

stuff, which was cute. I love the way he holds onto me when he kisses me. It's not tight and suffocating – there's a soft, assured quality to his hugs, which makes me feel safe. He fell asleep after that. I stroked his hair and played with his floppy ears and giggled at how cute he was. Then, after a few minutes, I was like 'Enough! WTF are you doing? This is so wifey. You're not that girl. Stop being such a loser!!'

He was snoring by then and I was still wide awake. There was no way I was going to sleep for ages. And I knew if I tried to read about Higgs boson, or whatever, that (a) I'd be too tired to focus and (b) it would just keep my mind turning all night anyway. So instead I did the inevitable and went online. Snap was the same and nowadays FB is just full of really annoying vids that people have shared about politicians doing dumb stuff, or animals doing dumb stuff, or people cooking dumb food. So I decided to read my book . . . Only kidding. I did what any good, self-respecting, self-flagellating, insecure person does annnnnnnnnnd . . . went on Insta. I scrolled through everyone's Stories for like the fourth time that day and, of course, found nothing new and exciting.

Then my eyes turned into squares and I began tearing up with tiredness because I had searched and re-searched every girl (and boy – don't tell Stephen) in my class and strategically liked or not liked all of the thousands of face-tuned, filtered posts on their profiles, just getting more and more depressed and having more and more FOMO, even though I knew full well that IRL none of it's actually true. I decided to allow myself some peace and go to sleep. But not before skipping over to the discover page just once, just for good measure.

A new video started playing, and it caught my eye. I

don't know why it got my attention at first. I couldn't hear what he had to say over Stephen's earsplittingly loud snoring, and it seemed like yet another video of yet another young guy talking about absolutely nothing. There was an old piano in the background, squeezed in amongst a lot of bric-a-brac. When he went over to it, I sat up in bed to watch and turned up the volume.

I wasn't sure about the song at first, but as he went along, it became clear that this was someone who wanted to be a Somebody.

> *Hey Mr Big Shot, hey Mr, give me a job,*
> *Hey Mr Big Shot, hey Mr, give me a life.*

And then the chorus began, or I think it was the chorus, and the whole feeling changed.

> *Like a kiss must be planted,*
> *Like a door must be opened,*
> *Like a tide has to turn.*
> *We're kids, very young, this is our song,*
> *And it's a song meant to be sung.*

He was young, I could see that. And the words and the tune were, well . . . There was something there I can't put my finger on.

The account was 'JoshKidJones' – nothing odd about that. But one thing was really bizarre. I couldn't quite see it at first because the light by the piano was quite bright, but then when he went and sat on his bed where it was darker, I saw that right on top of the video, like superimposed, there were white numbers with a date and time, right down to hundredths of a second. I've seen that on pirated movies sometimes. But the date said March 11 2078. Right day but, um, definitely not the right year.

I didn't know what to think about that, still don't. But it seemed to go together with other things that struck me as just a bit off-key.

This Josh guy didn't seem to know how to do a selfie. When he was sitting on his bed he's holding the phone up next to his face like an idiot, obvs had it pointed at a mirror. As music videos go, it wasn't exactly slick, being able to see the back of his beaten up old phone all the time. Plus he was wearing a roughed-up jacket over a ragged shirt which was open at the top. It was the jacket that seemed different, it was so unusual. At first I just assumed he must be another wannabe influencer posting about vintage clothes and indie bands. Not this guy. It was like he had never been on Insta in his life – like he couldn't quite believe that he was using it at all. He seemed so unlike every other guy online. His hair was actually messy, it hadn't just been made to look like it was. His jeans had clearly been ripped doing things over the years, rather than in a factory before he bought them. His shirt was a hand-me-down or a charity shop find, not box- fresh from Topman.

The room he was sitting in was different too. It wasn't a bedroom, but you could see a bed, a kind of camp bed like they use in the army. There was stuff I recognized on the walls – a Coldplay poster; a Glastonbury Festival poster just like the one I have in my room; and some other familiar but weirdly anachronistic items piled up around him. Like DVDs, CDs, that kind of thing. I found those super-weird – why would someone his age have DVDs and CDs? Why wasn't he just watching Netflix? And what even are CDs? LOL!

It just felt distinct from any other bedroom I'd ever seen – almost otherworldly. It was full of things I recognized, but somehow they were arranged differently, or looked different. I couldn't work it out. The room was old, the stuff in it was old, but somehow, weirdly, it all felt really new.

He started talking.

'My name is Josh Jones. But most people just call me Kid.' He stopped for a second, stared into the mirror for a second so his face was full on. He had big brown eyes and a chiselled face. He seemed fascinated and scared at the same time. It was like he didn't know what he was doing, like the whole experience was completely new to him.

'I'm from London. Piccadilly Circus, in Soho.'

Piccadilly Circus? Soho? It looked like he was in a cave to me.

'I just want to say, whoever you are, wherever you are . . . I know this, um . . . I know it might sound stu . . . If someone's watching this, we need your help. A lot depends on it. People's lives.' He stopped for a second after he said that, he looked around the room like he was trying to find something – anything – that would help him. He looked back into the lens then and I saw the desperation in his eyes. And then he twitched his mouth and looked down and just said – like it was incredibly sad, 'Well, as if there's even anyone watching. Hardly likely, I guess. Forget it.' And the screen went black. The video was over.

I stared at my phone. I should have written it off as a practical joke there and then, shut my eyes and gone to bed. For a start, there was the surname. But on second thoughts it is ridiculously common. Actually it was the '2078' that really got me. For a minute I pretended to myself that this stranger – Josh Jones or Kid – was actually talking to me from the future. I almost believed it. It was the weirdest sensation, like I was in a daze. I got a little over-excited and things got a little out of hand. My brain began to whir and whir and my heart started beating faster. I couldn't believe what I was seeing.

But then I snapped out of it. Because I'm not the most gullible person in the world. I knew he wasn't from the future. Of course he wasn't from the future. He couldn't be, could he? It could all be explained rationally. He had created an Insta to make it look like he was who he said he was – Josh 'Kid' Jones, from the future.

But even then, wouldn't he have asked his friends to follow the page and stuff to get more traction and likes, and to give whatever he was doing more exposure? Comments? None. Likes? None. But then, like, at the same time . . . WTF?!! It all seemed strangely, worryingly . . . real.

I started to think about different time travel theories I've read about in New Scientist magazine and in the school library. There really are some serious ideas about how time travel might work, although no one's proven them.

Some people say that you'd need a wormhole with ends opening at different points in space-time – but a wormhole sounds pretty much impossible to build. Or you could use a rotating black hole, if you could get near one without being shredded by its gravity. OK, a bit more doable is Einstein's idea that if you went off in a rocket at the speed of light and then returned to earth, you'd kind of find you'd travelled into the future. But all that means is you'd have aged way slower than the people you'd left behind on earth, so they might all be like eighty when you got back – or dead. There's loads more, and much more interesting theories – LOL, if you're interested in the insides of the atom – but my brain is pretty fried right now.

And anyway, of COURSE you can't talk to people in the future – I'm not an idiot.

Still, after the video I just sat there, stunned, confused and feeling, well, a little bit excited TBH. He was just so mysterious and – even if he wasn't in the future – which he obviously wasn't – I wanted to know more; a lot more. I'd been yearning for something interesting and unusual and puzzling to get my teeth into.

I decided to contact him. Whatever, I thought. What's the worst that could happen? If he turns out to be a psycho-weirdo-pervert-alien-woman-killing machine I'll just block him. Simple, right?

The video only had 2 views, but even that immediately made me nervous cos, like, what if someone else had seen it and had already got in touch with him? I felt, well, kinda like he was my discovery, this Josh Kid Jones guy, and no one else was gonna get there first!

So, I decided to bite the bullet.

izzyParry05

Hey! Calling 2078 . . . LOL! Love to help. Kinda confused about how TBH but whatevs.

Cool jacket btw, will DM u 2!

Izzy.

PS. Better learn how to take selfies mate. Superuser tip: try the buttons below the screen ;-)

DATE:

Thursday 11th March 2021

And guess what?! I woke up this morning, after Stephen had snuck out, and this Josh or Kid or whatever had responded!! He'd actually responded.

JoshKidJones

Izzy! Thank you. So much. Though I don't actually know what DM means.

Kid

How can he use Instagram but not know about direct messaging? It's bizarre, like he's from another planet. But now

I've watched and re-watched this guy's video like fifty times, I just can't help myself. I feel weirdly, bizarrely connected to it . . . to him I guess. But how can I? He's a total stranger. But it's like I know him somehow, like we've met before. It's the strangest feeling and I don't like it. I can't get this guy out of my head.

CHAPTER 14

CONTACT

8:41pm, 14 March

Hey

How are u?

Hey

Fine. Thank you.

Not v talkative r u?

Sorry, this is strange for me.

LOL, can I ask u a question

Go ahead.

Why?

?

Why r u doing this?

Doing what?

This ... like ... pretending ur from the future

What?

2078

Well, it is 2078.

;)

What's that mean? The ;) thing?

U seriously don't know?

Never done this before.

Look at it sideways.

Oh. Wink? Winking?

lol. Yes winking.

Why?

;) ;) ;)

?

Like, wink wink, nudge nudge, I beliiiiieve you…

Oh, like, you don't actually believe me…
I don't get it. It's 2078. I'm from Piccadilly
Circus, in London, England. Where are you
from?

From London, ye. Piccadilly Circus?! Hey, you're just
down the road from Les Mis!!! I reli want to see it.
Have u seen it?

Don't know what that is. And there's nothing
just down the road from here.

Les Mis. Les Miserables. Gotta say it – u r a strange
boy, lol.

Miserables. Wait! I do know that! There's
a big old poster on the corner of Wardour
Street. Really old, just scraps left really. Took
me ages to figure out the words. There's a
little girl on it looking sad? That's Les Mis?
Anyway, look, why did you mention 2078?

It's written across your video.

It is?

Date and time. U didn't know? Maybe you've been set up? Someone's fraping you… hahah?

No one knows I have a phone. What Cell are you in? You're not in the Hab-Belt, are you?!

Cell? I'm not in jail, Mister 2078. And besides … why would I tell a strange boy that slid into my DMs where I live? North London, that's all I'm saying.

Slid into your what?

Oh stop it! Well, tbf I acc slid into urs, but…

U still there? Why r u pretending to be from 2078?

Just trying to get my head around why you keep saying the year.

Duh, this isn't 2078! Why do you keep saying you're from the future? And if you're going to pretend you are, you might have the imagination to make up some other date than March 14th.

U keep going silent on me.

Kid?

Sorry. I don't know what's going on. It is March 14. But let's say I'm from the future, if you want. I want to carry on talking to you.

OK. Happy to play along. Let's say u̯ r telling the truth (which ur not) and u r in the future (which u aren't) n ur name is actually Kid (which I highly doubt), why … like, I mean, why r u on Insta?! LOL!

Answer the question!

It's a long story. Tricky to explain.

I've got all day. Toss up between u n the Kardashians … I know, I know … Kardashians def more interesting. DW I can watch them later OD!

OD?

Seriously? On Demand!

Oh. Sorry. Right.

Pokes showed us an Episode of that once.

Pokes?

My counselor.

My teacher. She described the Kardashian show as both the most successful and the most pointless TV show of the entire 21st Century

Well ur teacher has obvi never actually watched it cos if she had she would looooooooove it

Haha

I used to watch a lot of vloggers on YouTube and they would sometimes invent fake characters and stuff. But never seen it on Insta ... Is that what ur doing? Or like, I dunno?

Wait r u being paid? Cos if u r I think that's kinda lame cos I'm soooo broke rn and don't wanna be a pawn in ur experiment if ur getting paid n I'm not ...

OMG! U Rrrrrrrr BEING PAID!

I'm not being paid

Can I be involved? Seriously tho I've been looking for

something like this, and if it's paid, even better!

It's not a project. I'm not a project

I know u hav 2 be all secret n stuff but I SWEAR I won't tell a soul

This isn't … This is real.

TELL ME! I JUST WANNA HELP YOU!

Hello?

Anybody thr?

11:08pm, 14 March

Hey, I'm sorry about earlier. I don't know what came over me.

I was being a total idiot n acted like a dik, so … yeah … sorry. :(

I hope ur nt mad cus I do really wanna help u, withwhatever ur doing.

I mean, I still dnt completely understand, tbh, but, well, but I want to understand, I really want to and

Hey.

OMG. Hey.

Thanks, but you don't need to apologize. When we spoke it made me realize what I was trying to do was stupid and, I dunno … Honestly, I don't even know what I was hoping for in the first place. Nice to meet you. Goodbye.

WHAT? No! Don't go. Please. I wanna know more, I wanna understand

I know ur there. Please. Try and explain. I won't be an idiot any more. Pinky promise.

Pinky?

LOL

Um … OK … Well … Pinky = little finger

We don't use that word.

In London?

Yes.

I use it – I'm in London.

What year?

Lol, what?

2021 ... obvi ...

How is that possible? I mean, I know you're having difficulty believing what I'm saying but

I want 2 understand u!

But I'm finding it difficult to believe you too. Time travel, time travel talking, internet messaging through time, whatever this is! It's impossible. Do you work for Gnosys?

What?

Just be honest. Is this a trap?

WTF? Noses?

R u human or AI?

K now ur beginning 2 freak me out a lil bit TBH.

Tell me. Right now.

Dude ... Seriously. Chill. Anyway, time travel... yeah, it's impossible but it is pretty interesting. Wormholes, entanglement, tachyons.

Do you know anything about them?

Hello?

Don't tell me u've

U've disappeared again, haven't you?

FFS! U suck.

CHAPTER 15

LOCKDOWN

11:32pm, 21 March

Hello?

Are u there?

It's late, you're probably asleep. I'm sorry.
About the other day. About not trusting you.

I do. Trust you, I mean.

I know you don't work for Gnosys. There's just no way you're AI or some kind of Specta goon. I don't know you, but, reading back over what you wrote to me, you obviously have a sense of humour. You're individual, the way you talk is original and . . . well the coders at Gnosys aren't nearly imaginative enough to create someone like you. No way.

OK, so now I'm actually starting to wonder. Whether this is what Leo meant about revisiting the past. Whether you're what she was talking about.

Who's Leo?

You're there? Oh.

Hi.

Who's Leo?

Why didn't you answer me?

I wanted to see what you were going to say, like whether you, I dunno, where you were going to go with the story next. Couldn't be bovd 2 get into another, like, back n forth wiv u.

What you said was kind. Thx.

Leo is my godmother. I saw her the night we met, the night you commented on my video.

I was confused and lost … something had happened, to all of us, where we live, something bad … I needed her advice.

What happened?

You wouldn't believe me, even if I told you. Besides, it's not important right now. I haven't figured out why you are relevant yet

Excuse me?

Why you fit, I mean.

What do u mean, fit?

There has to be a reason you found me and I found you. It can't just be by chance.

LOL. Duhhhhh! That's how the discover page works.

Soz. Dint mean 2 burst ur bubble.

When I saw Leo she told me to look to

the past to find answers, to fix the future. It sounded weird – just like I know all this sounds weird to you. I asked her what she meant, but she wouldn't say any more. Or maybe she couldn't. It was like she knew but didn't know, at the same time. But it reminded me about the box in my dorm, left to me by my mother, full of my past.

I'm sorry. About your mum.

It was a long time ago. My dad left us before that – I've never been very good at keeping parents around for very long, ha!

I'm reli sorry Kid. Can I call you that?

Everyone calls me that.

The box, that's where the phone was. I used to play with it when I was little. It's been passed down in the family. Dad actually got it from his mum, though he never knew her. So it's like ancient. I thought if I figured out how to switch it on, I might find some old photos. Revisit the past, like Leo said.

Wait a second. Is that story about your mum dying

and your dad leaving real or part of the act? And your dad's mum too? Coz ur sick in the head if it's a lie.

I don't really know what to say to that. I've never been asked something so insulting.

No, I didn't mean it like that. Things never sound right in DMs.

How else could you have meant it?

I'm so sorry. I mean that.

This is pointless.

No. Please. Don't go again.

What's the point – I'm talking to a brick wall. What does any of it matter if you think it's all lies?

I don't – I don't think it's all lies – but you said it yourself … This whole situation is impossible to believe in. I'm trying. So hard. So so hard. I reli am. Please. Trust that. Trust me. Even when I say stupid things.

The phone seemed like a dead end. There weren't really any old photos on it. Except one of me holding the phone, and on the phone in the picture is the same picture of me holding the phone. In fact there was nothing else on the phone at all except that and the camera and Instagram. And Instagram led me to you. Leo didn't say any of this was going to happen ... But it was like she knew, like she had planned it, or knew who had, or that this whole thing was, like, meant to be ... That's what I mean. There's a reason it's you, I feel it, like, I dunno, I just know it, I just can't figure out why though. Not yet.

Wow. Lol. I feel honoured. Actually. Thx.

I still think ur bat shit crazy but I feel honoured!

Kid ... !!! What did I say?

Look, I know you don't believe me when I say I'm from where I'm from, from the time I'm from. So you won't believe me when I call my life a prison. Me, my friends, every single one of us that refuses to log in. We're all in prison. Stuck underground. Rotting. When we want to get out, above ground, breathe the air, we either take the risk of dying from the pollution or being beaten up by the

Teeth. Offliners have been killed leaving the Cell before. Most people never leave, unless they're out on scav. And even then we have to travel in packs, and never go out at the same time of day.

The whole world's gone dark. I know you don't believe it – how could you, it's impossible to imagine.

But there is one thing you have to trust is true.

You're so lucky. You're so, so free. Free to walk the streets of London talking and listening and feeling alive.

Lol!

What's funny?

Oh no, just when you said free to walk around n stuff, I mean not reli, lol!

I don't understand. What do you mean?

lockdown, obviously!!!

What's lockdown?

Coronavirus precautions. They keep changing the rules, but it's a total grind whatever. So confused – don't know if we've had the second wave or are still waiting for it. Surely u – I mean, where do u live again?

London, the Ghetto

the ghetto? Where the hell is that?! Are you being serious cos it's not funny if you're one of those weird like conspiracy theorists who say it was all fake or invented in a lab or something, my Nan died from Covid-19 and so it's reli not cool for you to take the piss

Covid-19? you're in 2021, of course!!! you're living in the middle of the first of the great pandemics.

The first?

I'm so sorry about your grandmother

thank you but I still don't understand, you don't know about coronavirus

No I do, I do, Pokes taught us all about it in Counsel, taught us about all the pandemics

KID A HISTORY OF THE FUTURE

of the twenties, thirties and forties. To be honest without them we probably wouldn't be where we are now, the Upload wouldn't have happened I mean. They – Sorry, that sounds weird, saying they, it's you, or not you, but, you know I mean

I reli don't

What I mean is the governments couldn't stop the viruses. I don't really know much about yours, in 2021, if you are when you say you are. But governments definitely couldn't stop the worse pandemics – the ones in the forties were really bad – and even when they finally managed to find cures for the viruses, the air had become so polluted, that with every new pandemic, every new mutation, more and more and more millions of people were dying, because their lungs couldn't take it, people were walking around with lungs that didn't work that made them vulnerable without knowing it. Everyone – young, old, rich, poor – was sick without knowing it, just from living, from allowing the world to become as polluted and poisonous as it became. until they had no choice but to log in, to start a new world inside a computer and leave the old one, the real one, behind.

What the HELL are you talking about? Look I'm sorry, I reli, reli want to believe you but

But what?

Well it's impossible! You are talking as if you're ACTUALLY from the future! Like I know I said I believe you and everything but seriously, HOW can you possibly be able to predict all this stuff? I mean I'm not like that bothered or anything, I just, this is so stupid!

Forget it.

NO! I WILL NOT FORGET IT! NO! DON'T U DARE JUS DISAPPEAR AGAIN!

Why? I thought you weren't that bothered...

Well... maybe... I... oh whatever, sorry, carry on, I'll play along

it doesn't really matter if you believe me or not. It's going to happen, it's out of my hands and out of yours. But if I were you, back then, in your world, I'd get out onto the streets and preach. I'd tell anyone who'd listen. I'd tell everyone I could. Open your eyes and your ears and look at what is happening to the world! Stop polluting the air, stop going so fast that you don't notice what's happening, stop letting technology take over your life, BECOME YOUR LIFE. Because if you carry on the way you are now, the world as you know it is going to end.

Sorry.

No, no. It's… I jus dnt kno wht 2 say . . . So, if you are in the future, then you didn't experience like any quarantine or isolation, or anything at all over the past year…

I'm isolated the whole time. I'm in quarantine twenty-four hours a day seven days a week 365 days of the year! All of us are! I would give anything to live in Soho in your time. Gaz's, Trish's, Bar Italia, all the pubs, so many great pubs, The French House! The theatres! All the old music halls, Ronnie Scott's! Is it true that all the sex shops in Soho have been shut down and turned into Danish bakeries? Pokes – my counsellor Pokes – told me they were.

Loooooooool! Seriously? Im rly rly sorry … u have 2 stop! Like seriously this is 2 much! I mean, it's amazing, dnt get me wrong, but u cnt be serious about all this! Jus tell me … plz … where u are and who u really are … I swear I won't tell anyone. I really won't. I literally luv the whole story n everything n u r obvi so sweet and cute but seriously, im sorry u hav 2 understand what I mean! Jus tell me who u are … I wont tell. Swear on my life. Ur secrets safe wid me.

I should go. It's two in the morning. Goodnight.

It's two in the morning here too. Told u ur not in the future! ;)

Kid?

Kid plz, im so sorry, I didn't mean to … it's just all a little hard to believe, thts all!

I know you didn't. I believe you. But you have to respect how hard this is. You'd be able to have some empathy for my situation if I was just a character in a movie or a book. So why not when I'm real?

CHAPTER 16

NOTHING BUT BLUE

DATE: *Sunday 4th April, 2021*

He hasn't spoken to me for two weeks. I've tried to reach him. I commented on his video again and everything, which is super embarrassing, cos now I'm starting to look like a nerdy fan girl, which I'm not, at all. Of course I'm not. (Well, I'm not trying to be). I tried DMing him after he went offline. Nothing. The next day, it was a Sunday, Stephen and I went for a walk in the park and then saw a movie and then came home and had sex. It was a good day. Any normal girl would have been more than satisfied with it. Me? All I did was check my phone constantly to see whether Kid had replied, which is stupid, cos I knew he hadn't, cos I hadn't got any notifications. Between the walk in the park and the movie; during the movie; before having sex; after having sex. It's literally – I'm not joking – a miracle Stephen didn't notice.

I feel like an idiot. I can't shake Kid from my mind. Behind every conversation I have with someone; behind every task I complete during my day; behind every bite of every meal and every step I take, Kid's there, lurking in the depths of my subconscious. It's like I know him. Like we're connected.

And I went and screwed it up FFS! It's the fact he says he's from the future – obvi. It just annoys me, cos it's impossible and I know he's joking, but I thought I was different, I thought he'd tell me the truth and wouldn't mind me just asking, point blank, where he actually lived and what he was actually trying to do and why he was making all that stuff up about there being more killer viruses in the future?! It wasn't like I was calling him out on anything or trying to make him feel stupid or small. It's ridiculous!

But, the really ridiculous thing is I don't actually care whether he's lying or not. He actually seems genuine and kind and interested in people that show an interest in him. I just wish he wasn't so like intense about it all. I wish he could understand how hard it is to believe.

You know what I really, really wish, I WISH he actually WAS from the future and that he'd just go ahead and prove it to me. Then maybe every convo we have wouldn't end the same way, with him saying he has to go and being all insulted and boring and urgh.

Actually – you know what – I wish I'd never talked to him in the first place, cos now he's all I think about.

DATE: *Tuesday 6th April, 2021*

This morning everything changed. Kid posted a video on Insta of him singing a song and playing that old piano of his. At first I didn't know what the song was about or what the lyrics meant, but that didn't worry me, cos I never know what any song means until I listen to it ten times at least.

When he was singing the song it was like something had changed. He'd seemed unhappy in the first video he posted, asking for help and, since then, all he's posted are depressing, strange, odd photos of what he says is his world, with long confusing captions about the future. This thing called Gnosys and this big Flood thing that ruins Soho. IDK.

But this song he sang about 'Clouds' and the 'empty blue' made me stop and think. It reminded me of the empty white of the blank pages in this diary, of the way they'd made me feel. Happy and free at first, and then, all of a sudden, they terrified me. Maybe the way I'd felt, in my own stupid little life, about Nan's diary, was the way Kid was feeling about his life. Maybe my empty white was his empty blue. Maybe he and I weren't actually so different after all; maybe everything he had been saying to me, everything he had been saying to all of us – about the future, telling me this story – was just his way of expressing the terrifying reality of being an adolescent.

It was the first time I'd actually understood how he was feeling. I'm not saying that I now believe he's from the future. It's not that I know anything more about his actual situation. But the empty blue – I knew what that was and how that felt. It feels like being ecstatic and depressed at the same time. It's wanting something so bad you'd do anything to get it . . . then suddenly forgetting all about it and moving on to the next. It's being excited about what's going to happen tomorrow but being terrified of the uncertainty of it all. It's the empty blue of being a teenager. And I get it.

Whoever Kid is and wherever he is doesn't actually matter. He's a young person, just like me, and he's lost. He's lost and he doesn't know what to do. All he needs is a friend. He's like me; I feel lost too.

CHAPTER 17

THE FLOOD

10:45pm, 8 April

You never told me about what happened that night. The first night, before we talked. Why did you go and see Leo?

Have I ever told you about the Teeth?

The teeth?

White Teeth. Well, first of all, they're not called White Teeth, not officially anyway.

The official title is Mobile Intelligence General Service personnel or Migs, for short. They dress in black all-in-one bulletproof suits. They wear these masks, like digital gas masks, that are made from plastic that molds to their faces. Half the time the masks are see-through and half the time they're black. On every mask there's an identical white plastic breathing apparatus, which covers the person's mouth. That's why we call them White Teeth. Because they've all got identical faces with identical, pearly white teeth. Bastards. They're employed by Gnosys to guard all their Data-Qs

Data-Qs? What's the Q?

I dunno, oh, quantum I think. They house all the hard drives and employees dedicated to keeping everyone logged in and brainwashed. Some of them are in old empty buildings or Tube stations. Some are like big skyscrapers, probably twice the height of the biggest building in 2021. I've heard that some Data-Qs are even in Zeps – Zeppelins – for places where it's impossible to build, or to support Migs on military manouevres. The Teeth are also employed to protect each and every Perspecta user

Which is about 99% of London and probably 99% of the world now.

Kid?

Sorry, it's just, writing that makes me want to break something. Makes me want to scream.

I understand. Well, only carry on if you can …

At first it all seemed pretty innocent – the Mig program. They were kind of like something between bodyguards and IT specialists. When the Upload happened – it started around the time I was born – that's all the Teeth did. They guarded the Qs and made sure anyone logged in was safe and happy. But that all changed pretty quickly. As more and more people logged in, Gnosys needed more and more Migs to serve the huge Perspecta community. Not only were more people logging in, they were staying logged in for longer and longer. Soon the lines started to blur and the Teeth got sharper. If you catch my meaning. You see, being on the street's not illegal; being able to walk around minding your own business is still technically a human right, but not if you're an Offliner. Not to Gnosys and definitely not to the White Teeth. Gnosys believe anyone who doesn't use their product is void of human rights, which is another reason why they 'benevolently' agreed to take on the production and supply of Roxi after the Pittsburgh Pact … stop us second class citizens getting our dirty mits on it. The real world isn't the   REAL world any more. Our world, the one that the human race has lived in since the beginning of time, the one you're living in now, isn't the real world now, so why should us NORMAL human beings have any rights? The OUTSIDE world. The one you can really touch and really feel and really live in, that doesn't exist to them. Now the world's inside your head. Inside the Perspecta Universe. We're a threat to Perspecta. To them, they see us as the scum of the earth.

Did someone get hurt that night? Did the White Teeth hurt someone?

No, thank God. They came and they went without laying a finger on any of us. It's what they came for that terrified me.

11:11pm, 10 April

Tell me about where you live.

OK.

Well …

What does it look like?

It's a ghost town, full of ghosts of a different time. That's what Soho is now. All that life and all that colour you've told me about – gone. It still has its peculiarities, I guess … Teeth come in sometimes, and you get the occasional pop

There you go again. What's a pop?

A Holo-Pop. They're like walking 3D adverts. Mostly they look like they were made in a plastic factory. Except Rosie Rogers. She's the daughter of Hamilton, who's the head of Gnosys. Her grandmother Sylvia started it all. They have Rosie holo-pops.

Too many names!! What were you saying about Soho?

The thing about Soho now is that it's kind of

like our own little fortress, our wasteland, left to fester and crumble by all the people who want to see this world destroyed. We call it the Ghetto.

The ghetto? I remember you calling it that before.

Soho is nearly the last place in London people haven't logged in, where people aren't using Perspecta. Gnosys would say it's full of the dead-beat, offcuts of society. I like to look at it differently, I like to think we are the last bastions of society. Soho – the last fortress of human nature.

So there's no one there any more? In Soho, I mean. Well … Not many?

If you know where to look, down little alleyways and between the paving stones, there are still lights on, people talking, things happening. There are undiscovered people, places and things; there are still so many secrets, even now. There's Skull's where Leo lives, and Lucien's where we go scavving every week or two. He's even got a pub at his place where there's always live music, no matter when you go. He calls it Muriel's after some place where artists used to hang out a century or more ago. You can never know all of Soho's hidden passages and secret ways. They tried to destroy it, with the Flood, but they couldn't. Well, not quite anyway. You can move us and break us and kill us; but you can't turn off the light.

Oh yeah, of course, the Flood, you mentioned it before.

It happened in 2060, the year I was born. Everyone knew it would happen, just not as soon as it did. They say it was global warming, that it was caused by sea levels rising, but that's no excuse for what it did to the city. They wanted it to happen – it's like they planned it. This wasn't just climate change, it was sabotage. And it was the beginning of the end of the Golden Dusk. About ten years before it happened, they began building up the flood defences around London, like the old Thames Barrier, just much bigger and uglier. They installed these huge mechanical steel walls protecting the City of London that run all the way to Waterloo Bridge, and then – after a gap – carry on from Charing Cross to Westminster. And they put another wall opposite, on the South Bank from Blackfriars Bridge to Westminster. Every time the river rose up, when there was a bad storm out at sea, or just a lot of rain, the walls would come up out of the ground like pieces of giant toast popping up out of the toaster and they would keep the water away from the buildings. Apparently they had to use more and more as the 50s went on, and they worked.

This is amazing … You're amazing.

What do you mean?

I mean, I dunno, dnt worry. Carry on. Plz.

Weather's insane these days. Most winters, we only see rain or fog, never snow. But there are crazy blips too. There had been more snow than ever the year before the flood. Snow on snow on snow. Hah. Like the carol they used to sing – In The Bleak Midwinter. Do you still sing carols at Christmas?

Yes. Yes! Of course we do!

We do. We're made to. I guess if we didn't, they'd wither and die, like all the other wonderful human traditions we've lost. From what everyone says, it was the bleakest winter in living memory. And then, in January of '59, the temperature suddenly started to rise. Winter just stopped, just like that, and out of nowhere, five months too soon, summer arrived. I guess it must have made people happy back then – the elders say London in the summer used to be the prettiest place in the world. But the heat from the boiling hot sun melted all the snow in a matter of days and that's when it happened. Snow had fallen particularly heavily in the Cotswolds, the Chilterns and other ranges of hills where the river and its tributaries get their water. When it melted, the water began to rise and it didn't stop. That same week there was a huge storm in the North Sea, out beyond the Thames Estuary. The surge pushed a huge tide up the river and when that water met the water coming the other way, down off the hills, the Thames was suddenly two meters higher than normal. The floodgates rose in all the right places and they worked: they kept the water away from the South Bank and all the government buildings on the Embankment and all the bankers in the City stayed dry. The problem was, because it was coming in both directions the water had nowhere to go but sideways through the gap in the flood barriers. That meant Soho. The area just northwest of the Embankment, the Circus, Soho, Covent Garden – had been considered too far inland to need defending. They didn't think the water would ever get up that high. The thing is it wouldn't have, if they hadn't built the barrier walls and forced it to. Like a ginormous funnel opposite the South Bank wall, the Westminster wall and the City wall created a channel for the tidal surge. The river rose up and burst its banks at Whitehall Gardens. It was unstoppable, like a miniature tidal wave, all the way up Northumberland Avenue and on into Trafalgar Square. They say it was like a lake around Nelson's Column. It carried on, like water in a fast flowing canal, all the way up Haymarket, into the Circus and up into Soho.

Do you mean like a lake? I just … it's just hard to imagine anything quite like it

It was like nothing London had ever seen before. Except maybe the Blitz. The destruction was beyond anything. Even when the river calmed and the flood went down, they say it took weeks to drain the streets. Life gradually got back to normal and London began to move again. But the flood hadn't just soaked the roads and damaged the buildings, it had finally broken the way people thought about the heart of London. I know London had had its jolts – four pandemics I think and two dirty bombs in the previous 40 years – but it had always bounced back into shape. And I know people had been moving out to the suburbs ever since the railways were built, two hundred years ago; but someone had always moved in to take their place. Now almost everyone deserted it, like rats. The flood was the tipping point. People sold off their property in Soho and the other areas the flood had hit worst. If they couldn't sell – because no one would buy it – they just left it to rot, saying it was too high risk to stay, or that the buildings were too badly damaged and we should be developing suburban communities in the north, east and west instead. All the while, the suburban areas of London had been getting more valuable and more desirable than ever, thanks to the rise of virtual reality, which meant the death of travel. Soho didn't matter much to the rich, they hadn't lived there for decades. And it all made sense to the government: Soho and its surrounding streets had been on red alert for years thanks to the big terror attacks in the thirties and forties. The only people that cared were the artists and the actors and the writers who'd always made Soho their spiritual home. That's what I mean when I say it was too good to be true, or too bad, depending on how you look at it. I've always thought someone planned for Soho to be flooded; like they wanted it to happen. Why else would they have left a bloody great gap in the wall? Why else would they have left just one part of London completely undefended? The Upload followed hot on the heels of the flood and Gnosys encouraged people to move north, east and west, away from the centre, by building all of its Habs as far from Soho as possible. I've got no proof, but I'd be willing to bet it was Gnosys that developed the technology for the flood defence system and it was Gnosys that neglected to defend Soho.

Sorry. Long story. If you didn't believe me before, I'm sure you don't now. But it doesn't matter. You'll be alive when it happens. It's probably better you don't believe me. It's probably better you don't believe the horror of what's coming. Ignorance is bliss.

yeah, I mean, it is impossible, but, um, totally possible in theory. I want to be a scientist when I'm older – nothing is fact in my world until I have the evidence to prove it. But I want 2 believe u, so much … it seems equally impossible to me that you could be making all this up. It's so out of this world but also so plausible. It seems so, I, I don't … I. I just feel so confused. U could always just go out there and like, I dunno, record it somehow. What it looks like up above. Y don't u jus put it on ur story?!

my story?

you're insta story – on Instagram…

I don't know what that is

Well you're on Instagram aren't u?! A story is like a post but it only lasts twenty-four hours, it's in the top left hand corner of your profile, it wud actually be super good for ur whole thing actually, like the whole live aspect of it, that it deletes itself… OMG – u should go up above and do an IG LIVE!

Kid? R u there?

You said u live in North London, right?

Kentish Town.

You're not a million miles away from Primrose Hill.

I guess not. So?

I think I've figured out how I can prove all this to you.

What? How?

I've got a plan.

CHAPTER 18

STARS ABOVE SOHO

'Where is she?' I run down the stairs and very nearly collide with Michel coming up them in the other direction at Skull's.

'*Sacrebleu!*' He wears nothing but a dressing gown and an exasperated expression on his face. He's carrying a lantern high above his head. The light fills my eyes.

'Really sorry to startle you Michel, but—'

'It's past midnight!' He affects an angry tone. 'Who let

you in?'

'Who let me . . . ? No one let me in! Leo always told me just to knock.' 'To knock?' Michel raises an eyebrow as he lowers the lantern. 'Nobody ever knocks.' Half asleep, half confused, he mumbles some broken questions. Then his voice tails off and he shakes his head with comic despair. 'Maybe she *is* expecting you, maybe she isn't.' He says, with a heavy sigh. 'No one tells me *anything.*' He takes a second lantern from its hook on the wall and gives it to me. It's heavy and the metal handle is hot. 'Bedroom. You know the way.'

'Merci Michel. Bonne nuit!' Give the old man what he wants, I think. He always likes it when I throw in some French.

'Bonne nuit, mon ami,' Michel replies with a knowing smile, before disappearing up the stairs towards his room.

I've only been up to Leo's private quarters once – the second time I ever came to Skull's, when I was still only eight years old. I remember being lost for words as she led me through the apartment at the very top of the building. There are four rooms, their ceilings made of glass. The penthouse is overflowing with valuable and exotic artworks; artefacts of historical importance; and a myriad of other miscellaneous objects, which matter or mattered to something or someone, somewhere, in the course of time. The rooms are lavishly decorated, with walls painted in thick, substantial colours like pine green and currant red, and opulently appointed with antique furniture.

I wonder if anything's changed in the twelve years that have gone by since I was last up here in the penthouse. *Doubt she's altered it an inch.* I knock at the front door proudly.

There's no way I would've been let in if Leo wasn't expecting me, I hope. The door groans a little as it opens. I stay rooted to the spot and don't move a muscle; Leo is a very private person and this is the innermost sanctum of her private space. *She'll call me in. Won't she?*

After waiting for what seems like an eternity, very gingerly I push the door wider and step into the apartment's sitting room. Not a single thing has changed. *Really – even that stuffed turtle? Gross.* I feel a little disconcerted.

'Leo?' I call out. 'Anybody here?' The grandfather clock chimes one o'clock. I think of Izzy, waiting in the wet and squally April weather. Then, as is always the case, that anxiety gives way to yet more anxiety about something else. What if she's not there at all – at Primrose Hill, where we agreed to meet? What if she doesn't turn up? Then my mind races back to the Cell and everyone fast asleep inside it. I wonder if anyone noticed me leaving this time. Not even Pas was awake when I snuck out.

The fire hisses and fizzes and pops; the dense, smoky air tickles my nostrils. I try my best to ignore my anxiety over the task I've set myself and walk a little further into the room. I wheel around – still, no one there. I could swear that picture's watching me. Now I'm spooked.

'Michel said to—' I begin, speaking into the silence with no expectation of a reply. When it comes, I jump out of my skin.

'Michel is a fool.'

I turn around as quickly as I can to find Leo standing behind me, as if she's been there the whole time. She's wearing pyjamas – fine yellow silk – and a fedora hat.

'Leo! Jesus. You scared the living daylights out of me!'

'But he *was* right to send you up.'

My heart thumps like it's going to spring out of my chest. *You sure know how to make an entrance.*

'Have you been standing there all this time? I've been—"

'Do sit down my dear.' She ignores my question but gestures to a blanket draped over an ottoman. 'You must be chilled to the bone. Here.'

I wrap it around my legs. I've never felt something so soft in my life.

'Cashmere. Very fine.'

'How did you . . . ?' I look at her in disbelief. *Is she reading my mind?* 'How did you know I was coming? I didn't, well, I'm sure I didn't tell you last time how—'

'I've told you a thousand times before, dearest Joshua, and I'll tell you again, Soho is full of beady little eyes. I happen to know a few, that's all.' She smiles. Despite her searing intensity and peculiar appearance, I find her smile comforting and quickly forget about how strange it is that she should have known I was coming. She proceeds to offer me the usual pleasantries.

'Cigarette?'

'No.'

'Brandy?'

'No.'

'How are the twins?'

'Well, thank you.'

'And how is Ruth? And is Mungo still drinking? And I hear Yottam has discovered a new species of Bolivian owl living, previously thought to have been extinct.' And so on and so forth until Leo decides that she's had enough and says, in her rusty, bassoon-like voice, 'How can I help, my dear?'

Having rushed here brimful of determination, now I clam up. I don't know how to explain what's happened, it's so outrageous. At last I just put the iPhone in front of Leo, then gaze at the intricate wooden inlay of her table top as if it's going to tell me what to say. 'It's my dad's old phone, from the tin my mum left me.'

'So you have been revisiting the past,' she says with a feline smile. 'And what have you found?'

'The ph–phone,' I stammer. 'It's not just a phone.'

'Indeed, I remember these things. It has photographs on it, perhaps?'

'No, not really; that's not the point.' I cast my eyes desperately around us. The room is like a time capsule, looking exactly as it was all those years ago when I came to tea and, I'm sure, exactly as it would have during the Dusk, before my time, before even Leo's, perhaps. Being here is like stepping back in time, or rather, through it.

'Imagine,' I say, hesitantly, 'you looked out of your window one day and saw the old London, London in the Dusk.' I gesture feebly at the antique objects around us. 'Like the outside matched what's in here.'

'Well, that would be rather magical,' says Leo, innocently. Then she narrows her eyes shrewdly. 'But are you saying that this is how the phone has made you feel? This is what the phone has *done*?'

I just look back at her and nod. The stress she put on that last word makes me feel she's ready to hear anything.

Then it all comes pouring out. I tell Leo – in as much

detail as I can muster at this time of night – what has happened since my last visit to Liberty's a month ago.

I tell her about meeting Izzy, about how it happened and how, over the past weeks, we've talked more and more. I tell her how Izzy wants to know about me and the Offliners and the world as it is now. I tell her that she and I have become close.

'At least I think we have. I can't be sure. It's difficult to know what she's thinking, you know? I mean, over the internet. I mean across time. You see – that's the point – that's what's impossible. *I* don't understand it! How could *she?*'

Leo seems so calm. Nothing appears to surprise her.

'All I know is she doesn't believe me,' I finish. 'But I feel, deep down, that she's important, you know, in all of this.'

'Important how?' Leo raises an eyebrow; pink smoke rolls out in waves from the corners of her wrinkled mouth.

'I feel like' – I pause to find the right words – 'I know her, or knew her, or will. It's so confusing.'

Blink.

She just blinked. It was almost imperceptible, but I caught it. Leo didn't expect me to say that. That registered for her differently.

'Are you sure it's her?' She distracts me and I lose my train of thought.

'Her? Why do you say that?' It's like she knows something. 'What do you mean *her?*'

'I mean exactly that.' She parries my probing with a broad smile, as if what she had said were entirely natural. 'Are you sure it's her? Are you sure she's the one? You say you feel you know her – that she's important. Well, are you sure?'

But I'm not listening: something's caught my eye, something that makes no sense.

Her gravelly voice grows quieter and quieter until it is nothing more than an indecipherable wind blowing over my ears. All I can concentrate on is the multitude of stars through the glass above my head, each one more irradiant and flawlessly diamond-like than the next.

Stars? Above London . . . In my whole life walking London's streets, I've never seen more than the briefest glimpse of a star or two in the night sky, when the choking smog breaks momentarily. *How could . . . ?* I open my mouth to ask Leo how I could possibly be seeing stars in the night sky – thinking *it has to be fake, it seems almost virtual* – when I feel my jacket vibrating. Again. And again. And again. I put my hand to my breast, not wanting to reach into the pocket itself and expose the phone while it's buzzing. Suddenly I realize I'm deeply suspicious of Leo. The phone continues buzzing intermittently – message after message. It can only be one person.

I'm late for Izzy.

'I need you to help me get to Primrose Hill.' I say, jumping to my feet.

'Up through Fitzrovia, over the Marylebone Road and through the park. When you pass the zoo you're there.' She chuckles to herself, stabbing at the ashtray with the butt of her cigarette. Her fingers are leathery and her nails are yellow from the smoke.

'I need you to help me get to Primrose Hill, *undetected.* That's right under the Podd Way, and in the park I'd be totally exposed. I really don't want to run into any Teeth tonight.'

At that, she beams mischievously and gets to her feet. 'Why didn't you say so, my dear?' She walks over to one of the bookcases, presses gently on a book – the Arden Shakespeare *A Midsummer Night's Dream* – and the bookcase swings inward like a door.

'It's non-stop with you, isn't it?'

'Straightforward's no fun darling. Come on then.' She steps through the bookcase and disappears from view. 'Time to play dress-up.'

The lift is old and mechanical, like the rest of this place. Once I'm inside, Leo turns and pulls the handle of an accordion-like door of criss-crossed metal so it unfolds across the lift entrance. We face each other in silence – she just looking at me, grinning like a Cheshire cat – as we shoot down through the old storeys. Then, after a minute or two, *thud!* I have to hold on to stop myself from falling over. Leo endures the shock of the car stopping a little more gracefully than I do.

She slides back the rickety, groaning accordion door and we step out into the workshop I've previously only ever seen crammed with mannequins. It's strange: the room is absolutely empty now apart from a single one. A mannequin, I start to realize as I follow Leo down the long room towards her office, that is dressed in a Specta uniform.

Close up, I see that the mannequin is me. An exact, lifeless replica of me.

'Leo, why—?'

'Oh, Jonesy here?' She points at the me-mannequin. 'I've had him forever. Moons and moons ago, Michel came up with a way of mirroring people's genetic make-up and installing it in mannequins. Marvellous Michel! There's more to him than meets the eye. It meant we wouldn't have to take our clients' measurements over and over and over again. Oodles of time saved and, well, apart from anything else, I think they're rather fun. It's rather ingenious, don't you think?'

'What, Michel . . . ? So this—' I can't stop staring at myself. Never mind the ingenious technology or this completely unexpected side to the old Frenchman. Is that really what my nose looks like? Do I have a double chin? All of a sudden, I'm massively self-conscious.

'He grows *with* you. Look.' Then, seemingly without any command from Leo, the mannequin starts growing! It gets taller; its face elongates and becomes more defined; its muscles and stomach become flatter and its legs get a little longer. 'Meet your thirty-five-year-old self.'

'What the hell?' I exclaim, forgetting the manners that she has always insisted on. 'Sorry Leo, I mean . . . that's what I'm going to look like?'

'I think he's quite a dish myself.' Then, again without command, the mannequin begins getting younger. My face becomes more and more round and my stomach becomes chubbier and all the definition leaves my body. My hair gets longer and longer and molars become milk teeth and then, as if I'm looking in on my very own dream, there I am as an eight-year-old boy.

'That's who I was when Mum died.' I say the words without being conscious I have spoken aloud, utterly lost in the reverie of the moment. So many feelings rush through my veins. Seeing myself as I was then brings so much back. Suddenly, I think of how Mum was just before she died: the welts on her pale, empty face; the seizures; her last, nightmarish, harrowing hours. 'Stop it! Please! I don't want to do this any more.'

And – in a matter of seconds – the mannequin morphs back into its present-day form, as if by magic.

'I'm sorry. I—' It's the first time I've ever seen Leo lost for words. 'There isn't a day I don't think of your mother. Not a single one.' She takes out an embroidered handkerchief and dabs an eye – something I've never seen her do before. 'El Kellis was the most important person in my world. One day you'll understand that. One day you'll understand why.' She looks at me for a moment, her eyes boring into my soul.

I'll never understand you, I think, *or any of this for that matter. I'll never understand why I feel how I feel and think how I think.*

But her gaze is warm and comforting. I feel safe.

'I'm very grateful to have found *you*, Kid,' she says. 'It's everything to me, being in your life.' She finally drops her gaze from mine, turns to the mannequin and begins removing the white Perspecta suit.

'Stop. Look at me.'

She stops what she's doing.

'I need you to look at me, Leo.'

She does.

'Tell me the truth. Please.'

'The truth?' She's calm, her eyes smile and she comes closer.

'You *know* what I mean. I have to know why you know

me so well, why you always know when I'm coming, what I'm thinking . . . Just . . . tell me what it means.' She pauses for a moment.

'The truth is . . .' She cocks her head to the right a little, and then to the left, looking at me as a dog might its master. It's like she doesn't understand the question, like it doesn't compute. '. . . You don't have much time.' She pivots on her heel robotically and finishes removing the suit from the mannequin, then thrusts it into my hands. 'Go into my office and put this on.' I wait, hoping she'll say more, praying she'll explain herself. Nothing.

Disappointed, I take the suit into the office to change, beneath the walls of bookshelves that seem to tower endlessly into the darkness above.

Just before closing the door I turn back to look at her, but she's nowhere to be seen.

CHAPTER 19

CRUISING WITH DENIS AND BERNARD

That's weird. There's nowhere to disappear to in a big, white, empty room.

'Leo? Where are—?' Before I can go back into the workshop to find her, the door slams in my face.

'Leo!'

My heart's pounding. I start panicking. I don't know what to do.

'Leo! This isn't funny!'

I grab the doorknob. Locked. I hear a click and then

another, and another, and all of sudden I'm going up. *What the hell is going on? What's happening to me? Is this . . . ? Did I take too much Roxi?*

I hold onto the desk behind me for dear life. *This isn't good. This really isn't good.* 'Leo. Please! What—?' The floor is literally rising under my feet. I move up through the narrow, ultra-tall room like I'm standing on some kind of a hydraulic platform. All the thousands of old books on the bookshelves ripple and fold inwards as the floor passes over them, carrying me slowly but steadily up towards the glass ceiling. Suddenly I'm beginning to wonder whether Leo actually plans to hurt me rather than help me. *Maybe she's not who she says she is, after all. Maybe she's been lying all along.* The roof gets nearer and nearer. I check my pulse: my heart beats as if about to burst out of my ribcage.

'Approaching Regent Street,' a robotic voice comes out of the ether. 'Please keep hands and feet in the car until it comes to a complete standstill.' When I look up, to my bone-shattering horror I see that I'm about to smash through a glass roof.

'Leo! Please! Stop this thing, now! Please!' It's getting closer and closer. I crouch down on the floor and cover my head with my hands to protect myself from the glass as much as I can. I close my eyes and prepare for the worst – the glass crumpling and shattering against my body, splintering and piercing my skin. But nothing happens. I stay in the same place for a moment, cowering and praying, and still nothing happens.

'Podd Station 320078. Regent Street, London, where this elevator lift terminates. All passengers alight here.' Then the voice adds, 'Change into appropriate clothing before alighting.'

Jesus. The suit. In the madness of it all I had completely forgotten Leo had given it to me.

Well, whatever this is, if it's spitting me out on Regent Street, I'm sure as shit not gonna get out looking like this. I tear my clothes off and scramble to get the suit on. I finally zip up the white one-piece as the automaton drones angrily, 'Alight. Alight. Alight.'

I look around, to my left and right, then up: the glass has disappeared and all I can see is a muddy, black night sky – I'm out in the open. *Wait. I'm out in the open?* I scramble to my feet, trying to get my bearings and work out where the hell I am.

Woah! Looking down, I catch Leo's office falling away beneath my feet. Somehow, I'm now standing on the glass that only seconds ago I was lying beneath; it quickly mists up and ceases to exist. I'm not on the roof of Liberty's. I'm nowhere near bloody Liberty's. I'm right in the middle of the Podd Way at Regent Street – suspended high up in mid-air! How is that even possible?

I stand there, looking along the track, the Specta super-highway. This is not a normal road. In fact, here there is no road; only a ten-metre drop down to maglev boosters that keep the Podds aloft. I can see rusting boosters spaced out in both directions along the trench far down below.

Suddenly and seemingly out of nowhere a Podd is hurtling towards me at breakneck speed.

I have to get off the Way!

'Leo? Leo!' I scream out in vain. 'What am I going to do? How the hell am I getting out of this alive?' I'm hovering like a fly but as paralysed as someone in a nightmare – stranded, terrified and wind-blown, with nowhere to turn and no one to save me. 'How could you do this to me, Leo?'

Wait. Just wait. The words that come into my head are not in my own voice, and not in Leo's. It's the same voice I've been hearing in my head so worryingly often, speaking to me now like a guardian angel trying to still my fears. *Trust your instincts. Wait.*

But I am not reassured. 'What do you mean, wait?' I wail like an animal – I'm so confused and so angry. This can't be happening to me. I begin to despair. It suddenly dawns on me: I'm not getting out of this alive.

In the heat of the moment and numb with terror, it takes a minute for me to realize that my eyes are clamped shut. I open them and now my feet are on firm ground. I'm standing, swaying, on a concrete platform, moss-eaten and crazed with cracks, that terminates at a kerb beetling over the deep trench, like the old Tube train tracks at Piccadilly Circus, only deeper. Right in front of me, stopped, suspended in the middle of the Way, is a Podd. A totally deluxe one.

On a busy night in its heyday, the Podd Way used to hum with its traffic of metallic shells, shiny and glowing. But like everything else Gnosys built and left behind in the old world, even this – in its time the most advanced technological feat anyone had ever seen – now looks drab, unremarkable, and increasingly dilapidated. Traffic is patchy and most Podds are scratched and battered, generally with several lights out of action. People say they look like squashed rugby balls flying through the air, but I think their beaked bonnets make them look more like a flock of constipated ducks. A flock of shabby, constipated ducks. Give something scary a goofy personality, Mum would always say, and it immediately stops being scary. So I did.

Well, that didn't exactly work this time, I think as my heart pounds and I stare in a daze at the sleek round vehicle in front of me. There's not a speck of grime on its gleaming shell, like it's been lovingly hand-polished or actually came off the production line an hour ago. Its gullwing door is open; its black leather interior radiates with the warm light of the onboard Streem display.

For me? This Podd is for me?

'Hello K.I.D.19.4, my name is Denis. I'm your Perspecta Companion. It's a great pleasure to meet you sir. Welcome to the Universe. Please, do feel free to get into the Podd. The climate on board is set to twenty-four degrees Celsius, which I have determined to be the optimum comfortable room temperature for sedentary adult humans. I must say, sir, it does feel awfully cold outside.' A posh British gent – like someone you would've heard reading the news on the BBC during World War II – speaks to me from within the Podd.

There's nobody inside.

'Do, please, feel free to get in. This is your own personal Podd, sir. Serial number XS 56.'

I look again, certain that the plummy voice is coming from inside the vehicle. Still, nobody there. The centre console doesn't indicate that any onboard computer is talking to me either. It bears only the revolving Gnosys logo, which sends shivers down my spine. I back away from the machine and wait for the new voice to say something else. I want to make sure I'm not going completely mad. I want to make sure this voice is not inside my head too.

But I think it is.

'Serial number XS 56. However, in previous conversations between the two of us, the onboard Streem Artificial Intelligence System – that is to say the computer system that runs this vehicle, sir – has told me that it does not go by its serial number but prefers to be called Bernard.'

I just stand there shell-shocked; totally confused. For all I know, I could have died and gone to heaven. Or hell, depending on how you look at it.

'Sir, if you'll forgive my impatience, I really must advise getting into the Podd. In just under seven seconds the Podd Way's self-monitoring system will have observed that there is no obstacle to traffic, your Legend command will be over-riden, and a normal pace will resume. As bad luck would have it, there are now two other Podds waiting behind, and Bernard here will be forced to move on, sir, with or without you inside.'

'Legend command? What's a Legend command?' I query, still dreaming.

'Six.'

'Five.'

'Four.'

I can't get in there . . . It's a trap . . .

'Three.'

'Two.'

Trust, have faith, get in. Get to Isabel. The more familiar voice, in my head, rings out again.

'One.'

Here goes nothing! I slide in under the gullwing door just in time – it almost closes on my arm. It locks shut. The Podd's engines whir; two black seat belts snake over my shoulders automatically, locking me into the leather bucket seat and forming an X across my body. It begins to move, rising from platform level up to cruising height as it gets up to speed against Regent Street's backcloth of decaying grandeur, and I'm off. To God – and possibly Leo – knows where . . .

In the beginning, way before I was born, the Podd Way was designed as a brand-new system of public transport available to anyone that was a Perspecta user. They called it the SmartCity programme, made out to be some kind of a gift to London. But it's very obvious now that this was nothing more than a ploy to get people to log in. And now they have, it's rare for actual Spectas to use the Way these days. Why would they when they prefer to live in deaf, dumb, digital bliss in the Hab-Belt?

These days, all the Podds and their Podd Way are good for is to transport the many Gnosys personnel required to work away silently in the background to keep the Perspecta Universe going. Mostly these are T-Class Migs – technicians and engineers – tasked with maintaining the Gnosys Data-Qs. The Data-Qs themselves are Gnosys's big link with reality. Turns out you can't stick your head permanently in the clouds without keeping your big fat boots planted squarely in the real world. Data-Qs are used to house and manage the material necessities behind the virtual world, such as power generation, data storage, quantum processing and all that. I sometimes wonder why we ever see Podds down Regent Street. It's a dead end, blocked off by the Wall at Piccadilly Circus. *Guess they're planning a Data-Q somewhere along here,*

I think – just as the BBC voice interrupts my reverie again.

'Welcome sir, I'm enormously pleased to meet you and I must say it's a great honour to be your Companion, sir. I've waited a long time for this moment.' The 'thing' sounds genuinely excited to meet me. His tone is that of someone greeting a celebrity or a hero, like it's a privilege to know me. 'Please do let me know if you have any special requirements or questions, about anything at all. I am here, after all, to serve you. For now, sir, I'll leave you in peace. Journey time is approximately fifteen minutes.' For a moment I just sit there, my hands either side of me, gripping the supple leather tightly, stunned by what is happening to me. For the first time in my life, I am at a loss for words. The world around me is going faster than my brain can process.

'How can I . . . Where . . . Where are you?' I say, my eyes bulging out of their sockets in wonderment and terror.

'I'm very grateful for your question, sir, and delighted to oblige you with an answer. However, the solution to the problem "Where am I?" is twofold. I am embarrassed to admit, sir, that, in reality, I do not exist anywhere. That is to say I have no tangible, physical existence. In other words, I am nowhere to be found or held or felt, although if I were invested with a humanoid form and features I have always imagined I would look like George Michael, who was a popular singer and gay icon at the end of the last century. Forgive me sir – I digress. Having said that, I exist *intangibly* in two places; my code exists in the mainframe computer at Gnosys's Data Q-1 in Manhattan, New York City, which is a city in the United Sta—'

I interrupt the thing, growing impatient. This has gone

too far and I don't have the time. I don't need a geography lesson – I need answers.

'Just tell me how I can hear you? Why I can? Can you read my mind? Is this you, Leo? Is this part of some sick game? Please! Can someone just give me a straight bloody answer?!'

'Sir, I understand your frustration.' The thing takes a whiney, offended tone. 'But there really is no need to take it out on me. I really am trying my best to explain but, as I'm sure you will appreciate, the conundrum of existence is not one that can be solved in three sentences.' *Wow*, I think. *A thing with a thin skin.*

'Okay. How about this, Denis?' I imagine the thing will respond well to be called by name. 'Or is it Bernard? I'm confused.'

'No sir. Bernard is the name that the Streem Artificial Intelligence System on board this Podd prefers to be addressed as. Denis is—'

'You're Denis. All right, all right. Well Denis – it's nice to meet you.'

'The honour is all mine sir, a great honour indeed.'

I'm beginning to get your number, Denis, I think.

'Why,' I spell the words out like I'm talking to a baby, 'can I hear you when I can't see you? In *simple* terms.'

'See me, sir? Oh my!' The voice gets weirdly, worryingly excited, its plumminess getting even plummier. 'What an extraordinary honour. I'd be overjoyed to oblige you, sir! One moment!' There's silence for a moment, then a man, dressed impeccably in old-fashioned tails, his hair slicked back into a perfect parting, appears on the central display in front of me. The little digital figure starts waving at me, then raps his knuckles on the screen, like he's knocking on a door to come inside. Before I can take a closer look, suddenly the whole Podd is filled with a bright kaleidoscope of light as the man who had been just some pixels on a screen apparently steps out of the computer, one foot after the other, and sits next to me in the passenger seat, brushing himself off and cricking his neck. *What. The. Hell.* My mouth is wide open, but nothing's coming out.

'I cannot thank you enough sir: our situation is really quite cramped inside there, as I'm sure you can imagine. My display settings are typically set to their default position, meaning I remain inside the Universe, a figment of your imagination sir, a voice inside your head.'

'But . . .' Nope. Still nothing.

'But you sir – charitable, generous you – have altered the settings and elected to have me take my human holographic form!' He smiles a sickeningly excited smile, his eyebrows so high in his forehead that they connect with his fringe.

Then he snaps his fingers and says, 'Mirror, Bernard, if you please.' What had been the computer screen immediately turns silvery and reflective. Denis pats his hair, brushes some invisible dust from his lapel, and leans jauntily across to check himself in the mirror. He gives a sharp intake of breath, stiffens, and straightens up in his seat, now looking ashen-faced.

'Well, George Michael might have looked like this if he had been fortunate enough to live another twenty years, wouldn't you agree, sir?'

'Did you say universe? Which universe?' I say, regaining

control of my jaw and ignoring his question. 'In. Simple. Terms,' I add quickly.

To give Denis his due, he seems to recover remarkably quickly from discovering that he looks more head waiter than heartthrob. 'In simple terms, sir, I am your Perspecta Companion. I cannot read your mind, but you can, if you wish, address me by thought alone. I exist inside your Plug, which is what allows you to access the Universe sir, the Perspecta Virtual Reality Universe, where "the surreal is your real!"' Denis uses his holographic fingers to put this final quote in inverted commas.

'This is completely impossible! I'm not logged into Perspecta! I'm not, I—'

'Far be it from me to contradict you, sir, but if you were not logged into Perspecta you would not be able to hear me. Do you mean to tell me you are not wearing a Perspecta Two Plug in your ear, sir?'

Once again, I'm speechless. My mind goes numb and I can't make sense of anything. If I'm not logged in, either I'm going mad or someone has logged me in without knowing it. Leo didn't, did she? But without a Plug? Is it part of the suit?

'Sir . . .?'

'What did you call me? Before? When you stopped.'

'I addressed you by your Perspecta ID, sir, K.I.D.19.4. You will have selected it upon logging in.'

'It doesn't make any sense.' I think out loud. 'I'm not logged in, I've never logged in. I'm an Offliner for Christ's sake – I can't log in! But . . . My name, my birthday . . . K.I.D, that's my na—'

'I'm terribly sorry to interrupt you, sir, but Bernard has

just informed me that we have arrived at Docking Station 320040 – Primrose Hill. It is now safe for you to disembark. Are you still intending to alight here?'

I snap out of my reverie. Whatever this is, whatever is going on, I'm going to get it out of Leo once this is done. Now the only thing that matters is getting to Izzy.

'Let me out, Denis. But you're not going anywhere. We'll talk on the way back.'

'Oh yes, sir, certainly, how wonderful! I will patiently await your return, sir!' The gullwing doors hiss as the hydraulics release them from their closed position and I am let out of the Podd.

CHAPTER 20

PRIMROSE HILL

After the sleek luxuriousness of the Podd, it's back to reality. The docking station is dank and empty. No attendant. No Teeth. Only a few parakeets dozing with their heads tucked under their wings. It's eerily quiet, except for the wind rattling away at some broken fencing. I can't imagine a big green hill is a particularly popular destination with vegetating virtual-reality zombies. And at this time of night I don't suppose I'm likely to run into any Offliners from the nearest cell, the Lock in Camden. I walk away from the docking station and the Podd as the gullwing door closes.

How could I have been logged in? How can I be? My mind wanders, until the old voice in my head draws my focus back to the task at hand – Izzy. We agreed to meet at the top of the hill at 1.30. She in 2021 and me in the here and now. The clock on the iPhone – which I'm clutching so tightly I feel I could snap it in half at any moment – reads 2.15. *I'm so late. Shit.*

Even in the pitch darkness of night in the smog-bound city, I am immediately transported back to being a four-year-old, running around this park with Mum and Lilly, our dog. Our flat used to be over there, just down at the bottom, overlooking the park. I remember looking out over the city as it was; and I reflect that still, somewhere down there amongst all of the sick, silver mess Gnosys has created, is Soho. It'll always be the heart of this city – my city, my heart.

My mind cycles through a series of people, places and things, landing back on Izzy. All roads lead to Izzy. Everything. There's no more time to waste; I have to see this through – it's the only way I'm ever going to answer any of these questions.

My phone's buzzing repeatedly now. Another text from Izzy, then another, and another. *No time.* Phone in hand, I begin running as fast as I can up the deserted hill.

3:57am, 11 April

Kid! Whr r u?! I'm FREEZING MY ASS OFF HERE!

Sorry! I'm so sorry! I just left Leo, she gave me a ... I just had the weirdest – I don't know how to describe it. I don't know what anything means any more.

Well I know my nose is about to fall off so if you wouldn't mind getting a move on, that would be great.

Coming up to the top of the hill now. Feeling weird. Feeling very weird, actually . . . need to get up to the hill. Need to get to you . . . Well, you know what I mean.

I don't mean to be rude but we haven't actually proved anything yet, and I'm about to leave, so I'm not really interested in

OK, OK. I'm almost there. One minute!

She gave me a suit! She put me in a Podd and logged me in! I mean, at least, I think it was her, it couldn't have been anyone else.

A pod? WTF?

I dunno how to describe it. It's how the Spectas get around. You sit inside this metal bubble, with no wheels, and when the Podd gets going the thing just floats at like 60MPH up above the ground. About treetop height

I suppose, if there were any trees around the Podd Way. Never been in one before. Usually they look pretty manky but this one that picked me up – I think you'd probably say it was the Rolls Royce of Podds! And I had a companion called Denis with me and he knew my name. This is the craziest night of my life.

OK. You know what? I'm actually reli freaked atm. Just get to the top of the hill so we can get dis over n done with. I chose something small, not telling you what. Like I said. Still can't believe Im doing dis.

It'll be worth it.

Here. I'm standing on the top of Primrose Hill at the observation point.

Do it. Now.

I've dug the hole. Burying the things now.

Tell me where to look.

Jus covering it.

OK. Face the city. Turn right. Walk along the path till it splits. OK?

I'm there.

You're at the corner of a little triangle of grass with paths on all three sides, yes?

Yes, yes, I'm here – triangle of grass, paths on all three sides.

Go and dig. Right in the middle of it.

Kid?

FFS!!!! KID!!! Put me out my misery! PLZ!

Wait a second . . . Wait no, Izzy, I can't dig there. Maybe I'm in the wrong spot???

Why? Why can't you dig?

Because there's a bloody great oak tree where you buried the . . . where you buried whatever you buried. Whatever it is, it must be right under the roots by now! I'll never be able to dig it up!

Izzy!!! please, we just need to try somewhere else.

Can't you see?

Izzy?

You know what. Fine. If you won't have faith then I won't bother. I don't even know why we bothered in the first place. You think you feel stupid? I just almost died for this!

Wait. Kid. Check your phone. I just sent you a picture of what it is I buried . . . I don't believe this. I can't believe it. It's impossible – I mean, I DO believe it, believe YOU, finally!

Checking the pic now

Izzy . . . Hahahahahah!

Acorns! Izzy, you're real, you're you, I'm

we planted a tree!

PART

TWO

CHAPTER 21

LEGEND

We just sit there, in total silence, Izzy in 2021 and I in 2078. We must have been there for an hour, maybe more, until it's now almost time for the sun to come up over the crest of Primrose Hill. Neither of us can believe what has happened, but now we don't have a choice. We've proved ourselves right; we have to accept the truth. The future and the past have been connected, tied together. We bent time tonight. This inanimate thing – this phone I'm talking on, or through, right now – actually bent the fabric of time. Weirdly, I've never felt as close to anyone as I do to Izzy right now. Except Mum, I guess, when she was alive. But it was similar. It was that same feeling, the same bond. I guess that happens to people when they share extraordinary experiences. I guess it's normal.

Izzy is the first one to speak.

'So, what now?' she says. I just burst out laughing. What else am I supposed to do? In one night I've travelled in a magic lift, been nearly flattened by an ultra-posh Podd, discovered I was logged into Perspecta, *and* proved time travel was possible. Possible, that is, if you've got this phone. There was nothing else for it, I have to laugh.

'Guess we just wait and see,' I say, once I'd got over my terrified, nervous, confused hysterics. 'There's a reason why this happened to us – why it's you and me – and I'm determined to find out why. I'm certain it's got something to do with Leo. I just have to work out why and what she's doing and, more importantly, find out whether both of us are safe.'

She asks me what I mean by safe and I tell her, honestly, I don't know. I don't know who to trust any more; I'm so confused by everything but I have nobody to help me see things clearly.

'Apart from you,' I say to Izzy. 'Honestly, you're the only one I can talk to. I trust Pas and Eliza, of course I do; but this is all so strange and mad and weird, who knows how they would react?'

She's silent for a moment. No messages come through. Then, just 'Sorry'. She's sorry that she ever doubted me. I tell her she's being stupid; I've been just as doubtful as her. She says she still doesn't understand it and goes on: 'I feel so close to you, in a way that I don't feel close to Stephen, or to Mum and Dad or anyone like that, and I feel like I've been here before, like I know this moment, you know, like I've actually lived it.'

I'm silent, then I say, 'I agree, it's like a deep, intense déjà vu.'

We say goodbye to each other, promising to talk every day, or as much as we can. We vow to work all of this out and solve the mystery of this phone, of her, of me, pledging to solve it all together. Then she goes offline and is gone, lost to me once more, somewhere in history.

The temperature must be dropping near freezing by now – a rare thing nowadays – and my steaming breath reminds me I must get to clean air quickly. I run back down the hill towards the docking station. Back in the Dusk, if Izzy is looking out over London from the same place, she must see glittering pinnacled lights beyond dark treetops, even while the rest of London sleeps. As I look out now, all I see is black emptiness. I stop and shrink behind a tree as the spotlight of a Chariot or Zep, hidden somewhere in the clouds, suddenly reveals the winter-like waste that was once Regent's Park. But then it flickers onto the crumbling streets beyond. It isn't coming my way, so I run on again down the hill to where the Podd is waiting, its gullwing doors splayed open: a strangely inviting, glowing womb-like thing. The leather belts snake over my body once more and I'm locked into the bucket seat, imprisoned in the nightmarish puzzle that in recent days has become my life.

Sure enough, Denis is waiting there, in the passenger seat beside me. He wastes no time getting straight to the point. *Unusual for you*, I think.

'According to my calculations, sir, you are currently using a beta version of the Perspecta software not yet registered in the system.'

'What! How? You mean like Perspecta Three? That's impossible. Has someone drugged me?'

'I've run a local systems diagnostic check, sir, and both the hardware and software – that is, your nervous system – engaging you with the mainframe are far more advanced than that of Perspecta Three. However, as may seem paradoxical, the code used to write your programme is, in computing terms, truly ancient. I can only say that mere vestiges of it remained even in Perspecta One, sir, which was created in 2022. Indeed I'm appalled to admit, sir, that I do not precisely understand how it is that you and I are communicating in the first place. However, sir, if you have approximately twenty-three hours, forty-seven minutes and eleven seconds, I would be immensely pleased to run an entire sweep of the Universe to see whether the code used to write your programme, sir, has been used anywhere else.'

'Approximately?'

'Twenty-three hours, forty-seven minutes and eleven seconds, sir. Yes sir.'

'Jesus. Just get me home, Denis.'

'Oh, certainly, sir. It would be the highest of privileges, sir.'

But I can't stop myself asking questions. I read *Alice In Wonderland* in Counsel as a kid, and I feel like Alice now.

None of it makes any sense and, even worse, the voice in my head – the one that had always seemed to guide me before – now seems silent, absent and unable to help me, just when I'm in need of *real* guidance.

'Earlier you said I'd said something that slowed the Podds down. You said I used a—

'A Legend command, sir.'

'You must be able to tell me what that is, at least.'

'Well, sir, I must confess – and I must apologise at once for this most embarrassing gap in my data – that I am rather at a loss myself. All I can say with certainty is that your Perspecta ID furnishes your status as "Legend"' – again, he uses his fingers to make little quote marks in the air – 'and that this status has been invoked twice since we met: firstly, at the docking station when you slowed the traffic on the Podd Way, and secondly, during your entire journey by Podd and on foot, when you have been – how shall I put it? – "invisible" to what we may call "outside" observers inside the Universe.'

I look at him, blank.

'Someone *not* logged into Perspecta could see you "plain as day", as you might say, sir, but to anyone logged in and therefore unable to view the real world, you would not register at all.'

He raises his eyebrows and looks at me expectantly, but again all I can do is stare back blankly.

'I suspect, sir, that you require a little more context. Invisibility is not part of Perspecta's conventions, sir. It is not within the capabilities of the Perspecta user. Both you and your Perspecta Companion – that's me, sir – are currently nowhere traceable in the Universe. And that, as you might put it, sir, is impossible.' He knits his brow as if musing. 'What's more, sir, a very brief scan through Perspecta's many-faceted history does reveal one curious conjunction between the power of Perspecta "invisibility" and the term "Legend"—'

'Can you stop it with the air-quotes, please, Denis? I'm finding this hard enough to follow without you waving your fingers around every other word.'

'Please do forgive me, sir. I thought that the—' he stiffens as if he's forcing himself to keep his hands on his lap '—air-quotes would help.'

'You were saying?'

'Indeed sir, the curious connection between being invisible inside Perspecta and your mysterious "Legend" status. Early in the development of Perspecta, when it was primarily an educational tool developed by Sylvia Rogers—'

I groan. 'Educational? She knew it wasn't for education!' I've heard the story before, in Counsel with Pokes and from some of the elders, but they always talk about it with scepticism and suspicion.

But I'm getting distracted, so I take a breath and decide to let it go. Denis resumes.

'*Legend* was the title of a game that enjoyed such success in schools of the Twenties that few children in Britain can have been unaware of it. The *Legend* player adopted the persona of a hero from myth or legend – Atalanta or Anansi, Brunhild or Cuchullain, and many others – and could earn points through various achievements. Notably but, alas, controversially, the game featured "goodness points"—' He stops, seeing me roll my eyes. 'Oh dear, sir, I am so sorry sir, I won't do it again.'

'Goodness points, Denis, yes?' I say, patronizingly.

'In the game *Legend*, sir, goodness points were awarded for acts of amelioration.'

'Amelia who?'

'Acts of betterment, sir; acts that improved, for example, the environment or the well-being and happiness of others. But all this is by the by, sir. What I have been steering towards perhaps a little erratically is this: having gained a certain quotient of points, the hero would attain what was called Legend status, and among its benefits was the ability to move, at will, invisibly through the Perspecta Universe.'

'Hard to imagine what some fifty-year-old school game has to do with me, Denis. Can't you find anything else about this supposed Legend status of mine?'

'Indeed, sir, this is merely a first "stab in the dark", as you would . . . erm . . .' Beside me, Denis lowers his raised fingers as if hoping I haven't noticed them and lapses into purse-lipped silence.

I wrack my brain for something else, anything to help me understand all this. 'What about how I got this Legend status – how I got into Perspecta?' I ask. 'Could it be to do with Leo? With Leonora Skull?'

'Sir, I'm afraid that name is unfamiliar to me. She does not appear to be a registered Perspecta user, which makes your suggestion seem improbable.'

I can't think of what to ask next – my brain is like spaghetti. Suddenly I'm no longer curious, just scared – utterly confused by what Denis is saying, tired, and overrun with emotion. All I can think about is being back in the Cell, in my bed. Safe and sound and ignorant of all of this. Being normal again: a regular Offliner.

That's what leads me to the scariest realization of all.

'Wait. What about Hamilton Rogers?' My voice trembles. 'He must have a higher status, or whatever you call it. Denis, answer me as quickly and as simply as possible. Is he a Legend too?'

'I can say at once that no Legend status attaches to Mr Rogers.'

'What if this is all just a trap he's laid for an Offliner like me to walk straight into? Does he know about me?'

'I cannot answer that, sir. Would you like me to enquire of his Perspecta Companion?'

'No! Stop. Don't do anything! But surely,' I continue hurriedly, 'surely he invented me – I mean invented it. He's the boss, he's the only one that could have given me this status.'

'That does indeed seems plausible, sir. Though two facts argue against it. Firstly, Mr Rogers' forte is business; he is not personally a programmer or even a designer of computer programs. Secondly, as I mentioned earlier, your programming code is older than Perspecta One, and Perspecta One, launched in 2022, is a little older than Mr Rogers himself.'

'But still,' I go on, desperate to know whether my worst fear is finally coming true, 'Hamilton could have given it to me, this Legend status?'

'Well, naturally Mr Rogers has programmers at his bidding. And although your Perspecta code is anomalous in its antiquity, sir, it was not until 2062 that you were logged in and promoted to Legend status.'

'What? That's not possible. None of this is possible!' My cheeks start to tingle and my head throbs. 'I . . . but that's . . . I was two years old.'

He pauses, then says, 'I agree, sir, it does seem a little out of the ordinary.'

I've had enough. Everything in the Podd begins to spin into a blend of multicoloured lights.

'Stop! Let me out!'

'Sir, we are only a few seconds—'

'Now!'

The Podd dives and stops very suddenly. The belt clicks open, throwing me forward so the side of my face smashes into the Streem display, cracking the glass. The gullwing door flies up, I roll out onto a Podd station platform and vomit in a rank patch of weeds.

I'm empty. I have nothing. Nothing in my body and nothing in my brain – nothing is certain and nothing is real. I'm completely lost. All I can do is go home. I'm not safe out here on the Podd Way – 'Legend' or not.

CHAPTER 22

EMINENT DOMAIN

It's the middle of the night,
between anxious dusk and hopeful sunlight
It's when my terrors all come out, unresponsive to my calls,
Invisible to you all.

In the prison of the night
I'm alone in all-consuming black,
can't see no white.

My lights fade out.

But I know there's still a flower, set high up on a hill
Fade me up, fade me up, fade me up

Let's go to the hill
Let hope refill our cup
Let's go to the hill
Make them look up

When I wrote those lyrics I was feeling renewed by what had happened on Primrose Hill, full of optimism. Now even though only a few hours have passed, the surge of positivity has pretty much disappeared. Guess it's the fact that I haven't slept all night – impossible after everything that happened with Leo, on the Podd Way, at Primrose Hill. I'm in my dorm staring at the iPhone and recording an Instagram story, and when I've finished singing the song all I can say is, 'Honestly. I feel alone.'

I'm speaking to whoever's listening, whoever's out there. I don't care whether there's anyone out there or no one at all. In fact, I'm certain there's no one out there now, in 2078, because the other day Pokes was giving a history of Gnosys and she said it had swallowed up all the social media platforms around in the first part of the century like a big fish gobbling up the little ones. It turns out there used to be loads, like Twitter and TikTok and Slanda and Gas, but they all came and went. Pokes says that's why books are best – because if they hadn't been written down on pieces of paper that had been printed out and put on shelves in the homes of people all over the world, but had just been lines and lines of code in an intangible online universe, all those billions of words would've just been wiped away in an instant when the companies went down. It means everything I see on Instagram now is from Izzy's time. Not that I get to see very much of it – I can only use my phone in secret, when I'm alone; and despite my hunger for the Golden Dusk, I find that browsing Instagram leaves me with a hollow feeling. I guess all I really want to do is shout, not surf.

I just need to let it out. I have to get this off my chest. 'I mean, I don't know, imagine something happened to you in your life, which made you question everything you ever thought you knew. All the stuff you'd always been certain of, the stuff you relied on to get up in the morning and go to sleep at night. Imagine something happened to you that made you doubt all of that. And then imagine you couldn't talk to anyone about it . . . You know what, imagine you had travelled in time, but you couldn't tell a soul.'

I sit on the cold, hard floor back at the dorm holding my knees close to my body. Taking the chocolate tin given to me by my mum, I put the iPhone back inside. I slide the tin underneath my bed and its red flowers and gaudy design are swallowed by the gloaming darkness. *Is it really safe there?* I'm getting more and more nervous about being discovered using the phone. But it's the memory of last night's events that actually makes me feel sick. *Please, God, not again.* I stand up quickly, the blood rushes out of my head and I'm disoriented. I run down the corridor to the freezing cold bathroom and hurl into one of the old china sinks. The white has chipped and faded away over the years and now the colour of the basins matches the concrete walls. I look up from the disgusting, brown-yellow soup I've just deposited in the sink, to my face in the mirror. I can hardly see myself, the glass is so dirty. But somewhere, in amongst the polka-dotted scuffs and cracks and abrasions, there I am, ashen and spent. I've got no energy left; there are no thoughts in my head. Everything's silent; and the plain of my mind is naked, unpopulated: a slab of lead.

'Come quickly! Everybody to the Ticket! Stillspeare's making a special announcement! Come quickly!' Jimmy Dolby – a blond-haired boy, probably not more than twelve – comes sprinting down the corridor, pausing only to stick his tiny head and boggle eyes into every dorm. He reaches the bathroom. 'Ugh, yuck, what d'you do that for?' he says with a smirk. I don't even look up from the mirror.

Very reluctantly, I clean myself up as best I can and make my way to the Ticket, feeling like death. By the time I get up there, the place is already full. I scan the room for Pas and Eliza. Eventually, I spot them on the other side of the crowd. *There you are. Boy am I glad to see you.* I'm so fixated on getting to my friends and elbowing and squeezing through the jam-packed round, I don't even notice who's on stage.

'Oi! Losers!' I call out to my friends as I get close. Only Pascale hears me. He turns to look but it's like he's looking straight through me, nothing in his eyes. Eliza doesn't look around at all – she's fixated on the stage. Something's wrong. I get stuck about four or five people short of the twins – a metre or so separating us – and turn to follow everyone else's gaze.

On the stage, in her chair, sits Ruth, flanked by the other COOs a few steps behind. She looks tired, browbeaten almost. Every time she catches the eye of an Offliner below she looks away. It's like she's ashamed.

A tall woman with blonde hair cut into a perfect, triangular bob, wearing a navy-blue pinstripe suit, stands to Ruth's left, towering over her. Her skin is like brushed plastic and her lips are bulbous and unnatural. She looks more like a Tooth than a human. Like them, she seems to be wearing a mask. Sure enough – as if I conjure them up just by thinking about them – to my horror there are four Teeth standing immediately to the left of the woman. They glower down at us all, like a pack of wolves observing their prey from higher ground. I look back at Eliza and Pas. Pas looks at me almost instinctively. Eliza, however, remains focused – her eyes glassy, her face fierce – with pinpoint accuracy on the unidentified woman in pinstripes.

'Good morning.' Ruth speaks, her tone uncharacteristically empty. The entire crowd raises and crosses their forearms and we proudly bare our marks, none more proudly than Eliza, who looks like she's ready both to cry and to fight. Ruth and the other COOs reciprocate, albeit with a little less gusto. At this, our unwelcome guests flinch a little. Whispers wend their way through the crowd. Something isn't right.

'This is Sally Smee,' Ruth continues, 'a representative

of the United Nations Cyber Council and our Minister for
Offliner Liaison.'

Our Minister? Offliner Liaison? There haven't been any
ministers since the Pact, eighteen years ago. There couldn't
have been: there hasn't even been a British Government since
then: that was when the UNCC took everything over. Besides,
we've never been recognized as a real organization. Why would
there be a government minister assigned to 'liaise' with us? I
look at Eliza again. She continues looking ahead. Her frown
says it all – this is a lie. Even Ruth seems unconvinced by what
she's telling us.

'A month ago the representatives from Gnosys to my
right made us a proposition.'

The representatives from Gnosys to my right? I marvel that
she can speak so calmly about the Teeth that stand inches
away from her.

She goes on, 'We have since considered the proposition.
Last night, Mrs Smee and the personnel here from Gnosys
returned to discuss the proposition further. The other COOs
and I conferred with Mrs Smee at length, along with the
individuals employed by Gnosys. And we believe, *I* believe' –
Ruth stresses this, trying to give what she's saying some kind
of affected, personal touch – 'we have reached an accord that
both parties can be satisfied with.'

It's like the oxygen is sucked out of the room, like
everyone's taken their deepest, longest, final breath. No one
stirs in the vastness of the Ticket.

'I'll let Mrs Smee explain the agreement further.'

Clip, clop, clip, clop, clip, clop. Like a rouged and ribboned
show pony, the bobbed blonde trots into centre-stage, her

stilettos clacking on the podium. Snapping like piranhas.

She stands directly in front of Ruth and clears her throat. I swear I see the Teeth stiffen for action, scanning the crowd for anything threatening. *Bastards! What makes you think we'd give you the satisfaction?*

'Friends! What a pleasure it is to stand before you all, and may I say how simply terrific it is to be invited finally – and welcomed so warmly – into the London Offliner Cell. *Your* home.' Her voice is pursed and nasal and a smile seems permanently smudged across her smug face. Semi-audible murmurs begin surfacing in the crowd. *No one invited you here; no one wants you; you are not welcome.*

I've never seen Ruth look so uncomfortable. Mungo is even redder than usual, his face full of rage at the injustice of it all and the hubris with which Smee carries herself.

The woman clears her throat again, still smiling falsely, and waits for the murmurs to desist. Strangely enough, they do, and silence washes over the Ticket again.

'Long before Gnosys successfully united our divided world, the United States Government went some way towards initiating the unification of people everywhere and establishing a respect and understanding between the people and the Government. One of the ways in which they established this feeling of understanding was by instituting into law the principle of "eminent domain". Eminent domain meant that the Government could take over any private property it desired, provided it paid the correct price for it or made arrangements for sufficient alternative habitation. It used to be used in Britain in a small way, when it was called compulsory purchase. By making eminent domain law, the US Government was able to take back land from the likes of the big banks and corporations and make it public, thus providing for the common man. They called it "draining the swamp".'

At this, she purses her lips and claps her heels together, as if to say *Don't we think that's clever? What a clever quip!* Then she pauses, waiting for a cheer, or perhaps applause. She gets nothing more than silent resentment from her audience. I feel my face screw up and my jaw clench tightly in disgust. If there's one thing that's been drilled into us in Counsel since day one, it's the story of when and where it all started to go horribly wrong.

The period of American history – world history – she's talking about didn't just plunge the world back into the social and cultural dark ages, it set a precedent for how much governments and corporations worked together and how much they could be in each other's pockets. Before, governments and more specifically politicians at least *pretended* not to be the puppets of the rich and the powerful. Afterwards, they no longer needed to pretend. Presidents and prime ministers no longer bothered to relinquish any of their business interests. Politician after politician was more openly corrupt than ever, going so far as to make light of the fact in their public addresses. Politicians have always been frauds, but now they brazened it out as if it was a virtue. Without those leaders and their policies, and the less powerful governments that blindly followed them, there's a good chance the Pact would never have been signed, which would have made the Upload impossible.

'Eminent domain,' she continues, 'was a key part of the Pittsburgh Pact, the document that has, in the years since, saved so many millions of lives and made better the lives of billions more.' She purses her lips and inclines her head a little, paying homage to the ruinous deal. 'The eminent domain clause in the Pact stipulates that, wherever necessary, the UNCC may appropriate private property for public use if it is in the interest of the people. Eminent domain, dear friends, is what has allowed *us* to come to an agreement that will favour all. The UNCC wishes, on behalf of Gnosys, to take over the land the Cell currently occupies, in order to make room for a new and essential Data-Q—'

An audible gasp runs through the Ticket and the terrified hum starts up again. I can't believe my ears. Leo was right, Gnosys don't care about what happens to *us*, they want the Cell itself.

'A new and essential Data-Q,' Smee continues, 'that will allow Gnosys to properly serve the ever-growing population of Perspecta users; a Data-Q that will allow the world to move on to an ever-brighter Perspecta future. The entirely revolutionary and long-awaited Perspecta Three is coming and it will change the world immeasurably for the better. But such change never comes without the united efforts of the community. Without a little help from our friends, as the old saying goes.' When she says this she clicks her heels against the stage – *clickety click*, *clickety click* – desperately pleased with herself, bracing herself for her grand finale. 'Thanks to the work begun so long ago by Sylvia Rogers, Lord rest her soul, data storage and processing capacities have taken a literal quantum leap. But data transmission on the scale demanded by the Hab-Belts and by Perspecta Three requires much more space, much more connectivity. The data must flow! The 2060 Flood left the old London Underground network grievously damaged, but Gnosys engineers have rescued it from otherwise terminal decay, installing more than a million kilometres of cabling and converting many stations into Data-Qs. Less than a kilometre from here in each direction, Oxford Circus and Waterloo are now almost ready to go online! Piccadilly Circus is the missing link in the chain.'

CHAPTER 23

HIC MANEBIMUS OPTIME

Smee starts talking again but my mind is in shock and can no longer process what she's saying. Something about relocation, Gnosys funding, a brand new state-of-the art Cell, unlimited Roxi supplies for the Offliners. Peace and cohesion. I'm too much in my own head, my heart is pounding too painfully, fear is rising through me.

'It has been put to my colleagues here,' Smee says, touching the shoulders of two Teeth as if they are her bosom buddies, 'that alternative routes might be found for this vital data connection and for the new Data-Q. Alas! Not so. Perspecta Three is on its way and we do not have the luxury of time. We thank you for salvaging this former Underground station from ruin and making it ready to house a state-of-the-art Gnosys facility. My dear friends, you have many admirable qualities. But as Offliners, you contribute nothing to the Perspecta economy and therefore can hardly expect Gnosys to pay hand over fist to help you stay in the luxury to which you have accustomed yourselves, occupying prime real estate that was never yours to use in the first place. But, with the help of our comprehensive and generous Offliner Relocation Package, by making way for the future, you now have the chance to make history.' She smiles yet another terrifyingly insincere and unnatural smile. 'I have absolute faith that the wisest and most foresighted among you will welcome your new role as both an honour and a privilege.'

A shadow grazes my peripheral vision. Someone or something is moving, and fast, towards the stage.

How could Leo possibly have known? What are we going to do? Where will we live? We'll die up there, out in the open. My mind spins like a Catherine wheel. I go cross-eyed, my brain too busy processing what's within to concentrate on anything without. There are shouts and heckles in the distance, out there in devastating reality. There's a ruckus on the stage. I want to look up. *Look up!* Yet still I can't take in anything going on around me right now. *We have to do something. What is Ruth thinking?*

'How could you?!' someone screams. It's a young voice, but full of wisdom and strength and anger. I look up and see Eliza now standing in the middle of the stage looking straight at Ruth.

'Eliza . . . !' I hear Pas shout somewhere. Eliza transfixes me. She's like a warrior. *She's also on stage with four Teeth.* I pull myself together. Filled with admiration and anxiety for her, I push my way violently through the crowd towards my friend standing on stage. If something goes down, I want to be there.

'How could you do this to us?' She howls like a banshee in Ruth's direction, holding nothing back. Her passion stills the wild, emotional crowd. Ruth says nothing. 'You know there's no alternative Cell, no Gnosys funding. Gnosys funding! Free Roxi for all? Are you mad? No, actually, are you stupid?'

Mungo, ever Stillspeare's most loyal acolyte, shouts at Eliza to stop, but she ignores him. He moves to get her off stage but, to my great surprise, is waved back by Ruth.

Hold on, I marvel; *did Ruth want this to happen? Did she want someone to do this?* Eliza seems to notice too. Suddenly, she stops berating our leader and turns towards us. I see Pascale closing in on the stage, looking like he has no intention of allowing his twin sister to go through with this.

'All of you need to realize what this means. I mean, what it really means. They want us out. Not moved to *greener pastures*,' she says with a sneer. 'They want us thrown out on the street to rot like the animals they think we are. The animals *she* thinks we are.' She spits the words out, pointing at Smee. 'This isn't about needing extra space! They want to build a Q in Soho, in the name of the blessed holy Sylvia? My arse they do. The only thing they want is no more Offliners.'

She turns to the COOs. 'Our very own leaders would have us slung out on our arses like careless Seekers! Like we haven't fought and died and slaved for the Cell – our Cell, our home – for the last twenty-five years!'

Some of the Officers are scared for themselves, others seem scared for her. But their expressions betray their true feelings. Eliza's words are too compelling.

'Just because they come in here with their platoons and their power, that doesn't mean you don't have a choice. Sure, they might outgun us one thousand to one, but since when was standing up for yourself about whether the other guy is bigger or smaller than you? Standing up for yourself is about making a choice. It's about choosing to fight injustice.'

She pauses and takes a deep breath.

'Maybe you just don't want to *admit* to yourselves that you have a choice. Because admitting *that* would mean being prepared to die for what's rightfully ours.' She stares long and hard at each and every one of them – Mungo, Suzannah, Yottam, Ruth . . .

She turns to us one final time.

'Because they know what *our* choice would be! We would choose to fight! For this! Our home! Our land! It belongs to us! To you! *Hic manebimus optime!* You know what that means!'

There's a clamorous cheer from the crowd, which makes Smee flinch, the permasmile slowly disappearing from her synthetic mouth.

'*Optime! Optime! Optime!*' The roar is deafening. Five hundred souls, standing up for what they believe in, what is rightfully theirs.

Hold on a second. I look around and realize that, in fact, the whole crowd isn't crying out for their freedom, only a third of them – my third, the youngers. I watch as the elders – who make up most of the crowd – go from patronizing contentedness to horror as they watch Eliza basking in shouts of *freedom* and *power to the people* and *fight for the next generation* from the youngers. The elders don't agree with Eliza, I see. They agree with the officials on stage. They don't think we have a choice.

Eliza is like a general talking to her troops before battle. It's painted all over her face: she is interested only in the fight, in doing the right thing. I feel an intense surge of pride shoot through me.

'And you,' she looks straight at Smee, 'can take your offer of friendship and union and march it all out that door. And take your goons with you while you're at it!'

She makes to jump off the stage, then stops, and turns back to face our unwelcome guest. 'You know what? Actually, do me a favour, will you?'

Smee nods curtly, terrified.

'Pass a message on to Hamilton Rogers. From. Me.'

A look of grave concern crosses Ruth's face. Now the elders, clearly terrified of the consequences for them, have begun protesting to Eliza. 'It's not for you to decide,' says one. 'We have COOs for a reason,' proclaims another. 'It's not the youngers' call. What the elders choose will be what's best for everyone.'

Eliza disregards their protests. 'The only way Hamilton Rogers is getting us out of here is by coming down here and dragging us out himself!' She jumps down off the stage and is immediately accosted by Pascale, who grabs her arm and pulls her away to a corner of the Ticket forcefully, out of sight. *Away from the Teeth, her adoring fans*, I think, as I watch the demonic half-men watching her.

Up on the stage, Ruth approaches Smee cautiously, flanked by the other COOs. *Damage control*, I think. Momentarily, the Teeth surge towards the COOs in attack formation; but Smee calls them off and Ruth is allowed to come forward. She wheels herself over to Smee. They begin talking, their expressions grave, rushed, and guarded.

Unable to make out what the two women are saying to each other, I turn to seek out the twins. The atmosphere is descending further into angry mayhem. Youngers and elders are arguing everywhere I look.

I find Pascale glaring at Eliza. 'What the hell were you thinking?' he rasps, pulling his hands through his hair. 'You're going to get yourself killed!' Seeing me at their side, he shoots me a look: *don't get involved.* I keep my distance. This is just between the two of them.

Eliza shrugs defiance. 'They don't scare me.'

'They don't scare you?' Pascale seems close to tears. 'You're not scared?'

'That's right. That's what I said.'

'And you think that makes you strong?'

Eliza looks away with an exasperated sigh.

'Not being scared isn't clever or strong,' Pas resumes. 'It's dumb. Sorry to break it to you, Napoleon, but that – what you just did up there – was plain dumb!'

Bristling with defiance, Eliza gets up in his face.

'Hey, stop, come on,' I interject. 'Stop guys!' But they both ignore my pathetic pleas.

'You're a coward. Just like them. All of them, cowards,' spits Eliza.

'What? Not wanting to die makes me a coward? You're more stupid than I thought!' Pas shouts back.

'You know what I said was true. *Someone* has to say it! Why can't you just back me up, Pas? Why do you have to be such a weed all the time?'

'Maybe you're right. Maybe it *is* true that they want us to rot in hell. Maybe they do want to cleanse the world of rats like us; maybe that's just the way it is. But why, for God's sake, does it always have to be *you* that points it out? Why do you always put yourself in the firing line? One day' – his voice cracks – 'you're going to get killed "speaking the truth" and I'm going to be left sisterless. Why don't you think about that before opening your big mouth next time and going all Winston Churchill on us? Huh?'

Eliza stares at him, long and hard. 'Sod this.' Then, wrenching her gaze from his, she storms towards the exit.

'Oi! Eliza!' I shout. 'Where you—?'

Too late. She runs up the stairs out of the Cell.

'Don't bother,' Pascale huffs. 'There's no point.'

'She'll be fine.'

'No! She won't! That's just my point. She won't be fine. None of us will. We can't win. I mean,' he gestures towards the Teeth, 'look at—'

But suddenly they're leaving, and Smee too.

What? I think. *Why would they go to all that trouble just to leave empty-handed?*

'You see!' Pascale turns back to me, his face red. 'She was wrong. Smee and the whole lot of them are going away, we're not dead, and nothing's going to happen to us. But Eliza – she's got a target on her back now, wherever she goes, whatever she does, they're—'

He stops suddenly as the Teeth walk right by us, escorting Smee out of the Ticket. The ghoulish soldiers are close enough to touch. As one of them looks at Pas and me for a moment, I see my face reflected in his visor.

Pas turns and leaves.

'Pas, wait—'

I go to grab his arm, but before I can my head is split in half with an incomprehensible wail. I screw up my eyes in agony and suddenly the wail is more than a sound, it's an image . . . images.

Aaaakhkhkh100111001111010100zzzzrrrrrr!

Numbers. Letters. Symbols. Sounds. Pictures. Flashing through my brain, paralysing me. I drop to my knees, momentarily disabled. It's like having the worst migraine imaginable. It's like I'm . . .

I come around and look up. Two black leather boots march away from me. It's the Tooth that looked at me. *It's like I can hear them, like I'm communicating with them . . . the Teeth!*

Then there is another sound in my head, a more familiar one. *Eliza*, it says. The voice in my head is speaking up again, after all this time. *Eliza.* It talks with urgency, like it's calling me to action, telling me to find her. The Tooth looks back at me just before disappearing from view.

Eliza! The voice booms.

Then, suddenly, as if I have no control over my body, I jump to my feet and speed across the Ticket towards the exit, chasing after the White Teeth. I run up the stairs but they've already left and the door is locked shut again. I pull hard on the lever. The door opens, painfully slowly, and eventually I get out into the evening gloom. Visibility is terrible and I can't see a thing. The Circus is filled with smog. I begin coughing uncontrollably, choking on the noxious air.

'H–h–help.' A whimper in the smog.

'Eliza? Eliza is that you?!' A terrifying realization dawns on me.

'Help m—' It's her. She's hurt. *If they have so much as touched her. If they've done . . .*

'Lizy! I'm coming! Stay right there. I'm coming. Just . . . Just keep talking.' It's impossible to speak with enough volume; I'm suffocating. She continues to make as much noise as she can and I follow the noise. She's obviously in a lot of pain. *I can't bear it. I can't . . .* I circle around the back of the entrance to the Cell and see a white trainer on the floor. It's Eliza's; I'd recognize it anywhere.

'Lizy! Are you there?' I speed over and see that the white shoe is connected to my oldest, dearest friend. Eliza lies slumped up against the railings surrounding the entrance, barely conscious. She looks as if she has been beaten to a pulp. Her eyes are closed and swollen, her eyelids are the colour of ripe plums. She is completely covered in blood. I try to get her to her feet but she howls with pain. Bones are obviously broken. She can't move. Her body is limp and leaden.

'It's okay. It's going to be okay. I'm going to get help. I'll find . . . *help!*' I cry out. 'Anybody!'

Tears stream down my face. Pascale was right. He'd been right all along.

I take off my shirt and press it firmly against a large, bloody gash on Eliza's cheek.

Crgghsssssjshdrlahxhs10011100111101010!

'Arghhhhh!' I fall back and hit the floor, thrashing around in agony. The pain is unbearable. Suddenly, I hear the thunderous hum and whir of powerful electric engines. I look around and see a Chariot lifting off into the air – the kind that Teeth always use, which looks like a giant metallic manta ray. The massive, shining cargo door of this enormous airborne people-carrier slides open and inside I see a Mig – the same one as before, I'm certain – looking at me once more, his matte black eyes boring into my soul. Next to him is Smee. She smiles at me, that same sickening smile she had flashed on stage, as if it has never left her lips. The MantaRay Chariot's engines blast, blinding me with dust and smog as it soars off into the murky sky.

CHAPTER 24

THE SAN

It's like I'm blind, the world a blur. I see familiar faces and hear friends' voices, but nothing registers, none of it means anything. People push and pull and offer to help. Youngers rally around me, tugging at my shirt, propping me up. It all seems incoherent, nothing matters any more. I move through the Ticket carrying Eliza's unconscious form, her head dangling, her eyes rolling around in their sockets, and the whole room spins around me like I'm at the centre of a roulette wheel. I am in complete and utter shock. Nothing but the present – nothing but the body in my arms – is of any consequence to me. My friend is hurt; my oldest, closest friend.

The gash on her head bleeds profusely. What if she dies, how am I going to feel? How am I supposed to explain it to Pas? How am I supposed to tell him that it wasn't his fault? It wasn't; it wasn't anybody's fault.

No! I'm suddenly filled up and overwhelmed with hatred. *It was somebody's fault. It was Gnosys's fault. Their fault. The enemy's.*

I look down at Eliza, I feel the muscles in my arms ache under her weight. She's not heavy, thin as a rake, but here in my arms she weighs the whole world.

Eliza is hurt. She is badly hurt.

I'm in floods of tears, the salty droplets make me want to vomit. The whole thing makes me want to vomit. I want to throw up. I'm going to be sick. Then, suddenly, my mind skips and I recall the migraine, and the Tooth and the way it looked at me. Having forgotten everything – who I am, where I am, past and future – my brain unexpectedly thrusts me back into the moment and consciousness resumes. What is happening? What am I? Who am I?

I reach the Chute and look down at Eliza's purple, pulped face; and the voice in my head says, *If you don't get her to Yottam now, she's going to die.*

'We have to hurry!' I try to shout. Several elders rush over to help.

'I'll strap in,' I tell them. 'You hand her to me and

then pull, all right?' I thrust her into the arms of two of the stronger, less frail-looking men who have come to my aid. 'Here!'

There's a crowd forming around the Chute. I jump in and secure myself in the harness. When they see that I'm safely in the swing, the two elders hand Eliza back to me, almost dropping her down the twenty-metre hole in the process. 'Careful!' I take her across my lap and, using the excess rope from the harness, fasten her body in as best I can. My head's spinning. I'm on autopilot.

'Pull!' The two men, helped and cajoled by the large audience assembled around the Chute, unlatch the down rope and tug violently. 'And someone find Pascale!' I call out, my stomach flying up into my mouth as I'm swallowed by the black hole, the horizon of terrified faces receding in a blur of speed. With the added weight of Eliza's body I feel like I'm dropping faster than I've ever dropped before. All I can think about is how terrified I am that my friend is going to die before I can get her to the San.

By now I feel pathetically weak. At the bottom, it takes every muscle to lift Eliza and myself out of the harness. I make for the westbound Piccadilly, where Yottam has his Sanatorium. *What if he's not there?* I suddenly think. *There's always a nurse on duty, surely?*

As I run through the various tunnels and passageways, Eliza's head drooping dangerously close to the concrete floor, I realize that the last time I spent any real time in the San was the day Mum died. A rush of different emotions overcomes me. Chief among them is anger. This stupid, shitty, disgusting world . . . This stupid, selfish mess of a world . . .

You took my mum from me, you've taken so many people from all of us, I will not let you take Eliza too.

She's getting heavier in my arms. I make it to the Sanatorium's arched entrance, whose giant oak door – scavved years ago by Rory Stillspeare – is closed. I bang hard but the old wood absorbs the shock and my fist makes barely any noise.

'Yottam! Please! Somebody! She's gonna bleed out—' The door flies open and, sure enough, standing as tall and as proud as a giraffe, there is Yottam Yellowfinch, the doctor.

Like some kind of effete adventurer, he wears a matching tan-coloured shirt and trousers above knee-high leather boots, which he keeps so buffed and clean that light seems to reflect off their mocha-coloured skins. A red polka-dot neckerchief perfectly frames his chiselled, stubbly face. It's a kind face, set around the bluest eyes you could ever imagine, filled with a history of exciting escapades and the never-ending possibility of another wicked, wonderful adventure.

'Kid!' he says in his Canadian drawl, smiling broadly. Then the twinkle in his eye vanishes. 'Oh my goodness,' he says, faltering slightly as he takes in the terrifying sight of Eliza's bloody face and tangled body. 'Give her to me!'

In a flash, he takes Eliza from me and carries her, like she's lighter than a feather, over to an empty bed. I collapse in the doorway, all my energy spent.

A distant voice calls out. 'Where is she? Kid? What happened? Kid! I came as soon as I heard.'

Turning, I see Ruth calling out as she and Ursula rush down the corridor towards me. Ruth wheels herself at a pace; her mother hobbles behind, barely able to keep up with her disabled daughter.

'I . . . I . . .' My body's gone into shock.

'Out of the way! Now!' Ruth's voice is commanding.

I can't move, can't you see? I can't even manage the words.

'Joshua.' Ruth glares, spitting from her chair. 'Get. Up. Now.' I struggle to get to my feet as quickly as I can. She wheels herself past me. When she sees Eliza, her warrior-like determination gives way to abject horror.

'Oh . . . Oh God, I can't bear it. The poor little thing !'

Ursula reaches the door and sees Eliza lying there on the stretcher, barely breathing, tended to by Yottam. She gasps and duly bursts into floods of hysterical tears.

I need to be strong, for Eliza, for everyone. I try to compose myself. I catch my breath and take the old lady's arm. Together we walk inside, onto the platform.

The Sanatorium is long and vaulted, its walls and ceiling completely covered by an enormous mural depicting animals from *The Story of Babar*, a French children's storybook about a world of friendly elephants, written in the 1930s. Yottam once told me that it had been his favourite when he was a boy. For half the length of the platform, the sunken train-track area is boarded over, allowing more space for beds and for the medical equipment that has been scavved from deserted hospitals around London. It looks so old and antiquated. Alongside the far half of the platform a train still stands. It has never moved in my lifetime. Its carriages extend beyond the platform and into the tunnel, furnishing Yottam with even more space.

There's more space above, too. At the same time that the Ticket was remodelled, the Piccadilly Line platforms were modified to fit double-decker trains – though they were never built because the Podd Way came along instead. But Yottam got Rory Stillspeare to make use of the extra headroom above the platform. Hoisted above the train, on winches anchored to the vaulted ceiling, are suspended even more carriages, with a staircase running up to them.

You only get the full extent of Yottam's mad genius when you come down to the San. It doubles as his own personal zoo, full of the most unbelievable collection of flora and fauna, none of which would have survived up above or without his help. The animal conservatory stands beside the two carriages at the far end of the long vaulted hall. A huge glass structure houses a menagerie of peculiar and remarkable creatures that he has procured, he says, from all four corners of the globe. It's extraordinary to behold – all that life and colour and variety here, down in the murky depths of our underworld. The commotion around Eliza is redoubled by the squeals of monkeys and chattering of parrots, as if they share our horror at the savagery we have witnessed.

I leave Ursula standing a little way away from the bed and slowly approach. Eliza is convulsing violently and foaming at the mouth. My stomach lurches and my throat closes up. How can this be allowed to happen? Tears stream down my face.

Yottam does everything he can to quell the heavy bleeding whilst an elder nurse tries to insert an IV drip in Eliza's right arm. Yottam shouts incomprehensible instructions at her and another two assistants who attend the ancient medical machinery pumping and fizzing and clanking and popping behind her bed.

'What's that? What are you doing?'

The nurse looks up at me but makes no response, then looks to Yottam, who doesn't look at her. She returns to her search for a vein.

'Hey! What's in that?!' In my heart I know they are doing everything they can, but I'm so distraught, I can't bear anything to touch her. Ruth looks at me as if to speak.

Yottam gets there first. 'We're inducing a coma. She's losing too much blood.'

'A coma? You mean you're putting her to sleep? How is that going to stop the bleeding?'

'A deep sleep, yes.' It's the way he says it, something's not quite right. 'It'll slow her heart, so slowing the flow of blood. It's really the only way.'

'And then what? How d'you wake her up?' Yottam looks to Ruth for guidance, but she is deadpan, focused on Eliza's chattering lips and cramping jaw. No one gives me an answer. It's the uncertainty on the nurse's face that gives it away.

'No!' The blunt word just comes out of my mouth. 'It's not up to you. It's up to her family, to Pascale.'

'Kid,' Ruth snaps, 'didn't you hear the doctor? There's no time.'

'There's always time!' A single tear rolls down my cheek; its bitterness tastes like helplessness. 'She'll keep fighting, I know she'll—'

'She's fighting too much!' The doctor begins losing his patience. Sweat is building on his brow as he works overtime to treat all her clotting cuts and gashes. 'That's exactly the point! She's got *too* much fight left in her! We *have* to calm her down, Kid . . . She's haemorrhaging.'

I stare at my friend – at her unrecognizable face –

and decide that I have lost. My heart slides down into my stomach like an oyster. *We've lost, they've won. This is it. It's over.*

'Where is she?' Pas – red-faced, crying and panting like a hyperventilating dog – rushes into the San and over to the bed, pushing past all of us. He grabs her arm and falls to his knees, wailing in despair. 'What's . . . Why . . . ?' He looks at me. His stare cuts into my soul. *He wants to blame me. He needs to blame someone – he should blame me. I can take it.*

'It was them,' I say. 'It was the Teeth.'

He looks long and hard at me. He is squeezing Eliza so hard that his nails are digging into her skin.

To my great surprise, he says, 'Thank you. For being there.'

And in that moment I have more love, respect and gratitude for Pascale than I have ever had for anyone in my life. *But . . . he isn't blaming me. I would blame me. I would need to blame me.*

'Pascale, we need to put your sister into a coma now.' Yottam cuts through the intensity of the moment without sentiment. Pas looks at his sister thrashing and fighting.

'Will she definitely wake up?' Pas asks, visibly marshalling his courage.

The doctor breathes in deeply.

'Be straight. Can you promise me?'

'It would be foolish to promise anything at this point, except that I will do my best and induce a coma immediately.'

A sunken expression comes over Pascale's face. 'I need five seconds with her.' He leans his whole body over the bed, covering his sister's face from view. He takes both shoulders in both his hands and holds them tight. He kisses her forehead, whispers something in her ear and lets the weight of his body fall on hers.

'Careful,' Ruth says nervously.

The doctor signs to her to wait, his eyes on Eliza. She has stopped her convulsive thrashing and jerking.

Pascale's calming her down. It's working!

Yottam suddenly springs to action. 'Nurse – dressing and stitches. Quickly. Everybody needs to step back.' A renewed hope glints in his sapphire eyes and he looks at Pas. 'Thank you.'

Pas steps away from his sister tentatively, clearly still terrified by what's in front of him. I take his arm gently and lead him away from the bed. Naturally, he's reluctant to go very far. We sit down on one of the old wooden benches fixed to the wall. I keep hold of his arm. He doesn't take his eyes off his sister as Yottam does his work. Eliza appears calm, breathing normally though with the help of a respirator. The nurses treat and stitch up her wounds and, after what seems like an eternity, the blood gradually stops spilling from her.

CHAPTER 25

EXIT STRATEGY

We sit there in silence, watching as Eliza is slowly cajoled back into the land of the living. Ruth is now at the other end of the San by the conservatory, joined by Mungo, Pokes and Suzannah. The four are deep in conversation about something, all their faces full of grave concern except Suzannah's, whose darting eyes make her look as distracted as ever.

'What do you think they're—?'

'It's the only way.' Pas cuts across my question. He doesn't look at me, but is still fixated on his sister.

'What?' I'm confused.

'She's right. I hate her for it. But she is right.'

'Pas,' I probe gently, not wanting to upset him any more than he already is. 'I don't understand.'

'We have to fight.' There's anger in his eyes.

Stumblingly, I ask, 'What about what happened to Lizy? I saw the Teeth, Pas. I looked straight at Smee. She's not messing. They're not going to stop.'

'No,' he turns to face me, 'you're right, they're not. If they're willing to do that,' he points at his sister, 'they're not willing to help us, they're not our friends and they sure as shit aren't going to find us somewhere new to go once they've ransacked this place.'

He pauses, looking back at Eliza. 'She's—' He holds back tears. 'That's the real message: we're coming for you whether you like it or not, and if you stand in our way we'll rip you apart – who you are, what you stand for, all the people you love in the world.' He fixes me with a look. 'Don't you get it, dude? She's the proof. If we fight, they kill us. If we surrender, we die out there up above like rats anyway.' He looks as possessed as Eliza had earlier in the Ticket.

'But don't you think, like, I mean, you could look at it another way . . .' I falter, trying to think about what I do and don't believe. But what do I really want to say? Is there any chance, any possibility in hell, that Smee was telling the truth? Is Gnosys willing to work with us, really? They never have before; we've always been third-class citizens to them. So why would they now?

I look at Eliza. I see the heart monitor slowly beep, beep, beep, by her bedside. I remember the look in Smee's eyes, the pure evil in them; the blood pouring from the side of my friend's head; and the total abject horror of it all. *Just business.* A sour, sinking feeling washes over me, like a thick sludge filling up the holes in my heart. Some people *don't* care. Some people really are just in it for themselves, whatever the cost; some people are just plain evil.

I turn to Pas. 'It's just business to them. You're ri—'

'Pascale,' Ruth's voice cuts in. 'I'm so sorry.' She's left the others and is now in front of us. I swallow my words along with my newfound vitriol; this isn't the moment.

'I take full responsibility,' she says. 'This heinous crime will *not* go unpunished.' It sounds like a platitude, weirdly fake.

'Eliza was right, Ruth,' Pascale responds resolutely.

Her face contorts a little. 'Look, I can't begin to—'

I can't help myself. 'Ruth! You heard what he said. You know it's true. It's the only way. It's our only choice.'

'Kid.' She looks at me sternly. 'This conversation is between Pascale and myself.

'You're not serious,' I fire back. 'I just carried my best friend all the way down here from the Circus, for God's sake! I'm not saying I'm some kind of hero. But if she'd been up there much longer she would have died.' I've never spoken to any of the elders like this, let alone the COOs or Ruth herself, but I can't stop myself. Anger ramps up in me. 'All of that, this mess, up there with them, is your fault! You let Smee and her Teeth down into—'

'Do you think I had a choice?' she spits, trying very hard

not to raise her voice. 'You think I wanted this to happen? Listen very carefully, Joshua. I've dedicated my life to the Offliner movement and to the lives of every single Offliner in this Cell. I watched my father build this place with his bare hands. The last thing I want in the world is to walk out the door and hand the keys to Gnosys.' She takes a breath and looks at Pas sympathetically. 'The last thing I wanted in the world was for an Offliner to get hurt at the hands of a Tooth.' She whips her head back around to me. 'Mark my words. What happened tonight is my very worst nightmare. And it's because it *is* my worst nightmare that I will *not* let it happen again.' Her eyes are dark. 'Do you understand?'

Understand? I understand perfectly. You don't want to say in front of Pas that you won't fight back, because that would mean saying what Eliza did was in vain, that she almost died for nothing, that Eliza was wrong.

'I respect you so much, Ruthie; so does Kid.' Pas looks at me as if to say, *Stand down.* 'You're so good to every single one of us, always have been, but there's no way I can let this go. You must see that? There's no way they get away with it this time.'

Now he is calm and collected. There's no anger or disappointment in his eyes, only thought and meaning. *You want revenge*, I think to myself.

'You're responsible for hundreds of people, I know,' he continues. 'And you've got to do whatever you think's right by all of them. But I'm only responsible for one person. She's lying over there and tonight she was almost killed. I've got to do what's right by her. That's my journey. If Gnosys are prepared to do what they did to her, there's no way they're on our side. There's no way they're our allies. That isn't what a friend does. That,' he points at Eliza but continues looking at Ruth, 'is the work of your very worst enemy.' He gets up and returns to his sister's side.

I get to my feet but before I can say anything he holds his hand up. 'Don't worry. I'm fine.'

Ruth turns back to me. 'Can you sit down, just for a minute?'

I do. Her voice is quiet and less angry now. The truth is, I will always respect her, even if we disagree.

'I know you're angry and I know you're in pain. What you just saw will be haunting every corridor of your mind. It likely will for the rest of your life. For that I will never forgive myself. But listen. Listen to me,' she says softly, gently. 'Smee talking about Sylvia Rogers and her so-called philanthropy isn't going to wash with me. Never has, never will.'

Ruth gestures towards the old Tube tunnel at the end of the San. 'They only care about the Hab-Belts, and Perspecta, and putting up Data-Qs to keep it all running. They can't just stick them out in the countryside, because they still have to grow food – and the climate catastrophe means that's nigh on impossible now. Deserted cities cost money to demolish or adapt. But these tunnels, our tunnels, are perfect for their network – they're telling the truth about all that. But they're lying about everything else. So I agree with Pascale. Gnosys is our enemy, not our friend; and no, I don't believe they intend to help us. I believe they fully intend to take what they want and give nothing back.'

Her eyes are drilling into me. 'Where I disagree with the two of you, however, is when you say that to fight is our only option. Fighting, Kid, just isn't an option.' She lowers her voice, her eyes burn into mine. 'Fighting is suicide—'

'We know that,' I interrupt, 'but leaving is suicide too.'

'See, that's where you've got it wrong. You remember the night the Teeth came into the Ticket? I was in the middle of reading out a letter from Stefano Ceccarelli. I'd made contact with Rome. We've been working together to find a new location for the Soho Cell.'

I open my mouth, about to protest. *There isn't another habitable place in this city to fit five hundred, not underground anyway!* Ruth silences me with a look and I keep the thought to myself. 'Have faith in the Offliners, Kid. We've survived a long time, given the odds. We can survive this.' She takes my hand and squeezes it hard. 'But we can only survive if we work together, if we move together, all of us, towards a shared goal. The only goal there is – to relocate. We play for time – as much as we can get. And we keep this as quiet as possible while we figure out the practicalities. But we're moving out. It's decided.' I follow her gaze over to Eliza as she adds, 'I can't let that happen to any more of you. I won't.'

She takes a breath. 'Help me, Kid. Please. Help me persuade the others. The other youngers all look up to you. I need your support. I'm nothing without it.' She wheels herself away, back to Eliza's bedside.

You want me to go against my gut. You want me to go against my friend and against my own gut. The only goal to relocate? Give up our home? I sit there for a moment, in a daze.

It can't be the only way. It can't be.

Find a way. It's like I'm in a trance. *Find a way.* A hundred voices sound in my head, all the same voice, all saying the same thing. *Find a way.*

Wait a second.

Snapping out of it, I ask Ruth, 'What did you say, before, about a shared goal? You said we need to have the same goal . . .'

'We can only survive if we work together,' she repeats, sounding perfectly sincere. 'Working as a team is our only hope.'

'That's it!' I'm suddenly on my feet as an idea springs to the forefront of my mind.

That's what Leo meant when she said, 'Are you sure she's the one?' Why I have the phone, why I met Izzy, why all this is happening. Revisit the past to save the future. We have to work together – her in the past, us here, in the future – towards the same goal!

'Sorry Ruthie, have to go.'

I wince inwardly and wonder whether Ruth is going to ask me where I'm off to in such a rush. There's no way I could talk to any of the COOs about using the phone – not even if it was just for calling someone in 2078. But apparently Ruth's just happy that her pep-talk has spurred me to some kind of action, and isn't about to ask me what exactly it is. Running over to Pas, out of earshot of the COOs I say, 'Come here, there's something I have to tell you.'

CHAPTER 26

FIND HER!

9.56pm, 13 April

Jesus! What did he say?!

Nothing. Not at first. You'd have to know
Pas; he's a very funny guy, he never takes
things too seriously. So normally … well, not

normally, because I don't normally go round saying I've got a phoneline to 2021 ... But if he hadn't been about as serious as he's ever been, he would've just ripped the piss out of me. I was still expecting him to. Or to be angry with me for talking crap when his sister was out cold on a hospital bed. But he just looked at me and listened, like he was too knackered to do anything else. Then he just said, well that's great man, I'm pleased for you, but I've gotta get some shut-eye now.

That's it?

He didn't say anything else all next day or most of today either. Nothing out of the ordinary. Then he told me he'd known me since he was four, and knew when I was joking or lying or babbling – I sometimes have these waking nightmares, you know – and he was pretty sure I wasn't doing any of those things now.

So he believed u? He believed everything, about us? Jus like that?!

Not JUST like that. But it didn't take as much persuading as I thought it would. I walked him through it again, showed him the phone, showed him us talking on Instagram. I was terrified, because making any digital connection out of the Cell is totally against the rules. But Pas just raised his eyebrows at me, and then said he'd never understood how phones worked anyway, or Perspecta, so it all seemed like magic to him. And you know what? I told him about the oak tree … and today he said he'd seen it. He'd been to Primrose Hill. Guess what he said next? He said, why didn't you get her to bury *Never Mind the Bollocks*, Sex Pistols, been looking for one of them for ages.

:-) :-) :-)

He didn't really go there because he wanted to check my story. It's just he's been out walking around for the past two nights, thinking about Eliza and Gnosys, and he went that way just for an excuse to put some miles in. I guess he still has more important things on his mind.

Of course he does . . . I'm so sorry btw, about Eliza.

Thank you Izzy.

It's still so raw to me, this whole thing. Us, the

Offliners, ur world n everything u've told me. I mean. I believe u, all of it. But I guess jus now this and Eliza getting hurt. I dunno, I jus feel so, it's sad, it's like really scary n

That's why we met.

?

That's the whole point! I didn't get it before, why we were the ones that connected, you know, why it was me and you specifically, but now I do! It's for precisely that reason.

Cos it's scary? I mean, it is, but Im not like cryin or n e thin

No! Not because it's scary! Because I NEED YOUR HELP! We all need your help! To stop what's coming! We need YOU to stop all this in your time. In history! I mean, in your present! You need to find Sylvia Rogers and tell her what's coming! You need to find her and tell her NOT to start Gnosys! That's why we were put together, why our paths crossed and tangled in time! Because you're gonna save us from the future in the past!

Izzy? You there?

Ye

What's wrong?

I guess . . . I guess it's just a lot is all

But you'll do it? You'll find Sylvia?

Kid. WTF. Ur talking 2 me like I'm sum kinda like Offliner hero! Im jus a science nerd doin her best @ school! Like im a geek . . . I don't hav any friends. Think you've got the wrong idea. Whatever you think, I'm definitely not special n I'm not a HERO ffs!

I'm your friend.

And, besides, you said it yourself . . . You're looking for an adventure . . . You want to be a Somebody. Doing this makes you a somebody.

Don't guilt trip me.

Izzy I'm not guilt tripping you. Please Izzy! I'm asking for your help. You're the only person who can stop what's coming because you're the only person in the world, in history, who knows what it is. Before it's too late! For us it is!

Did Eliza ask u 2 do this?

Eliza doesn't know about any of it yet. She's still out cold. I only told Pas. He says he's going to tell her when she wakes up – tell her everything – but he supports this. This is coming from both of us. And Eliza will too, yeah, when we tell her.

I dunno. Like I dnt even kno whr 2 start

Pas wanted me to get you to kill her, Izzy.

WTF?! WTF r u on about!

That's my point. Just listen to me. That's coming from Pas. From the most peaceful person I've ever met. If he's saying stuff like that then you know it's important. You know it means something. You know it's a matter of life or death for us. Otherwise I wouldn't ask.

So what exactly do u want me 2 do?

Find Sylvia Rogers, try and speak to her, befriend her, get to know her, and then when the time's right

I'm not killing ANYONE. This is ridiculous and youre scaring me. I'm going.

When the time's right, connect her with me and we'll persuade her, me and you, to stop before it's too late!

Iz...

So . . . You in or you out?

CHAPTER 27

PEPPERMINT TEA

We're back in the San beside Eliza. Another day, another long vigil. Mercifully, she'd surfaced from her coma relatively quickly and was conscious five days after the attack, thanks to Pas calming her convulsions and Yottam being the genius that he is. But she's very weak and still mostly asleep. Which is a relief from the confusion and the fits of terror when she's awake. The constant background chatter of

the menagerie seems remote, and the only noise that penetrates my mind is the intermittent whirring and beeping of
her monitors and the occasional low conversation between
Yottam and an orderly. I look at Pas and see he's exhausted,
so I steer him to his dorm. I hope he's able to sleep. I know
I won't be. In fact, after last night I'm afraid to try. I spent
the whole night rigid with panic, drenched in sweat. And
yet there's nothing I can latch onto, nothing I feel able to do
except come back down to sit with Eliza. That's where Ursula
finds me when she comes back in from the Galley after over-
seeing dinner.

'Dear boy,' she says in her wise, velveteen voice, 'get
some rest. Eliza's in good hands, the very best.' She pauses
and looks at me with a face full of what must be the most
comforting, maternal smile in all of London. 'She'll be good
as new, sooner than soon, you'll see.' Then she begins busying
herself once more. 'There's leftover hotpot on the stove. You
could make her some broth. Take your mind off things.'

I just sigh and my shoulders sag. I feel drained and
bewildered: helpless, no matter how hard I try to feel the
opposite. There's such a weight, a heaviness, to places like the
San, and to situations like Lizy's.

After a moment – as I stare into the middle distance
and she pretends not to notice – Ursula looks at me
shrewdly. 'They're all here, aren't they?'

I nod forlornly, knowing exactly what she's referring
to. She puts an arm round me and holds me. 'Ghosts and
memories is all there is here for us.'

I begin crying softly.

'I remember the night your mum passed on as clearly

as I remember the night my Rory died. I remember standing here with you, by her side. I remember taking you up and tucking you in – or trying.' She chuckles sweetly. 'You weren't going to leave your mummy for love nor money, were you my boy? No.' She leans towards me, our temples touching. 'Of course you weren't. A son as good as you never could.'

She takes a long pause; her breathing is slow and loud and shallow. Then she looks over at Eliza once more and says. 'Their fate isn't hers, Joshua – your dear mum's, my dear Rory's. It isn't her time to go, sweet boy.'

She looks up and begins talking as if to the ceiling, into thin air. 'Eliza'll not be joining you yet, gorgeous ghosties!'

Then she chuckles a bright, breathy chuckle, releases me from her embrace, and makes to return to the Galley. 'It's up the wooden stairs to Bedfordshire for you, my boy! Don't make me send my daughter after you!' Before she reaches the arched doorway, she turns to me once more. 'Oh, and Joshua, I'll be dropping something off for you in the morning.'

Sure enough, when I wake up there it is, sitting on my piano stool: a battered old tin labelled *Fortnum & Mason's Peppermint Tea*, with a scribbled note from Ursula on the inside of an old cardboard cereal box. With everything that's been happening, I've totally forgotten what day it is today.

Dearest Joshua, happy 18th birthday! I always meant to give this to you today, but I had to have a good rummage around last night to find it. Turns out someone had tucked it away at the back of the larder! Sorry there's no tea in it. She just loved her old tins, did your mum. xxxxx

As I pop off the lid , the scent of peppermint rushes out like a wave of nostalgia. I can smell it in my imagination – it's the sweet smell of my mother's breath – so vividly it is as if she's just walked into my dorm. Pulling the ragged red ribbon off the tight roll of paper inside, I unroll it and see Mum's handwriting – pages and pages of it.

Immediately, it's like I'm back in the old flat overlooking Primrose Hill Park. I don't know whether I exactly remember the whole scene, but I certainly remember Lilly, the dog we left behind. And I remember, even while Mum was talking excitedly about going on an adventure, that weird sadness in her eyes.

CHAPTER 28

THE WITCHING HOUR

'Here . . . Here with me.'

I took your little head in my hands and knelt down. I pulled you towards me gently, so that our noses would touch and you could smell the hot, dry sweetness of peppermint tea on my breath. You didn't know then that my breath smelt of peppermint tea. You had no idea what tea was, let alone peppermint. But you'd have recognized the smell anywhere:

my kisses were always full of it. That hot, dry sweetness meant things were going to be okay. At least I hope it did. I hope it meant you were who you were and I was who I was and that everything was what it had always been – safe, warm, happy. I hope, in that moment before everything changed, I made you feel all those things. It's all I've ever wanted you to feel: normal.

'Listen to me . . . Are you listening my love?'

You didn't answer me. I imagine you were far too busy trying to work out why my voice sounded so excited but my eyes looked so sad.

'We're going on an adventure! I can't tell you where, not right now, but that's part of the fun, isn't it? It'll be like a surprise! Like—'

I paused for a moment, desperately trying to ignore the throbbing anxiety that was pushing in on my temples like a hat too small for my head.

'Like when Lilly takes us for walks up on the hill and it's windy and rainy and we put our coats on. We never know where she's going to take us, but we always find our way back in the end. Everything always turns out all right in the end, doesn't it my love?'

I was talking a lot, and fast. You weren't used to that. With every new word, I'm sure you became just that little bit more confused.

I remember you turning your head away from me to look at Lilly all snuggled up and cosy by the stove.

'Listen to Mummy.'

You turned back to me and I began to cry a little. 'Everything's going to be okay,' I said to you, trying to smile.

Really it was myself I was trying to reassure.

'An adventure! We're going on a big adventure.' I took a deep breath and tried to stifle my tears. 'Even better than the ones we have with Lilly! Just you and Mummy; just the two of us, okay? We're going to . . .'

I remember beginning to say something else. I was desperate to explain what was about to happen, but the words wouldn't come out. Besides, it would have been pointless: I had no idea what was going to happen next, so how on earth was I going to explain it to you?

That was the first time I had really thought about it, considered the gravity of it all. In fact, it wasn't until that moment, as I stood there struggling to explain it to you, that I'd ever really processed any of it – the Upload, Perspecta, the Offliners – or considered that any of it was true. I never wanted to believe it; I suppose I'd never really had to. It wasn't until that precise moment that I'd ever so much as entertained the possibility that what was happening might actually be forever; that this was going to be the very last time I was ever going to see my books, my furniture, my art, my bed, my home.

I kissed your forehead. As I did, I noticed one of my tears fall onto your cheek. I remember wondering what must have been going through your mind as I watched it run down your face and onto your lip. You'd cried before, and tasted your own tears. But it had only ever happened when something was wrong; when you'd fallen over and hurt yourself or when I gave you cornflakes for breakfast instead of Frosties. I watched you lick your top lip, cocking your head to the side, confused by the saltiness of the tear. Mummy's tears tasted exactly the same as yours, which must have led you to the conclusion that they must *mean* the same thing too: that something really bad was happening, or was about to happen.

I felt sadder and more helpless than I ever had as I watched you struggle to process what was happening, using your recently acquired concepts of past, present and future. No one was hurt. The dog was in her bed and I'd given you Frosties for breakfast. Why could Mummy not stop crying?

I got to my feet and grabbed the suitcase I'd spent the whole day packing and unpacking. I had no idea what we'd need in our new home, never having actually been there. I didn't know whether it was going to be a home at all. You watched me in silence as my shoulders rose and fell and rose and fell. Now I was really crying. Now you could be in no doubt that there was something wrong, that I was in pain. I didn't cry, I still don't, especially not like that. Not unless things are very bad. Still, I think I could be forgiven: only a week previously my husband, your dad, had walked out in the middle of the night without so much as a word.

I could feel your big brown eyes bearing into me from behind as I dabbed mine on the sleeve of my orange cashmere cardigan. Thinking how your dad had given it to me for Christmas two years before, I let out a tearful laugh.

Christopher leaving was not only devastating, it was bewildering. We were utterly in love, and I'd always been able to rely on him. Somehow the affair theory just didn't add up. It seemed like such a pathetically simple explanation; so clichéd and unlike him. He was clever, your dad – freakishly clever – and never did anything in the conventional way. So, I always thought, if he was going to have an affair it would be complicated and there would be Gnomes and letters and a trail of breadcrumbs for me to follow. It would be a puzzle – he loved puzzles. No, if your dad were going to have an affair, it would be methodical and scientific and meticulously planned. He'd never just run away like some fugitive in the middle of the night, never to be heard from or seen again. That would be far too impulsive and poetic and . . .

At least that's what I'd always believed, until it actually happened.

Of course I was distraught and in pain. I was hurting more than I'd ever hurt before. But strangely enough, I was hurting more for your sake than for mine. After the night your dad disappeared I sat in bed all day long crying, thinking of you; about the world you were inheriting. The Flood, the Pittsburgh Pact, the Upload. I'd always tried to be a positive person, to make the best out of every bad situation, but this was different. This was like a bomb had been dropped on our life, like a martial artist was kicking me repeatedly in the stomach. This was too much: we were being forced to leave our home. The only thing I had from which to draw any comfort was the feeling that things were at rock bottom and couldn't possibly get any worse.

Your dad and I met at Peter's, a music hall, four years before the Flood, when London was still a relatively busy place. It wasn't the vibrant city I had arrived in ten years previously, pulsating with excitement and throbbing with movement. Not by any stretch of the imagination. But at least people were still walking the streets in the two or three hours of the day when it was possible: after the noxious swirl kicked up by the morning storm had cleared and before the thick, oily air pressure of night rolled in again, making it nearly impossible to see.

When I'd packed acting in – or rather acting packed me in – and I had started working at Peter's, there were still some things that were impossible to do inside Perspecta. In fact, back then Perspecta wasn't even the only 'virtual reality'! Seems ridiculous, hilarious, to imagine now, but there were quite a few others competing in the race for a new world in those days. Microsoft had one – YuVu I think it was called – and Synapps had Mynd and Apple had the iVerse. There were other, smaller services too, but they were the only three that seemed to pose Gnosys any real threat.

But back then there were still reasons to exist in the real world, even if you preferred your 'alt-life'. High streets still had shop fronts, some of the shops were even open, and a lot of schools and universities were still yet to become VEAs. It felt like in London there was still a faint glimmer of hope that we could give the old world one last chance.

We all know how that story ends.

Peter's was the very last crumbling rampart of London's night life. It wasn't really old at all. It was a museum, a stage set; a kind of mini, murky, adult Disneyland, designed as a hideaway for the few analogue adventurers still pining for the past.

Before opening the bar, Peter Pember had been a well-known theatre producer. There wasn't a bar in Soho that didn't echo with his laugh. But throughout the Twenties and Thirties Soho fought a losing battle against the great pandemics that seemed, every three or four years, to rear their ugly heads, each one stronger and more vicious than the next. Shows closed; theatres went dark. As time went by, even if the theatres reopened, nobody wanted to sit in them any more.

Finally, as another new show bit the dust prematurely, Peter took out an advertisement in *The Stage* magazine that read, simply:

Peter Pember the player is dead.
Long live Peter Pember the publican.
The Old Phoenix Arts Club,
1 Phoenix Street, WC2H 8BU.

Peter's was born.

Everyone thought he was crazy to open a bar when fifty others were closing daily across the capital. But Peter had foresight. The more people abandoned the real world for the virtual one, the stronger nostalgia would grow for the rest of us. He would hold on as all the other ramparts tumbled down around him and the castle that was Soho returned to rubble. There would always be people crazy enough to brave the smog to drink and dance like they had done in the good old days.

I joined in '55. At thirty, I was by far the oldest of all the performers. But Peter seemed to like that.

'You have a class, darling, a panache these children can only dream of,' he would say anytime I got down about failing as an actor.

'Failed?' he'd hiss, one bushy eyebrow in the air, pouting with alarm from beneath his enormous handlebar moustache. 'But you're on stage every night of the year, darling. Not even Olivier at his busiest could claim that.

You're the star of Soho. The shining star. Work is work, my dear El. And a stage is a stage is a stage,' he'd say, bowing his head a little, his pout having turned into a grin, a twinkle in his eye.

And off I'd go, feeling better. He was good at making you feel like you were worth something. I suppose that's why the punters kept coming back too. Even as the air got worse and the city got quieter, coming to Peter's was a way of reminding yourself of how good things had been – of the richness and beauty of life during the Golden Dusk.

I hated the dancing; I hated the ogling, aging clientele; and the costumes were utterly ridiculous. But it could have been worse. Besides, I had nowhere else to go. My agent had dropped me. My 'BA in acting' had meant nothing to anyone when I was an actor and meant diddly squat now. I wasn't welcome back home in Dublin, having been a 'grave disappointment' to my dad, and I wouldn't have wanted to go back anyway. So Peter became like a father to me, the bar my home, and the girls my family.

Before your dad came along, that is. Before you, my darling, gave my life the purpose I'd always looked and longed for.

'Gentleman, and ladies, few of the latter though there may be, raise your glasses for the last virgin in Soho,' Peter would croon into the faux-antique microphone that hung in the corner. 'Put your hands together for El Kellis and the Witching Hours!'

And, scantily clad and singing, on we'd come. Peter visualized an homage to the video for 'Like A Virgin', in which Madonna – she was a superstar of the Dusk – wore a wedding dress. But, as ever, he hadn't the resources to match his vision. I looked more like a sexed-up Miss Havisham surrounded by a gaggle of ghoulish bridesmaids: The Witching Hours.

Often, for the encore I'd be left on the stage alone to sing the song that somehow became my signature tune: 'Movin' On Up', another hit from the Dusk that's managed to outlive its own era, even if no one now would remember who sang it. It's got those amazing lines from 'Amazing Grace',

I once was lost but now am found,
Was blind but now I see . . .

but the old liberation hymn is a solid-gold weepy, and 'Movin' On Up' brings out the joy. It was one of the first things Peter and I really connected on, our love of the music that came out of the 1990s. Primal Scream, who sang 'Movin' On Up', were a favourite of mine. And when you listen to the song, you can't help but feel hopeful. 'Sing the Scream, sing the Scream!' he'd yell now and again from his little dark corner when the Witching Hour was up. So I'd launch into it – a slowed-down version, smoky and jazzy. And as times grew darker, it was something to hold on to.

On a good night the lights went down around two in the morning. If I changed quickly enough, I could be out ten minutes later. I tended not to stick around and drink with the other girls. I lacked their inclination and stamina to endure and engage with the vultures that hung about the place, stinking of booze and desperation, hoping to continue on into the witching hour with one of the Witching Hours. No, I liked to get home, get into bed and read a book –

made out of paper, controversial though that was. I had been collecting them, rather hoping that I might one day sell them for a lot of money. That would be my pension, once the virgin bride was dead and gone.

The Tube was always shut by then. Peter said he couldn't afford to send me home in a taxi every night, but he did buy me a full-face respirator with a night-vision setting. It meant I could ride home to Shepherd's Bush without crashing, or suffocating – though I'd arrive covered in black soot and stinking of ammonia. Very occasionally, I would leave my bike at the bar and walk up to the Euston Road, which had recently transformed into the first branch of the London Podd Way. I chastised myself every time. I had protested against the Way when it opened in '54.

Publically, the idea was to just get rid of traffic jams on the Euston Road. People would park their cars in new car parks miles away to east and west, and take a Perspecta-Operated Designated Driver – or PODD – to their destination. The stations on the old Hammersmith & City Tube line had been turned into docking stations where people could get in and out of the Podds.

Before it was opened, the Euston Road had been closed and hidden behind hoardings for about a year. No one knew what it was going to look like. The hush that came over our little band of protesters when the Mayor cut the ribbon wasn't one of wonderment, it was one of fear. They say the Upload began in 2060, but that was the moment it started for me. It was the very first time I felt I could really see into the future. And I found it terrifying.

You wouldn't notice a Podd now, even if it ran you over.

But back then it was an actual shock to see – suspended in the air high above a deep magnetic trench where the road used to be – those sleek silver machines, like hundreds of polished steel bullets. It looked straight out of a sci-fi movie. It looked like the future coming not to help but to steal our lives away.

It was part of Gnosys's SmartCity initiative. The tech giant gave the city bits of expensive infrastructure – like the Podd Way and the flood defence wall, the Toaster. In return it was allowed to build as many Data-Qs as it wanted, wherever it wanted, no matter what priceless edifice had to be demolished to make room. SmartCity was nothing more than a disgusting bribe, a shameful, shady, backhanded deal: *We'll give you a brand-new transport system and defend you against floods, but in return you have to let us invade your city and change it forever.*

Even with quantum computing efficiencies, it took serious, physical real estate to store all the data and run all of the systems for Perspecta – for the new world in 'the cloud'. Turns out this cloud was made of concrete and that in order to colonize the virtual world, Gnosys needed to buy the real one too. London was the first to sign up to SmartCity but soon other metropolises were falling like dominoes. No other company could compete and no city council or government could resist what Gnosys offered.

After all this, I'm ashamed to say that the night I met your dad was one of those nights I decided to catch a Podd. Actually no, I'm not ashamed to say it. If I hadn't taken one look at the foul weather and turned back downstairs to leave my bike behind the bar, Dad and I might never have met.

And you might never have been. As an alternate reality, that doesn't bear thinking about.

Just as I turned to leave again, Peter called out to me, 'Beastly out there. Fix yourself a drink, sweetie. Unless, of course, you've a pressing prior engagement.' He knew full well that the only pressing engagement I had was with my book and my bed. The tiny club was very quiet, with only one or two punters left; the girls had all gone home. *What's the worst that can happen?* I thought, poured myself a pint, and plonked myself down at the long, glowing, art deco bar.

I didn't really like beer; I only drank it to make a point. Stephen King liked to drink it. He was the most famous novelist alive in the early 2000s – him and J. K. Rowling – and there weren't really any novelists left by the Fifties. I guess I felt like I was doing the world a favour, living like the virtuosos of the Golden Dusk.

I hadn't been sitting long when a man sat down at the other end of the bar. He was about my age, I thought, maybe a little older, with a mop of very curly auburn hair. It had been parted messily on one side and slicked down a little with product, as if he had wanted to try and make it look straight, cool even, but had given up halfway through. It made me chuckle, imagining this man at home in front of the mirror, struggling to restrain his unruly tawny locks.

This, my darling, was the first time I ever clapped eyes on your dad, Christopher Edward Jones.

He wore a brown corduroy suit – straight out of the 1970s and dreadfully uncool, even by my low standards – underneath a long black overcoat, which was bizarre in itself as it was stifling in that basement. All topped off by a burgundy scarf – the 'Christopher Robin', as it later came to be known. I called it that because he was never without it and it was red and sweet and seemed to me to be your dad, perfectly summed up, in woollen form.

He was fiddling with the paper napkins in a bar-top dispenser. I looked over at him and caught him looking at me. He promptly went the colour of his scarf and turned his attention guiltily back to the napkins.

'Why did you do that?' I teased.

'What?' He managed to muster the word but couldn't look me in the eye. He was cripplingly shy, your dad. Even shyer then.

'Woman sits alone at a bar, man comes to the bar too but chooses to sit at the other end folding napkins!' I can't quite believe how obnoxious I was.

He laughed a little bit, still staring at the napkin he was now gathering into a perfect octagon. 'Sorry,' he said, smiling sheepishly, 'never been good at—'

'What?' I was now drunk.

'This – um – this sort of thing.'

'And what sort of thing might "this" be, Mr Nobody?' I said, laughing nonchalantly, but actually quite enjoying having a flirt.

He'd already had way too much interaction for one night. 'I'm sorry, I should go,' he said. And he went.

I was surprised; the men in the club were usually desperate for whatever they could get. And truthfully, I was a little insulted. But I was tipsy too, and so I took another sip of beer and thought nothing more of it. If Peter hadn't later drawn my attention to the octagonal origami that

Christopher had left sitting on the bar, I would never have thought about him again. And we'd never have had you.

Sorry — no good at small talk. Better at writing on napkins. I work at Imperial College, the robotics department. There's a great cafe around the corner called Fleet Kitchen which I visit every day around 2pm. If you ever happen to find yourself there, I'd love to buy you a coffee.

Christopher Jones
P.S. I'm your biggest fan.

And that was that. I went the very next day. We sat in a little café just off the Old Brompton Road. He had coffee and I had hot chocolate.

And we were married a year later in St Patrick's Church in Soho Square, a month before it was subsumed under the Virtual Diocese of Central London. We chose the church because it was near Peter's.

CHAPTER 29

TWINS

'You're doing so well. Almost there. Deep breaths. Breathe.
Take another deep breath. Good girl. Well done you. Good
girl – that's it. You're doing so well. Almost there. Deep
breaths. Breathe. Good girl. Well done you. Good girl – that's
it. You're doing so . . .' Medi-Migs were commonplace in all
but the most complicated and risky medical procedures by
then. Often when you went to the hospital, you were hard-

pressed to find a real human being anywhere.

For the most part I hated the way technology had taken over our lives, but could appreciate the positive effect the Migs had had on healthcare. The soft-edged, soft-spoken doctor drones weren't liable to human error, which meant fewer mistakes during operations. They self-sterilized, which meant almost no infections. And they were devoid of emotion, which meant they made decisions based on the facts of the case, rather than the feelings of the patient or their family.

The problem was that I wasn't sick, I was pregnant. Actually, by this point I was in labour and needed a real, emotional, feeling human being – preferably female – who could understand intimately the horrors I was going through.

'Just. Stop. Talking. Please!' I screamed at the robot.

It simply continued repeating the responses it was preprogrammed to give when in midwife mode, occasionally changing tone depending on the heart rates of the humans around it. 'You're doing so well. Almost there.'

I couldn't take it any more. I'd always meant to have a water birth anyway.

'Chris, get that thing— Get it out of here! I can't deal with it.' And then I think I subsided into half-animal screams about you. It was too late to do anything about the robot. You wanted to make your entrance.

You were born Joshua Jones in St Mary's Hospital, Paddington, at one in the morning or thereabouts on 19 April 2060. At six pounds and three ounces, you were a very small baby. You had dark, olive skin, deep brown eyes and one premature curl protruding from your little bald pate.

How could something so beautiful have come out of me? All the hysteria of labour disappeared as soon as I saw you. The horror of what's happened to my beloved Soho in the winter floods – all vanished from my mind. In fact nothing else mattered as soon as you arrived. From then on it was all about you.

An hour into your life things were calm and quiet once more and we fell into a peaceful slumber.

I was the first to wake up some two hours later, with you sleeping soundly in my arms. I smiled sweetly at your dad, who was now snoring away, Christopher Robin scarf on, his head lolling from side to side, making a squeaky sound on the back of the plastic-covered hospital chair.

'Good job, Mr Nobody,' I whispered. 'We did it!' I remember the sound of my voice made you stir a little; I immediately panicked and felt guilty, as one does about every little thing when one has a child. 'There, there, it's okay . . . little Josh, darling boy. Everything's going to be okay.' You went straight back to sleep, of course, without a care in the world. I, on the other hand, had more difficulty.

The room was a glass cube, one of about thirty on the maternity ward, spread out across the third floor of the hospital like perfectly placed blocks of ice. For privacy, the glass could be frosted and unfrosted at the touch of a button. The space was sparse, populated only by the bed, two chairs and a coffee table with a vase of sunflowers sitting on top of it. The sunflowers weren't real, of course. Like every other surface in the room, the coffee table doubled up as a computer. It was automatically logged in to the patient's home system and could project holograms of elements of home life into the room. This allowed each patient to stare at some fabricated memory of life before hospital on loop during recovery. When we arrived in hospital the day before, I had scrolled through the options, suddenly anxious that we weren't at home, that I wasn't having you in the warm familiarity of it all.

3D videos of Lilly were the only exportable memories available. *Lilly in the park. Lilly makes Chris fall over. Lilly runs and jumps into the canal.* It was lovely to see them. I hadn't for ages, not since your dad had taken a brief interest in photography and made the dog his muse. But actually, with the birth of my first child a matter of hours away, I felt that having the puppy in the room with me – even if she was just a hologram – would be less than calming. So, reluctantly, I settled for the flowers, artificial though they were.

Once I'd spent three or four hours in the sparse room, staring at you and kissing and stroking you, all for you to do nothing but sniff and *goo* and *gah* and fart in return, I was ready to engage with something else. Not that I don't adore you, my love.

Almost as soon as I'd had the thought, the glass wall facing the bed suddenly unfrosted, became solid black, flashed bright white, then displayed the words

So computers are reading minds now. That was my immediate reaction. *Streem? Please . . . I've just had a baby. Streem
definitely isn't going to be the first thing my son hears, second
only to his mother's voice! It's dreams he needs: dreams that'll
set him free from all this.* So, being careful not to wake you,
I reached for the touchpad on the wall next to the bed to
switch off the feed.

I pressed the button, but nothing happened. It wouldn't
turn off. I tried using voice commands; still nothing
happened. The logo remained, big and bold, front and
centre, almost like it was teasing me. Then, all of a sudden, it
dissolved and made way for a message.

ATTENTION
This is a public service announcement
brought to you by **STREEM**®
on behalf of the United Nations
ATTENTION

She was sitting in a beige-coloured room. A ticker
running along the bottom of the screen told us she was the
Secretary-General. The room had nothing on the walls and
only one flag bearing the blue crest of the UN, which hung
limp above her head. There was something about the way she
was sitting, or where she was sitting – in a room so plain it
was severe – which said all that needed to be said before she
even opened her mouth. She was a short, slight lady, dressed
in a lilac suit. Her blonde bob perfectly framed her pale face;
her grey eyes seemed ready to cry.

'I am speaking to you,' she said, 'from inside a secure

location in New York City. With a heavy heart and with great sadness I must tell you today that an act of global sabotage and cyberterrorism has been perpetrated against innocent civilians all over the world. As most of you will now be aware, two hours ago the firewalls of the United States Social Security Administration, the Home Office in the UK, the People's Bank of China and the Ministerio da Saude in Brazil were breached. Sensitive information pertaining to more than one-and-a-half billion private citizens has been stolen. It is suspected that the hackers have also been able to harvest sensitive information on anyone who has ever travelled to any of the four nations. The full extent of the leak remains unclear, and not all the individual breaches have yet been sealed.

'I have already consulted the heads of state in all four targeted nations, as well as other world leaders, and I have taken advice from representatives of global security agencies and cybersecurity experts. I am advised that there is no way to know exactly what has been taken, who has taken it, and what or who their next target will be. It is for this reason that I must invoke, with immediate effect, a state of global emergency.

'Representatives from all 193 UN member states will convene here in New York in one hour, in order that we may come to an immediate global solution to this catastrophe. One that will keep us safe and unite us against the invisible and ruthless enemy we now face. Thank you. God bless you all.'

The Secretary-General's face was faded out and, for a moment, there was nothing on the screen. Just blissful silence. I remember smiling. Yes, I'd been to America – I'd even had a visa once. My personal information was probably being sold to the highest black-market bidder as I lay there. But I didn't care. I was looking at the bigger picture, thinking of my newborn son. *Finally*, I thought, *they're all going to realize the problem with entrusting your whole life to computers, putting all your eggs in one basket. Finally! They're going to realize how stupid they are, putting all their faith in a bunch of zeroes and ones they don't even understand.*

The United Nations endorses use of

GNOSYS TECHNOLOGIES®

No. 1, Sunday Times 'Unhacked 100', 2060

The dark room was filled up with painfully bright white light once again. The silence was broken.

The UN endorses Gnosys? The smile was wiped from my face. No government or diplomatic coalition had ever endorsed the use of one company over any other company, not publicly at least. It just didn't happen.

I was right about one thing – this cyberattack was going to make people realize the problem with entrusting your life to computers.

But I was wrong to think that people would turn away from computers at last. Totally wrong. No one could have predicted what happened next.

CHAPTER 30

FIGURES IN A LANDSCAPE

'Mummy. Are we seeing Santa?'

'What?' I spun around. You were still standing there, staring up at me. I'd fallen into a kind of trance, a dreamless emptiness. I'd been doing it a lot that day. Seconds had passed, maybe minutes, and I had just been standing there with my back to you, my fingers gripping onto the handle of the suitcase so tightly that my knuckles were turning white. I could see how confused you were. I thought you might be about to cry. Those big brown eyes were so full of love and wonder . . . and trust. I could hardly breathe.

I let go of the suitcase, came over to you once more and smiled as big a smile as I could.

'What was that, my sweet?' I said, my voice croaking.

'Santa?' You said softly. Your eyes were like giant saucers.

'Oh well,' I said in my best everything's-going-to-be-fine voice. 'You know as well as I do how busy Father Christmas is at this time of year. Besides, his sleigh goes so fast it's very difficult to see him for long enough to get his attention.'

'But . . . writed him a list,' you said, your eyes filling up with tears. Father Christmas had always visited you, ever since your first Christmas. There can't have been any doubt in your mind that Father Christmas would visit you again.

'Oh my love! Don't cry! Of course he's coming. Of course Santa will bring you your presents! All I'm saying is he might not have time to stop and say hello . . . That's all!' My heart broke. I had tried to fit all the new Christmas gifts I'd bought you in the suitcase, amongst all your clothes and your books, but there was no way. *He doesn't need any of this. It's not going to mean anything to him if he's never seen any of it. If this is going to be the last Christmas he's ever going to get presents, I'm going to give him something that will mean something.* In the end I decided to leave them all behind.

Instead, I found an old Cadbury's chocolate tin and filled it with memories of your life. The life you were about to leave. The items inside the box included a blank book of music manuscript paper, on which I thought that one day you could write some songs; your raggedy old comfort blanket; an old book your father loved as a child; and a picture of him and me. I also put in an old iPhone that had belonged to your dad and, before him, his mother. A relic of a bygone age, an antique from the early 2000s, when people still used mobile phones, it was your favourite toy. I never understood why, but you would play with it constantly: prodding it and fiddling with it for hours on end. Even when it was switched on, there wasn't much you could do with it, but you didn't care. You just loved to stare at your own reflection in its little glass screen. That part fascinated me: I couldn't help but wonder what you were thinking about, what was going through your mind. Your dad always seemed less confused by this behaviour. Indeed, he encouraged you to play with your little toy, to get to know it, almost as if he believed it would be good for you in some way: a kind of good luck charm that – carried with you always – would let you come to no harm. Anyway, there it was, and still is, in the Cadbury's Roses tin.

'Do you understand, my love?' You nodded, your tears subsiding and a shy smile creeping back onto your face. 'But remember' – I was now very conscious of time – 'he only comes to very good boys. So, stay by my side, do exactly what I say, never let go of my hand and I promise, I promise Santa's going to leave something at the end of your bed tonight . . .' The shy smile became a big grin. 'Good boy. Go and kiss Lilly goodbye then we'll go.'

I'd been steeling myself for this, knowing that however much I couldn't bear the idea of leaving her, bringing Lilly would make getting down to Piccadilly Circus ten times as difficult. But when it came to it, I choked, hardly able to get the words out. You must have seen immediately that something was wrong. Instantly your eyes were like saucers full of water and you were wailing a deafening wail.

'Shhhh, shhhh, of course Lilly's coming with us, darling,' I said, trying to smile through my tears and holding you to me tightly, like I'd been joking. You calmed down a bit when you saw me clipping Lilly's leash to her collar, but you'd been right to cry, to protest. How on earth I felt like I could have left her behind in the first place is horrifying. I suppose it just goes to show how horrible it all was, how confusing and confused.

I put on my coat, got the suitcase, led you both to the door, and turned out the light. 'Time to go.'

There were no taxis. No rides. There was no need; people had already stopped moving around by then. They definitely didn't leave the safety and security of places like Primrose Hill to venture into town – into the Ghetto.

Zooooooom! Zooooooom! Zooooooom!

Three Podds shot past us. The last one, swooping down way too fast as it headed for the nearby docking station, only very narrowly missed you.

'Where we going, Mamma?' you enquired as we began trudging south towards Regent's Park, through the dark urban sprawl, barren and mostly deserted since the Flood. Snow lined the streets and encased the cobbles in the little mews behind our house. It made the old stones look like box-fresh white bathroom tiles.

'It's a surprise, remember?' You did, I think, but weren't actually very interested in the answer. You skipped from cobble to cobble, fascinated by the prints your feet made in the cold white blanket that had fallen from the sky. Besides, you knew I wouldn't let you down. I was all too aware of your faith in me. It panicked me even more. I hate feeling out of control now and I hated it more then. I liked things to be just so, to go the way they should.

'We going on 'venture!' You squeezed my midriff tightly.

We reached the park. What was once Henry VIII's royal hunting ground, and later one of the most beautiful London parks, was now nothing more than a desolate No Man's Land that separated the burbs from the Ghetto.

This was it. There was no turning back now.

'Just a bag of essentials, El; leave everything else behind,' Peter had said. 'The most important thing is you get to the Cell.' As far as I knew then, the Offliner Cell was a kind of refugee camp for anyone not logging in. 'Are we seeing Santa?' you asked again, as we walked into the terrifying darkness of the park and I looked back at the burbs for the very last time.

'Darling, I—' But I had nothing left to say. I had no more energy. Of course you thought we were seeing Santa. To you, it could have been the only possible explanation for getting into your big red puffer, putting on your woolliest hat and scarf, and going for a walk when it was dark and freezing outside. I don't suppose you'd even begun to consider the suitcase: that would have been one thing too many to get your heard around. After all, it was Christmas Eve and you were only four years old.

CHAPTER 31

DEADROOM

I'm in a circular room with walls of glass, high up in the clouds. Where there aren't windows, there are smooth white walls, and white shelves of old books.

A very large desk stands at one end, with a very large black chair behind it. On the desk is a single picture frame, the photograph facing away from me. In the centre of the room, four black leather armchairs are arranged around an old green trunk. Moving closer to see, I feel like I'm floating. Letters are painted in white on all four sides of the trunk:

S.S.S.

S.S.S.? What is S.S.S.?
I cast about for some clue to where I am. There's nothing, only – as I walk past the trunk – a name written very small beneath the initials.

SYLVIA SCARLET STERTON

I don't recognize it. Reaching the desk, I look back at where I've come from.
There is no door. Just windows, walls, shelves.
How did I get in here? Where IS here?
I feel strange, dizzy. My right hand is holding the iPhone, but I feel strangely disconnected from it, from my whole body. Clutching the phone tightly with fingers that don't feel like my own, I sit down at the leather-topped desk and pick up the picture frame in my equally alien left hand. Heavy silver, it holds a black-and-white photograph of a young man in a linen suit, standing outside a grand old

building. A cathedral, perhaps a castle? There is an inscription at the base of the frame.

James Rogers
1993–2058

James Rogers?

Suddenly I hear voices from outside the room, too muffled to be understood. But I can tell there's a man's voice, then a girl's, shouting at each other. They're echoing like they're in a corridor, getting closer all the time.

Heartbeat yammering like a guard dog that's just been woken up, I jerk back from the desk, shoving the big chair aside. The heavy frame drops from my disembodied grasp with a dull clunk, leaving James Rogers face-down on the desk like he's pinned down by the weight of a fallen cathedral. For some reason, I'm momentarily aghast at the horror of the idea. In fact, I'm so sickeningly distracted that it's a few seconds before I register the other thing.

I've dropped the iPhone too. It's like I have to press rewind so I can watch it skitter out of my hand, bounce on the leather top of the desk, and cartwheel over the side onto the floor, out of sight.

The phone!

'—lutely not. Not till we're in the deadroom.' The voice of the man is sour and angry and much louder than before, like he's just ten paces or so away. The sound is still muffled, chopped up, but the word was definitely *deadroom*.

I whirl round. There's only the walls and the windows and the high clouds beyond.

'—the deadroom? Just talk to me here.' The girl's voice.

'Inside!' the man says, coldly.

Deadroom? I ponder for a fraction of a second. But there's no time to think. I just know they're coming in here. I can feel it in my prickling hair.

I look around again. *Maybe I missed something.* But there's still no door, no way in.

And no way out!

The realization jolts through me sickeningly.

Only the trunk. S.S.S.

Does it have to be the trunk? I think.

The voices are getting even louder.

It does.

A place without doors. How can a room have no doors? Is that what a deadroom is?

Everything still feels surreal. I quickly set the picture frame back on its feet, run to the trunk and try to open the lid. But it won't budge. Then I feel something heavy in my pocket and reach inside. A key. A key that wasn't there before.

What? I think. *Impossible.*

The key is made of gold and fits perfectly into the lock on the trunk. I turn it, lift the lid, and – all in one go, as if it were the most natural thing anyone could ever do – I climb inside the trunk and pull the lid closed, folding myself into the tiny space—

And then I remember the phone.

My line to the past, to Izzy!

In the inky blackness the voices seem even louder, drowning out the sound of my own pulse, my own heaving breath.

And I know the girl's voice, without a shred of doubt. It's hardly muffled at all now.

'So we need to be in your magic room before we can talk? Gosh, Daddy, I wonder what could be so important. Or is the word *embarrassing*?'

'Don't be so idiotic, Rosie. You're old enough to know how things work. Get inside. Now!'

Hamilton!

I can't leave my phone out there.

They'll find it! Hamilton will find it. And he'll get to Izzy!

The enormity of the idea almost crushes me. He has so much power already, in the real world and in Perspecta.

Oh my God, what if he could reach back in time too?

Without a further thought, I arch my bent back against the heavy lid and push it open, then pour myself out onto the floor and dart back towards the desk.

I can't see the iPhone.

Where the hell—?

'And I'm old enough to do what I want,' says Rosie. The room's still empty, yet she could be right there behind the desk, she sounds so close.

'You're a Rogers,' her father comes back at her, danger in his voice. 'A Rogers does what needs to be done – no exceptions. In!'

There's a grunt of expelled air like someone's been shoved, violently.

Impossibly, coming through the wall as if it isn't there at all, a shoulder and a blonde head of hair appear – then halt. Rock-solid, resistant.

Rosie.

I'm torn between the thought of Hamilton getting my iPhone and Hamilton getting physical with Rosie. Then her voice hisses, 'Don't you lay a hand on me!' She sounds like a cobra. Like she can look after herself.

She's going to have to, I decide. *It's all I can do to look after myself.*

In the nick of time, I see the phone case gleaming by one of the desk legs. But just as I step over to retrieve it, there's another grunt, another shove, and Rosie is backing rapidly through solid wall, propelled by Hamilton's arms.

I do the only thing that's left to me. I kick the phone, sending it spinning across the floor and under the book-shelves, out of sight. Then I hurl myself so fast backwards towards the *S.S.S.* trunk that I feel something wrench in my torso muscles. The lid's still open and I literally dive in head first – no time to pull it closed on top of me.

The voices are right next to me, like they are in the room.

They *are* in the room.

'Daddy, I don't want to.'

'I don't care whether you want to or not, Rosie.'

'You don't care whether I want to or not? You don't care if your daughter doesn't want to log out and fly to London so you can pimp her out to a load of old salivating reptiles? Great father you are!'

'Your ingratitude is remarkable. Don't you dare speak to me like—'

But then abruptly Hamilton stops. Silence once more.

'You left your grandmother's trunk open?'

'I haven't touched it!'

I look up, Rosie's voice ringing in my ears.

Two faces peer in, black against the bright daylight coming in from the windows.

This is it, I think, suddenly calm, resigned. *It's over.*

Then the lights go out.

CHAPTER 32

LOSS AND RECOVERY

Blinded, my other senses open out. The air feels suddenly different, colder. I reach out for the side of the trunk but it's not there, only a brick wall, chilly and slightly damp. I shut my eyes and rub them with my knuckles. The two silhouetted heads are still there, like afterburn inside my eyelids. And my brain has belatedly connected the dots: Sylvia Sterton became Sylvia Rogers when she married James. But I'm not in her trunk at all. I'm in my dorm in the Cell, panting in the darkness but awake.

'I can't do this any more!' I shout at the wall, sitting up in my bed with a start. *This has got to stop.* In, *two three*, out, *two three*. I try to breathe normally to calm myself down. It's a panic attack – my fifth since the day Eliza was beaten up. *Another panic attack!* I can't seem to shake them off since I carried her away from the deathly ghouls. 'Why is this happening to me? What the hell is wrong with me?' I sob. 'I have to know what's going on.' I have to make sense of the tangled, sickening confusion inside.

As I sit here sobbing, my shoulders rising and falling in gentle waves, all I can think about is my mum: how much I wish she were here to comfort me, to tell me what to do, to guide me.

Reaching under my bed, I pull out my old tarpaulin bag and reach in for the *Roses* tin. There's my comforter again, but it's no comfort, just a reminder of all that's been lost. There's Mum's little memoir, but I don't want to read it again now. There's—

The phone! Where's the phone?

The iPhone should be in here. This is where I've been stashing it for safekeeping at night, at least since I realized I wasn't about to get an instant progress report about the search for Sylvia Rogers. It's been two weeks now since I asked Izzy to find her. For a week I slept with the phone under my pillow waiting for an Instagram alert. But I was always afraid it would fall bleeping to the floor and I'd be hauled off to explain to Ruth why I was sleeping with an illegal piece of tech. So into the bag it went, switched off, while I slept.

It's not there. The phone is not there. I can't believe my eyes. I rack my brains for what else I might have done with it. Did I leave it or drop it somewhere earlier in the day yesterday? No, I definitely checked for messages from Izzy last night.

Pas! Pas knows about it! He must be messing with me. I pull on my shirt and trousers and march barefoot down the corridor into his dorm. He's not there. Instantly my suspicions gather like a thundercloud. *Where the hell is he? It's not even seven yet.* I rifle through his stuff but I know it's futile. If Pascale has nicked my phone, he'd hardly leave it lying around.

I'm just leaving my dorm again, shoes on this time, when Pas comes barrelling into me and nearly knocks me flat. Before I can even open my mouth to let out the accusations, he's got me by the shoulders and his beaming face is an inch from mine as he yells, 'She's good! She's— Yottam's down there now. She's okay!'

He doesn't need to explain more. In moments I'm sitting on the edge of Eliza's bed with him and she's smiling dreamily, telling us how she's been on a beautiful boat drifting lazily along the Amazon. That's all she can say about the time since she stormed out of the Ticket more than two weeks ago. Seems like she's had a more peaceful time than me. I suppose I could feel bitter about this, but I only think, *Good.* I'm glad, just deeply happy and relieved for her.

It's not till I come back up from the San and I'm standing outside the Galley, last in line for breakfast, that I remember the phone. The idea that Pas might have taken it as a joke, in the middle of his worries over Eliza, has evaporated. I turn my dorm upside down, twice, but can't find it and can't think of anything else to do. Totally stumped, but exhausted from the switchbacks between relief for Lizy and anxiety over the phone, I finally just try and forget the phone, bury the thought of it, like I'm tucking it deep in the tarpaulin bag of my subconscious.

Eliza isn't completely right, not for a week. There are relapses into chaos and darkness. She seems catatonic when she's asleep and sometimes, too, when she's awake. It's like she's a different person. I'm terrified she'll never properly come back to us.

But there's something about the San. You'd never imagine it was once a Tube platform where rush-hour commuters in the Dusk would cram into trains like sardines. Those tunnels used to carry people off to offices or shops or bars or museums; now they stretch away silently into darkness, empty apart from the creeping tentacles of Gnosys's subterranean data network. But you hardly ever think of them, hardly even remember you're underground.

It's the birds, mostly. When the lights go up for the day, it's dawn chorus for the next half-hour, but after that it's just the birds chirruping and tweeting and warbling gently like they're having an endless conversation. Against that background, the growl of the solitary panther, the chatter of the monkeys and the trumpeting of the pygmy elephants somehow sound like they all fit together.

Gradually Yottam seems happier and happier with Eliza's progress. One morning I come down and hear Ruth talking to her about the day Smee called on us, and I'm amazed at how calmly she takes it.

She's calmer than me, anyway. I'm bugged to hell by the

thought of Izzy and what she's up to, and how I can't find the iPhone, can't possibly reach her.

In the end I decide I have to talk to the twins. Eliza knows nothing yet, but I reckon she'll be strong and calm enough now to hear the news. It's time to bring her up to speed with the weirder side of things.

I head to the San with Pas on our lunch break, between going out into the Ghetto to scav for some replacement copper piping – needed by Ursula in the Galley – and our afternoon Counsel session with Pokes. Yottam's busy tending his birds and beasts, so we have some privacy.

'Lizy, erm . . . there's something important I've got to tell you,' I begin, hesitantly. Then I realize Pas is laughing at me.

'Already told her, bro,' he says. 'She knows it all.'

I bristle inside. *This was my story to tell!* But I manage to hold in my annoyance as the penny drops that Pas has done me a favour. She'd never have believed me, especially now I've no phone to show her, no Insta messages.

For now I decide to keep that little detail to myself, but it doesn't make the conversation much easier. Instead of being incredulous, Eliza is furious.

'Why didn't you tell me about this when it happened? Before I got my face smashed in?' she barks at me from her bed, where she's still hooked up to myriads of ominous-looking black and green wires connected to big, clanking machines, bells, and whistles. She still looks extremely frail in her blue hospital overall, but she hasn't lost any of her characteristic pluckiness. 'I'm your *best friend*, me and Pas!'

Pas rolls his eyes.

'I didn't think,' I say stumblingly. 'I guess I just figured it was best to keep it under wraps, for now.'

'The fact that you can communicate with someone sixty years in the past using your amazing technicolour dreamphone? The fact that you can time travel—'

'I can't time travel. Don't be ridiculous! I can talk to her, that's all.'

'That's all?' Her eyes bulge in her head. Pas giggles a little bit, happy to see his sister back to her good old exasperated self. I just sit there, with a lump in my throat, looking down at my lap like some kind of naughty schoolboy.

'That's *all*?' she says again. 'You *can* time travel, because you have her! She's you in the past as far as I'm concerned . . . Oh my God.' She looks away from Pas and me and into the middle distance for a moment. 'This is absolutely huge! I mean, so you've asked her to find Sylvia. But she needs to find her and kill her. You do see that, right – that it's the only way we can stop the future and what's happened?'

Pas looks at me and I feel a pang of pressure edging its way from my head down my neck and into my back, then beginning to ache in my belly.

'I said the same thing,' Pas tells her. 'It has to be done.'

'Look, I know what you mean and I get that you're angry—' I begin.

'Angry?' Eliza squawks. 'That's the understatement of the year.'

'Lizy, I get it, okay?' I lean towards her, like I'm talking to a child. I can see from the flash in her eyes that this annoys her, but somehow it eases the pressure I'm feeling. 'I was there, remember? I brought you down here.' The pain in my back begins to subside and I sit back a bit in my chair. 'I agree, it is going to be difficult for Izzy to get close enough to Sylvia to persuade her to ignore her life's work. For Sylvia, I imagine it's kind of like a primal impulse or instinct: she *has* to start Gnosys.'

'That's exactly why she needs to kill her.'

'Eliza!' I suddenly feel very angry. 'Listen to yourself, for one second! You're asking someone – a normal girl, who has never heard of Gnosys, never experienced one of our morning storms, never seen a Tooth, who goes to school and does her homework and has a boyfriend, in the year 2021 – to murder someone! You're asking her to throw away her entire life for us.'

'Yes. That's exactly what I'm asking,' Eliza says, her face stern and resolute. I can see some doubt creeping into Pas's eyes after what I've just said, but he isn't going to argue with his sister; not right now, not after everything that's happened to her.

I know that now would be the time to fess up that I don't have the phone. But I'm still too embarrassed, so instead I argue back. 'I'm not going to ask someone who didn't ask to be caught up in all this – who lives in a completely different age – to ruin her life. And besides, who knows what would happen between then and now if she did put a knife in the back of Sylvia Rogers in 2021? It's messing with the fabric of time so drastically and irreversibly that anything could happen. It'd be total bloody madness! Surely, I mean *surely* you understand that?' I'm trying to sound principled and intelligent, but I just feel shrill and stupid.

'Surely *you* understand that even talking with her is

messing with the fabric of time!' laughs Eliza scornfully. 'Maybe "anything" has *already* happened. This Isabel of yours, she has to kill Sylvia.'

'Well I'm not going to tell her to do that,' I snap. 'And anyway—' I choke '—I haven't got the phone any more. I've lost it.'

Eliza looks at me aghast, like she can't fathom which is worse: my disloyalty or my stupidity. Or my weakness – because I'm now sitting here with my lower lip quivering, like a child waiting to be sent to the naughty step.

Into the silence, it all comes spilling out. I tell them how I had the phone one day and it was gone the next. I say I've looked everywhere. I even admit that I searched Pas's dorm.

At the end of it all, Eliza looks less aghast but no happier. 'I'm tired and it's giving me a headache thinking about it,' she mumbles and turns over in her bed. And that's that. Conversation over.

Pas and I troop out. Dejected, I follow him into his dorm and continue to spill out apologies and self-recriminations. When I've finally run out of steam, he leans over and puts an arm around me. 'Kid, you're okay. You did what you thought was right. Lizy'll come round. Your 2021 girl isn't going to do anything she doesn't want to, anyway. If she tracks Sylvia down, that's a start. We'll look for your phone together, but till it turns up you might as well just – I dunno, chill. When it does, then we'll see where we are, and how things have gone down in Izzyland.'

I wish I could believe that were possible now, but I don't any more.

CHAPTER 33

WE REGRET TO INFORM YOU

Kid?
How do you know my name?
Kid . . . ?
Yes.
Josh Kid Jones?
Yes . . . How do you know my . . . What is this place?
It's a nice name. Kind. You have such a kind face.

I don't understand . . .

My name's Rosie.

I know your name. Everyone knows your . . .

This is my father, Hamilton . . . Daddy, this is Kid; he's my friend.

Wait! Rosie! Watch out, he's—

Daddy! Stop! Please stop!

Get off her!

I wake up. Another crazy dream. *Why am I dreaming about her?* Sweat pours down my face. *I'm boiling.* I watch the hot air shoot like jets of steam from my nostrils as it hits the freezing cold air in the dorm. My heart beats at an alarming rate. I check my pulse. *And so amped up?*

The other day a couple of youngers said they'd seen me walking out of the dorm at night. I've no memory of it. So apparently I've started sleepwalking now too. I feel so messed up and I hate it all. I hate my life. *I hate all of you. Mum, Dad, everyone!* 'I hate you all, for letting me down!' I scream. People would have heard that, I worry for a second. Then I stop worrying – 'I HATE YOU ALL!' It's too painful to think of Mum, so I search desperately in all the weird, dark, lonely cloisters of my mind for something, anything else to focus on.

Rosie. Rosie. Rosie.

Without warning I begin to overheat again, and the voice in my head echoes thunderously like a pinball around my mind. *Rosie! Rosie! Rosie!* It ricochets as if propelled by the memory of the terrible dream I just had. Then everything comes momentarily clear and I know what I need to do, even if I don't know why.

Suddenly it's like my brain is completely empty, all the ideas and memories and clarity gone, leaving just barren silence. I look around my dorm room, mirroring what I'm doing in my head: a miniature me, lost, searching, hopeless, in the middle of my vacant skull.

But then the whirl of sensations starts up again and it's like I'm going round the same rollercoaster, over and over. Suddenly, miniature me is reaching out for Mum's hand, but can't quite get to it. The smell of peppermint curls phantas-mically in my nostrils; but before the smell becomes taste, it's gone. Though it's nearly three weeks since I read her memoir, the scenes from it are still running through my mind like they're on a loop.

Leo! The roar is so startling that I immediately jump up out of bed and stand there naked, shivering, like a fevered inmate in a jail cell. The old voice, again. After that Perspecta trip to Primrose Hill, I don't know if I trust Leo, and I certainly don't understand her. But I know she was once Mum's closest friend, and I know what the voice is asking me to do. *Just give her a chance. One more chance. Give her a chance. A chance. A chance. A chance.*

'Okay!' I pull on my clothes, shoes and scarf as quickly and as painlessly as possible. It's the middle of the night. It must be. The dorm's black and I'm absolutely bloody freezing. It's May! The weather is so messed up these days. I leave the relative comfort of my room and go up the Chute, through the Ticket, past Mungo, who snores away bliss-fully unaware of me and my surging anxiety. I stop at the gate to look at him for a moment, as if I might find some inner peace in his slow, soporific snore. No. No chance of that, I realize, getting out my Roxi disp, inserting a pellet and taking a big hit. I crank the heavy gate open, leaving the Cell and throwing myself out into the dangerous, toxic black. The still silence of the Ghetto now seems terrifying. As I make my way through it, I can't help but think about everything – Eliza, the Teeth, their indecipherable, deafening screams, the panic attacks and dreams, the lost phone, Izzy and whatever the hell's happening with her mission to find Sylvia. It all begins to overwhelm me as I skulk, unnoticed, down Great Marlborough Street towards Liberty's.

'My dear, how good of you to come!' The rose-coloured smoke from Leo's pink cigarette curls around her head in a perfect spherical plume. She is both imposing and congenial in a black suit, very tightly fitted around her tiny, brittle frame. I stay still and silent, a stern look in my eyes. She raises an eyebrow. 'Oh dear, you've got yourself into a terrible tizz, haven't you? What on earth's the matter? Sit down, over there.'

She's sitting behind a small antique writing desk in the corner of her drawing room, the candlelight darting back and forth across her face like a shadow puppet show. I do as she suggests and take a seat on one of the two luxurious burgundy sofas in the middle of the room.

'Tell you what,' she says, 'why don't I come and sit down with you over there? We'll have some tea. It's far too delicious a meal to be taken at such an uneventful time of the day. Besides, Michel makes the most divine tinned tuna tartines. Crustless of course.' She comes over and takes a seat in the matching sofa, opposite me. 'To die for. Michel!' she bellows, making me jump. *'Nous aimerions avoir du thé et des sandwichs dans le salon toute de suite!'* Her French sounds flawless, but what would I know? Is there anything you can't do? 'In fact,' she says, changing her mind, 'perhaps something a little stronger befits the mood. Michel! On second thoughts just bring the brandy!' Brandy? Where on earth, where in London, could you possibly get brandy? I think to myself, my suspicions growing, my blood beginning to boil with impatience. She sits back, lighting one of her pink Roxi cigarettes nonchalantly, and smiles at me.

Now I'm seeing red. 'Enough is enough! I've got some questions and I know you have the answers, so I'm not leaving until you tell me what I want to know. Firstly—'

She reaches into the inside pocket of her double-breasted purple velvet suit jacket and removes a manila envelope, which she hands me. It's blank on both sides, crumpled, and obviously very old. I stare at it, resting it in my hands and fingering it gently. A letter.

'It doesn't contain all the answers, but it may help you focus your questions. Open.' She lights another cigarette, watching me closely. 'Read.'

Office of Hamilton Rogers,
Gnosys Q-1, 175 5th Avenue, NY
December 19, 2064

Dear Mrs Jones,

We regret to inform you that, subsequent to your husband's disappearance, his contract with Gnosys (henceforth 'the company') has been terminated. As a result of the unusual circumstances of your husband's departure – leaving without giving written or verbal notice – any severance benefits assigned in the terms of his employment with the company are nullified and rendered void. Therefore any property, health plans or retirement packages belonging to or provided by the company must be returned to the company and/ or terminated within the time periods stated below. The items are as follows:

- Property at No. 68 Regent's Park Road, London NW1 7SU
- Retirement/Severance package totaling £250,000/ annum until death of former employee
- Complete G-1 Employee Health Insurance Cover for former employee and family of former employee until death of each respective individual

Please vacate the above property by Christmas Eve of this year (December 24, 2064). Please also be aware that any retirement packages or health plans listed above will be terminated within a week of your receipt of this letter. Moreover, any attempt by yourself to withdraw any remaining funds (paid in by the company) from your husband's bank account will be looked upon by the company as an act of theft, investigated, and prosecuted accordingly.

However, as a gesture of thanks on behalf of Mr. Rogers himself, for all the good work that your husband did for the company when in its employ, Gnosys would like to offer you and your son a unit in one of our brand-new Habs, free of charge. Once situated, you will have nonstop access to the Perspecta Universe – our hyperrealistic virtual reality – in which you will be able to live and work without interruption.

Our Hab units are designed around a single purpose: to allow our users a completely safe, undisturbed life inside the Perspecta Universe. The Habs are sealed and secured from both the outside world and the wider Internet, giving you complete peace of mind when it comes to the physical and cyber safety of you and your loved ones. Our specially designed XoGno2000 Haptic Rigs come fitted with lavatory function as standard. Fully immersive, the rigs enable users to stay logged into the Universe for up to twenty-four hours, after which time government regulations stipulate one hour of physical exercise outside of the Universe. Depending on your needs, our London Belt contains single, double, triple and quadruple rig units.

N.B. Since the Paperless Post Act of 2061 we are no longer able to accept letters sent via the United States Postal Service. Should you wish to take Mr. Rogers up on his kind offer, or if you have any other questions regarding the contents of this letter, please respond via GNOME.

Kind regards,

Gregory F. Manning
Executive Assistant to Hamilton Rogers
GNOME: 212.477.0947

CHAPTER 34

CHRISTOPHER EDWARD JONES

I drop the letter on the floor and look up at my godmother, my eyes as big as soup bowls. I can't think, I can't move, I've forgotten how to breathe. Leo hands me a glass of brandy. I clasp it in my right hand, completely still. I am a zombie, a prisoner inside my head; and Leo with her letter holds the key.

'Michel came and went,' she says. 'I didn't want him to disturb you whilst you were reading. He bids you *bonne nuit*.'

I stare, mouth open wide. She allows me the moment, she gives my brain the time to catch up.

'My father worked for Gnosys.'

'Yes.'

'My father *wasn't* a computer engineer and he *didn't* run away with another woman.'

'No.'

'My mother lied to me.'

'Your mother saved you.'

'What?' I spit, snapping out of the daze.

'If you had known the truth you wouldn't have survived a year after she was gone. You would have told one of your friends who would have told someone else who would have told an elder who would have told a Stillspeare, and before you knew it you would have been slung out of the Cell coughing up black gunk in a doorway on Lexington Street. You know as well as I do the punishment the COOs give for colluding with Gnosys. Exile. Your mother did too. She knew she could never tell you the truth about who your father was; she knew it the moment that letter came through the door, the moment you became an Offliner.'

I'm in a rage.

'She lied to me, Leo. She didn't just leave me, she lied to me! My whole life, everything I've ever thought about my father has been a lie. I've spent my life hating him! Do you understand what that feels like? Despising his memory! It's her fault. She left me on this planet alone, fending for myself, armed only with a lie. She ruined everything.'

Then Leo looks at me with an expression I don't recognize. *Is that anger in her eyes?*

'Never,' her voice booms and her face becomes dark, 'ever talk about your mother that way. Do you understand, young man?'

Young man? I'm suddenly frightened. She's angry. It feels like she could blow at any moment.

'Your mother sacrificed everything for you, including herself. Her body, her brain, her life. Everything. She didn't lie to you; she freed you from the terrible reality of her situation so that you could live a good life, the best life possible.'

I say nothing. My mother's face comes to the forefront of my mind, her beautiful, kind, brown eyes, full of love, looking down at me from above. *Sleep well my love, dream as many dreams as you can, your dreams will set you free*, she says, stroking my hair, wishing me goodnight. *Go, my darling, and be free.* Then the image begins fading to grey. I squeeze my eyes shut and try my best to hold onto it, but the precious scene grows more and more dim in my mind's eye until eventually it's gone completely.

'I'd almost forgotten.' I look at Leo, my eyes full of hot, stinging tears. 'It's been so long I'd almost forgotten.'

'Forgotten what?' Her voice returns to its normal, gravelly, soothing pitch.

'How much she loved me.'

Leo nods. 'You're not angry with your mother. You're angry with your father. He left. She didn't.'

I process this and decide that she is right. I knew she was right all along. My mother loved me more than any mother's ever loved a son. *It's Dad*, I think. *It's the not knowing, the nothingness that surrounds my memories of him.*

'Indeed,' Leo continues gently, 'your mother knew

almost nothing of your father's work. She knew, of course, *where* he worked, but beyond that she had only suspicions and hypotheses. He couldn't talk about his work and she wasn't interested. Until this.' She points a long, spindly finger at the letter on the floor. Instinctively, I pick it up and begin studying it again, reading every line twice; trying desperately to find anything to connect the company with his disappearance, any evidence of foul play. Nothing. *He just disappeared*, I think, *and they took back all his benefits.*

But I am not satisfied. 'It still doesn't explain why he left.'

'Not explicitly, no, but one could be forgiven for inferring.'

I look at her as if to say, *Go on . . .*

She clears her throat. 'Look what they did to Eliza.' Whatever Leo's sources, she has evidently heard all about Smee's visit to the Cell. 'Your father loved you and your mother more than anything else in the world. He loved you with everything he had. The two of you were his salvation. It's wisest,' she tilts her head towards me, her eyes full of love, 'to imagine the worst and hope for the best. Again, look what they did to Eliza.' She virtually spells it.

They killed him. It hits me with such force that the words lag behind the thought. 'They killed him.'

The idea blows me back like I'm a leaf in a gale. Then, suddenly, it all starts to make perfect, horrible, stomach-churning sense.

'They killed him because of me,' I cry out like I've been shot through the stomach. My heart races, my brain's on fire, my body boils, my skin stings. 'Leo, it's you that doesn't understand. I'm logged into Perspecta. Someone logged me into Perspecta when I was two years old. And that explains the dreams, this whole mad telekinetic trip I'm on, the voice I always have in my head. And it explains why they killed my father. I'm *still* logged in, without a Plug at all, without ever needing to have a Plug. I hear things, I see things, I can communicate with the system . . . Do you get it? I thought I was hallucinating when it started but now . . . It's all too real, it all makes too much sense, and absolutely no sense at the same time. I have a Denis, Leo; I mean, I have a . . . And I'm in deep, Leo. Deeper than I think you understand. Please, Leo. What is happening to me?'

At this the corners of her mouth wrinkle as if she's about to smile, or as if she's smiling in her head. 'No, I do understand. I understand . . . *mostly*. You're not hallucinating, Joshua, not at all. You're very much logged in to Perspecta. Not only that, but in their world you exist as—'

'A Legend.'

She blinks, surprised by my knowledge.

'Indeed.' She pauses, processing her surprise. 'Do you know what that means?'

'Not a clue,' I say in frustration. 'Well, okay. I think it means I can be invisible, or something, inside Perspecta. And maybe it was Hamilton who made me this—'

Another panic attack, the worst yet. I can't breathe.

Leo gets up quickly and kneels in front of me. She holds out her hands, palms upward, and tells me to do the same. She tells me to breathe and I do; at least I try. She tells me everything is fine and that I will recover and that things are as they should be and, very gradually, my breathing begins to stabilize and the cramps subside. I begin to feel normal again.

'There are indeed things that are hard to understand, Joshua,' she says. 'And not understanding is frightening, I know. That's why I felt it was time to begin your education the last time you were here. You had a taste of Perspecta then, didn't you dear, when you asked me to help you get to Primrose Hill? Was it fun?' she says, a mischievous grin surreptitiously curling its way from one corner of her mouth to the other, as the smoke from he cigarette curls its way around her face's feline frame.

I just stare at her, my mouth open, remembering the crazy lift ride through the roof of Skull's that left me miraculously hovering above Regent Street waiting to be sent flying by a speeding Podd. Looking at Leo now, I wonder how she can be so blithe about such a terrifying experience. It's like she's talking about a fairground ride.

'Shall I tell you a secret?' She asks theatrically, knowing very well that secrets are all I'm in the market for now. 'We don't live in a capsule, here in Skull's.' She goes on. 'We need the outside world, even if our needs are quite modest. We trade with Lucien Loffabond, like you do, and also with Seekers, Roxi Runners, all sorts of Ghetto folk. However, much to his chagrin, Michel must sometimes venture beyond the Ghetto. We know how to run up a rather splendid Specta suit, as you know, but there's still the need for transport: for Michel to use the Podd Way. But it's getting to the Way that's the problem. As you may have noticed, dear, the area between our front door and the nearest docking station is rather a mess.'

I picture the colossal tangle of twisted girders and shattered masonry just next to the old Liberty's building – all that's left of a whole block of shops and offices from the Dusk. I've always just thought of it as a useful barrier against the world outside the Ghetto, a bit like the Wall at the edge of the Circus.

'Alas, clambering over rubble is not quite Michel's style. And nor, frankly, is being a butler. He's severely underchallenged here.' She looks away for a moment, a forlorn expression on her face, almost like she feels sorry for Michel, bad about his skills not being put to good use. 'He likes a project, see – such as the ingenious mannequin you saw. That's Michel. One of his best, I think! Another of his inventions is an adapted service tunnel below ground that allows him to ride to the docking station in style, avoiding all the oomska as he does! That's how you got there.'

'The lift went up.'

'And that,' says Leo, 'is where Perspecta came into play. You were already partly inside the Universe. You'll recall we had a beautiful starry night, quite impossible these days as you know.' She leans in a little, a knowing expression on her face. 'Perspecta.' She whispers, before leaning back and carrying on. 'You will have seen the bookshelves in my office elegantly folding themselves away as you set off.' She stands up and sits back down on the sofa opposite. 'Well, although you were actually travelling down below the base-ment, then along Michel's secret tunnel and up again to the docking station, you *felt* as if you were simply going up. With the right equipment, a smidge of imagination and a willing participant, virtual reality not only looks but also feels like, well, real reality.'

'It didn't feel like reality to me. The lift – it went through the roof!'

'Through the roof, Joshua?' Leo looks truly puzzled.

'It went through the roof. And the next thing I know I'm floating in mid-air like a Podd. About two storeys above Regent Street.' I wipe my sleeve across my nose. 'The lift's completely vanished and I'm either going to smash down into the street or get hit by a Podd.'

Leo looks so appalled that I check my sleeve to make sure I haven't left a green trail on it. But she's evidently not thinking about my manners. 'I'm very sorry,' she says, hesitantly. 'I now begin to see what you meant when you said you were on a – how did you put it? – a "mad telekinetic trip". What you experienced when you left here that night was certainly not the plan. And yet you did end up catching a Podd, yes?' she asks, concerned, quizzical.

'Somehow, yes. Don't know how. I just ended up on the station platform and then it turned up, just for me. But hold on.' I rush to get my words out. *So many more questions to ask.* 'Why would you want me in Perspecta anyway? Why – I mean it's everything that's wrong with the world? You've said it yourself!'

'Can someone have known you were there and interfered?' She ignores my question.

'Denis says I'm invisible in Perspecta.'

'Well, perhaps.' She squints at the ceiling for a moment and leans forward. 'D'you know, Joshua? I think you are a deeply emotional young man. We have seen that already this evening. It's not necessarily a bad thing. Indeed, some of the best kinds of people are deeply emotional people, but it does mean you cannot always control yourself. And you have powers, potentialities, in relation to Perspecta, which you do not understand. Which, indeed, I myself do not. Perhaps it's possible that in your fear, your panic, you altered the Perspecta experience that had been designed for you.'

I just shake my head in confusion.

'No, I don't know either, Joshua. But look at me,' she says, her voice now as quiet as I've ever heard it. There's no pomp and circumstance to it any more. 'As to why Perspecta, well, I cannot give you the whole story because . . . I simply can't. Your mother took what little she knew to her grave in order to protect you. And your father, well . . .' She trails off. 'However, there are some things – some absolute empirical certainties – that I can and must now convey to you. It's time you knew the truth, at least that part of it which I am able to share.' She gulps. The first time she ever has. I gulp too, mirroring her, knowing now, finally, that she means to give me the answers I crave.

'You're afraid that it was Hamilton who gave you Legend status. No, Joshua; he has nothing to do with it. In fact as yet he knows nothing about Legend status.' She puts out her Roxi cigarette calmly before immediately lighting another.

'Your father, Christopher Edward Jones' – she sounds out the words slowly – 'logged you into the Perspecta Universe as a very young child. And he gave you your Legend status.'

I close my eyes, not sure whether to cry, not sure whether to laugh.

'I can't tell you why, I wish I—' She pauses, like she's

choosing her words, but then just says quickly, 'I don't know why. Nobody knows why. But the fact is that you've been given the access you have, and you continue to exist both inside and outside the Universe simultaneously without having to use a Plug. Your father meant for you to use the privilege for a reason.' She crosses her legs quickly and leans forward, raising an eyebrow. 'Your father – whether he's alive or dead now, near or far – gave you more than just his own genetic code, he also bestowed upon you an altogether different and much more dangerous kind of code—'

'It's inside me.'

'It exists wherever it exists. The point is, it exists, and the reason it exists—' She stops talking very suddenly, and just stares at me, glassy-eyed, almost like she's in a daze, like she's making a decision. Or rather, I suddenly feel, like something inside her – separate almost – is trying to decide what to say.

'Yes?' I ask. I can feel my pulse throbbing in my temple. 'Why did my dad make me a Legend, Leo – and why did he log me in to Perspecta in the first place?'

'To destroy it.' Suddenly she's palpably back in the room, snapped out of her daze and sitting up straight like a meerkat.

'What? What do you mean, to destroy it?' I feel vulnerable, like there's a spotlight on me. Like all of a sudden, with just three words, I'm no longer with my godmother in the safety of Skull's but somewhere else, somewhere dangerous, expected to be someone new. It's the way she's looking at me as if she means every insane word.

'Have you gone completely mad?' I say, harshly, standing up. 'Destroy Perspecta? Have you lost your mind?'

'Isn't it obvious?'

'That you've lost your mind? Yes. Very obvious actually!'

'The girl in the past, the dreams of Rosie Rogers. Your father logged you in so that, when the time was right, you would be able to see the truth in all these things. So you could connect them.'

'My father ran away, died, whatever he did,' I say, my throat dry, fighting back tears, 'and left me and my mum with nothing but a stupid old mobile phone.' I bow my head. 'Which I've now gone and lost.'

She fixes me with a powerful glare, like a tractor beam. 'Lost?'

Stumblingly, I repeat what happened, or at least what I know about it – which isn't much. 'One day I had it, the next it was gone.'

There's a moment's dreadful silence during which I think she's going to summon Michel and have me thrown out. Ripples of unreadable emotion cross her features. Then she seems to compose herself.

'But you did have the phone, Joshua. And where did it lead you?'

'To Izzy, it led me to Izzy Parry in 2021. You know that already!'

'To Izzy Parry in 2021. Indeed. Your father left you a phone that connected you to a girl alive at exactly the same time that Perspecta was being invented. So that you could use the past to save the future.'

'I've told her, I asked her, Izzy; I get that! But I'm not going to destroy anything, not here in the present day I mean! I'm— The best I could do was convince her to convince Sylvia Rogers to stop or do something different or . . . I don't know! But me? I don't have anything! I can't actually do anything. It's not like I'm some kind of—'

Legend. The voice resounds in my head. *Legend.*

Then silence.

'There is no one else.' Leo says quietly, like she can see in my eyes what I'm hearing in my head. 'You and Hamilton Rogers are the only two people in the universe – in both universes – with the ability, the power, to do what has to be done. Switch. It. Off.'

She takes a long draw on her cigarette without releasing me from her gaze, then resumes. 'But when Hamilton gives a speech tomorrow night at what used to be Parliament, he certainly won't be talking about switching anything off. That, I'm afraid, is something he will never do. Besides, you have two gifts he doesn't. You have the gift of insight, and even if you've lost the phone and can't speak to Isabel now, you've already shared that gift with her, to do with it what she will. And you have another gift, your Legend status, even if you don't yet understand how to use it.'

She leans forward and says, quietly and with sweetness in her voice, 'Those tasked with changing the world never know why they have been chosen. Why it should be them leading the vanguard, crying the battle cry. It is not your destiny to know why. It is for others, time itself, to show you that. All you can do is trust the signs, the voices, the dreams, the people you meet along the way.' Then another long pause. 'Your father meant for you to fix the future, Joshua.'

I pick up my jacket and slowly make for the door.

'Joshua?' she says.

'I love you Leo.' I stop at the door and turn to face her. 'Thank you for being honest. Maybe you're right. Maybe it's all true, maybe none of it is coincidence. I can accept that my father – the man who abandoned my mum and me when I wasn't even five – left me with some kind of computerized curse. Maybe I'm a robot' – a single tear rolls down my cheek and I back away out of the door as Leo gets up and comes towards me – 'but I *refuse* to believe I'm hell-bent on some "save the world" mission that I never asked for, that I could never succeed in!'

Leo's voice follows me as I run down the stairs away from her. 'The phone is gone, Joshua. The Houses of Parliament, tenth of May, eight o'clock. That's tomorrow night – well gosh, no, actually it's tonight since it's past midnight already. Go there! It's time to use your other gift.'

CHAPTER 35

GNOSYS
VIRTUAL LTD.

DATE:
Sunday 18th April, 2021

I didn't know what to feel when Kid asked me to find Sylvia Rogers. At first I was just like no – no way – there's no way I'm going in search of some strange woman to tell her I've seen/met/talked to the future and it ain't happy with her.

'Hey Sylvia! How's it going?! Cute skirt. Oh, BTW, the future's a cute boy with olive skin and he says you're, like, totally mad and you know this whole Gnosys thing you've got going on? You do? Oh great, well, basically, um, it's a bad idea and you should probably just give it all a rest TBH, cos it's gonna be a baaaaaaaaaad vibe for a bunch of really crazy people called Offliners that live in Tube stations. That cool?' Cos obvi Sylvia – my bestie Sylvia Rogers – is totes gonna turn around and be like 'OMG, babes, what do you mean? Of course, I'll give up on my thing – the thing I'm most passionate about in the entire world – and pack it all in . . . Just, ya know, cos you asked.'

I mean, WTF was he thinking?!

I just left the whole thing alone and didn't message Kid and tried to forget about it all for a few days and focus on me, on the here, the now and the present. LOL, it's still weird saying that. Especially when I haven't been able to stop thinking about the really mindblowing problem, which isn't the Offliners' situation but WT actual F is letting us chat just like he's in London 2021?

I tried to make the question go away but I couldn't, and kept finding myself disappearing down rabbit holes on the internet. A rabbit hole is like a wormhole but doesn't take you anywhere. I went to the library too, straight to the shelf with 539 as usual (that's the Dewey number for 'modern physics'). There's nothing like a book. But eventually I realised that even the nuttiest quantum theorist doesn't have what I have – proof. That's where I win. Even if it's just acorns and oaks and Future Boy, I know it's true. It's like Billic Eilish or Kim K has walked through the door and is having a cup of tea with me, right here right now, but I'm not a fan girl any more, I'm a friend.

So I've been thinking a lot about quantum entanglement and tachyons. They seem the best bets. Oh dear, diary, you don't know what tachyons are, do you? Should I have turned you into a multicolour particle physics chart after all? Tachyons are subatomic particles that go faster than light. So a message using tachyons would arrive before you sent it. Pretty mindblowing, hey?! And entanglement is where two different particles act like they're the same particle, so if you do something to one, you do it to the other – even if it's light years away in the galaxy, or years away in the future. (See, told you quantum physics was wacko!) So say you had a bunch of photons and someone else had another bunch that was entangled with them, maybe you could message each other???

So I've been doing pretty badly at thinking just about the present. And in the end I kept coming back to Future Boy and how he wants to, um, entangle me with Sylvia Rogers.

I agreed to nothing when he DM'd me, so I didn't feel like I HAD to do anything. To his credit, he did say he'd understand and respect my choice either way. I felt for him – I feel for all of them, the whole time – of course I do. I mean, this is the most incredibly weird and wonderful thing that's ever happened to me – that's ever happened to anyone, ever, maybe. The problem is, not being there, it all feels abstract. How bad things really are, you know. How really, actually awful life is for the Offliners.

Kid's told me all about their lives and the way they're

forced to live. He's talked more and more about the Teeth and Gnosys and Perspecta and Hamilton Rogers. Hamilton Rogers. In fact for a bit now he's been talking about HR more than anything or anyone else, about how evil he is and how much Kid loathes the man and would love nothing more than to see him dead. And when the Eliza thing happened I guess shit got that little bit realer for them, especially Kid. I can't imagine what that would be like. I can't imagine how horrifying it must be to see your friend lying on the floor, beaten to a pulp and close to death. Let alone having to carry her without any help, knowing that, whatever happens, whatever you do, you're her last chance. Her life-or-death-person, you know?

The problem is, however much Kid and I talk and however much he tells me about his life – about how hard things are – and no matter how much I believe it all and know, deep down, in my heart that it's all true . . . well, if I'm completely honest it all still feels like a movie to me. Like an epic fantasy which could never ever have anything to do with me. No way, you kidding me?! Little ME?! LMAO!

Then last night I realised something, why do I care FFS? I mean, what does it matter? Like, seriously, why does it matter whether it's real or not, whether it feels right or not, whether I feel like it should be someone else talking to Kid instead of me, like someone else would be better suited to this crazy dream? Even if it DID turn out to be just a crazy dream, it's better than sitting doing sod all with Stephen. Better than being a Body not a Somebody. I don't want to be pushed around by any boy. But I don't have to actually tell Kid about it any more than I have to tell

Stephen. What's he gonna do, come back from 2078 and yell in my face? Whatever I do, I'm going to do it because I want to.

How, dear diary, did I come to this resolution? How, I hear you ask in your weird paper voice, did I do a complete one-eighty and arrive at the conclusion that, actually, I would find Sylvia Rogers? That's all thanks to my dear, darling boyfriend. (LOL, yuck, gross.)

When I say it's all down to Stephen, I don't mean that in a good way.

'D'you think it's possible?' I asked him when we were watching that old movie Back to the Future in bed.

'What?' he grunted, looking at the laptop.

'Time travel!' I said.

'Oh. Um. Dunno,' he said.

'Do you WANT to know?' I said, deliberately sounding a bit more exasperated than I actually was. I mean, I wanted to chat for once, about something that interested me, something that MATTERS to me.

'What?' he repeated, turning his head away from the screen to look at me and screwing up his eyes a little so that he gave himself little crow's feet.

'Doesn't matter,' I said, turning over in bed so that I had my back to him and the laptop.

'Baby . . .' he gushed. Boys are so so so gullible! LOL! 'Baby, c'mon, what's up? Yes . . . I mean, no . . . What was the question?'

'Nothing. It doesn't matter.' Wait for it, I thought.

'Baby! Please!' He grabbed my shoulder and pulled on it gently, turning me to face him. I started giggling. He smiled.

'I'm sorry, what was the question? I really want to know!'

'I just wanted to know what you thought about time travel. Whether you think it's possible for a person to revisit the past or go to the future, or, I dunno, TALK to the future.' He looked at me sweetly, genuinely thinking about it. I paused for a moment, the real question I wanted to ask on the tip of my tongue, wondering whether I ought to ask it. 'I mean, what would you say if I told you I was in touch with someone from the future? A boy from the future.'

'Haha! Baby!' He just started laughing at me. 'You're so funny.' And, with that, he tweaked my nose patronizingly and turned back to Michael J. Fox and Christopher Lloyd. That's when I saw red.

'I'm so funny? What do you mean I'm so funny? What's that even supposed to mean?' I just went for him. 'I'm so funny because I ask questions about things that interest me? Or am I funny because I don't just sit and watch something and glumly – mindlessly – digest it like it's plain old, boring white bread. I mean seriously!!! What's the stupid point in us doing anything together if we're not gonna talk about it?! Like, FFS Stephen!' And so on and so forth until I pushed his buttons just that little bit too much and we were in a full-on fight.

The fight was fine; I mean, I'm sixteen, he's seventeen, like, fights are always gonna be stupid, dumb and meaning-less, but it was what he said right at the end that really hurt. He said it just before he left and stormed out, back to his. That was what changed my mind about all this stuff, this weird, trippy business.

'Why do you always have to do this?' he said. 'We can

never just chill and watch a movie or just be quiet and, like, do nothing, because you've always got some crazy, weird idea you wanna talk about or some annoying question you need to ask. And then when I don't know the answer, or I just giggle at you because it's cute, you get all pissy with me and make me feel like I'm stupid cos I don't mind just being normal. That's the thing with you! Why can't you just be satisfied being a normal girl in a normal part of normal London that goes to a normal school and has a normal boyfriend?! Instead of wanting your life to be like some crazy sci-fi movie?!'

I didn't respond to him and so he walked out of my bedroom, slammed the door (arsehole, he did it deliberately – he knew it would wake up my parents) and just left.

I sat on the end of my bed for ages. I didn't cry. I didn't want to. I didn't see the point. All I could think about were his final words as he stormed out – 'What's wrong with it the way it is?!' I turned them over and over in my head until I'd worked myself up into such an effing state that, as far as I could see there were only two options: break up with Stephen for being such an unimaginative, unadventurous moron, or find Sylvia Rogers.

I took stock of the situation and a few big, deep breaths and decided to go with the latter. I'm not gonna give him the satisfaction, I thought, I can't be arsed to see him beg.

I grabbed my laptop and went straight to Google. 'Sylvia Rogers' was my first search and it just turned up pages of people who couldn't be her. Funny, I thought, to know someone's gonna be famous before they actually ARE famous. Then I searched 'Hamilton Rogers'. Still nothing.

Then I realised Hamilton Rogers probably isn't alive yet. I actually felt mildly embarrassed, like someone could see me and might be laughing. But more than that I felt weird. I'm not used to feeling older than anyone, let alone knowing someone's gonna be born that isn't yet. Jesus Christ. I think I'm losing my mind. Then it hit me – I was being stupid – Kid always told me Gnosys started around now, like a couple of years ago, 2019 or something. So there must be a website or at least, like, some kind of company registration or something.

And BINGO! 'Gnosys Virtual.' I found it! I clicked on the link – www.gnosysvirtual.com – and it took me through to the site. It was pretty basic TBH, after everything Kid's told me about the company and the things they've done and the shit they're doing. I was expecting something with a little more BANG, you know?! All it had was a little blurb about what they do over a white background. Guess you gotta start somewhere.

Then, just below that, there was a description of their latest invention, which they would be rolling out into primary and secondary schools in Oxford next year, with the hope of getting the technology into schools nationwide by 2024. They were calling it 'Perspecta'.

It blew my mind, in a way that it hadn't been blown when I sat on Primrose Hill last week, and planted those acorns and, minutes later, received a photograph from the future of a giant oak tree standing in exactly the same spot. When Kid proved he was from the future, somehow it all felt normal, or at least, rational . . . natural . . . I dunno what the word is. Maybe it was just the fact I was suffering from mild hypothermia at thc time.

But this, Sylvia's website, her boyfriend who I KNEW she

was going to marry, their plans, their future . . . somehow this was the real thing. Now it was completely real. Now it was my life. I could read about it, look at it, follow it, touch it, get to it.

But how?

Then there it was, like a gift from God, my way in. My ticket to Sylvia.

We're Hiring!

Young, clever, imaginative, creative, hard-working? Interested in a career shaping the minds of the future?
Gnosys is for you!

Click the link below to find out about our internship programme!

Internship Opportunities

CHAPTER 36

PETRA

Who does Leo think she is? I rail in my head as I run as fast as I can from Skull's. *Telling me to risk my life on some hunch she has that it's going to be me who singlehandedly brings down Gnosys, the biggest corporation in history. Me who persuades the whole world to log out from the universe they've willingly embraced. Me, an eighteen-year-old nobody Offliner with nothing!*

For the first time, I'm suddenly glad the phone has gone. But I still long for the safety of my life before it, before Izzy. And I promise myself that – regardless of phone, Izzy, voice, dreams and coincidences – I will not be going to the Houses of Parliament.

What did Leo, or my dad, ever do for me? I rage in the thick, noxious murk of night. She just gives me sardines. All he left me was a stupid, useless, crappy old—

'Shit!' I exclaim, skidding on the rubble and falling over on my side. There, about ten metres up ahead, where Carnaby Street meets Beak Street, is a group of about fifty Seekers, all huddled together in a circle. They are right in my way. Don't think they saw me, I say to myself, dodging into the darkness beneath the bedraggled awning of an abandoned Vans shop. The night-time wind wails as loud as ever in the narrow street; I could scream and still they probably wouldn't hear me. I stand there in silence, but it isn't long before I am overcome with shivers. The weather is so messed up these days. Summer's not far off, yet it's suddenly turned much, much colder now than it was on Primrose Hill the night of the oak tree. The wind makes it feel glacial.

I try to reassure myself that these Seekers may not be starving or angry or crazed; that they may not bother me if I stroll past them just minding my own business. But the odds don't look good. It's not that Seekers are bad people, or out to get wandering Offliners; but it does something to a person, the terror of living up above, breathing in poison for too long. In the Ghetto, it's dog eat dog. Either saints very quickly become sinners, or they die.

I can't die up here. In under a minute, my chattering

teeth have given me a splitting migraine. If I stand here too much longer, my Roxi will run out and I'll be full-length on the paving stones, my pockets being emptied while I cough up tar and quietly succumb to exposure. If I'm a gonner, it's not going to be hiding from Seekers.

Three. Two. One. 'Arrrrrrrrrghhhhhhhhhhh!' Roaring, I charge towards them with my head dropped like a rhinoceros's and my hands in the air like I'm an avenging phantom.

Heads spin round. But they do not scatter. Usually Seekers are skittish, nervy people who either dart at the first sign of trouble or bare their teeth ready to fight. This group does neither. Seeing at the last instant that they are never going to disperse, I skid to a halt about a metre from them.

Their cracked, emaciated faces look at me expressionlessly, like I'm an irrelevance. Then, gradually, they all turn in to the circle again, blocking the width of the street. There's nothing else for it. I begin pushing through the tightly packed crowd, jostling them out of the way one by one. They barely register my presence as I bump and knock and shove my way towards the break in the middle of their circle. It is then that I hear singing, or what I think initially is singing. Their ring is not formed for warmth around a fire, as I imagined; it is this sound that has them captivated. Finally, when I break through, I find that what I've heard isn't singing, but crying. It brings me to a halt.

Sitting cross-legged on the floor is a young woman, not much older than me. She rocks back and forth, cradling a child – a little girl, whose head lolls from side to side with the motion. Out of the woman's mouth and her eyes – running in tears down her cheeks – comes a kind of pain I've never seen in another human being. Yet I recognize it as something I once felt myself. She is crying in exactly the same way I cried the night that my mum died. The scene needs no further explanation: the little girl is dead and this is her mother.

I fall on my knees and come face to face with the woman. It's completely involuntary, like I've been pushed by invisible hands on my shoulders. As she looks up at me, I feel a pang of recognition. The woman's eyes meet mine. Her lips are cracked and her face covered in boils.

Suddenly, overlaid like tracing paper on the tragedy in front of me, another scene replays itself in my mind. *A little girl. Her mother lurking in a nearby doorway. Necklaces made of chicken wire and broken brick. Denim dungarees.*

The woman at the heart of the crowd stops crying. Her cheeks glisten with tears that look like they're freezing to her face. Ever so gently, she turns her daughter's cold, lifeless face towards me. The blood covering the little girl's neck – black like she's coughed it up from damaged lungs – sparkles with frost.

Three spare Roxi pellets, I remember. And a whisper: *Kindness. Good. Thank you.*

I have seen them both before, on this very street only a few weeks ago. On my way to Skull's the night after the Teeth had first come into the Ticket.

My heart pummels my ribcage.

The mother lets go of her daughter's head and it flops back into her lap. The girl's eyelids part a fraction, as if she is looking at me. The pupils are tiny and grey, like the heads of nails beaten flat by a hundred hammer strokes. Then her eyeballs roll back in their sockets.

I put my hand to my heart, not knowing what to say or whether the girl's mother will understand me. 'I'm so—'

The woman reaches out her hand and takes my other hand in hers, placing it on top of her daughter's, which lies cold and limp on the girl's chest. As I squeeze the tiny hand, a tear rolls down my cheek. *Don't cry,* I tell myself. *It is not for you to cry.*

Then the woman pulls my hand and the girl's away, revealing the child's midriff.

'What happened?' I gasp.

There is a very small hole in the front pocket of her denim dungarees, not big enough to put a little finger through. Around the hole is a circular patch of red, wavy around the edge, dark. It looks like the rose on the lid of the tin my mum gave me before she died.

The girl has been shot in the stomach and the blood gushing out has seeped through the denim and crystallized around the wound, like black frost. It is the most horrifying thing I have seen in my life. My eyes go back to the face of the murdered girl.

'Who did this?' I can barely get the question out. I am not even looking at the mother, and I don't expect the answer from her cracked lips.

'Teeth.'

I stare at the girl for a moment, immobile. I can't believe my ears. At last I look up at the woman, my eyes red from the icy wind.

'We went down to the Q by the river, the Embankment, looking for something to eat,' the woman says. Immediately, she begins to cry again; a cry from somewhere deep inside. Shaking, looking as if she is suffocated by her pain, she struggles to speak.

'I knew – I knew they wouldn't listen to me if I went to them, if I asked . . . So I sent her.' She wears an expression of unbearable guilt. 'I thought they would be kind to her, to a little girl. I stood back. Sh–she walked towards them, slowly and smiling, singing. They told her to stop, but she walked on. She was fearless, fearless! She even had something ready to give them in return for—'

Sobs rack the woman before she can carry on.

'She reached for her pocket, and they— She fell down. She—'

But the woman can't speak any more. She has nothing left.

Suddenly, with thin fingers, she begins prodding desperately at her neck, like she's lost something precious, something utterly priceless to her. As she finds it, her breathing calms. A necklace of chicken wire and broken brick.

I unwrap the scarf from around my neck and unbutton the top of my jacket to show her the identical necklace her daughter gave me the last time we met. Then, wiping the tears from my face, I go to wrap the scarf around the woman's neck. In the bitter cold, she looks as if her grip on life is almost gone.

She puts out her hand. 'No, thank you.' She looks down at her daughter. 'You have something to keep warm for. I don't.'

I can see she will not be persuaded. But suddenly impassioned, I tell her: 'I lost my mother. To this, to the future.

And now I think it's my job to make sure she didn't die for nothing.' I look at the little girl lying there dead. 'To make sure *she* didn't die for nothing.' I want to stay with them both, but I know it isn't my place.

Getting slowly to my feet, I look around at all of the terrible, terrorized, poor people around me and think: *No more needless dying. No. More.*

Then I look down once more at the woman and her little girl and whisper, 'What's her name?'

'Petra.'

'And yours?'

'El.'

'What did you say?' I can't believe my ears. *It's impossible.* My mind in a spin.

'Em. I'm Emma,' the woman repeats, her voice cracking.

'Oh,' I say, more an exhalation of breath – a sad sigh – than a word. 'I, my mother—' But it is pointless to go on, so I just tell her, 'Good luck Emma.'

And I run off, as fast as my legs will allow me, for the Circus.

PART

THREE

CHAPTER 37

THE WALL

The piano plays itself, or at least my fingers tinker on their own; uninstructed by my mind they move unconsciously across the keys. I've been sitting here in the dorm for hours now – numb – playing whatever my hands want, going with them on their journey over the soft, white ivories, wherever they so desire. It's always been my happy place, sitting here at the piano, singing my songs. It's the closest I've ever got to feeling properly secure. It's more of a release than an exercise. Touching a key here and a key there, hearing their corresponding notes, adding another two notes to the first and giving life to a chord – it's visceral and transporting. It takes me out of all this and delivers me somewhere else entirely. I don't know where exactly, but it's opposite to my own reality in every way, far away from this hard and infinitely complicated world. Playing just feels good, kind and straightforward. Then, when I sing over the top of the harmonies, something else happens. The songs seem somehow to give life to that new world – that beautiful, alternate reality – like the music itself is its foundation and the words are its bricks and mortar. I sing about a better world – for a better world – like I'm calling for it, wherever it is and however far away and unlikely it might seem. Whenever I sing for it, it feels that little bit closer every time.

I'll do it one day, I think to myself, putting the lid down on the piano gently and getting up to leave. *First I'll try and get to play at Muriel's, if Lucien will let me. But my real dream is the Albert Hall. One day I'll play to thousands of people, happy people, living in a REAL world – one where people sing and dance and are full of life and love. One day.*

I pick up the preloaded Roxi disp sitting on top of the piano, put it to my lips and inhale, feeling its protective gas freeze over my alveoli, one by one.

'Bit late in the day to be heading out on a charge, *mon brave*, what!' Mungo barks suspiciously as I approach the exit. His pipe juts from his mouth like a gun barrel from a turret, trailing vinegary ant-tobacco fumes.

'Late scav, Mungo. You know the drill.'

He frowns, not buying it. I lean in and whisper in his ear. 'All right, if you insist. Pie night. Ursula's out of pigeon, she didn't want to bother anyone, so I offered to help her out.'

'Ahhhh! I see! Right you are my boy, good of you to be a sport and give the old girl a hand! You'd better get to it, soon be getting dark out, and none of us want to go hungry on pie night, what!'

And that's all it takes. Or so I think.

'Just a minute Jones! Funny get-up you're sporting tonight, old boy!'

Shit. Double shit. Smugly pleased with my easy lies, I've been clinging onto the hope that Mungo will somehow just not notice I'm wearing the Perspecta uniform Leo gave me. I turn around, my mind going like the clappers as I desperately try to work out a response that will satisfy Mungo's curiosity.

'Like you said, Mungo . . .' I come closer to him, leaning in, doing my best impression of a clipped military manner. 'Covert operation. Can't be too careful up above these days. You're much better off running into a Tooth dressed like one of them than dressed like one of us, don't you think?' *Nudge, nudge, wink, wink.*

He's silent for a beat – seemingly confused – and then his crinkly old smile appears. He doesn't say anything, just taps his nose. He unlocks the steel portal, which has now been made even more secure.

'Mum's the word,' he says, and bids me good luck out in the toxic air. *Jesus, poor Mungo.* I suddenly feel kind of guilty lying to him. How the hell can a dude his age be so gullible?

It's already dark out. No surprise there. But I can hear the drone of a Chariot somewhere to the south – exactly the way I want to go if I'm going to get to Westminster. I strain to see as my eyes get used to the bleak, eerie gloaming. No, the engine noise is west of me now, Piccadilly way . . . And again it's off to the south . . . to the east. *Damn it!* Whatever I said to Mungo a few moments ago, I'm really not up to being picked up by a Mig patrol. *Gotta be Regent Street*, I realize.

I feel genuine fear as I cross the vast, empty Circus. A lump grows in my throat. *Never been this way, not on my own*, I think. The Wall always gives me the heebie-geebies. Distant clangs and ominous creaks. Whistling and moaning noises that could be the wind or . . . something else. Dark tunnels. Dark winding stairwells. *You could go in and never come out again*, I say to myself, even though I've memorized the through-route enough times so it feels like it's etched on my hippocampus.

You only need look at this side of the Circus to realize that whatever's on the other side of it isn't pretty, not for an Offliner. Where the grand old boulevards of Regent Street and Piccadilly once converged – back when this was the busiest place in the world – now a huge wall marks the border between the Ghetto and the future. It is made of old red Routemaster London buses, standing bumper to bumper crosswise across Regent Street, completely filling the gap between buildings on its south and north sides. They are stacked in tiers, one atop the other, till the Wall is four or five buses high at its very top – a roost for watchful pigeons. Battered and worn and covered in obscene, angry, anti-Gnosys graffiti, the buses were piled there by a coalition of Seekers and various other outlaw groups sometime in the middle Sixties. It was a kind tit-for-tat response to the way that everyone was leaving the inner city behind during the Upload, a kind of 'if you don't want us, we don't want you' two-finger salute.

The sheer size and complexity of the makeshift barricade is a testament to the hatred people have here for the establishment, for the future. Some of the buses were filled in with concrete to make the structure more stable, with huge metal shafts going up through the middle of them, like pins precariously holding it all together. The doorways and decks of the others form a labyrinth, constantly turning left and right, up and down, with innumerable dead ends. The Wall has other sections too, like where Wardour Street meets Oxford Street, twice as high as the Regent Street Wall; and where Shaftesbury Avenue crosses Charing Cross Road. All of them are constructed in a similar way, all with only one route you can take through, between the Ghetto and the outer streets. And only if you know the way.

How on earth did they get them on top of each other? I wonder. But I'm only trying to distract myself from the anxiety of the task ahead.

I reach the door to the Routemaster where the route through the labyrinth begins, and I climb the stairs to the top deck. *I know the way and I'm going to be okay*, I rhyme to myself. Then, *I've got a bad feeling about this.* My stomach ties and unties itself in knots over and over again.

Looking back one more time at the devastatingly drab but familiar Circus, for the first time in my life I'm not one hundred per cent certain I'm going to see this place again. It's a strange, empty feeling, but I know I'm doing what I have to do. Getting through the Wall is just the first step. Westminster is the real unknown. I know I have to find out the truth, once and for all. I know I have to do it for Petra. For all of us.

CHAPTER 38

ARRESTED DEVELOPMENT

I'm looking down on Regent Street from a bus high on a shoulder of the Wall. There's almost nothing to see in the gloom. The wind gusts in from outside like I'm in a wind tunnel. But as I make my way between the worn old seats, ripped and bedraggled, the ghosts of old London seem to come alive around me. I close my eyes – just for a second – and imagine the impossible: it's 2021 – Izzy's time – and

I'm riding the bus down Regent Street on a summer's day. Babies cry, mothers coo, businessmen chat chat chat away on their phones as the crisp English sun shines in through the windows. There's life everywhere. Real life. I open my eyes again, praying it's not a daydream. But of course it is. And Izzy's year is pandemic time, so maybe there's not much real life going on anyway, I remind myself.

After a few more twists and turns, I pause in another bus, hair prickling on the back of my neck.

Can't get spooked now, I remind myself. Too much at stake.

'Who's there?' I call out.

A noise to my immediate right; a kind of rattle amid the moaning of the wind. 'Someone else in here?'

Cautiously, nervously, I turn to investigate, heading down a side passage into the darkness. A dim light appears up ahead, and soon I'm in another bus where, to my surprise, the cabin strip lights are illuminated. Then I see it.

There, at the other end of the bus, a large tarpaulin covering two or three banks of seats flaps furiously in the wind. Wait a second, what is that? Then I clearly see, sticking out from under the sheet, the butt of a very old rifle. Guns? A pile of old guns? I go towards it and gently lift up the tarp and look underneath. Sure enough, piled precariously on the old bus benches are hundreds of old weapons, from way before the Dusk. Shotguns, hunting rifles, bayonets, even a Gatling gun. All of it on top of an enormous pile of ammunition. What the . . . ? It's like a mini antique armoury.

Click.

Suddenly, all the lights in the bus go off. I drop the tarp

and stand stock still. *Shit*. It's totally pitch black. I can't see a thing. *Double shit*.

'Tickets please.' What the hell? A voice – a young girl's, or perhaps it's a boy's – somewhere in the dark.

'Sorry . . . Who's . . . What d'you mean tickets?' I grab hold of the railing next to me and steady myself. Terrified now.

'Tickets please!' Suddenly another voice, somewhere else in the bus, joins the first. 'Tickets please!' Then again, in a totally different part of the bus. 'Tickets please! Tickets please! Tickets please!' And again and again and again. The voices seem to come from a different place every time, getting louder and quicker, until eventually it's a cacophony of voices coming from every corner of the vehicle. I stand frozen, unable to move a muscle.

Click.

The lights are thrown on and I'm momentarily blinded by the brightness. Then, to my horror, I see I'm completely surrounded. Boys, some teenagers, some as young as ten. Everywhere! Emaciated, hollow-eyed, gangling limbed, they come at me from all sides. Ten, twenty, there could be thirty of them now – it all happens so fast I can't see to count. They come at me from above and below. Where are they coming from? What the hell is happening to me?

'Tickets! Tickets! Tickets! Ticketttttttttttttssssss!'

They jump and howl and spit and claw at my clothing like rabid dogs. The speed of it, the intensity of it – I'm paralysed by fear. It's like a nightmare, like a tide of cockroaches scuttling my way, crawling all over me, flailing there insect-thin arms to scratch at me.

I cover my face with my arms to shield my eyes and begin making for the back of the bus. I'm backing towards the exit, pushing, pushing, pushing. If I can just get to that door! I turn and try to barge my way through the human barrier, but to no avail. They're coming at me from all sides, baring their young teeth like fangs, giving out feral yelps and barks. I lose my footing and fall to the floor, cowering against the back wall of the old bus. They are more like animals than boys. It all happens too fast for my brain to process. Now they're so close it's like I can hear their bloodthirsty little hearts beating out of their chests.

'Someone! Help!' I scream at last; a hopeless, impassioned plea. This is it, I think. It's over. They're going to tear my limbs from their sockets and rip the flesh from the bone like piranhas.

'Stop!' A voice – this time I'm certain it's a girl's – issues from the other end of the bus.

The boys stop immediately, but not before the one nearest me – all sunken eyes and acne – bites into my arm. I pull away immediately and cry out in agony. Skin and flesh rip; the boy draws blood. '*JESUS!*'

Wincing in pain down on the floor, I open my eyes again and find the foremost attackers retreating innocently, almost apologetically, into the panting mass behind them. The one with the overactive jaw looks at me with a peculiar expression of regret. It's almost sweet. *Sweet? Who am I kidding? What ARE these things?* I press my shirt against the wound on my arm to absorb some of the blood. 'That hurt, *a lot*,' I say, scowling back at him.

'My boys, bitta spunk from a Specta! Who'd a thunk it?'

The driver's cab door opens slowly. As I gawp in bewilderment, a young girl comes out and walks towards me very slowly. She's the same age as the baying wolf pack that surrounds me: somewhere in the netherworld between childhood and adolescence. As she moves her head from side to side, examining me, her childish blonde locks swing around her pretty face. She's wearing denim dungarees and a pair of old yellow crocs, and when she turns to smile at one of the boys from her loyal pack I notice that she's only wearing boxer shorts underneath them. You must be freezing, I think, trying to distract myself from the abject ridiculousness of my predicament. She draws closer and closer; the boys part like the Red Sea to let her through.

'Wait a second. I'm not . . .' But of course: the suit! In the blur of the bizarre ambush, I've forgotten that I'm marked out by the white Perspecta suit. That I stand out like a sore thumb. 'There's been a mistake, I'm not a Specta, I'm just dressed like one,' I protest. 'I mean I'm trying to—'

'We like spunky.' She cuts me off, withdrawing a rolled-up cigarette from somewhere in amongst the golden tangle of her hair and putting it in her mouth. All without taking her eyes off me.

The boys – her minions – cackle. She strikes a match and at once the wild chorus falls silent. She stops a couple of metres away from me and draws hard on the cigarette. I look at her and she looks at me – long and hard. Piercing.

More than anything I'm confused now, mesmerized even. They're kids; she's a kid. Feral or not, she can't be more than thirteen. It's surreal, almost magical. There's something amazing about her poise. She's both lioness, ready to pounce on her prey, and little girl, desperate for love and attention – all at the same time.

She kneels and crouches down in front of me, bringing our eyes level and her face within centimetres of my own. Her breath smells of liquorice, sweet and hot. I manage to maintain eye contact. She cocks her head to one side and raises an eyebrow. 'Bit spunky, ain't we, Specta?' Casting her eyes around the crowd of boys, she adds, 'I think spunky Specta here's got lost, my Terrors!'

'Terror! Terror! Terror!' the boys wail over and over in a deafening echo. The girl puts up her hand and immediately they fall silent. She lowers it slowly and starts swaying from side to side, like she's sizing me up.

Wait a second, I think, something's off. Her movements, her words, her attitude: they're exaggerated, affected. They don't quite fit her body, her face, her age. It's like she's modelled this dangerous, intimidating badass on films she's watched. She's acting; this is a performance, a show, a front.

All right then – I crack an imperceptible smile – two can play at that game.

'What are you?' I snigger. 'Ten?'

Actually I reckon she's two or three years older than that, though small for her age. But the smug smile is wiped off her face. Her eyes, still only an inch from mine, dart left and right as she tries to see how the boys have reacted to my affront. She's been caught off guard. She's trying to see if she's lost face. The boys look shocked, like they don't know how to react.

Gotcha! I think to myself.

She sniffs loudly, composing herself; bites her lip, then says quietly, 'Old enough.'

She turns and walks away.

'Wait a second, I need to get to the other—'

'Take it away, boys!'

Her parting command is all I hear before – in a surging, leaping frenzy and with bloodcurdling whoops and screams – the boys pile on top of me. *Maybe not such a good idea to mess with little girls. Sod THIS!* It takes everything I have to throw enough of them off me for long enough to get to my feet.

With the recklessness of wildcats, they continue the attack. One of them – particularly small – launches himself from the staircase leading to the top deck and tackles me around my neck, bringing me crashing back to my knees like lead. Once more I'm on the bottom of the terrifying scrum. I'm running out of energy fast.

'Argh! You're crushing—'

My arm gets caught under one of their legs; the bone below my elbow feels as if it's about to break. I tense my forearm as hard as I can and push with all my might, but it's no use. This is going to hurt.

CHAPTER 39

THE TERRORS

'Stop!' It's her voice, the girl's. The boys obey, backing away immediately, recoiling like springs and retreating to the edges of the old bus. Then, suddenly, she's running at me from the other end of the bus like she's possessed. She gets to me and goes straight for my arm – the one that had just been about to break. But instead of trying to hurt me, she grabs it and examines my tattoo, my mark, fascinated by it. Then she looks up at me, wide-eyed and in awe. It's the first time she's actually looked her age: the first time she's looked like a child. 'Your arm . . . You're an Offliner.'

'Yup,' I say, sitting up. 'Like I've been trying to tell you since I got here. And what in God's name are you?' I look at the boys behind her. They gawp at me too, like I'm some kind of deity. 'Actually, first, who or what the hell are *they*?'

'I'm Jemma. But you can call me Jem for short,' she says with a smile, in a voice a lot more childish than she had a few moments previously. 'They're the Terrors and I'm the boss! We patrol the border. Have done since Ivan died.' When she says this, the Terrors – now assembled like an audience around us – bow their heads and begin whispering solemnly to themselves, as if they are venerating some kind of celestial being.

'Ivan?'

'The Terrible,' she says, straight-faced.

'You're kidding, right?' I ask, raising an eyebrow and chuckling to myself.

'Why would I be kidding?' she says, apparently oblivious to the irony and confused by my laughter.

'All right,' I say, 'And you and your boys thought I was a Specta?'

At this, the Terrors begin crowing and screaming and beating their chests.

'Give it a rest, would you!' I bellow. She flinches. Some of the boys go red; none looks sure how to react.

'Sorry. It's . . . been a long week,' I say. Jemma just continues to look at me. The pack is nervous and skittish now.

'I, um, how – tell me, why are you here?' I ask, as gently as I can. If I want to get past them, I now see, I'm going to have to engage them.

'Where else would we be?' Jemma spits.

'Well, yeah, okay, but what I mean is how did you end up *here*?'

An inscrutable expression passes across Jemma's face.

'You first,' she says.

'Me first?'

'You got on our bus, we didn't get on yours. And we're not the ones dressed like goons.'

I think for a second about making up a story, some elaborate lie as to why on earth I should be here in the Wall, an Offliner dressed in a Perspecta Suit. But in the little time I have to think, nothing even remotely believable comes to me. *What's the point*, I think, *already too many lies to keep track of back in the Cell. Besides, even kids wouldn't believe someone could do something as stupid as this.*

'Oh, you mean this?' I say, putting my hands in the pockets of my suit and fanning them outwards. 'I'm, um, going to Westminster, to get into the Houses of Parliament, where – well . . .' I'm suddenly overcome by the same sense of doubt that consumed me as I left Leo's last night.

Petra. Petra. Think of Petra. Think of the future, the voice in my head rings out. I'm about to talk back to it, aloud, when—

'What?!' Jemma shouts, obviously totally bamboozled by the insanity of what I've suggested. 'The Houses of Parliament? Why? How? Are you—' She looks at me with the kind of expression that only a child can sport, one of genuine, bewildered fascination. She taps her index finger on her temple. 'Are you all right in the head?'

'Honestly, I don't know. Someone told me to—'

'Oh . . . right! Hear that boys? Someone "told" Spunky here to jump off the cliff, so he's doing it!'

The Terrors wail mirthfully, some knock their knees together excitedly, others strum their fingers against their chins, thrilled by the stupidity of the suggestion. Jemma has regained her ringleader cockiness.

For crying out loud! I think. *If I don't get out of here now I'm never going to make it! No time to explain, they'll never get it*, I decide, reminding myself of the madness of my mission, of the fact that even I don't really know what to expect on the other side of the Wall.

At that, the thought strikes me. *Mission? Missions! Kids love missions!*

'Look,' I say in a confidential tone, 'I wasn't going tell you this. I *shouldn't* be telling you this, but since you're allies . . .' I lean in.

Jemma and the Terrors mirror my movement; some of the boys at the back are climbing on the others, craning to hear.

'I'm undercover. Secret Offliner business. I'm infiltrating Perspecta.'

They look at me, their eyes massive, globe-like, like I've told them the Earth is flat.

'I'm a spy, for the resistance.'

'No way!' Jemma says, eyes wide with wonder. Finally she's showing herself as she truly is: an excited tomboy. 'Perspecta?' Almost without a pause, she adds, 'We'll come with you!'

'No, that's not going to happen.'

'Why not?' She puffs out her chest.

'Because—' I try to think of another excuse. This is becoming too much.

'We'll be your backup. Every spy needs backup!'

'Because you're children, for Christ's sake!'

Jemma says nothing. The Terrors fall silent. Their eyes, as bright as stars just seconds ago, are now dull and watery.

'You're just kids.' Again the image of Petra pushes its way into my head. Petra with a rose painted in her own blood on the denim of her dungarees.

The burble of excitement dies.

'Yeah, we are.' Jemma says, something like sadness in her eyes. And then she looks at the boy closest to her, a particularly young, skittish one with ginger hair and very fair, freckled skin. 'Show him,' she tells him.

The boy rolls up his sleeve to reveal a deep, horrible scar on his forearm.

'How did you—'

It is Jemma who replies. 'My brother, Ivan, was a Mig captain.'

'A Tooth?' I say, gravely.

'That's right. Guard class.'

'Your brother did that?' I say, pointing at the scar, horrified.

'Yes.'

'How could—'

'To save his life.' She pauses. 'How much do you know about how a Mig becomes a Mig?'

'The only thing I know about Teeth,' I say, defensive, 'is

that they're the enemy. Every single—'

'*Ivan! Ivan! Ivan!*' the Terrors erupt, screaming his name in my face. It's terrifying.

'Enough!' Jemma puts her hand in the air. The boys fall silent. 'Not every single one.' She has a steely look in her eye; direct, adult. 'Before the Upload, people joined the Guards: it was a job. You were trained, you served, you got paid, you went home. That's how it was when Ivan enlisted. After a while they made him captain. Put him in charge of training cadets. Big bro was so good at it they took him out the field in '65 and put him on staff. Cushty office job in a new department. "GPRS" they called it; still do. Gnosys Paramilitary Recruitment. Based in the Belt. He figured he'd be convincing people to sign up. An example of all that a Tooth could be. The model Mig.' She laughs a sad, empty laugh. 'But, when he got there, it quickly became clear that recruitment didn't mean recruitment at all. It meant cultivation.'

Disgust in her eyes, she pauses, looks around at all the boys and then back at me. Then, still holding my gaze, she orders, 'Show him.'

All the boys roll up their sleeves and, just like the first, every single one has the same deep scar on his right arm.

'What happened to you all?' I gasp.

Jemma grabs the ginger-haired boy's arm and holds it aloft.

'A Tooth's Plug isn't an earpiece; it's an implant.' I lean in to get a closer look at where the Plug used to be. The old wound is big and cavernous. 'And Plugs were big in those days.'

'Are you saying,' I address the boys, 'you were going to be Teeth?'

'Would have been,' Jemma continues, 'if Ivan hadn't saved them. There's a big problem with virtual worlds – 'side from all the other problems – and that's virtual babies. Most Mig departments are fully botted – Tech, E-Class, Medi. But guard-class Migs, Teeth, are the only all-human Gnosys security department left.'

'G. P. R. S.' I spell out the letters slowly, suddenly realizing who these boys are, how they came into being. 'The S stands for Surrogacy, not Services. It's a breeding programme.'

'Way to go, Spunky.' Jemma says. 'There is something between those big ears of yours!' She sniggers and so do the boys. But the humour goes over my head. I'm completely blown away. Disgusted by the idea of Gnosys breeding human beings, shocked by the discovery. 'Breed-a-Mig,' she chuckles darkly. 'There ain't a game the Spectas aren't in.'

'I'm so sorry,' I say to all the boys. They just go on staring at me; I don't know whether they understand or care.

Turning back to Jemma, I ask, 'How did he do it? Your brother, I mean. How did he save them?'

'He couldn't take 'em all. There are hundreds, maybe even thousands of 'em in there. So he piled as many cots as he figured he could fend for, bring up, ya know, shoved them in the back of a Manta and flew off into the sunset. Well, the gloaming.'

'Didn't they come after him?'

'What do you think?'

'What did he do?!'

'He'd picked one of the crappiest nights he could –

hurricane of '65 – and in the storm instead of flying away from London he flew straight down this way. Landed on the roof of one of the big buildings up Regent Street. Hamleys; you know it?'

'Used to be a toy shop,' I chip in.

'Good place to bring a bunch of kids.'

I only nod, transfixed.

'But Ivan had it all planned out, see? D'you know you can fly a Chariot by VR?' she asks, relishing the opportunity to tell someone else – someone new – her story. 'No, 'pparently nor did Gnosys! My bro was pretty damn smart. Soon as he'd carted the cots under cover in the building, he hunkered down inside in his rig and remote-flew the Manta right out of town, over the hills and far away. Didn't take long for the Teeth to spot it now, but he took them on one hell of a wild goose chase. Ended up ploughing it into the Atlantic somewhere off Scotland in the middle of the storm. So—'

'Gnosys assumed all the kids were dead anyway.' I finish the thought for her.

'No shit, Sherlock. And they all lived happily ever after, totally offline, raised by Ivan. By himself. Dunno how many places they lived before he got them set up in here.'

'What about your parents? Are they – dead?'

'Might as well be.'

'They're logged in.'

She just nods.

'And you?' I ask.

Her voice firm and clear, Jemma resumes. 'I'd been logged in as a baby. Perspecta was all I'd ever known. Ivan sprang me out of the Belt. Physically I was a vegetable, but brain-wise I was still young enough to be able to learn new ways. He didn't have long left then – just a couple of years – but he taught me everything I know. Not just how to live in the old world – to survive out here in the wild – but also how to take care of my boys.' She squeezes the hand of the ginger boy.

She says nothing for what feels like a very long time, and then: 'Ivan's lungs gave out eventually. He managed to secure small amounts of Roxi on the black market, but not enough to keep us all alive, and him.' Sadness and loss fill her eyes.

Mum, I think, my mind's eye suddenly seeing her as she was at the end, her face pale and hollow, her breath a faint whistle. At that moment I realize we're kindred spirits: me, Jemma and the Terrors. Each of us is only alive because of the ultimate sacrifice of someone who loved us.

I look at Jemma for a moment, then at all her lost boys sitting and listening patiently and dutifully behind her.

'You're crying?' she says with a look of bewilderment.

'No, I'm not,' I say, turning away so that they won't see. Looking at the sickly, emaciated faces of all these young boys, condemned to death by a future they didn't ask for, I can't help myself.

She gets up and, to my great surprise, stands to attention. The boys jump to their feet – all of them – and do the same. 'The Offliners, your people, they're like us,' she says. 'The fighters. The free. We're with you.' She salutes. The boys do too.

Suddenly overwhelmed by the unexpected show of solidarity, I feel compelled to salute back.

'What do we call ya?' she asks.

'I'm Kid.'

'Kid,' Jemma says, thoughtfully. 'Knew you were one of us.'

'Thank you.'

'And . . . um . . . sorry about the arm. Ponzo gets overexcited easy.' The acne-faced boy who took a chunk out of my arm looks over at me and pushes out his bottom lip apologetically. 'He's a bit trigger-happy. More used to joyriding Podds than being pent up in buses.'

Wait a second – joyriding Podds? I want to know more, but suddenly I'm aware of how much time has ticked away, and I still need to get to Westminster.

'I've got to go,' I stutter. 'Um, no worries Ponzo. Goodbye, all of you. And thank you!'

'Good luck Kid. If you ever need a bit of a fright,' she winks, 'you know where to find us!'

I turn and walk towards the exit, still fighting back the tears, and step off the bus onto the crumbling edge of the Podd Way.

CHAPTER 40

SCORCHED EARTH

'Denis!' I call out as I stand on the concrete platform just by the bus door. I don't know whether I need to shout his name or think it – *I don't know the rules!* What I do know is I'll never get to Westminster in time on foot and panic is rising inside me like someone's turned on a tap. I'm feeling giddy and more than a little nauseous. *Woah!* I steady myself. *Don't want to topple into the Podd trench and get flattened.*

Where the hell is Denis? 'I need a ride, dude,' I shout into space. 'Like now!'

And then, just as before, there it is, my Podd, hovering gracefully in front of me.

'Goodness! I'm ever so sorry sir!' says a familiar BBC-inflected voice, as disembodied as when I first heard it. There is no man in a suit now, which makes the following two-way conversation even more confusing. 'Bernard and I came up against some surprisingly busy traffic around the Marylebone Road. Forgive us, won't you? Well, forgive Bernard; in point of fact, it's his fault entirely. What was that? I'm terribly sorry sir, Bernard's taking issue with me. Excuse me? Will you stop? Are you or are you not the operating system in charge of this Podd? Oh, sir, do please forgive me, Bernard is being quite ghastly! Yes! Yes you are! You are totally unreasonable and I find your comments deeply unpleasant—'

'Denis.'

'Sir?'

'Open the bloody door and let's go.'

'Quite right sir. Bernard, do as you're told.' The gullwing door swings open gracefully and I jump in. Inside, the Streem display is already showing the Houses of Parliament as my destination; ETA, five minutes.

I've never had an aerial view outside the Ghetto before, unless you count flying over what used to be Regent's Park to Primrose Hill and back. When we set off now and get up to height and speed, I ask Denis to unfrost the Podd's shell. As the metallic carapace shifts from glowing opacity to brilliant translucence, I see that the Way is surprisingly busy tonight. The aluminium bubbles of Podds, glittering like bullet-nosed Christmas baubles, all seem to be flying at great speed along various routes. Some are in ones and twos, others are bunched like strings of pearlescent shells, reflecting each other's kaleidoscope of lights. *Must be something going on; they're all heading in one direction. And these are some amazing-looking Podds!*

Before I can think any further, my eyes stray from the pretty lights to the dim landscape around them. I'm faced with a dreadful realization: what's left of London between the Ghetto and the Belt is nothing more than a burnt, blistered, rotting carcass. My mouth hangs open and my eyes water as I pass the barren, broken emptiness of this once great metropolis. I know we have sibling cells out here: the Bush and the Scrubs. But they're small and, apart from messages of solidarity sent to our anniversary gatherings, we hardly hear from them year to year. Now I see why. It looks just like the photos in Pokes's old history books – like Ypres, Dresden, Aleppo, Srinagar – all tumbledown tower blocks, broken domes and spires, rows of houses half-collapsed beside crazy rubble-strewn streets.

I always felt hard done by – always felt like we've all had it real bad in the Ghetto – but in reality it's the exact opposite. Living in Soho all my life, I've been afforded a strange privilege. We're the only people left who have even the faintest idea of what things might have been like before the Upload. Soho's not a ghetto; it's a museum, it's a shrine and a tribute to what things were like in the Golden Dusk.

We fly over a wild, unkempt mix of scrubby trees and battered grass and then out onto a wide boulevard with what looks like a battlefield at one end of it. I raise a hand and the

Podd slows as if Bernard has read my thoughts.

Another Podd rushes up behind us and – just as I think it's going to slew to a halt or smash into us – it rises suddenly and leapfrogs us. 'Rather discourteous of them, if I may be so bold, sir,' observes Denis, with the superior air of a restaurant *maître d'* disappointed in the quality of the diners. 'Podds like theirs – or indeed yours, sir – are equipped with jets and rotors to free them from the electromagnetic Podd Way at need. Such things are essential if, for example, you own a large country estate. But really, sir! Here in London? There are *protocols* for travel in a busy metropolis!'

In the illumination of the Podd's passing lights, I briefly glimpse the outside world more clearly. And now I realize what's in front of me. We're above the Mall, and Buckingham Palace stands a ruin, black with soot, its right wing completely destroyed. Above the Palace, an enormous holo-pop burns bright in the black sky, a huge Gnosys logo revolving slowly, casting beams of light on the dere- lict mansion. The dazzling shards seem to cut into the old stone, hacking away at it, breaking the place down, brick by brick. I'm thrown to one side as we swing around the old Victoria Memorial in front of the Palace. The personifica- tions of Victory, Constancy and Courage, whose gilt bronze once gleamed over the Mall, now look like the black vultures of Gnosys, ready to pick off anyone who venerates the past. Before shooting towards Westminster across the burnt turf that was once St James's Park, I look back up the desolate Mall one last time. If I didn't know any better, I'd think I was the last man left on earth.

'Sir?' Denis pipes up, shocking me out of my morose reverie.

'What?' I bite back.

'I'm awfully sorry to disturb you. Only, I wanted to clarify a few things with you before arriving at the Houses of Parliament, sir.'

'Okay. What's up?' I reply.

'To begin with, sir, I'd just like to confirm that, upon arrival at Parliament, you do in fact mean to attend the Gnosys annual London shareholders' meeting?'

'Shareholders meeting?' I wasn't expecting that. Then again, I don't know what I was expecting.

'That's absolutely correct, sir. The company holds an annual – offline – gathering of its shareholders in all the capital cities of its major marketplaces. A sort of Gnosys grand tour, if you will.' Denis chuckles to himself; a bit too facetiously for a computer, if you ask me.

'Offline?' I don't have time for small talk. I'm also conscious that another Podd is now nosing so perilously close to the rear of ours that its occupants might as well be planning a boarding party.

'Ah, yes, my apologies, sir. The conference is conducted outside the Universe. Those in attendance must perceive it through an augmented reality, at the very least. Mr Rogers certainly prefers that it be conducted entirely offline, but that can prove a little too much for users not used to existing outside the Universe – that is to say, the vast majority of them.' He laughs an even heartier laugh this time, as if he's having a joke with himself. Again I notice the Podd from before, a battered-looking thing, jostling close behind us: too close for comfort. But it doesn't seem to faze him.

'He's going to be there – Rogers?' I ask.

'Mr Rogers attends every shareholder meeting, sir. It is where he presents all the company's brand-new technology for the year and outlines his goals.' I feel beads of sweat erupting from the pores along my hairline. Hamilton Rogers is going to be there. We're going to be that close.

'And Rosie? What about her?' A beat of silence. For the first time since I met him, Denis seems lost for words.

'Er, yes sir, Miss Rogers is *due* to be in attendance, sir—'

My heart skips a beat and my palms begin to sweat. *Due? What does that mean?* 'I need to know if she'll be in the building.'

Another long pause. 'Yes sir, Miss Rogers is currently at the Houses of Parliament.'

My pulse goes up and my mind races. *I'm going to meet Rosie. I'll be able to speak to her, to tell her she has to help us, to* . . . I suddenly remember the horror of my dream, of her cry: *Daddy! Stop! Please stop!*

Denis interrupts my racing thoughts. 'But, sir, with the greatest respect, I must advise against any contact whatsoever with Miss Rogers. She is heavily guarded. Engaging her could draw unwanted attention, sir.'

His voice fades out to a dull hum in the back of my mind. All I can think about is Rosie. Every dream I've ever had about her, every fantasy of seeing her.

'Sir!'

I snap out of it.

'The Palace of Westminster. You have arrived,' says Denis.

CHAPTER 41

CHAMBER OF HORRORS

The Houses of Parliament stand right there, Big Ben to my left. The vast Gothic facades and pinnacles have been exquisitely maintained and restored and, up this close, must be just as impressive now as they were in their day. But there are two crucial differences. The four clock faces at the top of Big Ben are now giant billboards, advertising the building's new purpose:

INTERNATIONAL INSTITUTE OF TECHNOLOGY

TONIGHT, 10 MAY:

GNOSYS®

ANNUAL SHAREHOLDERS CONVENTION

And the 21st-century docking station covers part of the front of the 19th-century building. I think back to Counsel with Pokes, and photos she's shown us of what it looked like when this was the oldest seat of democracy in the world. *Hey, wasn't there a lawn here, with a statue of that guy, what was his name? Oliver Cromwell?* It all comes back to me, that lesson. A king tried to overthrow parliament and plunged England into civil war. But he didn't succeed. Instead, this guy Cromwell overthrew the king and had him killed. Pokes made a big deal of the statue: she said it was there as a warning against any would-be tyrant of the future. As it is, Cromwell's now been carted away, and Hamilton Rogers is coming to talk about world domination.

As the nose of my own Podd kisses the docking station's electromagnet, the engine powers down, and we come to a stop, I start to realize quite how much of an event I've inadvertently found myself attending.

The docking station gleams with white marble, polished

mirror-smooth. At least two hundred Podds are docked in a line alongside my own, each in its own little U-shaped bay, like boats at a marina. *That's it*, I think, *this is where all the Podds were headed; why there were so many Spectas on the road tonight!* With only a handful of exceptions – notably the grimed and graffitied heap that tailgated us on the way here – these are deluxe machines. Polished to a flawless sheen, many are customized with spoilers, baffles and bumpers you'd never see on a London Podd.

The Podd immediately next to mine is elongated, like a stretch limo. Suddenly, its gullwing doors slide seamlessly back, revealing the interior. I swivel my seat around and crane to take a closer look. *I can see out of my Podd and into theirs, but they can't see in while my doors are closed*, I reassure myself.

Four empty velvet seats face each other in its enlarged passenger area. I've never seen anything so luxurious; the cabin is enormously spacious and finished in dark mahogany, with perfectly pleated curtains lining the windows. Whereas even in my own prestige Podd there is only one Streem display, in this machine the entire interior casing seems to be one giant computer screen. As I scan the rest of the cabin, a central console rises up in the middle of the seats, revealing a bottle of champagne on ice; the cork comes off with a little pop and the contraption pours out a glass on its own. *Self-pouring champagne? You've got to be kidding me.* The only object that seems oddly out of place amid all this luxury is a rack at the back that would look more at home in an ambulance. Turning my head I see a matching rack in my own Podd. *Stretchers? Why?*

Out of nowhere an old man, previously hidden from

view, emerges from the driver's seat of the other Podd. He has white hair and bushy white eyebrows that protrude from beneath a pair of dark, moon-shaped sunglasses. He snatches the glass of champagne and drains it in one motion.

He can't see me, right? Surely he can't see me. I swing my seat around and look straight ahead inconspicuously, just in case. I catch a glimpse of his suit in my periphery – it's a cross between a tuxedo and the regular Specta garments, like the suit I'm wearing. A glowing purple bowtie turns like a fan beneath his chin. *Who is this guy?* Very cautiously, I turn my head back in his direction. *Shit!* He's out of his Podd and his face is right up against the side of my own. He looks straight at me, over his glasses; his eyes are horribly bloodshot and his pupils are tiny.

'Denis,' I say, very slowly and quietly, trying not to move my lips. 'Why is that man looking at me?'

'That, sir, is Gregory Potman. Entirely harmless, I assure you. A multibillionaire from the North of England, Mr Potman is a major shareholder in Gnosys. His business is, and has always been, dealing with primary waste disposal for the residents of the Hab-Belts.'

'Toilets?'

'Not precisely, sir. Avid users of Perspecta have proven reluctant to leave the Universe in order to perform those, ahem, little daily necessities of human life. His organization, Potman Percutaneous, is responsible for installing the Percutaneous Endoscopic Gastrostomy System into the haptic rigs of every Perspecta user in Europe. Without that, things could often get really rather messy, sir, if you catch my meaning?'

BANG!

I look around to see that the old man has fallen onto our Podd and that his face is squished right up against the window. *Jesus!* It's terrifying; he looks like the living dead. His face is so saggy and grey that it is almost impossible to make out any of his features; the skin around his eye sockets has wrinkled so much that where his eyes would once have been, now there are merely black holes. His lips and chin hang off his protruding jawbone to such an extent that these particular features look drawn on, cartoonish, dreadful. I turn away and face forward, trying to keep calm and ignore Potman as he peels his face away from the window with seemingly herculean effort.

'Ca-can he see me?' I ask Denis, too scared to look back and find out.

'Oh no, sir! Not to worry! Mr Potman loves Perspecta so much that he holds the record for most consecutive hours spent inside the Universe – ten years and three months! Would you believe it?! UN guidelines stipulate that a user mustn't spend more than twenty-two consecutive hours in the Universe without taking proper physical exercise. These annual meetings are the sole exceptions to his strict regimen of immobility. Potman's reluctance to log out has caused him to go very nearly blind. And besides, it is impossible to see inside a Podd if its door is closed.'

'So why does it look like he can?'

'I'm afraid I can't give a definitive answer to that question, sir. Suffice to say – and I do hope the gentleman in question would forgive me – Mr Potman is quite the eccentric. Like a great many of our shareholders, sir. Totally harmless, though, I assure you, sir.'

Reassured, I look around and see Potman slumping

into an automated wheelchair and then being escorted by two Teeth into the building. Indeed, looking down the long platform of the docking station, a great number of people – mostly old white men in dark tux-like suits – are also being escorted in chairs by pairs of Teeth. *Never seen this many pigs*, I scowl. *This is gonna be fun . . .*

'Might I suggest, sir, that you begin making your way inside? If you don't want to miss the beginning of the keynote address. I will do my best to guide you through the event, sir, and will always be by your side or, at least, in your ear—'

'Denis,' I caution, to stop him going off into his usual verbal tailspin.

'Forgive me, sir. It'll be an honour to assist in any way I can. The only thing I won't be able to help you with, sir, is how to act like you've been logged into the Universe for as long as the assembled company have.'

'Right, thanks,' I say anxiously. 'Any top tips before I go to my almost certain death?'

'Slumbersome, sir.'

'What?'

'Sleepy. My advice would be to act very, very sleepy.'

'Sleepy.' I sigh, resigning myself to whatever horrible fate lies ahead of me.

I leave the Podd and head towards the main entrance. *Sleepy, okay.* I walk slowly, zombie-like, one leaden foot in front of the other on the lustrous marble. Then, halfway down the platform, two figures move in on either side: Teeth reaching to grab my arms. *Hey!* I surge towards panic, my instinct to pull away.

'No sudden movements, sir,' Denis whispers before I

do, and I resist the urge to look at my unwanted escorts. 'Allow them to take your full weight. It's what they expect you to do. No need to worry sir! This is a good sign, they're buying the act!' Denis sounds like a little boy up to no good. I feel like telling him to shut up, but don't, not wanting to draw any unnecessary attention to myself.

My head suddenly starts to throb, but this time I'm ready for it. It's the same feeling I got when the Teeth came into the Cell. I can feel it coming – the numbing, terrifying blackness of another attack – and so I focus every ounce of my energy on clearing my mind and ignoring the beeps and squawks and white noise of my surroundings.

'Once inside, your retina will be scanned and you will be cleared for entry. I've communicated with the scanner's operating system and entered your code.'

My heart races. My breathing breaks into short, sharp pants. I'm so hot in this suit.

'Relax, sir. Ignore everything. Focus only on me. Focus only on what you mean to do.'

The Teeth guide me through the main entrance into what seems to be a black hole. I look around, trying to work out where I am. A door slides closed on what I realize is a gigantic, spherical body scanner. My feet are clamped to the floor and a mask is placed on my face. Bright laser beams shine in my eyes and the clamps around my feet force my legs to buckle and my body to fall back into a metal armchair that rises from the floor beneath me. The facial recognition mask disconnects from my face with a positive *ding*. Denis obviously did his job. As the sphere begins spinning faster and faster around the armchair, I stay absolutely still.

'Denis…' I whisper, close to inaudibly, out of the corner of my mouth. 'What the hell's happening?' The sphere continues to whir and whir around me at dizzying speed. Before he has time to answer, its walls are pulled up and away and, to my utter disbelief, I am sitting on one of the green leather benches in the House of Commons. The walls of the scanner reconnect above my head and form a sphere once more, before flying away like a great big balloon. Hundreds of other balls – just like the one I was just inside – fly around the chamber too.

The great chamber looks just as it does in the pictures I've seen in Counsel. Grand and gaudy, it has been perfectly preserved. An audience of hundreds of Spectas – Gnosys shareholders, mostly aged – fills the ranks of tiered leather seats. Then, all at once, I feel a gust of fetid, chilly air coming from above me. I look up and see that the spheres have gone, revealing one major difference between the chamber now and how it was during the Dusk. The high top of the vaulted ceiling is rolling back, smooth and silent. Above us the tar-black night sky is being uncovered.

Then there's a thunderous roar: a sound I'd recognize anywhere; a sound that would send chills down the spine of any Offliner. Four immense black masses block out the sky as Gnosys Chariots loom over the heads of the crowd like great behemoths, metres above the building. Their doors slide open and Teeth hang out of the sides of each craft, their e-cannons trained on the people below. Snipers. *So you don't even trust your own. Or maybe*, I gulp, *you're expecting trouble.* Monstrous fan-jets in each Chariot's whale-like fuselage rotate to keep them hovering in mid-air, meanwhile forcing the London smog down onto us in reeking waves.

CHAPTER 42

HIJACK

A thousand questions rapidly flicker through my head. *Why show them the sky? Why are you trying to suffocate your own people?* Then suddenly I see it. Clear as the sky is black. *Ah, that's the whole point. You're not showing them the sky, you're reminding them of the world that they escaped. Reminding them of how you saved them from the poisonous, polluted past.* I feel my blood boil and my heartbeat quicken. *A world you helped to poison! That you destroyed!* I feel like screaming. I begin coughing violently, rasping for air. *Forgotten my Roxi. Shit.*

'Bear with, sir. I'll have the Central OS instruct one of the attendants to provide you with a breathing mask.'

Sure enough, almost as soon as Denis has said it, an attending Medi-Mig is fitting an oxygen resp to my face. Once it's on and I'm breathing normally, I realize other people in the audience are having masks fitted too. It's the first time I've really looked at them all; the first time I've had the opportunity to study the faces of the veteran Spectas up close.

The first thing that strikes me is how they all look remarkably – spookily – similar. Their faces are ghost-white and wrinkled, like they've spent too long in water. Their eyes are bloodshot and their bodies are saggy and thin. Their movements are slow and lagging. A few look utterly bewildered, like fish out of water. I realize these are the ones who are actually conscious, logged out of the Perspecta Universe and trying to make sense of the real one.

Soon I'm beginning to suspect that there was no need for me to panic about getting here on time. Droves of Spectas continue to be deposited on the green benches, many of them apparently fast asleep. It's like a vast sleepover for the terminally decrepit. So much so that I find myself struggling to stifle my yawns.

Then a voice blares out of hidden speakers around us. 'Ladies and gentlemen, the meeting will begin shortly. Welcome to reality.'

Hundreds of tiny red lights blink on, off, on, off around the chamber, looking like little fireflies.

'I say, now that *is* interesting!' Denis's voice suddenly exclaims in my head. 'Everyone in the audience has had their Plug set to idle, sir, and the chamber is now entirely offline because the keynote is about to begin. And yet you remain logged into Perspecta, sir, or I would not be able to communicate with you now. Most unexpected!'

The sense of anticipation in the chamber is more than palpable. It's a sight both awe-inspiring and terrifying to behold. The man next to me starts moving back and forth, like he's having a fit. The man on my other side tries to clap his hands, flopping them together unsuccessfully, as if they were fins. Both men begin rasping, like they are trying to say something, like they're trying to cheer. I look around and realize everybody is doing the same thing – some more successfully than others. I join in, copying the man on my right; the one on my left is making almost no sound at all. By now the entire House is filled with a peculiar cacophony of half-cheers. None of them has the lung capacity for more than that; this is the best they can do. 'Still', I say to myself, 'who'd have thought so many half-dead people could make so much noise without saying anything at all?'

'It is a strange thing, to be sure sir, but as a sad side-effect of living in a virtual reality, one's body simply stops working as it should. There is, I'm afraid, no way around it. That, sir, is why every Podd is equipped with its own set of stretchers. Emergencies are all too frequent.'

'But how do they live? I mean why aren't they dead? You know what I mean, they look dead, sound dead, but—'

'—are not in fact dead, sir,' Denis finishes for me. 'It is indeed curious sir, this business of virtual reality. Perspecta users who are fully logged into the system at all times – living in Hab-Belts and existing in haptic rigs, that is, as opposed to logging in and out using portable devices – may be living lives beyond their wildest dreams. But dreams come at a price, sir.'

'You turn into a zombie?!' I cut in flippantly.

'Not exactly sir, but this is what happens if one does not use one's vocal cords – does not move a single muscle in any meaningful way – for as long as these men and women.'

If the keynote is coming, it's taking a hell of a long time about it. Soon I'm bored and listless. I scan the chamber for Rosie. *Where is she? And if she's not here, why the hell am I?* My backside aches on the green leather; I'm not used to sitting still so long. Time seems to spool out endlessly under the roiling sky, and before long I'm struggling to stop my head nodding. I'm really beginning to feel more than just drowsy.

I'm startled awake by Denis's voice, sounding like he's battling heroically to keep his composure.

'Forgive my intrusion, sir, but we are being boarded, sir.'

'Boarded? What?'

'Someone is attempting to enter the Podd uninvited, sir. An intruder, sir!'

'Enter it? Who?!'

'I say! One of them has slipped something into the locking mechanism.' Denis's pitch shifts upwards. 'Hey, you! Young fellow! This is a private vehicle. I really must protest!'

To be honest, I think to myself quickly, *if someone spoke to me that way I'd probably ignore them.*

'Sir?' says Denis. 'In principle I don't wish to publicize

your presence here, but really this demands the attention of Gnosys security.'

'Teeth, Denis? You must be joking, what—'

'Oh, oh, sir! The young vagabond has the door open now! The whippersnapper!'

I glance around nervously, feeling alarmed now, worried it's written all over my face and hoping nobody's noticed. But thankfully all eyes are on the floor of the chamber, where an array of holograms is now parading. It seems to be some kind of historic pageant: a woman with a long blonde plait leaning over a keyboard; a classroom of children wearing headsets like oversized blindfolds, all leaning and reaching and gesturing in smiling unison . . . A creamy voiceover on the chamber loudspeakers reels off names and dates and other details, but I'm finding it impossible to pay attention.

'Sir! Sir!' comes Denis's screech. 'I believe the Podd is being hijacked.'

On the chamber floor, holo-pop clips replace each other in rapid succession: sports games, educational games, some kind of superhero game. The woman again, older now, coalesces out of the darkness with a dark-haired man. They're holding a huge plastic ear between them, with an earplug in it.

The creamy compere's voice compete's with Denis's tone of increasingly affronted hauteur.

'Sir, Bernard really is most put out. He'd like you to see what's going on – and so would I, sir. With your permission, sir, we will relay the signal from the onboard closed circuit surveillance system.'

Before I can respond, I hear a babble of voices.

'Quick, in 'ere before they see us!'

'Blimey, swanky set of wheels this is.'

The Podd interior appears in my mind's eye, half-obscuring what's going on in front of my eyes in the chamber. Denis is beaming me a view from somewhere above the dashboard. Huge, shadowy figures are piling in through the door. Big hands are all over the Podd, stroking the svelte seats, pulling and pushing at buttons.

Hey! I yell inwardly, suddenly as outraged as Denis. The sensation is bizarre – having my field of vision split like this, augmented – but the emotion surging through me is even more alien. It's a moment before I realize what it is. Possessiveness. Before now, I've never owned more than my Walkman, my clothes and what's in my Roses tin, but suddenly the Podd, my Podd, is being invaded, and I'm balling my fists in rage.

'Upholstery like a baby's bum!' says one of the hulking intruders.

'What's this do?' says another, yanking at a handle.

''Ere, give us an 'and, will yer! I reckon you can open this,' says a voice from the rear of the Podd.

'See any food? I'm bloody starving.'

'Better than food!' A shower of small objects erupts suddenly into the air. 'Chocolates! Bloody champagne!'

I hear the pop of a cork and the babble becomes a blur of noise. In the midst of it all I can now just about hear Denis's voice, addressing not me this time but the hijackers.

'Oi!' comes a yell over the hubbub. 'Keep it down, will yer? There's something in 'ere. Tryin' to say somethin'.' There's a sudden sound of shushing and giggling. *Giggling?*

Whatever goes on next is drowned by a burst of applause in the chamber.

Then Denis is back in my ear. 'Sir,' he says, 'I must confess that I find it a little difficult to credit, sir, but the, erm, visitors claim to be friends of yours.'

Friends of mine? My mind races.

'I'm terribly sorry madame, would you repeat that?' He seems to be talking to someone else. More muffled consternation and then, to me again: 'Do you happen, sir, to know anybody by the name of Jemma?'

Jemma!

I look again at the image being relayed into my head from the Podd. The hulking brutes aren't huge at all. They're children, their likenesses vastly distorted by the on-board camera's fish-eye lens so they seem to fill all the available space.

Recent memories flash through my mind: Jemma declaring *We'll come with you, every spy needs backup*; the dejected faces when I said no; the battered-looking Podd we saw almost riding our rear bumper on the way here.

Oh shit! My mind reels. *The Terrors have followed me to Westminster. What the hell are they planning to do? Stage a coup?!*

Just as I'm scrambling to think how to respond, the Commons loudspeakers cut in louder than ever, booming across the chamber.

'Ladies and gentleman, Gnosys CEO and President, Hamilton Rogers.'

The space is plunged into pitch darkness and the whole place falls silent. Then, four spotlights shining from the bellies of the four hovering Chariots run back and forth over our heads until the beams meet in the very centre, focusing on the old table where prime ministers once spoke. I've seen photos of that table with old books of English law lined up on it, but now it's bare. As the Chariot beams cross, simultaneously four herculean holo-pops bearing the Gnosys logo emerge around the old table.

I know I should deal with the Terrors but I also know that I need to focus everything I've got on what's going on in the chamber. There's sudden excitement in my peripheral vision. My heart rate increases as I see Hamilton Rogers emerge from a door at the back of the chamber.

'Denis,' I whisper inwardly. 'Really, really bad timing. But yes, Jemma is a friend. They're not a threat' – *at least I bloody well hope they're not a threat* – 'and you'll just have to keep them in the Podd and keep them quiet.'

'Quiet, sir? I don't think the champagne is conducive—'

'Denis! Just . . . sort it out. Sorry, I have to concentrate.' I don't know how to tell him to stop the video and audio feed to my head, so I just say, desperately, pathetically, 'Over and out.'

'As you wish, sir,' Denis assents stiffly. My head clears of everything except the sounds and sights of the Commons chamber.

CHAPTER 43

THE GREATEST SHOWMAN

Hamilton is walking towards the table, mounting steps I can't see just behind it. Standing on the table like it's a podium.

I can't take my eyes off him. This is the first time I have ever seen him in the flesh . . . the first time I've been a matter of metres from my worst enemy. I feel strangely filled with emotion.

He's a tall, lean, good-looking man in his fifties. His hair is thick, golden-white, and parted on one side. His face is much more open than I imagined it would be – the kind of face you would feel comfortable talking to, sharing with, entrusting your entire life to. *Guess that's the genius*, I think, my eyes fixed on him. His suit is a deep blue and his shirt is made out of the crispest possible white cotton. In the solar brightness of the spotlights, I make out a herringbone pattern stitched into the suit: expensive, almost regal, somehow saying *trustworthy*. This man is unlike all the other tech billionaires who came and went during the Dusk. You'd never see him touched by facial hair, I think, or in sweater and chinos, or carrying himself like an ordinary geek though wearing a suit. This is the one that prevailed, this is what a grown-up tech billionaire looks like. He is corporate to the core, and wants you to know it. If I didn't feel so incensed I might even be a little impressed.

He basks in the strange ululations of the packed House for a few moments, before raising his hand and bidding the Spectas fall silent.

'My friends!' The richest, most famous man in the world speaks as if he really *is* addressing his closest allies. His voice is soft but somehow amplified throughout the huge space so that it feels like he is whispering in your ear, speaking only to you. 'It's that time of year again!'

The audience tries – and fails – again to show its praise. Hamilton nods in deep appreciation, nonetheless. *This is so weird*, I think. My eyes must look like saucers.

'Yes!' He smiles broadly at us, like a father might smile at his favourite son or daughter. 'Once again, it's my huge privilege and great joy to tell you – my most cherished, loyal supporters – what the future holds.'

He puts up his hand before anyone can start trying to cheer again.

Not your first rodeo, is it mate?

'Before I continue, I'd like to apologize for putting you through the agony of leaving your Universe. London is not quite Apeiron, is it? Trust me, I know all too well how unpleasant *this* world seems when you live in ours!'

You make me sick, I say to Hamilton in my head. *And I wish you could read my mind, so you'd know.*

'As I say every time, I can't stress how important it is to me that we all come together, just once a year, in this, the old, dead world, to celebrate the beautiful new one which we have had to leave for the evening . . . and which we will all, very, very shortly, be returning to.'

He gives a cheeky, politician's grin. The rasping breaths and dead-man's splutters erupt in the crowd again.

'Calm down, calm down. You all know Perspecta will never cease to exist. There is *nothing* I care about more than protecting and maintaining the new world – *your* world.'

He stops, like he's thinking, retracing his thoughts, then puts his index finger in the air. 'Perhaps there is *one* thing I care about more than maintaining Perspecta.' He pauses again, smiling, looking around the great room. 'And that's protecting the future of Perspecta.'

The audience attempts to clap, like a trained troupe of arthritic seals.

'Now, we all know why you're here!' A supercilious grin creeps across his face slowly, from one tanned cheekbone to the other. 'We know you didn't come for the canapés!' A smattering of breathy chuckles runs across the chamber. The man to my left actually snorts.

'No, no, no.' Hamilton has every single person in the room in the palm of his hand. 'You came for a revelation. What, I hear you all ask, can he possibly do next? What, you wonder, could the most revolutionary hardware in the history of the world be?' He folds his arms, purses his lips. His eyes narrow: the greatest showman. 'Well, I'll tell you one thing. It's going to send the value of your stock soaring through the nonexistent roof!' The monstrous reptiles that surround me begin flailing and rasping again in utter delight.

The sales pitch continues, but now it dawns on me that this is actually the only thing he's going to say about the new Plug – or whatever it will be. There's no detail, just big, vague abstractions. Third-generation Perspecta will be completely different to second-generation. It will be a seamless experience. It will be so discreet you can't believe it. Yadda yadda yadda.

Even some of the shareholders are starting to look impatient now, their fat fingers drumming on flabby knees.

'Yes, I know,' says Hamilton, suddenly informal as a man talking to his family at the breakfast table. 'This has taken a while. Longer than any of us wanted.' There's a rumble of agreement and a thudding of heels and walking sticks against the wooden floor. 'But sometimes, folks, you just can't hurry the future. Not a future as incredible as this one, at any rate.'

And he's off again, ramping up the rhetoric, mostly as empty as before. But when he says Perspecta 3.0 will be 'unbreakable', he seems to be making a genuinely new claim. And his conclusion has me wide awake with alarm. 'Not only is P3 the next logical step in the evolution of the virtual-reality user-experience, it is the next step in *human* evolution.'

What the hell does that mean? I wonder. But before I can begin to speculate, my thoughts are scattered like ninepins.

'The most beautiful thing about P3?' he asks. 'It protects the future. When I talk about the future, I'm not talking about you or me or what I will be unveiling to you here tonight. No, when I talk about the future, I'm talking about her . . .'

There. Right there – not more than a few metres away from me – there she is, Rosie Rogers, walking confidently but dutifully, up the steps of the podium-table to join her father. She looks smaller and slighter than I imagined, with a kind of unworldly innocence. A simple pale yellow cotton summer dress falls around her slim frame. As far as I can see – from this distance and without the benefit of a giant holo-pop – she isn't wearing any makeup. But the spotlight beams make her features look as sculpted as any model's. My eyes are greedy. I can't focus on anything but her; nor can I focus on any particular thing about her: the light of her eyes, the line of her nose, the curve of her lips, the dapple of her freckles. I want to take all of her in, all at once, as if she might disappear at any moment. I'm babbling in my head. I'm mesmerized.

But I'm not too stupefied to recognize that all this beauty must be obvious to everyone, to some degree. That's why she appears everywhere in holo-pop Gnosys advertising.

Actually what tops it all off for me is the imperfections. Those freckles are there to remind me she's a human being and not an angel sent from heaven. It's how she's always looked to me in her hologram form: perfectly imperfect.

She lifts her dainty, perfect hand in the air and waves at us all. I almost wave back, I am so enraptured, so under her spell. She's as composed and comfortable in the spotlight as a princess; just as you'd expect the most famous person in the world to be.

'Hello London!' she says. 'It's so great to be here!'

Like her father's before, her caramel voice is amplified perfectly, making it feel like she is talking only to me. Remembering her holo-pop on Shaftesbury Avenue, which I've stared at for hours and hours over the years, I always figured she was only ever talking to me. It takes me by surprise to realize that the geriatric zombies think she's talking to them too. If the reaction they gave her father was good, the way they respond to her is nothing short of extraordinary. For Rosie, they manage to produce enough noise to make you think they're actually normal.

She takes a step back, allowing her father to take centre-stage once more.

He points again at Rosie and the crowd smacks its cheeks in delight. 'That is the future. Standing right there before your eyes. And if I have just one duty, one responsibility, one single reason to be on this planet, it is to protect the next generation from all those forces of evil we have had to contend with for far too long. P3 means that the next generation – the future – will never have to experience the ugliness of the old world and its many terrors, as we did for so long.'

Wheezy cheers erupt again. Loud cheers. The crowd is working itself into an asthmatic frenzy.

'You'll have seen my Rosie – *our* Rosie – quite a lot lately.' He looks over at her, beaming, sickly sweet. 'My little ambassador.' At this, Rosie's face blooms with happiness. She looks like a pageant-winner who's unexpectedly toppled all the frontrunners.

'I mean, come on, who could resist a smile like that?!'

I know I need to hear what Hamilton's saying. *But her eyes, man. Jesus Christ.* For a moment, they blind me to anything except her, however hard I try. I screw my face up as tight as I can. *Concentrate. You have to concentrate.* I open them again and fixate on Rosie once more, but manage to take in what her father is saying.

Now he has a big, warm grin on his face.

'Even our friends the Offliners are blessed with the occasional sight of our Rosie.'

Hamilton pauses long enough for the Spectas to feel each others' discomfort, then resumes, 'No, no, I know. I don't like to think of them either. And if I had my way, we none of us would *ever* have to think about them again!'

Now there's noise: a ghastly sound like feet in mud as hundreds of withered lips smack together in relish.

'But you see, like all of you here tonight, my darling daughter has always been much more patient than me. We mustn't abandon our responsibilities to those less fortunate, she tells me time and time again. We must be understanding of those who decide to dwell in the dark. That's why, day in day out, Rosie's been going into the godforsaken ghettos of London and New York, Rio and Delhi, Tokyo and Beijing.'

Again the audience shifts. But Hamilton soon puts them at ease again. 'Not in person, of course! I'd never dream of putting her life at the mercy of the disease and filth and bestial instincts that run riot in those places. But at her request, there she is in holo-pop form, to offer a hand up to all those poor benighted souls, to remind them that there is a better world, if they want to take it. And those people love her! Oh they adore her! Actually, I get a bit . . . uncomfortable when I hear just how much they do.' He crooks an eyebrow and there's a smattering of lascivious seal-barks. Something flickers in Rosie's eyes. *Wait, was that . . . disgust?* I wonder. But if it was, she has it almost immediately under control.

'But you know what?' Hamilton bellows so suddenly that the massed ranks all jerk back in unison. It's the first time since Rosie got on stage that I'm able to peel my eyes off her for a moment and back to her father.

'No matter how often we reach out, even with the help of Rosie here, all the Offliners offer in return is . . . ingrati-tude. Ingratitude! Have you ever talked to these people? No? Count yourselves lucky. *It ain't pleasant, people.*' He affects an American twang. Then, continuing, 'As my dear mother Sylvia might have put it – God rest her soul – they've got a bloody nerve. Always questioning, always querying. They are *doubters*. The Perspecta Universe, they say, is a lie. Theirs is the real world, they say, and ours just a fantasy, which has done nothing more than blind the human race and must be stopped.' He pauses and looks around the great room with a terrifying anger in his eyes. 'Our noblest intentions, our peerless technology, our years and years and *years* of hard work, our great civilization, the future we cherish – all of these things, into which you have poured the generosity of your hearts and wallets – is to the Offliners nothing more than *cloud cuckoo land.'*

He looks down, clasps his hands together as if in pained thought, and talks for a moment as if to himself.

'You, my friends, have been superhumanly patient. You have been kindness itself. Truly, you have gone beyond the call of duty and honour and mercy.'

He raises his eyes and looks at Rosie. There are tears in them. Then he looks to the audience and raises his hands, palms together, as if in supplication.

'So it hurts me now, to have to beg my beloved daughter – kindness personified – and all you tender-hearted souls, to accept the truth of our situation. To ask for permission to let what is right finally run its necessary course. Not,' he adds quickly, 'that it will hurt your bank balances. Be assured it will not.' He opens his arms wide, pivoting on his heels so everyone can see his broad smile. 'You *know* something's right when it makes moral *and* financial sense. And I'm talking *real estate* here!'

Suddenly I'm feeling queasy. Cold sweat breaks out on my forehead.

Hamilton's smile becomes a wolfish grin, then disappears altogether. He looks out and scans the audience, almost like he's looking for something. *A rat*, I think, wishing I were invisible.

'What are we to do with them, those monsters of ingratitude, those shirkers who never worked a day in their lives, those haters who'd like nothing better than to tear down every Hab-Belt on this planet and plunge us back into nightmare?'

He cocks his head and casts his eye about as if looking for hands raised to offer answers. But of course there are none. This audience only knows how to lap up what it's given.

'If we're to protect our loved ones – our future – the time has come to face an unpleasant truth. That truth is this. After years of trying to unite the old world and all its many barbaric factions, years of trying to bring all these different people into our new world and welcome them with open arms, it is with a heavy heart that I must admit it. We have failed. *I have failed.* These people do not wish to be helped or united, they do not wish to live in the future, they wish to cling onto a past, an old, dead history that is long gone.'

His eyes narrow.

'This is not a problem for them. They're happy in their misery, it's obvious. But it damn well is a problem for the rest of us! This is the way I see it – and I've given this a lot of painful thought. After all the help we have given and the offers we have made, if you choose not to log in to Perspecta, you are not merely choosing a different way of life, you are rejecting the *only* way of life, the *only* one that works, the way of life of the future. By refusing to log in, you not only threaten *our* way of life, you threaten *our* children and *our* future. And that, friends, leads me to the most important announcement I will make today.

He pauses solemnly for a moment, and then suddenly he's jabbing a forefinger at the dark skies and yelling as if he wants to call down the lightning.

'What will we do with those stinking, filth-loving

gutter-lickers, those drug addicts, those inbred thugs, those rapists and child molesters, those terrorists? Those vermin, those sewer rats – we're going to find them and trap them. We're going to clear them away. Starting right here and now, we're going to flush out that vast, seething reservoir of anarchy, insanity and disease. And I'll let you in on a little boardroom secret: we know exactly where we're going to begin.'

My world seems to reel. *They're coming for us, they're coming for us now.* The beached sealions all around shake their pale, fleshy dewlaps and spatter themselves with spittle in sheer delirium. But there's a roaring in my ears like the thunder of massed storms sweeping in. A rage unlike any I've ever felt boils up inside me. I am close to standing up and screaming.

He looks up at the banked benches again, as if he's looking straight at me. Shivers shoot down my spine. There's no denying it now, no shying away from the reality of our situation. He means for us to be eradicated. He means for the Offliners to be extinguished – just like that – and removed from the face of the Earth.

'Either you are with us, or you are against us. There is no middle ground. So to those who have rejected the Perspecta vision and the protection it gives us all, I say this: log in, or be brought to justice.'

CHAPTER 44

ROSIE
THE RIVETER

There's silence as he gazes around the room with a beatific smile on his face. A few seconds later, with a clacking of heels, a tall woman steps up to the side of the table he's standing on. Plastic face, plumped-up lips: I know her instantly.

'Friends and fellow shareholders,' says Sally Smee, 'thank you. As head of Gnosys security for London, I'll be tasked with the Offliner clean-up operation. So Mr Rogers has asked me to take questions for him now.'

She told us she was Minister for Offliner Liaison, I rage inside. *Now we know what they mean by 'liaison'!*

'Mr Potman,' says Smee as the spotlight falls on a face that looks, in that harsh light, almost exactly like someone has drawn eyes on an elderly backside. The noise that comes out is almost impossible to interpret, but Smee is ready.

'Thank you, sir. Mr Rogers, Mr Potman asks if there's anything his company can do to help, since they're experts in removing human waste.' There's a bubbling froth of laughter, and Hamilton's eyes gleam, but silence falls quickly now.

Smee orchestrates as more comments, sounding increasingly rehearsed, are offered by the audience. Praise, another gag or two; no questions that actually require an answer. Yet I'm less aware of what's being said than of the sounds of sporadic coughing and flab shifting on leather seats. Without Hamilton's rhetoric to wind them up, the shareholders seem uncomfortable.

Suddenly as the spotlight roves towards yet another shareholder, it stops in its tracks.

'Daddy, if I may.'

Rosie steps to Hamilton's side. As the spotlights focus on her belatedly, a flicker of surprise crosses his face. But then he smiles indulgently at her. 'My dear, of course.'

That's weird. Did she think it was getting awkward? I wonder.

'No one is prouder of what you've achieved than I am, Daddy,' she says, golden smile matching her golden voice. 'And of Gnosys, which depends on all of you here. We're never happier than when we're in the Perspecta Universe, are we?'

Belches of agreement all round.

'The wonder of our lives in the Universe, the joy of the friendships we have with each other there. We wouldn't be without it. Indeed, we'd be nothing without it. The only thing that could be better, and it hardly seems possible to me, is a better Perspecta. But it is possible. And it's coming.'

A beat. 'Eventually.'

Hamilton's smile freezes.

I lean forward, riveted. *She's holding something in, I know it! She's furious.*

'No one,' Rosie resumes, 'knows better than you, Daddy, how long it is taking, what a strain the wait is. Every morning I see it in your face at breakfast. And I spend every day wishing I could wipe away the wrinkles from that furrowed brow. And so I want to plead with you all, our great Gnosys family, to look at that face and see the weight of responsibility. It's a weight we must all share.'

'Thank you, darling,' interjects Hamilton. 'But there really is no need to be worried, though I do appreci—'

'Oh, but there is!' she cuts him short. 'I'm really worried, Daddy. Worried for you and for all of us – Gnosys share-holders, Perspecta users, and Offliners too.'

Hamilton's arm comes up and for an instant I think he's actually going to cuff her around the face. Instead he's got her shoulder and is trying to steer her towards Smee, who's reaching up from the foot of the podium. Then he registers the noises from the tiers – bellows, thwacks of sticks against wood, farts erupting in incontinent surprise.

Hang on, the shareholders want her to stay. They want her to keep talking.

He freezes, and Rosie turns to him, seemingly strengthened by the support from the crowd. 'Daddy, the greatest thing about Perspecta is that it gives *us* infinite choices. And to the Offliners we offer just one simple choice: join us if you want. And yet, just because most of them say no to that, should we really be taking away their right to choose, completely?'

Hamilton's lips are locked in a rictus but his hand is now gripping Rosie's arm in a vice-like grip and pushing her again, pushing hard.

'Should we really be taking away their homes?' she says, and her voice breaks. With an air of resignation, she gives under the pressure of her father's hand, walks towards the steps, then raises her head and delivers one last question. 'Should they really be made to suffer, Daddy, just because we're all frustrated with how long Perspecta Three is taking?'

As she steps down to the floor, Smee is on her like a raptor. I can't see clearly what's happening; they're obscured by the table and by Hamilton, who now turns to the shareholders with a jovial shrug, his self-command recovered.

'Out of the mouths of babes!' he laughs. 'There's no one I love more than my darling Rosie, but I sometimes forget she's only seventeen. Let's all give her a round of applause and cut her some slack. She'll see sense when all this is over. And ladies and gentlemen,' he begins to wrap up, 'I am so grateful to you all for everything you do for this great company we have built together. I am so grateful to you all for logging in. I am so grateful to you all for being a part of the future. Thank you.'

Hamilton leaves the podium-table and seems to relieve Smee of Rosie, who sweeps ahead and vanishes behind the Speaker's chair, the way she came in. Several White Teeth detach themselves from the shadows and follow.

By then, without a thought for how I'm going to do it, I'm already getting up from the green leather bench to go after her.

CHAPTER 45

FACE TO FACE

'Denis!' I whisper inwardly. 'Denis, something's up. D'you see that?'

'I presume you are referring to the three Migs that just attended Miss Rogers, sir.' He sounds even stiffer than usual.

'Attended? I'm not sure that's the word for it, Denis. I think she's in trouble.'

'I must say sir, I don't disagree with you. But sir, if I may now draw your attention back to your young friends—'

Before he can finish, I'm walking down the aisle that leads from the end of my tier towards the chamber floor, and turning for the door Rosie went through. I see Hamilton exit in front of me.

'Sir, I can appreciate that you have no attention to spare for what's happening here in the Podd. But I really, really must implore you to refrain from going through there or making contact with Miss Rogers! This is not the time, sir! You are in very dangerous waters!'

'Denis, I want help, not an argument. Can you do anything to distract the Teeth, and Rogers? And can you show me where she is?'

'Oh!' Somehow Denis manages to sound as if he's wringing his hands. 'If you insist, sir, while I keep your, er, guests entertained with some Fred Astaire. It's impossible for me to refuse a Legend command.' His voice in my head suddenly ratchets up an octave. 'Sir! In front of you!'

I quickly step to my right to get out of the way of an elderly red-headed woman in an oncoming auto-chair, almost colliding with it, its passenger, and its two accompanying Teeth.

'Well, thank God for you, Denis. Close shave.'

'I can only agree, sir. Now, through that door ahead, down the corridor, and Miss Rogers is in the fifth room on the right, waiting for transport to her next destination, sir. Inside right now are four Migs, sir. I am using the OS to override their instruction to attend Miss Rogers and send them to another part of the building, where there has been an accident that needs attending to.'

'Accident?'

'At the turn of the millennium – that period you so thoroughly appreciate, sir – I believe they referred to it as a "clean-up in aisle four".'

'Ahhhhhh,' I smile to myself. 'You bloody genius.'

'I do my best, sir. Er, sir?'

'Yes?'

'Reluctantly setting aside the situation here in the Podd with your exuberant friends and their remarkably short attention spans, I must warn you that I cannot be certain how long the Migs will remain distracted. And although I am also providing a distraction for Mr Rogers, I do not know how long that will work, either. He is currently walking to his daughter's dressing room. You need to hurry.'

'Done.'

I put on my best zombie-sprint – an awkward contradiction in terms, and painfully slow – and make it across the central aisle of the chamber and through the door without so much as a scratch. On the other side I find a wood-panelled corridor, lined with dozens of portraits of old prime ministers. *Fifth on the right. Gotcha.* But there's Hamilton, fifty feet ahead of me. Something in the way he's rolling his shoulders makes me think this won't be a happy father–daughter chat. A deep, throbbing anxiety pulses through my veins.

Then I hear the pony-clop of heels coming round the corner behind me and I dodge through the nearest door as fast as I can. 'Sir!' comes Smee's voice, and her footsteps hurry past. 'Would you mind joining me in here, sir.'

At the sound of a door shutting to, I sidle out into the

now-empty corridor and flit past the oily gazes of Hecate Horrocks, Tony Blair, Margaret Thatcher, and various other premiers I don't recognize.

'I need to speak to my daughter. What is it?' I hear Hamilton bark.

'Of course sir, very sorry, this couldn't wait,' I hear Smee saying, through a door on the left. 'I have to ask you to log back in immediately. Something appears to be interrupting the Mig chain of command—'

'Denis!' I yell inwardly. 'They're onto you.'

'So you might think, sir, but Sally Smec is responding to an alert I placed in the system. A little double bluff. They will be busy for a moment or two establishing that the alert is an error, and then for another few moments establishing that the Migs' communications have indeed been scrambled.'

'Denis, you're a star. I'm going in.'

I barrel onward to the fifth door on the right and turn the time-worn handle very slowly. The door opens as if I'm a character in a slow-motion movie.

And sure enough, there inside sits Rosie Rogers, in a humble old wooden chair, in front of a mirror surrounded by a bright arc of lightbulbs. She holds a shaking hand to her mouth, gnawing at her nails. Her other hand is on the table, clenching into a ball then opening, like she's a Fury flexing her claws. She mutters inaudibly through clenched teeth tugging the jag of a fingernail; she's like a woman possessed.

Is she in Perspecta? I wonder. *Or talking to herself?* Then I see a small black object on the dressing-room table next to her open handbag. She's not wearing her Plug.

Suddenly Rosie pitches her voice like she's five years old. 'Of course, Daddy. Anything for you, Daddy. Whatever you say, Daddy.' And then she's snarling low, 'Daddy, one of these days I swear—'

The door hinge creaks and she turns, her face morphing with quicksilver speed into a look of delight as she does so.

It's like the sun rising for the first time. No holo-pop smile could have prepared me for this, the real thing. Her irises are the colour of washed-out denim jeans; flecked as if with entire galaxies of stars.

'Hi!' I say, brightly. Then, in my head, *Really, 'Hi'? God you're so lame.*

'Hello,' she replies, and I feel a rush like I've never felt before, somewhere close to ecstasy. She said hello to me!

'I thought—' She pauses, the paranoid anger that was on her face a moment ago flashing again for a second in her eyes, 'I thought you were my father.'

My bubble bursts and my cheeks flush. Suddenly I feel like the intruder I am. The delight wasn't meant for me, and it was fake anyway.

'How can I— Who are you?' There's an accusatory note, though she doesn't seem scared so much as confused.

'Well, I'm . . .' Then it hits me. For the first time I realize that, although I've seen her face every time I'm out on scav, and I dream about her every night, and I feel like we've known each other all our lives, Rosie Rogers has never thought of me once before now. I've never existed to her.

'I'm Kid. Your friend.'

'No, I don't think we've met before,' she says, suddenly assertive. 'I'm so sorry, I think you need to leave.'

A shout from Denis breaks my attention. 'Thirty seconds, sir! You need to leave *now*!'

'No. Please no. Stall him, please.'

'I'm afraid that's not possible, sir. You must leave now or face—'

Desperately, I summon up the memory of everything Rosie said out there on the podium. Looking her full in the face I say, without premeditation, 'Come with me. Come with me, now!'

She looks uncomprehendingly back at me. 'As I said, I think you need to go back to your Podd. The meeting is over and this room is private.'

I look down at my Specta suit in frantic despair. 'No, no,' I scrabble around for the words, trying to explain the inexplicable, 'you don't understand, I'm not a Specta, I'm not like them, I'm from the Cell – the Circus. I'm Kid, I'm an Offliner and we haven't got any time. You're not safe. None of this is good, none of it's real – your father, his plans. Perspecta. I'll explain later, but . . . just . . . just come with . . .' I reach out a hand.

Rosie says nothing, neither flinching away nor taking my hand, but gazing at me still with that curious and wary look, like a cat cornered by something it doesn't recognize. From what she's said in the chamber, she should understand what's at stake here – understand that this is the moment to act. But then the reality dawns on me. *She's not going to understand, is she? There's no way she can. She lives in a different world, for Christ's sake! The Offliners are just an abstraction to—*

'Sir,' Denis says very quietly in my ear, 'you've left it too late. I'm so very sorry, sir.'

'What, why—' I reply, confused.

Another voice cuts in. 'Rosie, we need to—'

Hamilton Rogers bursts through the door and looks straight at me. I look at him. We hold each other's stares for what feels like an eternity and, for the first time in my life, I know what it feels like to look death square in the face.

CHAPTER 46

I'M SORRY

DATE: Sunday 2nd May, 2021

I'm sorry a fortnight has gone by and I haven't written anything. I've been, I'm just, it's . . . stupid. Saying sorry to you is stupid. I mean, what can you possibly do for me? How can you possibly care what's written in you – all my secrets and thoughts and feelings – when all you are is a collection of pieces of paper, bound together? Some blank, some filled in, but all useless in the end.

If it's any consolation I haven't written to Kid on Insta either. Well, I tried a few times when I really needed a shoulder to cry on, but no answer. At first I was like WTF!? Now I'm just tired of it. I wouldn't answer even if he called me. Maybe.

I started writing in you, little book, because Nana told me Oscar Wilde once said: 'I never travel without my diary. One should always have something sensational to read on the train.' I started keeping a diary because I wanted future me to read that I had been a Somebody, had adventures, been kick-ass, done cool shit. I wanted to tell you, dear diary, all these amazing stories that you, in turn, would tell back to me, fifty years from now. Tell back to my own family, my children . . . But, well, the thing is, when I began this I thought I was doing YOU a favour, as stupid as that may sound. I felt it was like some kind of massive privilege for you – my audience of one – to be privy to the amazing-but-not-really-day-to-day-adventures-of-Izzy-from-Kentish-Town! Because if I hadn't seen it that way, I probably would never have written anything down at all! I mean I don't need to tell you this, you know it all too well, better than most, but I think I can be pretty self-centered at times, or have been, was, could be. Before . . . now.

Back then I felt I was doing you a favour, but now I realise it was actually the reverse. I now know that the honour and privilege is completely and totally mine. The pages, the clean, fresh, white space in which you allow me to keep my secrets, are yours. The time I spend boring you with the doldrums of my day-to-day, yours. It's your selflessness and loyalty and patience that has kept me going these past three months. You know everything – all the stuff that goes on in my head, stupid, not stupid, big, small, whatever – and you never, ever judge me and you never tell me I'm stupid or I can't or I shouldn't or I should or I won't or I don't. And you love me, you must love me, you have to because you've never let me down, ever, not once, and please, please, please, please, please, please, PLEASE NEVER LET ME DOWN OR LEAVE ME!!!!!

Because now, here with me, not some guy in the far flung future but here, in my room, in my hand, you're the only one left.

You know, when you're young —

(It's funny. A minute ago when I was saying 'you' I meant you, my diary, but now when I say 'you' I mean . . . me. I mean everyone except you. Yes, I do actually realise you've never been through these things and never will, and you can't actually know what I'm on about.)

Anyway, when you're young – sixteen, seventeen, eighteen, I dunno – and you start going out with someone, it's very easy to kid yourself, in an amazingly short space of time, that this person is going to be your one and only, your forever. When you're lying in bed with each other – maybe it's the first month, usually it's a few months down the line – and he says to you in that soft, assured voice, 'I think I love you Izzy', it's the sweetest, strangest, warmest feeling you'll ever have. I mean, obviously Mum and Dad say it to me, and Nana, and various uncles, aunts and friends have said the words 'I love you Izzy' over the years, but it never sounds anything like how it sounds when it comes out of his mouth. It's almost like they're not speaking in the same language, like they're saying something completely different.

In my case it was the first time, but I imagine it's the same feeling every time it happens. Until you realise, that is, that nothing lasts forever and, more importantly, that at this age those three words – 'I. Love. You.' – are as cheap and disposable as condoms.

Condoms . . . that's ironic.

I honestly thought Stephen was going to be my forever. He was – whether or not I admitted it before – my world. We did everything together, we shared our whole lives. I became him and he became me. By the end we were – as stupid and corny as it sounds – the same person. It's the little things that make it different, it's the names you call each other and the looks you give each other and the silly baby voice you put on when he's around. It's all THOSE things that give those words – 'I. Love. You.' – meaning. When it's just you and him, when you're lying next to each other and no one, ever, in the history of the world has felt like you are feeling right then and there, or has said what you just said right then, or has been held like he's holding you in that moment. But . . .

What you don't realise until it's all gone and you're sitting looking at your whole relationship in front of your eyes – the cute pictures on Insta you put up to show everyone how in love you were, the texts going back years on your phone, the sexy photos you sent him, the teddy bear he sent you on Valentine's, the cinema tickets and Polaroids up on your wall and the jumper that smells of his deodorant – is that none of it meant anything. None of it's original. They did it all before on Gossip Girl. It's happened to every girl in your class. To every boy. Look at Normal People!!! Look at Connell and Marianne! EVERYBODY'S DONE IT BEFORE AND IT ISN'T SPECIAL AND IT ISN'T NEW.

AND IT ISN'T TRUE LOVE. Nothing – however much it might feel like it in the moment – is forever. Not at sixteen. Not now. Not ever. When things really get real and it's the moment of truth and the bond you share is about to be tested to its limits, it all, inevitably, falls apart. It all goes to shit.

You know that thing you do when you're in a relation-ship and you superimpose onto your boyfriend loads of the stuff you really want in him or her? You know that thing? You do it so well and you get so good at ignoring the bad things and you've gone so far down the road to fooling yourself that there's really no turning back . . . That thing? Well I did that with Stephen. He WAS sweet, yes. He WAS kind to me. But now that I look back on it all, he wasn't really everything I thought he was. He wasn't the deep, emotional soul I painted him to be. That was what I covered him in. Beneath it he was a kind person, who didn't see the world like I did, who was always going to move on from our relationship as fast as he got into it.

'Izzy. Hi,' he said, when he answered the phone. It was last Thursday, when it rained all day without stopping. One of those days when no one can do anything, go anywhere, see anyone. Like one of those endless lockdown days. I had to call, I couldn't bear being trapped any longer.

'Er. How are you?' he said.

'I have to tell you something.' I cut to the chase, knowing that small talk was going to be impossible because he isn't capable and I couldn't deal with the burden of not telling him any longer.

'Ok . . .' he said. Awkward. 'What's up?'

When he said that I wanted to scream. I wanted to say: What's up?! WHAT'S UP?! FFS! Grow up! That's WHAT'S UP!

Instead I just told him, simply and honestly because there's no other way you can.

'I'm pregnant. I took a test a week ago, it came up positive. I've been to the doctor. I'm, it's six weeks, I can get rid of it. It's . . . fine.'

I don't know why, but I felt like I had to reassure him, like he was the one that was pregnant, like he was the one whose entire world had crashed into itself and in an instant, in the most terrifying way possible, been torn down.

He stayed silent, so I carried on. 'Sorry I didn't tell you. I just didn't really know how.' I couldn't deal with dragging it out any longer than that.

Even more silence and then, then there they were, those two words, the perfect storm in a couplet.

'I'm sorry,' he said. And then fell silent once more.

I wasn't hurt or angry or sad or even disappointed. I was shocked. It winded me. So I just hung up the phone.

He didn't call me back and I haven't tried to call him and, even though I feel lonelier and more lost and definitely more terrified than I've ever been in my entire life, somehow things in my head are clearer than they ever have been before. Though we haven't like broken up or anything, and he hasn't said either way whether he'd like to have a child or not, Stephen is gone. Stephen has made up his mind and his actions are screaming much louder than any words ever could.

Which, however sad, is a fact, an empirical certainty, like I am a girl and I have a baby growing inside me. I need certainties now. I have had so few – I've been sure of so little – that I have to cling on to the smallest possible fact, even if it hurts me.

I don't need him. I don't want him. What his emphatic, useless apology told me was that the real Stephen isn't the one I'd created in my head.

Besides, the worry of no Stephen pales in comparison with the worry of Mum and Dad.

I stopped being scared of my dad's bad temper when I became a teenager. But their views terrify me. They don't believe in abortion under any circumstances. It'll be: 'No, no, you'll have the child, Izzy. Quietly and disgracefully, where no-one can see you.' They wouldn't be able to have me live with them any more. They wouldn't want me there any more at all. No WAY.

The Christmas before last – the Christmas when Nana gave me this diary – Dad watched that film Philomena, you know the one with Judi Dench? Well, when she's sent to the convent and the nuns take her baby and put him up for adoption, my dad, Mr. Nick Parry, a teacher at a North London comprehensive school, said, 'It's probably for the best, best for her and the baby, now she can try and live a good life and forget it ever happened. Him too, the little boy.'

I. Shit. You. Not.

Needless to say dad's reaction at the end of the film when, fifty years later, mother and child are reunited, with Steve Coogan standing goofily by, was not a joyous one. TBH I think he switched the film on by accident because he thought it was a musical.

Yes, I know it's 2021. But now you understand why I'm not telling my parents I've got pregnant aged sixteen. They wouldn't accept it on the grounds of their religion. Their beliefs have always just been my normal – my breakfast, lunch and dinnertime. But now, writing it down, it seems like such an ugly truth, so damning a revelation about who they are, where I come from, that it makes me want to be sick. TBH, it makes me not want to be their daughter.

I couldn't go to relatives either, because most of them are either devout too or wouldn't want to fall out with Mum and Dad over me anyway. I'd have to try my friends . . . but it's not like they're old enough to have their own places with spare rooms where they'd want a mother and baby. Maybe no-one would have me. Oh yes, I guess there's always my new friend from Planet Perspecta. Like he could whisk me off into futureworld through his magic phone. Which apparently is permanently switched off now anyway.

That's what I'm talking about when I say I feel clearer than I've ever felt. Because now, really, I have nobody. Nobody except you, my most loyal friend, my Londoner's Diary. I may be pregnant and lost and scared and lonely, but I have you, and with every word I write down on your pages, things get that little bit clearer, that little bit less dark.

DATE: *Thursday 13th May, 2021*

Tomorrow this will all be ancient history.

I'm booked in, eleven o'clock at the clinic. Gonna take the day off school, sick, stay in bed, watch Netflix. I'm taking the pills. One really heavy flow – the nurse said that it shouldn't be anything much worse than that – and it'll all be forgotten.

No future. Not for this little baby. I'm sorry.

To: Isabel Parry
From: Sylvia Sterton
Date: 13 May 2021, 10:01PM
Subject: Re: Interview for Gnosys Internship

Dear Isabel,

I hope this finds you well.

Once again, thank you so much for applying for our internship. As I said last week in my response to your CV and cover letter, we would love to interview you for the position. Because we haven't heard from you, I'm just following up to see whether you are still all good to come to Christ Church College, Oxford at midday tomorrow, when we will be interviewing applicants.

Please do let me know that you are still planning to come.

If you have any problems, please don't hesitate to get in touch.

Looking forward to meeting you,

Sylvia

To: Sylvia Sterton
From: Isabel Parry
Date: 13 May 2021, 10:42PM
Subject: Re: Interview for Gnosys Internship

Dear Sylvia,

I am really sorry I didn't respond to your e-mail inviting me to interview for the internship position. It was really kind of you and I really appreciate it. It's just that this week has been really hard, for personal reasons, and I haven't been able to concentrate on anything else. And I'm afraid that tomorrow I now have an appointment in London at 11 and so I won't be able to come to Oxford for the interview. I am really grateful and flattered that you asked me.

Best wishes,

Izzy

To: Isabel Parry
From: Sylvia Sterton

Date: 13 May 2021, 11:30PM

Subject: Re: Interview for Gnosys Internship

Dear Izzy,

I'm so sorry to hear that. I hope everything's OK?

It's a great shame about tomorrow, as James and I thought your CV was excellent. I especially loved your essay idea that particle physics might one day allow two-way communication between different points in time. I'm very sorry not to have the opportunity to ask you the question that bugs me: If it was possible, wouldn't we have heard from the future by now?

As for the 'Body/Somebody' distinction in your cover letter to us, there is no question in my mind that you are one hell of a Somebody! I wouldn't say this before an interview, but I suppose there's no harm in it now.

Good luck. You will go far!

Sylvia x

DATE: Friday 14th May, 2021

I have moved my appointment at the clinic to Monday. I've been going over and over this in my mind. How can I possibly rationalize putting off having this abortion? And I've

come up with two reasons.
- Three days isn't going to make a difference.
- I refuse to let what's happening right now define my future. Or (if Kid's got it right) the future of the world.

GOTTA RUN! SKIPPED SCHOOL! CATCHING THE TRAIN TO OXFORD! XXX

CHAPTER 47

THE BEAR

Friday 14th May, 2021 (LATER)

It all began at Paddington Station – the 10:18 to Oxford – with a Starbucks and a copy of New Scientist. By a stroke of luck the cover article was all about the future of virtual reality, so I actually had a chance of getting my mind focused on what I was going to be interviewed about. (Obvi had Cosmo in my bag too in case I needed a breather.) Rather than my usual mocha-caramel latte, I'd got myself a BLACK

AMERICANO. I know, right – how grown up am I? It tasted disgusting. Actually WTF is it with coffee? What can people possibly see in this poo-coloured drink that tastes like tree bark?!

All that was me trying to feel positive after what's happened over the past three weeks, and with the clinic still to come. The thought of that, and the fact that I'm pregnant, never left me for a second. But Sylvia's final email last night helped massively. It landed almost as soon as I'd written to tell her I would be there after all. She seemed so lovely, so open and kind-hearted, so keen. It was the kindest, most encouraging email I think I've ever received. She seemed genuinely excited I was coming. I don't know how many other people applied for the internship, but I've definitely never felt so wanted in my life.

And this morning the journey helped too. A constant anxious hum was always at the back of my mind. But the train took me out of myself like taking me out of a tunnel. I've never been to Oxford before and the scenery from the train window on the way there was beautiful. Horses running around lush green fields. Little thatched cottages with chimneys puffing perfect, Gandalf-like puffs of smoke. Farmers herding sheep. Deep, green woods thick with beautiful old oak trees. I absolutely LOVE the countryside. I wasn't even in it – I was just on a train going through it – and yet it made me feel so free. Looking at it, I have absolutely no idea why anyone lives in the city . . . Also, I looked up house prices in the country compared to the city and it's so much cheaper to live in the countryside: it's absolutely mental. I thought, what a weirdo am I, like I'm suddenly making grown-up plans. And I looked at myself reflected in the train window, and I realised I'd made a decision. Seriously, you should see my Insta Story today, it's like a homage to the countryside. Everyone's gonna think I've moved house . . .

So the train arrived. Oxford was a slow burner. Turns out it's a bit like an onion. An off onion – gross on the outside and better and better as you peel away the layers. The town is kind of shitty on the outside (where the train station is) and then, very gradually, it gets more and more and more and MORE beautiful until you get to the centre, where the university is.

It's like, I dunno, like a magical, medieval megalopolis, perfectly preserved, with churches and libraries and grand halls and colleges and green 'quadrangles' ('quad', my first bit of Oxford lingo) and parks and turrets and tiny, secret passageways that lead to little old oak doors and vaulted archways. One more time? OK, if you insist: Oxford is completely magical. I was so transported that, walking through it, for a bit I even forgot about the baby growing inside me.

Then, it was the moment of truth, time for my very first job interview. I'd been due to meet Sylvia in a room at Christ Church, her old college. She left like a year or two ago but says former students can still use rooms there. Which would be better because, she said, 'I get way too distracted in cafés! A bit obsessed with cake ;)' But then she called at eleven o'clock to say there had been a cock-up with the registrar or something and the room had been double-booked. So she asked me to meet her at The Bear, a pub. I googled it and turned up a little bit early, so I ordered a lemonade and waited in the back room.

Sylvia Rogers – whoops, I mean Sterton of course! She came bounding through the door, almost hitting her head on the very low, very old doorframe. She's very tall and lanky, and seems to be constantly in motion, with this amazing, other-worldly energy, like a human hurricane. She was wearing a bright red mackintosh, flared purple cords, and this multi-coloured gypsy shirt with sequins and beads and stuff sewn into it. She seemed so awesome – everything about her! Her hair was goldilocks blonde and tied back into a long, thick plait, a bit like the braided loaves of bread you get in proper old bakeries.

'Can I tell you a secret?' she said, plonking a raggedy old canvas duffel bag on a chair. 'Everyone thinks I carry around hundreds of important, leather-bound tomes in this bag. Not a bit of it!' She began actually shaking and snorting with laughter. 'My dinner's in here!' It was as if carrying groceries in her bag instead of books was the most mischievous thing ever.

'I'm Sylvia', she said, and this enormous toothy smile made its way across her face – you could actually see it growing from right to left. 'You're Isabel! Or is it Izzy? You prefer Izzy don't you?' I just nodded – all I could do – hypno-tised. 'Well, Izzy, what are you having?!'

When Sylvia went to get the drinks, the strangest thing happened: I realised that for the first time I hadn't thought once about the pregnancy. It was like she was an antidote to all my anxiety. But when she went off to get two bitter shandies (her suggestion: it was revolting), all the pain and confusion came back like a rush of blood to the head.

Five minutes ago I'd met her, but it was already like I

needed her, her energy, around me all the time. When she spoke to me – just those few words – it was like basking in a ray of perfect sunshine. But when she wasn't there, it was like sitting in the corner of a dark damp room whose windows are all smashed in, the wind howling through. I'd never experienced anything like it in my life. I don't believe in fate. But the way I've been feeling lately, the way things have gone, with all the confusion and pain, meeting Sylvia felt as close as I have ever come to, I dunno, divine intervention.

And writing now from my bed, having lived today out in full, I can tell you, dear diary, that I seriously believe this was all meant to be.

Sylvia came back into the room, and again I immediately forgot about the baby, she was full of questions like where-did-I-come-from and how-did-I-get-into-science and who-is-your-favourite-scientist.

So I told her about Ada Lovelace and we talked a bit about Ada's idea that no machine could ever actually think for itself. Computers can KNOW HOW to do a billion things, but will they ever UNDERSTAND WHY? We feel filled with something we call consciousness, but computers seem empty in that way. How would we know if AI was truly thinking? Well, obviously Sylvia has read and thought about all this a lot more than I have, but she seemed really engaged by what I was saying. Especially when I said that consciousness might really exist on a quantum level – much more complex than computer-think, which is still basically in ones and twos.

That took us on to my application essay, where I must admit I felt a bit more uncomfortable. I had to argue my case about how quantum-entangled particles could be used to send messages to the past or the future, and a phone could distort time to let people in the future contact people in the past. But at the same time I had to pretend that phoning another time was just a wild theory. I reckoned telling her I'd been chatting with some guy from 2078 would have ended the interview pretty fast.

'It's all just a theory, like all the others,' I remember saying, trying my best to sound lame. 'And anyway, for it to work properly, you'd need the person in the past and the person in the future to be using exactly the same device. Like, the same phone would have to be in two places, two times, at the same time, if that makes any sense. Whatever, it's obviously impossible.'

Sylvia just shook her head and said no, no, it was fascinating and she hadn't been able to stop thinking about it since she read my essay.

But then came the killer question: 'Where did you go to university?'

That was when I began getting a really bad stomach ache and things began going downhill fast. Sylvia had been perhaps the nicest, most open person I had ever met, but when I told her that I hadn't been to university and didn't have a degree, she changed immediately. She started being really cagey, checking her watch all the time and saying that the requirements for the position were very clear on the website. It was almost as if she thought I was punking her, like taking her for a ride and messing her around. I tried not to show it but I was actually pretty upset about that. I asked her how she could possibly have thought I was postgraduate age, given my CV and how I look. She just kept repeating herself about how clear it was on the website and saying that this was really awkward for her and that she had loads to do.

And I could feel it coming. I tried so hard to hold it in but maybe it was Stephen's reaction, or maybe it was travelling all that way only for her to say I had let her down, or maybe I had just put so much hope and expectation on this moment, on her, and . . . well, that's when it happened. I burst into tears, really hysterical tears. I was whimpering through snot and saliva, but I told her flat out: 'I'm pregnant and I can't tell my parents but I don't want to kill a baby and I don't know what to do.'

No. Agreed. Not my finest hour. THANKS, hormones.

But what happened next was just mad. Rather than jumping up in disgust (and knocking herself out on the low-hanging ceiling), Sylvia burst into hysterical tears too. She apologised profusely, telling me how thoughtless she had been and insensitive. She said that her boyfriend, James, who was her business partner, was away on a research trip in Oman and that she had been left all alone to handle everything and was feeling very overwhelmed by it all. She was ashamed to have taken it all out on me.

She seemed to have done too much of a 180 when, a few minutes previously, she had basically said INTERVIEW TERMINATED. She asked so many questions about the pregnancy, about Stephen and my family situation. She said she absolutely understood why I couldn't tell my parents, but also why I now didn't want to get rid of it.

Yes, that's right. I'm going to keep my baby. That's the

big decision I'd made when I'd looked at my reflection on the train up to Oxford.

She seemed to get it all, to get me, my quirks, my weirdness. Once again, I felt like everything was OK, like this throbbing feeling of anxiety I've been having lately wasn't there any more. And she offered me the job right there on the spot. Just like that. Like by magic – almost like my being PREGNANT had something to do with it TBH.

But what about my age, about not having a degree, I asked. Oh, that didn't matter after all. In fact it made me pretty much the exact demographic she was catering for – it's all about helping kids before they even get to university. Anyway, we had connected so thoroughly and so completely that there could be no one else for the job and she was sure we'd be great friends.

She went on to talk a lot about what Gnosys were aiming to do at the moment and what would be required of me during the internship. I would be helping her in her lab, directly, just her and me, cataloguing her research, helping her design the virtual reality interfaces. I mean can you believe it, dear diary?! Cos I can't! I would be directly involved in shaping the Perspecta virtual reality Universe. And, she said, there might be a permanent position at the end of it!

Even more extraordinary, she said that I could stay in Oxford AT HER HOUSE – with her and her boyfriend! – for the duration of the internship! Only if I needed, of course, she said. 'If you don't feel up to the horrid train journey, I mean, you know, because of . . .'

I'd think this was all a bit bizarre coming from any other stranger, but she just seemed so open and genuine.

As she dropped me back off at the station, she said, 'Oh we're going to have such fun! What a summer we have ahead!' I waved goodbye and got on the train, brimming over, grinning from ear to ear, the cat that got the cream! I didn't feel lost any more, not a bit. I didn't feel frightened or small or at sea. She took it all away, with her energy and positivity and optimism. It felt like I suddenly had a guardian angel.

Then, well . . . then I remembered.

I remembered Kid, and why he'd wanted me to make contact with Sylvia in the first place.

I felt nauseous, and it was nothing to do with the baby. After everything that he'd told me about what Sylvia's plans are going to mean for the future. And I'd left her without mentioning so much as a word of what he'd wanted me to.

Though I was sick to the stomach with myself, somehow Kid and all the stuff that's happened between us, the fact that he's changed my life and everything in it . . . it all felt like a distant memory. It's not just because apparently he's not speaking to me. Now that I've met Sylvia, now that I KNOW she hasn't a bad bone in her body, now that I feel like we can do good together – well, to be honest, somehow Kid and the Offliners feel like a fiction to me. Or, if not a fiction, they feel like far away, small figures on a distant horizon. So much so I now have no clear idea of HOW I can possibly help them, I don't know how I can possibly change anything in their world.

Apart from to do the best I can in my new job at Gnosys Virtual. Apart from to change the future for the better and the good and, hopefully, for the child sleeping soundly, safe at last, inside me. Even after sitting on the train and realising I wasn't going to go to that clinic, I still wasn't sure how I could get through this whole pregnancy thing. But now, knowing Sylvia – seeing how she reacted to me, how at ease she was, how unfazed and excited she was for me – I feel like I CAN do it, I can definitely keep it. I'll work it out. I will work it out. WE. Will. Work. It. Out.

CHAPTER 48

IN THE CROSSHAIRS

I feel like I'm about to keel over. Hamilton's mouth is moving and chunks of noise are flying all over the room like buckshot.

'Who the hell is this?' He looks at Rosie as if I'm her fault, then turns his blazing eyes back to me. 'Who the fuck are you? What do you want with my daughter?'

'I—' My mouth opens and shuts uselessly. *Keep your cool,* I tell myself desperately, torn between wanting to run and wanting to stand up to him. *There's a way out of this. There's always a way out.*

To my astonishment, it's Rosie who provides one. 'Daddy, it's no trouble at all. He's harmless. Just wants an autograph. No idea how he got back here. I've told him this a private area, haven't I?' she says, looking at me and inclining her head a little – *haven't I?* – like we are in cahoots. I can't get any words out. My mouth is bone dry. So I just start nodding my head slowly at her and then more quickly in Hamilton's direction. 'And he's promised to leave as soon as he's got it,' Rosie says, both reassuring and authoritative.

Hamilton seems to put his steamroller rage on hold for a few seconds. 'One of your devoted legion of fans is he?' His voice is layered with charm and sarcasm, like oil floating on vinegar. He looks at me, studying me for what feels like an eternity, like a zoologist inspecting a new species of insect he's just caught in a jar. Then, to Rosie: 'Give him what he wants quick and send him on his way. You and I need to have a little chat, my darling.'

I steal a glance at her, no idea whether she'll react to this veiled threat with terror or defiance. Instead, she looks like she's been invited to champagne. 'Course, Daddy. I'll just give him a signature. Then I'm all yours.'

She's showing more self-control than I've ever seen in anyone. *It doesn't make any sense,* I think to myself, my heart about to burst out of my chest. I know she's lying through her teeth and covering up an almighty rage. Yet unlike her father, whose charm always seems carefully studied, Rosie looks and sounds absolutely genuine. *How the hell does she do it?* I wonder.

Trying to warm to the act, I pat the Specta suit's empty pockets and give Rosie a frantic look. Hamilton, like a man completely accustomed to ignoring everyone around him, drums his fingers against the wall and muses aloud, 'Never will understand why there are still people that prefer a name on a scrap of paper to a Perspecta autograph.'

Rosie takes pen and paper from her handbag, quickly writes something.

'Thank goodness you always come so well prepared, sweetheart,' Hamilton snarls with a venomous smile. Unperturbed, Rosie hands me the note.

I gawp wordlessly at the sheet, rich and creamy with pale yellow and blue flowers twining in a top corner.

> *For the kid with no name,*
> *love*
> *Rosie Rogers*

Instead of each *o* in her name, she's drawn little hearts.

'Roses and forget-me-nots,' she says, as if I've just expressed a keen interest in the floral design. Then she stands and injects her voice with a note of briskness. 'Now, I need to speak to my father, so I'll walk you to the gate.'

'No need for that, my dear,' says Hamilton. 'My officers will take him.'

Something in his tone fills me with sudden alarm. *'Take him'? Take me where?*

'Papa, really, don't be so silly,' Rosie chides with every

appearance of fondness. 'I'll go with him. I'll be perfectly fine. It's a labyrinth in here – wouldn't want him wandering into anyone else's dressing room unannounced now, would we?' she says, pitch-perfect.

She starts to get up, but he puts a firm hand on her shoulder and pushes her back into her chair. 'I said, the Migs will deal with him.' His voice is steely.

Abruptly I'm drenched in panic sweat.

'Now!' he barks into the empty air, one hand to the Plug in his ear, the other gripping Rosie's arm like a vice as she tries to wriggle free.

I want to bolt for the door and at the same time I want to tear him away from Rosie. But I'm rooted to the spot. Fear clangs inside my skull like the old bells of Big Ben.

Where the fuck are they? says Hamilton's voice. *If they're not here in thirty seconds I'll have them cleaning up nuclear spills.*

I stare in astonishment. His lips aren't moving.

It's like my fear, my panic, has opened a window into Hamilton Rogers's head.

It's a seething cauldron of venom and darkness. I wouldn't want to live in there. But I'm so amazed by what's happening that I squeeze my eyes shut in the hope that it will help me focus. Images, not words, come slewing out of the swirling dark. Migs hauling prisoners away . . . Iron doors clanging shut . . . Fists bunching around baton handles . . . Switches being flicked . . .

I flinch and open my eyes.

Now Hamilton is staring at me, eyes wide, mouth locked in a snarl of perplexity while his voice spits unfinished thoughts

– What the—? Can he—? – into my head.

With the words come more images. Hamilton in the mirror, sweat beading on his brow. The Commons chamber, viewed from Hamilton's perspective, as he painfully explains the delay in launching Perspecta Three. A test tube. A syringe. A bottle of pills. And finally me in my Specta suit, standing staring back at him right now. *Without a Plug! Who the f—?*

All this has only taken a fraction of a second. It's like time has slowed down. But Rosie, slipping from her father's grasp, surges to her feet and steps my way, frantically waving me towards the door and mouthing *Go! Go!*

Hamilton is after her straight away, yanking her back and striding towards me. But she's given me the impetus I need, and I spin away towards the door.

I lunge towards the carpeted corridor and suddenly my head fills with agonising noise.

Ssssgrkglkgrkglk10011100sssskrgh1101010!

There's a tramp of feet down the corridor from the direction of the Commons chamber, accompanied by a clacking of heels.

Unwillingly, I look left. Black-uniformed figures are marching my way, and with a visceral shock I find myself looking directly into the eyes of Sally Smee, not thirty feet away.

Her eyes open wide.

Shit! She knows me! In my mind's eye, I see her in the door of a Chariot as it lifts off from the Circus where I huddle protectively next to the unconscious Eliza. *It's her!*

'You!' Her shout rifles down the corridor.

Beside Smee, in smooth unison, four Teeth raise their

e-cannons. For an instant I wonder if Rosie is going to step out of the dressing room and stand in their way. But I can hear she's otherwise occupied now, cursing her father as he curses her back.

'Denis!' I yell inwardly. 'Help me, for chrissakes.' Then to myself, *Sod it! If I get shot I get shot.* With a jerk, I start running, screaming something I can't even recognize.

I try not to think about the fatal blast that's coming, but when the hollow chatter of the e-cannons begins, I know it's worse than futile. My legs feel like I'm in some ancient diver's suit, weighed down on the ocean floor by lead boots. My mind is awash with wave after wave of deafening white noise, the incomprehensible interference wail that comes from the Teeth.

Plaster rains from the ceiling. Pitch-black smears and bursts of flame appear on the carpet ahead of me from shots fired just too wide. Forcing my legs to keep pumping I see, fifty paces ahead, the pedestalled bust of some extravagantly bewhiskered grandee crash to the floor. A massive chunk of ceiling thunders down on top of it in a billowing cloud of dust. *Are they trying to bring me down, or trap me?*

'Denis,' I project again, trying to pierce walls with the thought. 'Where the hell are you?'

'Right here, sir!' comes his plummy voice.

'Denis!' If he were in front of me, I could almost hug the stuck-up old—

Instead I flinch and tumble as a gilt-framed portrait leaps from the wall in splinters and flaming scraps of canvas. Somehow I manage to register the face as it crumples. *There goes Boris Johnson.*

'Denis, what do I do?' I whine in desperation, clawing the carpet.

'Right here, sir.'

'Yes, I heard you. I know you're there. But' – I labour the words one by one – 'What. Do. I. Do?'

'My sincerest apologies if I wasn't clear the first time, sir,' comes Denis's voice. 'You must exit the corridor through the next door on your right. Immediately. I am deflecting the Migs' e-cannonfire but I cannot do so forever, sir.'

Like a speeding earthworm I wriggle to the doorway to the right just up ahead as bolts of energy pass above me. They leave the air so hot, I'm sure I can smell my hair being singed. I'm shaking, stunned and terrified.

But then somehow, as if employing some unknown strength, I'm through the archway and pushing myself unsteadily onto my feet.

'Now, sir, if you wouldn't mind,' says Denis's voice, 'please hurry. I am in need of assistance.'

'You want *me* to help *you*, Denis?'

'Sir, yes, please.' I can almost hear his lip quivering. 'Head straight along the passage, up the stairs, through the blue door on the left . . .'

My head whirls.

But just then I feel the wind knocked out of me as something barrels into my ribs. The passage spins in front of my eyes and I crash back to the floor with someone on top of me.

CHAPTER 49

DOWNRIVER

'Gotcha!' A voice is speaking right in my ear. 'Gotcha before the Migs did.' Then the mouth turns away and bellows, 'Vince, Frosty, give 'em something to chew on!'

The sound of shotguns, so close I cover my ears, is followed immediately be a renewed cough of e-cannons.

'Come on Spunky, stir yer stumps! It was a rugby tackle, not a bleedin' wrecking ball!'

A small hand yanks at mine, and I struggle to my feet, just beginning to comprehend.

'J-J-Jem!' I whisper.

'We're getting you out of here, boss.'

Then she barks, 'Pasha, Ziggy, grab old Spunky here while I give the bastards something else to think about.'

'Wait! D-Denis wants me at the d-docking station,' I stammer.

'The talking tinpot?' Jemma laughs. 'Don't worry about him. He's just scared his paintwork's gonna get scratched. Got in an almighty flap about us climbing on board. All we was doin' was ducking from the station Teeth. Ditherin' Den wouldn't have any of it! Wouldn't even let us move his precious Podd. So we had to go a bit pirate on him and moved it anyway! Then he reckoned you could find the Podd where it is now, but I reckoned he'd reckoned wrong. So instead, we came to find you.'

Small figures haul me away. Just before we take the stairs, I turn and glimpse Jemma pulling a fist-sized object from her oversized jacket to hurl it back into the prime ministerial corridor.

'Gotta go, old man,' pipes one of the Terrors, just as an enormous bang momentarily silences the e-cannons.

I'm rapidly herded by six or seven children left, right, up, down, through what looks like a huge kitchen, across some kind of ballroom, and into a stone corridor like something out of the Middle Ages. The small huddle grinds to a halt at a junction. Within seconds, Jemma is running up behind. 'Left, yer pillocks! Left! Jesus, Mary and – can't get the staff these days, can yer?'

We're out through a gothic stonework archway into the harsh, damp night. She shoves a Roxi disp in my mouth.

'Breathe.'

I do, willingly, knowing that if I don't I'll start coughing up black blood. The Roxi rush hits fast. It galvanizes me and suddenly I'm fully conscious.

I look around. We're on the other side of the Houses of Parliament, the side I haven't seen before – the old House of Commons terrace, where MPs used to swap chat and chicanery at open-air tables overlooking the River Thames. Now there is no river view; just a giant steel wall rising into the smog. A section of the Toaster, the enormous flood defence system installed before the Upload, before I was born. I've never seen it so close before; it looks impossibly high.

Heaving for breath, I suddenly think of Rosie and her father unleashing their mutual fury on each other; Hamilton yanking her; the Teeth letting rip.

Shit, shit, Rosie . . .

'Wait!' I push myself up further to look around. 'Rosie! We need to go back for—'

But Jemma interrupts me.

'No time for that, Spunky,' she says, and gives me a shove along the terrace.

There sit two Podds. One is mine. The other has sharks' fins and a big cartoonish decal of grinning sharks' teeth.

'Nice, innit? There it was at the station, all shiny and cool. Couldn't resist. I mean c'mon, no Specta deserves a flying shark.'

Jemma pushes me into my Podd just as I hear the

bloodcurdling crackling of cannon fire, like the sound of cancerous giants coughing their last.

'Sir! At last you're back!'

Denis is standing there as dapper as his look of sheer desperation will allow.

'Bernard, sir! Bernard isn't talking to me. First they broke in. Then they spilled champagne on his carpet, sir, and left chocolate stains all over his upholstery. And then—'

Jemma and a few of her boys are piling in around us as we speak. Not only do they ignore Denis completely, they actually walk right through him as if he wasn't there.

'Pump us up, Ponzo,' Jemma barks at a scrawny boy in the driver's seat, his acne-scarred face scrunched in concentration.

Ponzo the Terror, I realize. *Manually controlling the Podd?*

'And then,' wails Denis, 'as you can see, sir, they took control of the Podd, sir. I told them we couldn't leave the docking station without the correct protocols being in place, or without your Legend command. But this young tearaway here simply announced he had "hotwired" the vehicle, sir. Bernard – oh poor Bernard – was relying on me, and I failed him. And now the Migbots are going to come for us both.'

'Hit it, Ponzo,' shouts Jemma. Her expression suggests she can hear Denis's whining but regards it as an irrelevant distraction.

'Aye, aye, captain!' whoops Ponzo.

The doors slam shut and the jets throw us upward into the darkness with rocket-like force. The flying shark lurches after us, fast but wildly off-kilter. The cannon-fire blares on and our Podd jolts us to the right, then to the left, then shoots forward like a missile.

'Oh sir, they're doing it again!'

'Denis, I'm not blind.'

'But the Migbots, sir!'

'Migbots, Denis?'

The Podd drops alarmingly, leaving my insides to plummet after it a second later. Denis lets out such a high-pitched whoop of nauseous terror that I wonder whether he is programmed with a virtual stomach.

'H-how are you driving this thing?' I ask Jemma feebly, trying not to heave.

'Whatcha think Ivan was teachin' us all those years before he died? I'll give yer a clue: it wasn't knitting. Knew how to fly anything, he did. So whilst old wass-his-face, Mr Gnosys, was keepin' yer entertained with his chinwag in the old House of Commonzo, me and the boys was out here makin' ourselves useful, innit! Tinker here, a tinker there, and we managed to rip this hunk o' junk out of the main-frame! We're flying solo, boyo!'

And with that, before I can say anything further, the Podd's walls and ceiling de-mist, leaving the entire upper shell of the vehicle transparent. For a moment I can see only London's smoggy darkness. But then comes a dramatic splash of light – cannon-fire bursting somewhere too close for comfort. Another Podd glides in front of us, and then the flying shark is alongside – a squadron flying in level, if shaky, formation.

'Are they both . . . ?' I begin.

'With us?' Jemma finishes for me. 'Certainly are – them's our Spitfires,' she says gleefully.

With a moment to breathe, I turn back to my Perspecta Companion, who looks white as a sheet. 'Migbots, Denis? You were saying.'

'Gnosys security, sir, but operating in the Perspecta Universe rather than the physical one. The Migbots will come for us. Bernard and I are agreed on this point, sir. They will come for us and rip our code to shreds. They will scramble me up and leave me a useless, redundant, idiotic Level 80 Companion.'

I don't ask. I know Denis will deliver.

'The lowest level in the Universe, sir,' he sniffles. 'Entry-level.'

Our Podd banks sharply without warning and I cling to the edge of my stretcher. Another flash like lightning reveals not the sky but the Thames. The river is less than fifteen metres below us, so close that I feel as if one of its grey, foam-flecked waves could pluck us from the air. Nausea grips me. So does astonishment. I've seen so many old photos and films of the Thames, glimmering and stately as it pumped through the heart of the capital in the Dusk and before. Now all I see is an angry, churning mass. In the strobing light of laser blasts, it smashes and spurts against the colossal flood defences, making them look petty and diminutive. *This river must be thirty metres deep these days!* Another swerve, a huge explosion to our right, and I glimpse a dismal vista on the south side of the river: factories and tower blocks, terrace houses and train stations, all ruinous and forlorn in a land-scape of a thousand standing pools. *So much for the Toaster,*

I think. Now I understand why they say the Coldharbour Offliners go scavving in boats.

'Bernard,' sniffles Denis, 'will be lucky if he's repurposed for a golf cart – there are so few of those these days – but he's truly afraid he'll end up in Potman's human waste removal.'

Krrrrrrrhouaouh! Krrrrrrrhouaouh! Blindsided by cannon fire, our Podd is thrown violently off course.

I look behind and am horrified to see two giant Chariots closing in on us, flying low above the river.

'Watch out!' Jemma screams at Ponzo. Denis has vanished into the console, where I can hear him faintly whimpering.

Ponzo thrusts the controls forward just in time and the Podd somersaults over Waterloo Bridge, narrowly avoiding a collision. 'Keep yer bloody eyes peeled, yer plonker!'

Suddenly there's an enormous explosion behind us. It looks as if one of the Chariots has been led underneath the bridge by the flying shark. Smaller, daintier, the shark flits like a firefly narrowly past one of the supporting piers, but the Chariot is too big and crashes with an almighty burst of flame into the huge, derelict structure. The other Chariot pulls up and slows almost to a stop to avoid the same fate.

'Damn right!' Jemma whoops. 'You don't mess with the Terrors!'

She points to the third Podd ahead of us as it swoops upward, its lights briefly illuminating the flood defence wall, and then dives down over the other side, presumably on its way to the Ghetto. 'And it looks like the scumbags have given up the ghost.'

Our own Podd slews violently to the left and I'm hurled

against my seat restraints. The river vanishes, replaced by sheer walls full of broken windows, racing past at a colossal rate. Again the Podd banks sharply, careers along a dark funnel of half-derelict old buildings, and swoops over a wall of massed red buses.

'Landing in ten seconds,' Jemma shouts from the front of the cockpit. 'Looks like we're comin' in hot. Get ready to jump, people!'

A smooth, swift turn, a few seconds hovering, and then a rapid descent. There's a clash of metal, a screech from Denis, and an almighty clattering before we come juddering to a halt. I sit still for a few seconds wondering why I can't see, then slowly pry my fingers away from my eyes. We're down on the floor of the Circus, and so, it appears, is the statue of Anteros.

CHAPTER 50

CURFEW

'Lights out!' Yottam announces gaily the following evening, prancing up and down the corridor like an excited pony galloping around its paddock. Tonight's the first night of 'elder rounds', a new duty given to the COOs by Ruth as part of a strict curfew. It's resented by the youngers, and no doubt the COOs don't much like it either, but Yottam is taking it in his stride.

I'm not. For a start, I'm annoyed our 'tireless' Cell doctor isn't down in the San watching over Eliza. I know she's much better now but she's still not back in her own dorm.

I'm also tired and spent and frustrated after three hours in the Office of Identity being interrogated by the Chief, who is beyond furious with me for leaving Soho without asking. And now, every night of the week, one of the COOs will actually put us to bed, then check up on us periodically throughout the evening, as if we were little school children at a boarding school. Needless to say the new system stinks. And it's largely – sorry, entirely – my fault because I went on my little jaunt to Westminster.

'You know the rules, people,' continues Yottam in his unshakably positive way, as if he enjoys his new pastoral role. 'Lights out means lights out.'

I hear some hecklers shout out at him as he passes by, turning the lights off in their dorms one by one.

'I'm seventeen years old, Yottam. I don't have a bed time!' says one.

'I'm *eighteen*! Turn the light back on!' says another.

'You suck!' says a third, just as the doctor sticks his head around the doorway into my dorm smiling a broad smile. *Not really what I want to see, man,* I think to myself, scowling petulantly at Yottam from above the book I'm reading in bed. *Kind of busy.*

'Now, now, don't blame me, folks!' he shouts back down the corridor. 'I'm under strict instruction, just doing the boss's bidding!'

Then comes the cherry on the cake.

'You've only got Mr Jones to thank for this!' chimes

Yottam, like a standup delivering the punchline. With that, he sticks his tongue out like a stupid, annoying, mischievous child and yanks the cord, plunging the dorm into darkness. Even as I wince, I have a nasty feeling I'm going to have to get used to this. Yottam loves a running gag. I just know that every night he's on duty I'll be lying here silently mouthing the word *Please* and thinking: *Don't do it. Nobody needs reminding, dude.*

'Go to bed kids,' he yells. 'Lights out means the lights *stay* off. Doesn't mean turn them off, wait for Yottam to leave, then five minutes later get found sneaking through the Ticket on your way to the Circus to gawp at the statue Mr Jones knocked off its perch! It means go to sleep.' His voice trails off in a high-pitched chuckle as he leaves the now-silent corridor.

I don't sleep a wink that night, and things don't exactly go pleasantly for me after the Houses of Parliament night. That kind of inane banter is just the tip of the iceberg. I receive a fair amount of flack from pretty much everyone for inadvertently landing them in it too. I guess I deserve it. If life wasn't shitty enough for the youngers in the Cell before I stirred things up, now our every move is monitored. What little freedom we had to go up above and explore is almost totally gone.

'What I don't get,' Eliza barks at me from her own bed in her own dorm, 'is why you felt the need to tell Ruth you *left* the Ghetto? Could easily have just said you were out seeing Lucien or scavving or, I dunno . . . You didn't have to tell her *everything*!'

'Hold on – wait a second, I'm really sorry – I'm not totally sure what your point is,' I say. 'Are you saying I could have kept this to myself, even though there's a Podd out there with Anteros sprawled on the ground next to it? Or are you saying I should have kept all this to myself? You don't think the fact that Gnosys is planning to wipe us out is something the COOs might want to know about?'

I can't keep the sarcasm out of my voice. I'm not proud of it; she's still recovering and it's only been a month since her beating by the Teeth. Eliza is propped up on her pillows with a steaming cup of Ursula's ring-necked parakeet broth beside her. Everything should be hunky-dory. Yet instead she's belatedly joined in the chorus of condemnation and here I am, having to go over what she's missed – the whole Westminster trip and its consequences – and win her round.

'Obviously they need to know!' Eliza replies. 'All I'm saying is you could have told them you'd heard it from someone in the Circus or that you'd got some intel, or—'

'Intel?' I cut her off, confused as to how my best friend could be so unsupportive. 'Intel?! Suzannah hasn't provided anyone with any useful intelligence on Gnosys or anything else outside this Cell since she first took office! And where else would I have got my intel here?'

'Clearly I'm not talking about Suzannah.' She pauses for breath – she still gets worn out far too quickly – then adds, 'You didn't need to drag us all down with you so everyone has to be tucked up in bed like babies. That's all I'm saying, Kid.' She is seething with frustration at the nightly curfew and blanket ban on all youngers leaving the Cell.

'Wow.' I have to take a beat to breathe, such is my

shock. 'You're the last person I expect to hear that kind of shit from. I don't have to justify this to you, or to anyone in this Cell. I did what I did because if I had stayed quiet I'd never have been able to live with myself. And for what – just so I wouldn't get in trouble; just so we can all keep going out into the Ghetto on jolly little scavving expeditions? No! Things have changed, Eliza, this is real. They are coming for us. And you, of all people, should understand what that means.'

In the uncomfortable silence that follows, Eliza just stares at me. It hurts like hell that she is turning her fury on me. *What happened to the old Eliza?* I wonder. *The comrade, the fighter, the leader, the friend?*

Pas has remained characteristically silent, but now he asks quietly, 'What's going on with you?'

'What?' I turn to him. 'What's that supposed to mean?'

'All the secrets and the sneaking around and stuff. Just feels like something's up with you, that's all,' he says with his classic brand of irritating calm collectedness.

'Are you guys for real right now?' I say, groaning inwardly to find myself fighting on two fronts. 'Is this some big joke? Are you about to jump up in the air and say "No worries man, we're just messing"? 'Cause if you are, let me know and I'll leave you to it. I really don't need—'

'Eliza isn't going to be leaping up in the air for a while, Kid,' Pas interrupts, with something like a growl deep in his chest. I feel my cheeks flush, like I've been caught stealing from her.

'What's Legend, man?' Something about the way Pas says it, so direct and to the point, shows he isn't going to drop it until he gets an answer. 'I hear you shouting about it every night in your sleep, shouting and crying. At first I just figured it was one of your strange fantasies about the Dusk or something. But with all the other weird shit happening, I don't know. Yeah, we all hate Gnosys, but actually sneaking out to the Ghetto to go to one of their shareholders' meetings? Come on man . . . what's up? I've known you since you were four, and I can tell things ain't right. What's going on?'

My head is pounding now. Though Pas sounds calm, I feel like he's trying to beat down the door with his questions. I just want it all to go away. I wish I could get a bit of support from my inner voice – something, anything – but I haven't heard a word from it since getting out of Westminster a week ago. I wish I could see Leo.

'I can't tell you,' I say finally. 'You'd never understand.'

I look at him long and hard, then at Eliza, who is eyeing me with steely eyes, her mouth a flat line. We just stare, the three of us, like we were in some kind of standoff, none of us seemingly willing to crack. But after what feels like an hour of silence, Pas says, 'Sod this. I'm going to sleep. Might as well, before I get sent off to bed anyway.' He gets up and walks out without looking back at either of us.

I look at Eliza. Suddenly she no longer seems angry, only disappointed, which is even worse. 'Please,' I say quietly. I don't have the energy left to raise my voice. 'Please don't make it out like this is all on me and I'm bringing you down with me. You may've forgotten in all your righteous anger, but it wasn't so long ago you were standing up in the Ticket begging people to fight the good fight against the bad guys. This is on you as much as it's on me. Own it, and stop shifting the blame.'

'There's no blame, Kid. We're not angry you went to the shareholders' meeting. That's not the point. All we're asking is why, and what it all has to do with these nightmares you're having. We're your best friends. We'd do anything for you.' Then her voice turns bitter. 'He gave you the chance to explain, and you didn't. Why would you be like that? He's never been in this fight like you and me. If you're going to bring us with you it's—'

'I don't want to go blowing my own trumpet here or anything,' I snap. I can't help it any longer. It feels like the whole world is turning against me, and for no good reason. 'But have you forgotten who it was that saved your life when you decided to go up above and take on the Teeth all by yourself?'

She looks at me with a sad, lost expression. If she said *That has nothing to do with anything*, she'd be right. I know it doesn't and I know it's pathetic. But she just says, 'Never doubt for a second that I owe you my life. I never do. I will never be able to repay you for what you did for me that night. I'll never ask anything else of you, however much I might want to—'

'That's not what I'm saying, Eliza, I'm not asking you—'

'But this isn't about me, or you, or the choices we've made. It's about Pas – and he doesn't owe you anything. He's only ever been the most loyal, protective, trusting friend you'll ever have, and he's never asked for anything in return. Until now. Now all he's asking for is the truth. You owe him that.'

I'm tired, overwhelmed; but it isn't really that. It's the fact I feel I've let my friends down. She's right, I do owe him the truth; I owe both of them the truth. But after everything, feeling like I'm being attacked from all sides, I don't have the strength to tell them. I don't have the strength to be honest with them about who I really am; I barely have the strength to accept it myself.

Eliza turns over and pulls her pillow over her head. Loneliness like I've never felt before floods over me. First the old familiar voice and now my two best friends – they're all going silent on me. I sit and stare at the wall above her head like I'm hoping it will tell me what to say. But I've run dry. I get up quietly, turn out her light, bend and kiss the back of her head, and leave her to sleep. I know, then and there, I have to tell them everything. I know it, but I don't know how.

CHAPTER 51

THE OFFICE
OF IDENTITY

A few days later – a few dark days during which I speak to no one, keep my head down, and spend as much time as I can in my dorm – Ruth calls me into her office again.

My second visit to the Cell's one and only forbidden chamber is very different to my first. That first time, the morning after the Westminster shareholders' meeting, was such a terrifying whirlwind that though I went deeper than ever into the bowels of the Cell to meet with Ruth, I failed to take in the unearthly majesty of the tangle of tomb-like rooms that includes the Office of Identity. This second visit, I'm all eyes.

The tiny lift – a relic of London Underground days and the closest most Offliners have ever come to a glimpse of the Office of Identity – takes you down from the Ticket. At the bottom is a large, dank, and dimly lit stone hallway. Moss grows on its walls and it smells like a sewer. An iron door stands at the opposite end. I remember hearing from Pokes that, once upon a time, the Office had been a kind of recreation area or officers' mess for the people that worked here when the Cell was a Tube station.

I walk towards the door between walls lined with lighted candles that hiss in the occasional drip from the wet moss. Trying not to think about whatever tirade or cross-examination Ruth has in store for me, I imagine all the engineers and drivers, cleaners and ticket-office workers scurrying about their daily grind, back when things were good. At the door I stop for a moment and take a deep breath, preparing myself. *What's it going to be this time?* I wonder before rapping my knuckles three times on the cold metal. To my surprise, the door is opened not by Ruth, but by Suzannah Key, our reclusive COO of Intelligence.

'Hello,' she says in a whisper. I've never really taken a close look at her. Until Ruth introduced the new system of elder rounds, Suzannah was very rarely seen outside her quarters. She is wearing a green, ankle-length woollen skirt and a white blouse, buttoned all the way up to her throat. Her outfit reminds me of something the last queen might have worn when she was off duty during the Dusk. Suzannah is old, but her skin is soft and smooth, like she has taken care of herself over the years and spent little time in the sun (even when there was any). Her milky eyes dart around the hallway behind me, very rarely if ever making contact with my own, and then only in a clandestine, investigative way – as if she were expecting or hoping for someone else.

'Come quickly,' she continues, and then beckons me with both hands, like a squirrel digging for nuts in the ground. She turns and leads me into the main, circular atrium of the Office, from which all the other rooms are accessed. 'Sit down. Tea there. Biscuits here.' She picks up a silver tray, piled high with digestive biscuits – the plain kind – and scuttles over to me. Her movements remind me of Gollum in *The Lord of The Rings*, which we watched quite recently in Counsel.

'Shhhh.' She puts a thin, curled finger to her lips. 'Stillspeare treats. Not for youngers usually.' She cradles the tray like it's stacked with gold bullion, then stretches out her arm and offers it to me, almost as if I have some kind of disease she doesn't want to catch.

'Shhhhhhhhhh!' She snatches the tray away and replaces it almost as soon as I've taken the biscuit. *Jeeze*, I think, *relax*.

'Back soon. Ruth very keen to talk.' And, with that, she beetles out of the room through one of the eight doors. *Eight doors*, I think to myself. *I'm in the belly of a spider.* I gulp audibly, as I sit in one of the extremely eclectic collection of armchairs in the centre of the room.

The circular room reminds me a little bit of Leo's apartment – the place I've been longing to visit since Westminster, if only I could escape from petty Cell duties or sneak out at night like I did before the curfew. It's a lot shabbier than Skull's, of course, and much less well appointed, but pleasant watercolours adorn the rough concrete walls, and blue velvet curtains hang around every one of the eight doorways. It isn't grand by any stretch of the imagination, but it's clear that, over the years, the Stillspeares have made a big effort to make their waiting room look presentable.

'Now.' Suzannah pops her head back around the door. 'Come. Come, quickly.' But before opening the door completely, she glances behind her into the room I was about to enter, like she's double-checking whether I am to be permitted or not. Turning back to me with a grave expression, she says, 'Enter,' and she opens the door to reveal Ruth sitting in her wheelchair behind her desk.

The office is small, cosy and well lit, and covered in family portraits. The metal desk, more like a butcher's table than a bureau, is covered in stacks of files and papers, fastidiously organized.

'Sit down; we need to talk,' Ruth says brusquely, barely even looking at me. Suzannah retreats into a corner, her eyes still darting about almost preternaturally in their sockets. I sit in the chair opposite the chief and wait to be blasted.

'How are you?' she asks.

'Fine,' I say, tersely. Very obviously she isn't interested in the answer anyway.

'I understand the youngers aren't taking well to the new sanctions imposed as a result of your little escapade—'

'They shouldn't be suffering because of something I did,' I say. *Might as well try one last time to get everyone else off the hook.*

'They're not suffering. They're safe.' She pauses and looks at me properly for the first time. 'And they shouldn't be punishing you for keeping them safe.'

It is the first time anyone has said anything nice to me since the night in question, and to my surprise I suddenly begin feeling a little overwhelmed. The emotion is obviously written all over my face.

'Your friends will come around, Joshua. In time. And as for poor Anteros, we will not be restoring him to his pedestal in the Circus, but we'll be bringing him down into the Cell and I think we may be looking for somewhere else to put him. In connection with which, I've asked Suzannah to join us today. She's received intelligence that relates to the Gnosys event you attended last week, and what Hamilton Rogers said there about what he has in store for us.'

'Intelligence?' I query, my anxiety immediately spiking. 'What kind of intelligence?'

'Suzannah,' Ruth encourages her forward. 'Tell him.'

Suzannah steps forward, quivering. 'Mr Jones knows – he knows we do not discuss our sources,' she stammers, her voice quieter than a mouse. 'But, well, you see, it has come to our attention that there is a, a—' she looks at Ruth nervously, who gently bids her continue, '—a rift, between Rogers and a significant number of Gnosys shareholders.'

'Rosie.' The name tumbles out of my mouth unconsciously.

'What?' Ruth says, raising an eyebrow.

'Nothing.' I look at Suzannah, wishing I hadn't said the name. If there's a rift with Hamilton, it has to be because of what Rosie said at the meeting, but I don't want anyone to see how distracted I get every time I think about her. I drag my thoughts kicking and screaming back to the main issue and ask, 'So, when is Gnosys coming for us?'

'They're not, they're—' Suzannah fumbles for the words. 'They're not coming for us. Not for a few weeks, at least, and it's not decided yet whether they're coming at all. Rosie Rogers's intervention clearly had a big effect. A group of shareholders has refused to put their votes behind her father's plan. They've convened an emergency meeting, at the Institute of Technology – at the, er, House of Commons – next month.'

'A rebellion?' I ask Suzannah. *Rosie inspired a rebellion*, I marvel in my head.

Ruth cuts in. 'We've talked this up and down and round. We'd love to think that it's a serious challenge to Hamilton's power. Far more likely, it's just part of Gnosys internal politics and even if it's not resolved at that vote, it will be sooner or later.'

I'm about to say *I'll go*, or *We should get in there, see what's going on*, but then I glance at Ruth. A look in her eye seems to suggest that she isn't about to encourage me to go and infiltrate another Gnosys event. She has brought me here to tell me all this for another reason.

'Why am I here?' I say. 'Are you going to tell me there's nothing to worry about? Because obviously, there is. Hamilton Rogers is going to win his vote, and even if he doesn't—'

'You're here because I doubted you, and I was wrong. It's obvious from this new information that Gnosys *was* planning to launch an attack on the Cell, which aligns with what you told me the night you left the Ghetto. But—'

'Stop avoiding it, Ruth,' I hit back. 'It means we need to fight. The Cell is just the beginning. They're going to purge the world of anyone, anything, *everything* that's not logged in and dressed in white!'

Suddenly she's furious. 'Listen to me!' she roars, slamming her hands down hard on the table. 'For the last time, we do not fire on others unless fired on ourselves! We are not going to fight, we are not going to attack, and we are not *going to war*!'

She stops and the air in the room settles. Suzannah is cowering, almost curled up in a ball in the corner.

'Then tell me, Ruth. Why the hell am I here?'

'What we are going to do is learn to defend ourselves and – whatever the outcome of this emergency Gnosys meeting – we are going to prepare for the worst. And I need you to help us do that.' She sits back in her chair and sighs, and then I notice her eyes beginning to glow. She wants to smile, though I know she knows she can't, not in front of Suzannah; not in this kind of situation. 'Most of the people in this Cell are either too old to protect themselves or their first priority is as carers. Frankly, half the elders who are strong enough are either pacifists or pessimists. And when it comes to getting off their arses at a time like this, that's nearly as bad as being too old.'

Wow, I think, I *don't think I've ever heard you swear before*. Somehow I find it galvanizing, as if in that moment I see Ruth as a new person with a new attitude. As if finally, somehow, she is on my side. Right now, having anyone on my side feels astounding – but the fact that it's Ruth . . . My confidence comes bounding back so hard and fast, I'm not quite sure I can keep it under control.

Ruth apparently senses as much. 'I've said it before and – at risk of inflating your already oversized ego even further—'

'Hey now,' I deadpan.

'Here's how it is,' she says, ignoring my attempt at humour. 'You, along with your two friends, have spent more time out in the Ghetto than everyone else put together. You've had to deal with real dangers. Plus you're the only people here that the youngers truly respect. You're already old enough to know better, yet you look set to be perpetual teenagers, all three of you. But to them, that's what really scores the points. And,' she smiles, 'there's no separating you. You're already a tight little ball, and I reckon you can roll the others in – the Offliners that are able to fight. I wish Eliza were properly better, but at the very least she can help you plan. I want you and Pascale to marshal all the youngers you can to the cause and get them ready for the worst. If—'

I cock my head and raise an eyebrow at her.

'All right, all right,' she says, knowingly, '*when* Gnosys come knocking again, I want as many of us as possible to be ready to mobilize. I know we can't stand up to them forever, but that's not my intention.' She hands me a cream-coloured folder: *Top Secret: Open Only In The Event Of Unavoidable Evacuation.* 'The youngers need to be ready for us all to escape. They need to be ready to get everything we have – as much as we can take with us – out of the Cell as quickly as possible. That,' she points to the folder, 'was given to me by my father just before he died, along with several other documents that go with it. They took him years to put together, but, unbeknownst to all of us, the old dog managed to come up with a workable plan.'

She says it with a proud smile. 'It's all in there – well, all you need to know at the moment, anyway. If and when things go sour, that's the first stage of getting us all out alive. And they – the youngers, I mean – need to be ready when it does.'

I look down at the file once more. It's old and tattered. In the bottom right-hand corner is Rory Stillspeare's signature, its last letter tailing off in a thin line going downwards towards a spider in a web. *The belly of the spider*, I remember.

'It was his favourite animal,' Ruth says, noticing me looking at the inky arachnid. 'Most legs wins, he used to say to me when I was little. Ironic, huh?' She glances down at her wheelchair.

'You really want me to do this, Ruth?'

'I need you to. And one more point, Kid. The last thing we need is general panic. As far as everyone's concerned – elders and youngers – this is all a drill and we don't know if we'll need to do it for real.'

CHAPTER 52

REUNITED

'I kind of wish you were lying about all this, but it's all too weird to be made up,' Pas says.

I've told him and his sister everything. Not just what Ruth has asked us to do; everything. After I came up from the Office of Identity I took a long walk and a hard look at myself. I realized it was my fault that my friends and I were falling apart, because I was holding back just when I need to open up. I realized I needed to come clean with them, tell them what's been on my mind – for their sake, for mine, but most of all for friendship. So I've finally told them everything I can about Leo and my dad, and being logged in to Perspecta from birth.

'Lying? How come?' I ask Pas.

'Was hoping for a quiet week.' He's lying back against the wall of my dorm, that familiar old grin painted thick across his kind face.

After what's been one of the heaviest conversations of my life, the tension between the three of us suddenly seems to dissolve. Like she's been released from a coma again, Eliza leans over and hugs me tightly.

'I'm sorry,' she says. 'I was being vile. You didn't deserve it.'

'Yeah he did,' Pas pipes up, playing the fool as usual. 'He got us all in the shit, *and* he's a Specta!'

I start laughing so hard I can't stop and my sides begin to hurt. Pas's comment wasn't really that funny, but it's the signal that I have my friends back. The laughter is really an explosion of love.

'We start tonight then,' Eliza exclaims shortly afterwards, looking up from the file Ruth has given me. 'But we need a name for our little war band.'

I look at her quizzically. This hardly seems the most urgent problem.

'Esprit de corps, dude,' she goes on. 'Go and ask old Mungo about it. If your unit doesn't have a name it isn't a unit. Your mates the Terrors understand that, and they're still in shorts.'

For a few moments we toss names around rapidly: Tubeway Army, Piccadilly Relish, Soho Rising, Circus Freaks . . . The list is punctuated by snorts, giggles and, soon enough, sighs of frustration.

'This is going nowhere,' says Pas.

'The Younger Generation?' I mumble forlornly.

'Sounds like a 1970s dance troupe,' says Eliza, impatiently. 'In fact they all sound like old band names.' Then in a trice she brightens. 'The Scav Squad! What's good enough for us is good enough for the youngers. And that's what we'll call our merry men!'

'The Scav Squad!' Pas shouts.

'It's perfect,' I say. Then I feel the weight fall back on my shoulders. 'I don't think we have much time.'

Pas grows serious. 'Just keep us in the loop this time, bro. We're here for you and you're here for us. If this is going to get real, we need to stick together.' He pauses, his eyes piercing with determination. 'Whatever happens, those pigs aren't going to get away with what they did to Lizy. I've promised myself that.'

'Plus, Kid,' says Eliza, 'you're the only person we know that has the inside on Perspecta. So even if you feel like being a little jerk all over again and not trusting your friends with your stupid secrets, you're going have to spill, or I'll cut the secrets right out of you!' She grimaces in her own bittersweet way. 'All right.' She gets to her feet and goes to leave. 'I'm going to go and find all the dorm captains and call a meeting. They can help us get everyone together to arrange meetings and stuff.'

'Wait,' I say, then add in a low voice, 'Remember this is

top secret. None of the elders can know. Ruthie says they'll freak.'

'Copy that,' she says, winking at me and tapping her forefinger against her nose.

A week or so later, and the Scav Squad is a reality. It's been a relief to be busy doing something positive, rather than just cooped up feeling hated. To keep the whole operation out of the earshot of the elders, Pas and I talk to the dorm captains in Pokes's classroom. She might be a COO, but she's not an elder, and she's happily been sworn to secrecy. By way of a diversion, she's even spread it about that we've all decided we need to put in some extra work on calculus. As if.

The day's session is over and I'm left behind clearing up. I tuck the big roll of Cell blueprints under my arm, deep in thought, and walk into Pokes's cupboard.

I barely have time to register Pokes sitting on a stool with her back to me, stooped over something, when suddenly she's let out a squawk of surprise, and so do I.

'Joshy! Scared the shit out of me!' she says.

I squat to pick up the rolls of paper I've just dropped. She's on her feet facing me now, but I distinctly heard a clatter as she stood up, as if she's put something on the table behind her. I squint up at her. *Wait, is she blushing?*

Pokes bites her lip as if she knows I've spotted the colour rising to her cheeks. Then, as if she's made a spur-of-the-moment decision, she says, 'You can keep a secret; I know you can.'

I nod slowly.

'Look what I found. It was under one of the bookshelves,

behind some crumpled-up paper from the other day's test.'

As she steps aside and nods towards what she's just put down, my jaw virtually hits the floor. There on Pokes's desk is my iPhone.

'I've got to own up,' she laughs again. 'You caught me trying to switch the damn—'

Then she sees my face.

'You – have you seen this before?'

'My – my mum left it to me. It was Dad's.' Hastily I manage to add, stammeringly, 'I-I d-don't use it. There's no one to call. I . . . play with it. I mean, I used to.' Now I'm the one who's blushing.

'Right,' she nods, half teasingly. 'There's certainly no one to call.' She looks down at the phone, thinking – deciding – like a child reluctant to share her new toy. Then she looks at me again, a big smile on her face. 'Shame, always wanted one of these. I won't tell if you don't tell.' She winks, handing it back to me. 'You'd better take it and keep it safe. And, if you're ever feeling generous, I'd be more than happy to take it off your hands now and again!' She grabs me and marches me towards the door. 'Come on you nutter – it's dinner time!'

I can't escape back to my dorm like I want to. But I can hardly focus on what Pokes is saying as we queue up at the Galley and eat in the refectory. Someone took my phone and hid it under the school bookshelves? I try not to cast suspicious glances around me. But somehow it doesn't gel anyway. The only really crazy person here is me. Crazy, or in dreamland.

Then it comes back to me: my bizarre dream, the deadroom in the clouds, Rosie and Hamilton . . . and me desperately kicking the phone under the shelves there before diving into the chest. That was the night the phone disappeared, wasn't it? And a couple of days later there were people saying I'd been going walkabout in my sleep. I was so anxious about the phone being discovered, I must have taken it somewhere I thought was safe and hidden it there. And Perspecta wrapped it all up like some epic adventure.

After dinner I can barely stop myself from running to my dorm. As soon as the door is shut behind me, I fish out the charging cable and watch the phone as it switches on. It's been more than a month. The battery icon appears, then the white apple with a bite out of it, then the home screen lights up. Immediately, the iPhone buzzes.

It isn't a message; it's just an Instagram notification. Apparently the clip of me singing 'Primrose Hill' in my dorm has got more than one hundred thousand views. Any other time and I might be whooping and wondering whether that makes me some kind of celebrity in 2021. But right now all it does is make me want to speak to Izzy. I've so much to say, and I'm desperate to talk to her.

CHAPTER 53

SPLIT

10:28, 2 June

Not surprised . . . You saw all that destruction AND
you nearly got killed! In one night you met Rosie and
Hamilton and got into a chase with some Teeth AND
GOT AWAY WITH IT . . .

Wait? Actually, did you get away with it? I mean, have
there been any repercussions?

Well, I wasn't popular with the COOs. I came back and had to go down to Ruth's office, the Office of Identity to explain to ALL the COOs where I had been and what I had seen. I told them about Perspecta 3 and the delay, and about how Rogers doesn't just want the land, he wants a purge, he wants us all dead . . . I told them about Rosie standing up to him about that. And then Ruth banned all of us – all the youngers – from leaving the Cell.

But would it even be safe to leave the Cell any more? Is the Ghetto under siege?

That's the weirdest thing. The day after it happened – the day after I had come this close to being complete and utter toast and the Teeth were zooming up the Thames after us . . . it was like nothing had happened. I snuck up out into the Circus with Pas, just to see if the Teeth were still there . . . but there was nothing. It was completely silent. Like they had forgotten or something. Almost like the whole thing was a dream. Except that the Podd was still sitting there in the middle of Piccadilly Circus, all showroom shiny. Oh, and the statue.

Statue?

The statue in the middle of the Circus.

Eros, right?

Anteros, actually. Pokes says he's Eros's twin brother. Anyway, the point is we hit him with the Podd when we were landing.

You're shitting me. I thought you loved all that Olde London stuff, and you've gone and wrecked Eros?

Anteros. But yes. I feel terrible. And the elders are furious.

And since? I mean, have you had any REAL trouble? From Gnosys?

Haven't seen a SINGLE Tooth.

What? Isn't that just really spooky?

Right?!

So, you said you got back to the Cell and you told them everything. Like, you mean you had to tell Ruth about why you went and about your dad and all that?

Obviously I had to leave SOME THINGS out. I couldn't tell the COOs the real reason

I went to Westminster. "Oh, I've been on the phone to a girl from 2021 and by the way I'm a kind of Perspecta superhero too." LOL. Life's complicated enough right now without everyone in the Cell thinking I'm totally bat shit crazy. They wouldn't have believed what I heard at Westminster, but the thing they absolutely HAVE TO BELIEVE now is that Hamilton Rogers is coming for us.

So you didn't tell her about me?

No, like I said, it just, it wouldn't have helped. But don't get me wrong. This doesn't change anything. Actually going to Westminster has made sense of it all – of why Leo sent me, and of everything before that too. I realised EXACTLY why I was there . . . Leo's been right all along. She definitely meant me to hear what Hamilton was going to say, and maybe she even meant me to see Rosie for what she is. Rosie's not like Hamilton. If he hadn't come in I was going to try and get through to her. I still don't know Rosie, she doesn't know me, but I KNOW her. I know she's a GOOD person. It's in her eyes.

Ur makin me jealous now ;-)

No, don't be like that, you're just as important – MORE important . . . Listen. However much I wanna hate my dad and however much I can't bring myself to accept it, actually I can't avoid the truth . . . He set me on a path. He gave me a responsibility. He meant for me to meet YOU and he meant for us to fight, in the past AND in the future.

Izzy?

Izzy? How did it go with Sylvia . . . I mean, what did she say, when you told her about me? What was she like?

You there? Like I keep saying, I'm sorry you couldn't reach me, I'm sorry I didn't call. I lost the phone and I've only just got it back.

Izzy? What is it?

Nothing.

Oh, ok . . . so how was it? What did you say to her?

You know, was just like finding out what she was doing, sizing her up, stuff like that.

But you already know what she's doing. You read the website and stuff. Are you gonna meet again?

Yes! Yes of course. I took a job there, at Gnosys.

What?! That's kinda . . . awesome I guess . . . Deep cover!

Yeah, I guess.

I know something's up . . . I can tell. You're not being yourself

Nothing's up

What is it? What happened with Sylvia? Just tell me. What did she say to you?

Izzy! Tell me!

Nothing! OK? Nothing happened! I didn't forget WHY I was supposed to be there. But I couldn't do what you wanted. I tried to message you about things but you weren't there. I had no one to talk to. I had to make up my own mind. It's not that I don't care about you or the Offliners, before you accuse me of that, cos I know you will . . . It's not anything like that. It's because SHE isn't a bad person. She's NOT doing a bad thing and she doesn't WANT TO ruin the world. It's the furthest thing from that! Gnosys is trying to do good! She's trying to do right by people who have nothing! She's trying to help kids! Children! And you know what, I respect that! I'm not going to stop her. It wouldn't be right. I can't stop her from doing something good. And anyway, we can't FORCE anyone to change everything they're doing. That's how you just push them away. BUT what I can do and will do and WANT to do – BECAUSE I care about you and BECAUSE you're my friend – is I can guide her from the inside. What's happening in the future isn't set in stone. We CAN change the future in the past. I can HELP her to do the right thing. That's the point, that's what she needs.

Kid, don't do this. You don't understand. If you were here. If you were in my head, in my body . . .

In your body? What's that supposed to mean?

There's more going on than you think. More at stake. For me. I'm not just some stupid girl with nothing to worry about and no responsibilities. And I have morals and virtues too. I care about the next generation more than you could possibly understand. Which means I care about *your* generation. You. The Offliners. It's just . . . well, that's why I believe Sylvia is trying to do RIGHT. She cares about children, about the future, and so do I. I can't explain it, why I feel like this. It's personal. You wouldn't understand

I understand perfectly, but what's obvious to me now is that you don't understand at all.

don't say that Kid, you have no

This was a ridiculous idea from the beginning. I should never have expected you to do what needs to be done. I'm an idiot. I should never have even bothered you. The twins are right. The only thing we can rely on is ourselves. Thank you for your friendship, but this is too important to me . . . this is my life . . . just like yours is yours . . . and we have to choose what's right for ourselves in the end. Good luck.

Kid! This is ridiculous! I AM gonna help! I'm TRYING! Why did I meet her in the first place?! If I didn't care? Why would I have done any of what I did

You've gone, haven't you?

You know what Kid? You aren't the only selfless person that's ever lived. I have other people to think of too. Another person, to be exact, and I want that person to live in the kind of world Sylvia is going to create.

CHAPTER 54

TRAFALGAR

When I come to my senses I'm walking through the murk, gasping for Roxi. The narrow street opens out and a wide plaza lies in front of me.

My world has suddenly shifted in the course of a single Insta message. Yes, everything was chaos and Gnosys was coming for us, but Izzy . . . Izzy was going to fix it all. And now she isn't. I'm back in the hopeless darkness.

At last I realize I won't make it any further. I'm gasping. Sitting down against a cracked and mossy stone plinth, I take out my disp and drag desperately on it.

Izzy knows damn well Perspecta will destroy the future if Sylvia Rogers carries on her work. And now she isn't even going to try and persuade her to stop.

I cough helplessly. I'm too despondent even to curse Izzy. Looking up, I see the plinth is topped by a giant bronze lion, all covered in green tarnish and white streaks of pigeon shit. Dimly, I register at last that this is Trafalgar Square. *So that was where I was heading. The River. Waterloo Bridge.* I've only seen the bridge once before, from the Podd escaping from West-minster, but I remember how the dark water looked flowing underneath . . .

With a sharp intake of breath that leaves me spluttering again, I pull myself out of my head and back into the present, into the world, my world.

'Jesus, what am I doing?' I mutter, squeezing my fists into my eye sockets. *My friends. The Cell. I can't just give up on them all. Not now – especially not now. It would be like stabbing them in the back. And anyway, look at me, sitting here taking Roxi! Obviously not totally committed to ending it all, am I?*

I skip back past the conversation with Izzy to Ruth, sitting dauntless in her wheelchair with her useless legs.

'*You really want me to do this, Ruth?*'

'*I need you to.*'

It doesn't bring my courage rushing back. I have to force myself to my feet and start the slog back towards the Circus before I feel it begin to flow through my veins again. However hard I try to ignore them, Izzy's words won't leave my head. I roll them around and around in my skull, like I'm trying to despise them from every angle. Yes, I'm furious. I want to hate her. Maybe I *do* hate her. But maybe, I begin to realize, her reluctance and disloyalty are the kick up the arse that I need.

Eliza and Pas, I think, *I have to find Eliza and Pas!* I know I'll find strength with them. And knowing that makes me realize I have strength to give them, too.

No doubt I'll have to face Mungo on the way in; I have no idea how I managed to slip past him on my way out of the Cell in the first place.

The sun must be going down; dust devils swirl violently in the noxious air as I stagger into the Circus.

Just then the iPhone goes off in my pocket once more. *Izzy again.* It's at that moment I make my decision.

I can't see a thing and begin coughing furiously. *Damn it, not going anywhere in this.* So I just do it. I have to free myself of a false hope in the past. I have to let go of Izzy. At the top of the steps that lead down to the Cell, I put my hand in my pocket, withdraw the small metallic rectangle and throw the past, as hard as I can, into the dark, foggy future. I wait a second and think I hear the iPhone smash some way away on the edge of the Circus. It doesn't matter. It's gone. And I'm free. From now on, I'm only going to look forward, focus on the future, on what *we* can do – me, my friends, the Offliners in 2078. Not Izzy, not anyone in the past. They didn't understand and never could.

I lie here in the darkness, not able to differentiate between the whispers emanating from the other dorms in the corridor and those drifting listlessly through the corridors of my mind.

It's impossible not to think about what's going to be happening tomorrow, just down the road in Westminster. The Gnosys shareholders are going to challenge Hamilton Rogers about his plans to wipe out the Offliners. *Could someone at Gnosys really see us as worth a bit more than dirt?* I wonder. *More than the dust and dirt they're always trying to escape with Perspecta?* The hope seems so slim, so unexpected, it feels like vertigo. Whenever I let myself think that Hamilton could actually be in danger of losing his grip on Gnosys, I feel butterfly twinges. Then they're gone just as quickly. My head tells me there's no hope, I'm just clutching at straws, and Suzannah's sources will soon be telling her the date set for the crushing of the Ghetto.

Still, it's weird: I can't help but feel a change. It's not just here, down in the Cell, after weeks of anger and insecurity and doubt, that I feel it. I also feel a change in my heart. *What doesn't kill you can only make you stronger*: Pokes told me they always used to say that in the Dusk. Well, I'm not dead yet and, yes, I guess I do feel a kind of strength that I never have before. I didn't feel it even a month ago, before I realized that our world, as we know it, will be over very soon if we don't do something about it. I didn't feel it before Izzy abandoned us. I only feel it now, lying here in the dark and the cold reflecting on everything that's happened in such a short space of time. We're building the Scav Squad and whatever comes, whenever it comes, we're going to be ready to fight our corner.

Besides, Pas has just reminded me that we're going on actual scav tomorrow, due at Lucien's at five o'clock as fixed using the old *A–Z* code. And there's nothing like a trip to Lucien's to take your mind off things.

CHAPTER 55

MODERN FAMILY

DATE: Wednesday 15th September, 2021

I just realised something. In two days I, Isabel Parry, 17 years old, will be six months pregnant.

I thought pregnancy would make me way more conscious of time passing. You know, like, I thought I'd be superduper aware that with every moment that goes by I'm just hurtling ever closer to the day that will change everything forever, for more than one person, and make all the other days pale into total and utter significance. When I first found out, I was definitely really conscious of every day that went by. But I think that was probably because, well, back then I was pretty adamant I didn't wanna keep it.

Him. It's a he btw. YES! OK! I know I said I wanted it to be a surprise. I caved – I couldn't wait any longer. Doctor Harper told me at my last scan! A he! He's a he! A real-life little Bubba – I'M HAVING A BOY!

Now, the thought of it all makes me grin from ear to ear and go 'Arghghghghghghgh!' with fear at the same time. But back then I was just plain terrified of what was going to happen. And I was right to be. Before Sylvia and James, before the summer, the idea of giving birth filled me with a sense of doom and overwhelming sadness that I'd never ever felt in my life before. Back then I had three options as far as I was concerned.

1) Have baby, keep baby, leave school and raise said baby with little to no support from my family, whilst also enduring their shame and retribution. (NO THANKS).

2) Have baby, put baby up for adoption, return to school and live out the rest of my days thinking 'what if', 'where is my child, WHO is my child?' . . .

Or 3) get rid of the baby and have an abortion.

Well, even then, though my maternal instincts were already burgeoning alarmingly, I knew option 1 wasn't really an option at all. It just wasn't realistic. I couldn't bring up a child, not without the full support of my family. Which, like I say, I would never have got.

Option 2 was never really an option either. I've watched my fair share of 'Teen Mom' on MTV and if labour can last up to two days in some cases I'm not gonna push and push and kill myself having a baby (all by myself, may I add) only to give it away a day later.

So option 3 was, really, the only option. Getting rid of it.

Wow. Writing that, I just had the most horrible feeling in the pit of my stomach. Now, feeling how I feel, after everything that's happened, the thought of what I contemplated makes me feel truly sick.

Back then, when I found out, it WAS the only option. But there was still something – something in the back of my mind, guiding me, a strong, stirring feeling – that made me believe that there must be another way. And for that reason, day in, day out, I would keep putting it off, putting off option 3, the inevitable and horrible reality of my situation.

I believe in abortion, and a girl's right to it. I reckon I'd have thought like this even if I hadn't heard Nana's stories about women she knows who've been forced to have children in the most shitty circumstances. She had a sense of mission because of the faith. She left the faith and her mission was to help Catholic girls who'd 'got into trouble', as they used to call it. Girls who'd been raped or duped or who'd just got carried away. Girls who'd been forced to have an unwanted kid though they couldn't possibly support it, or it was terribly disabled . . .

But it wasn't all this that was on my mind. My putting it off wasn't based on any kind of moral stand I wanted to take. It was . . . just a feeling.

And then I was almost nine weeks and summer was on its way and something HAD TO BE DONE when Sylvia came, like a hurricane, into my life, turning that feeling into a conviction. Then the internship came along, and it became too late and too dangerous to abort my baby. And something magical happened. I no longer needed to have conviction in my beliefs or to worry about my three horrible and suffocating options. Because – only very recently, dear diary – another option has presented itself. It was Sylvia's suggestion.

Option 4: 'A Modern Family'.

I'm sitting in the little blue room – my room – upstairs and at the back of the little house in checked red and grey brick in Cardigan Street, Jericho, Oxford, that I've called home for three months now. I can't believe it's been that long cos, like I said, time has flown by and it's been the happiest period in my entire life. On June 14th I had the best birthday ever – just sitting on a punt in the sunshine while Sylvia and James took it in turns to pole the thing along the willowy river and pass me strawberries and chocs. I've never felt so free and so inspired as I do here. I don't have to hide my subatomic secrets from anyone – my muons and gluons are right out there for all to see these days! In fact, Sylvia keeps finding me new quantum physics books and I've got about five open on the bed right now. My brain seems to be heading into warp speed. And, rather than being a source of anxiety, in this house being pregnant has been a joy.

Sylvia and James have been so supportive . . . feeding me and looking after me, taking me to and from my appointments at the John Radcliffe hospital AND giving me the day off when I need it (my morning sickness was VERY VERY VERY bad at the beginning). More than anything they've been excited about the baby. Not excited in like a cutesy, cooey type way, but genuinely, actually excited for ME, about the prospect of me being a mother and of bringing a child into this world.

Their love and passion for children is extraordinary. And it translates to Gnosys, to Perspecta, to how they do business as a whole. I mean, It's obvious Sylvia doesn't think of the company as a 'business', but more as a kind of charitable cause, or, like, I dunno, a philanthropic exercise. She couldn't give a monkeys about money. Whereas James very much does see it as a business. He has a mind for that; he's just that kind of person.

But still, whatever bit of the company either one is focused on, they are both TOTALLY COMMITTED TO THE CAUSE: allowing children to learn through experience, through really, actually, properly GOING TO MARS, as opposed to reading about it in a book!!! I really believe that we have created something that will change the world. WE. Can you believe I just said 'we'? Actually – and I've been so busy I haven't even told you about this – we've already trialled Perspecta in some Oxford primary schools!

Schools outreach is a big part of my responsibility. Most of my days are spent talking to the head teachers of the schools we have already done trials in, and exploring the possibility of carrying out trials with new head teachers who we haven't yet worked with. Everyone is so responsive it makes the work really, really gratifying and exciting.

And it makes me think, you know, that I was right and Kid was wrong.

I really do believe him – believe that he wasn't lying about what happens in the future, what's going to happen next. But none of that is Sylvia or James's doing. It just

CAN'T be. So maybe, possibly, some dodgy politician or big boss in the future is going to twist everything my friends are doing now, everything they dream of doing with Gnosys and Perspecta. That still doesn't mean they should stop doing it altogether. I trust them. I know they're good. And I believe in their dreams, I really do.

Here's how I see it. So Charles Darwin, right, came up with natural selection in the 19th century? The idea that species that adapt best thrive and survive but other species don't and die out. And in the 20th century that got turned into the idea that there was a master-race that had a right to wipe out other races. Does that really mean Darwin should have kept shtum? That we would be better off without understanding evolution?

That's where I think Kid had it wrong. That's where I disagreed. My friends have every right to give the world their genius ideas. And however terrible things might be in Kid's time, who's to know what they'll turn out like after?

Besides, I tried to tell him I got the internship as soon as I did, but he never messaged me back. Never even read the message . . . And since we last spoke on Insta – horrible day – he's gone totally silent again. No DMs, no replies to mine. Maybe he's still angry with me. Maybe he's embarrassed because he knows I'm right. No Insta posts either, so maybe he's just lost the phone again, the klutz. Whatever . . . I believe in the here and now. I'm trying to do the right thing in the present day. I've even started thinking I might have to delete my Insta app, maybe my actual account, just in case Sylvia looks over my shoulder, so she never sees some of the things Kid's said about her and Gnosys and Perspecta.

It'd be totally unfair on her to have all that hanging over her head. Don't like the idea of not being able to see those convos again, maybe have to have another gander through them first. But in the end . . .

And TBH I dunno about you, dear diary. Everything I've written in you! I don't for a minute think she'd go snooping, that's definitely not Sylvia, but accidents happen. When I've filled your pages maybe I'll stick you in an envelope and seal you up, or bury you, or stick you under the loose floorboard in the corner over there.

The point is, I'm not going to be responsible for changing the future the way Kid wants me to. I'm living on my own terms from now on. As for the future, working with Sylvia and James is the best way to try and change it!

I loved Kid. I'll always love Kid. He became like a brother to me, like family, so amazingly quickly, and I think he'll always seem that way. But sitting here in Oxford and working for Gnosys in the year 2021 – well, all the rest of it, Primrose Hill, all of that, feels like some distant dream I once had. A faint and fading dream.

I still haven't told my parents I'm pregnant . . . I'd told them that when term ended I wanted to enroll in this 'Christian summer camp' in Oxford that was taking place from July to September. They were only too happy they'd be seeing the back of me for three months, and even set up a bank account for me with DOUBLE my normal pocket money to see me through . . . the good little Christian I am, LOL! . . . Then after all that it was back to Covid crisis. School closed early, in June, and – disaster! – the camp that I was supposed to be going to was cancelled. When my bump started showing at the start of July, I was terrified of what Mum and Dad would say. So I just bolted for Oxford and Sylvia and James. Even then, I guess I wasn't even sure I wanted the baby . . . I dunno, I was SO CONFUSED!

But I'm clear now. Clear on what needs to happen. I'm stronger and braver and feel more secure than I ever did before. And besides, that's exactly what option 4 is all about!

It's weird, cos it came about two days ago, and I caught it all on my iPhone, on the voice-recorder thingumyjiggy. I wasn't spying or anything! It was mid afternoon and we were sitting in the conservatory, having just come back from the lab at Christ Church. Sylvia was working on enhancing the User Experience in the Amazonian Rainforest World we created for the Perspecta Universe and, well, anyway, she always likes me to record our sessions when she's working you know? Because she always thinks aloud, like the whole time, and then forgets everything she's said. But if we record it, when she loses her train of thought we can just go back to it later on the phone.

We took a little break and got onto talking about the baby, and about how I didn't know how I was going to break it to Mum and Dad. I guess I forgot to turn off my phone and so it caught the whole thing. I'm listening back to it now as I write. Basically I'm talking about how I knew I had to tell them, that I felt strong enough to, but that I knew they would be furious and I knew it would change everything and that they wouldn't let me leave school and really, my only option was to put the baby up for adoption. I began getting super emotional and saying how sorry I was that I had put the two of them in this position – being an emotional burden on them and that it wasn't their problem, that I needed to just work it out on my own . . . when something weird happened.

'Can I tell you something?' Sylvia said. She cut me off abruptly, what she wanted to say had obviously been on her mind throughout the conversation. 'James and I have wanted to have a baby since we met in first year.'

'That's so lovely!' I said. Which in hindsight was stupid.

I remember she screwed her face up into a ball when she said the next thing, so that the tip of her nose and her top lip were touching. It wasn't the look of a happy expectant mum. And she'd seemed so happy moments before, so excited for me, for the future. This look was more like she was focusing everything on fathoming how I might respond. 'I hope this doesn't sound odd to you. But, in reality, it's you who is doing us a favour.'

I was totally baffled. It was super bright in the conservatory, and I thought I could see the faintest sheen in Sylvia's eyes. Was she crying?

'We've been trying – James and I – since we met. It's, well, sort of been our dream. It's the reason we started Gnosys in the first place. Our desire to have children of our own one day, and for the world to be a better, smaller, more easily accessible place for them.' In the recording she chuckles to herself, I guess for being so geeky and weird and amazing. Then she burst into tears. 'I'm so sorry, this is ridiculous. I can't believe I've turned this entire conversation around and made it about me. Oh HONESTLY, God, how shameless.' She got up, all flustered, and whizzed around the room like a yo-yo, trying, and failing, to find a tissue.

'What is it, Sylvia?' I said. I said it gently and quietly,

without taking my eyes off her, so that she'd stop what she was doing and calm down. I wanted her to know I actually cared, to make her feel comfortable enough to tell me whatever it was she needed to. 'What do you want to say?'

She looked into my eyes. I looked into hers. I think what I saw was fear. But looking back, deep down I already knew what she was going to say. Finally she blurted it out.

'I'm infertile. We can't have a baby. That's why you're doing us a favour. Well, mostly me.' Then she giggled a little bit, all nervy, before continuing in a quiet, breathy, tearful voice. 'That's why I'm just so desperate to do as much as I can and be as much of a part of your pregnancy as possible, as much a part of the baby's life as possible.' She paused for a long moment. 'If you'll let me, that is . . .'

I had always wondered why Sylvia had been so ready to help me, so eager to know so much about the baby. And right there I remembered the moment at The Bear when she had been about to say I hadn't got the internship and I broke down and told her everything – the moment when she suddenly changed her mind and, seemingly out of the blue, gave me the job.

'But . . . the internship,' I said, fumblingly. 'You do actually want me for the job?'

'Oh God, yes, Izzy!' she said, looking at me with eyes now bright with tears. 'I knew you were the right person as soon as we got talking at the Bear – your background, your ideas, the way you think! But when you said you hadn't been to university and all that, well . . . technically that WAS a problem. I just had to hide my disappointment behind my Ms Interviewer act. I'm sorry!'

'But—'

'And when you broke down about being pregnant, I couldn't keep up the act. The stuff about criteria all suddenly seemed so stupid and impersonal. And so . . . well . . . here you are.'

Sylvia's face was this amazing mixture of fear and hope.

So I just came out with it. 'You'll definitely be part of the baby's life. I can't imagine it being any other way.'

Instantly I could feel the sunlight through the conservatory windows shining on us again. 'I can't look after a baby on my own, we both know that, not right now. And you, well like you said, you want to be as much a part of his life as possible. You can't stop your work either, but we can share. Be like mums together, you know?'

Sylvia was stuttering. 'I-I-I'd be so honoured, I don't think anyone has ever trusted me like— '

'Actually I feel really selfish asking. But I've been going mad trying to think how I could manage on my own. I feel so naive and impractical. And maybe this sounds even more selfish, but I don't want to give up my work. Anything you could do to help would be just amazing. At least until I finish uni, and then . . .'

'But sweet Izzy,' she said, and now she sounded halfway between calm and tearful, 'you can get support at university – there are creches and things – so there's no need for all this. He'll need you, not me and James. You're his mother.'

'Well, that's what I mean. We can both – all three of us – bring him up together. Be a modern family.'

She didn't answer. At this point in the recording all you can hear is her crying. Really really crying. But there was this look on her face – she was smiling like magic and her eyes were so bright. And then you can hear me crying too as I realise she's agreed. And then it's impossible to understand what either of us are saying.

Until 'Hello.' James was suddenly at the door in his suit and Sylvia and I both go silent and James goes 'Oh dear,' in a smiling voice, 'what on earth's happened to you two?'

'Jimmy!' She ran over to him and gave him a hug and a kiss. 'Want some tea? Izzy and I have some news.'

And that was that. That was option 4. Sylvia Sterton and James Rogers will help me bring up my baby boy and together the four of us will be a very loving, modern family.

CHAPTER 56

UNREAL CITY

'One more for the road?' Pas says, refilling his own disp and offering me a second pellet, an impish glint in his eye.

'Think I'll pass.' I say, louche, my legs dangling over the side of the fallen statue of Anteros.

'It's funny. Fourteen years of hanging out with a bona fide comic genius and your banter's *still* shit. Did I say funny? Actually – that's the point – it's *not* funny.' He chortles, far too pleased with his own terrible joke.

'Wait a second,' I say, 'are you wasted already? Should we take you home?' I try very hard not to laugh when I say this, feeling my own rush begin.

'Yeah man, you got it, totally *wasted*,' he says sarcastically as he cocks his dispenser – *schlack* – and I hear the pellet cracking within it, the gas hissing as it fills up the reservoir inside. Before I know it, he's hunched, pulling hard, his lungs filling up with Roxi, his head filling up with colour. Facing away from me, looking down at the ground, his head lolls, limp.

Wait, is he . . . ?

'Dude, you all r—'

'Gottttttttttcha!' He throws his head back and opens his arms wide like he's performing some kind of ritualistic sun-worship. 'Hahahah! That's the good stuff! That. Is. The. *Juice!*' he yelps, his voice ricocheting off the sides of the empty fishbowl of the Circus.

'Gimme that!' I point at the pellet in his right hand as I jump off the sidelong statue into a gaggle of mangey parakeets, who immediately explode into the air. I howl with laughter as he dodges the panic-stricken birds, then load the little pill-sized pellet into my disp and take a hit. I come up straightaway, the second frozen dose popping and cracking in my lungs as my head begins pulsating, the already unusually bright day becoming a psychedelic swirl in front of my eyes.

We're standing in the very centre of the Circus, where we've stood a million times before, doing exactly the same thing, readying ourselves for another adventure out into our beloved Ghetto. But somehow today feels different. Despite everything that's happened – maybe *because* of it – I feel closer to my best friends now than I ever have before.

You're high as a kite, you plonker, I think to myself. But it's not that. We're always high out here; have to be. No, this is a real feeling. Like we've come through something and we're out the other side. Things might get worse, probably will, but whatever happens, we're together, the original Scav Squad.

'Shame sis can't come,' I say, unravelling the wire from my headphones. 'Properly beautiful day.'

'Never change, do you, Curls?' Pas says, mocking my sentimentality. 'Probably for the best. She hates Luci Goosey.'

'True.'

'Shall we?'

I open the lid of my busted CD Walkman and insert today's chosen soundtrack: *AJ Tracey* by AJ Tracey. An epically talented grime artist from the Twenties, he's a bit of a hero of ours. '"Ladbroke Grove"?'

'What else?' says Pas. It's our favourite song on the album. We press play and sprint off through the derelict dust bowl, on into Shaftesbury Avenue.

It's a beautiful day. *Must be windy up there*, I think, watching the whirling dirt clouds moving fast across the sky. Every now and then I even think I see a flash of the sun's disc. It's gone as soon as it's there but, with the juice flowing through me, one flash is all I need to feel like I'm going back in time. It's throbbing hot. I tie my jacket around my waist, though my scarf stays wrapped around my face. With winds like this, a storm could whip up out of nowhere in seconds.

'Quick detour?' Pas says, running past Great Windmill Street, the fastest way to Lucien Loffabond's joint – the old multistorey car park on Brewer Street. 'We'll take Rupert Street and cut back.'

'For sure!' I guess today Pas feels like celebrating.

He vaults the fallen awning outside the Lyric Theatre, pulls out a paint canister, and shakes it up so the ball bearing clicks and clacks inside. Then he sprays the Lovethorne family tag – a heart pierced by a thorn – in green paint on the crumbling theatre wall. With a smirk, he holsters the can and disappears off up Rupert Street.

Suddenly I hear the faintest hum of an electric charge. I skid to a halt, kicking up a suffocating daze of dust and trying not to inhale it.

Rosie, I think, expectant and excited. Same place, every time, where Gnosys plants its holo-pop sensors.

The hum gets louder and louder. The light, refracted and distorted, begins to dance in the dusty air. Before I know it, I'm submerged in a dazzling bath of brilliance – right inside the holo-pop. I wait for her voice, for her words, for 'I believe in my future'.

Maybe it'll be different this time, I think, exhilarated, *now that she's actually spoken to me. In real life.* And I'm lost in Rosie reverie.

'Imagine . . .' A male voice, booming.

That's not—

The Roxi rush is really taking hold, but I'd recognize that affected, oleaginous, media-trained purr anywhere. I stumble backwards out of the hologram. Towering like Godzilla over Theatreland, in Rosie's place, is Hamilton Rogers.

'Imagine . . .' He pauses, as if trying to find the words. *You fraud.*

'Imagine infinity.' An undulating, romantic piece of piano plays.

I know it's pre-recorded, but I feel nauseous. It's like he's speaking directly to me, looking into my soul. Like he knows me.

'Imagine infinite possibilities. A place with an infinite number of opportunities for you, your loved ones. A place where all cultures and creeds live together harmoniously, happily, healthily, into infinity. Imagine Apeiron.' And as he says the name, he vanishes, revealing a bird's eye view of what looks like the biggest city I've ever seen – an ocean of architecture, an entire country, a world. New, gleaming, unthinkably tall spires apostrophize the skyline. Temples from ancient times shimmer as if new-built. Half-familiar landmarks stand side by side with others I couldn't imagine in my wildest dreams. Parks the size of entire plains, some arctic, some lush, some desert. Seas bordered by giant mountains. Thousands of airborne craft, from hot-air balloons to intergalactic spaceships.

'A city where the impossible is a redundant concept.' Hamilton is back, flying over the city, walking on air like a god. It's like I'm going with him, watching, winged. Then with a swoop we are on the ground, in a boulevard of giant buildings, marble and stucco, a thousand shop awnings and gilded doorways. I recognize logos from the Dusk – luxury fashion houses, tech brands, food emporia that were either consumed or killed off by the Upload. Apple, WholeFoods, Ecovo, Spoot . . .

It's a kind of Elysium. In the shade of gargantuan multicoloured sequoias, thousands of people parade up and down. People? Some are human enough; others look like beings from far-flung star systems. But what feels most alien to me is the expressions on all these faces – all so happy, all oozing wealth and health, all unwrinkled and unfazed. It's in how they walk, too, as if unaware they are living in a dream world.

'Welcome to Main Street, Apeiron,' says Hamilton.

This is what it looks like inside the Universe. This is Perspecta.

My head has finally outrun the Roxi. But there's another rush going on inside me now, a warm glow I can't suppress.

'Do you like trees?' asks Hamilton.

It's like he and I are really there. I find myself nodding, entranced. 'So look up!' he says with a childlike smile, almost like a friend. 'This is Oakland.'

Pokes often shows us the old infomercials Walt Disney made in the early days. This is Hamilton now: a modern Disney, friendly family man, maker of dreams.

I look up and my jaw drops. At the end of Main Street stands a tree, two thousand metres tall and hundreds wide where the branches begin to spread. Its soaring trunk is not oak, but aluminium, steel, glass and stone, blisteringly bright, beautiful and complex.

The branches look natural, wooden and leafy, but they uphold a city. Tiny compared to the unbelievable metropolis all around us, the perfect green oasis basks in twinkling sunlight. Hundreds of extraordinary buildings rise towering from the branches or hang down like huge Christmas decorations – all shapes and sizes, a myriad different materials and styles. As we rise into the middle of this tree-city, I see a large circular screen like one of Big Ben's clock faces at the Institute of Technology in Westminster, carrying the words:

PERSPECTA 3.0

coming soon

Hamilton speaks. 'Oakland is home to Apeiron's most upstanding citizens, the men and women who have helped me and my family create the new world – the most inventive, industrious people in the Universe. It takes many years of hard work and dedication to reach these heights – it takes Perspecta passion, loyalty, love. But if you join us, if you help us, if you leave the old world for the new, Oakland could be your home too.

'Come on.' He offers a friendly hand, and though I know he isn't there I actually reach out to take it. 'I'll show you where we live: Rogers Tower.'

There, springing up out of the upper branches of the vast tree, like a glass fountain, is another skyscraper. And in a flash, we are at the very top, in a glass office overlooking the whole of Apeiron, and Hamilton is talking again – something about wanting to work with those not yet logged in, wanting to help those less fortunate than him and his disciples.

But I'm not listening. I've been in this room before.

The desk, the leather armchairs, and in the middle of it all—

It's the chest, the trunk. The one in my dream that night, where I hid when Hamilton and Rosie came into the room. Stencilled on the old green trunk are the white letters

S.S.S.

and, smaller,

SYLVIA SCARLET STERTON

I was INSIDE Perspecta.

The heat rises in me, my heart hurts, a wave of panic and terror crashes over me like I'm there all over again.

It wasn't a dream. I was in Perspecta, in the city of Apeiron, in Rogers Tower. I was there and it was real.

CHAPTER 57

LOFFABOND'S EMPORIUM

'Kid!' All of a sudden Pas comes barrelling through a dust cloud, the holo-pop vanishes, and I see Shaftesbury Avenue around me again. 'What is it with you and bloody Rosie Rogers?! I was halfway there before I realized *you* weren't. We're gonna miss our slot!'

'It wasn't Rosie.'

'What?' he coughs in the thickening air.

'It was Hamilton. It was like my dream, you know the one where I lost the phone. It was a holo-pop but I was there again – same room, everything. You know what it means? I wasn't dreaming that night! I was in Perspecta, actually really in it!'

'Get down!' Pas squawks unexpectedly, grabbing me by the arm and dragging me down to the ground, out of the light. 'You're timing! Jesus. Shhhhhhh.' He puts his finger to his lips. My head starts to burn, filling with a familiar, pumping kind of pain, and then noise.

11011101xxprrkkr01101010krrrr—

Sure enough, a patrol of two Migs marches out of the Circus, crossing Shaftesbury Avenue where we were a few moments ago but carrying on into Windmill Street.

'Shit,' I whisper, my headache immediately subsiding. 'Windmill Street? We should go back to the Cell.' I feel strange, distracted and scared after the holo-pop and the dream and now . . .

'Coming from the guy who escaped from all the Teeth in Westminster?' Pas chuckles, getting to his feet and brushing himself off. 'It's a routine patrol. We've spent our whole lives skipping them. Lucky I suggested a detour.' He offers his hand. 'Get up, you big baby. We'll take Wardour Street!'

Then he smacks me on the arm and runs off down the Avenue. 'First one to Old Compton Street's a Specta! . . . Oh wait,' he turns to face me but keeps running backwards, grinning, 'you already are one!'

I snap my headphones back on my head and we're off! It feels good to be running again, free, up above. But Pas is more right than he realizes, and I can't get it out of my head, what I now know: I can exist inside and outside the Universe, in the real world and in the virtual.

How do you control yourself? How do you decide when you're in and when you're out? How do you—

Oh for God's sake! Hold your horses, cowboy. I pull myself together. *You may be a semi-Specta, but you're not gonna start talking about yourself in the second person.*

I pound the cracked, warped concrete of Wardour Street, Pascale up ahead leaping from doorway to doorway like an alley cat running from the business end of a broomstick. We scuttle as stealthily as possible passed St Anne's churchyard. The hot gale blasting through the gaping church windows sounds like a Chariot's fan-jets. We whip past Old Compton Street, a mirage of broken glass and bawdy ghosts. And then we're on the corner where Brewer Street peels off to the left from Wardour Street, towards Lucien's.

Pas kneels cautiously in the doorway of the old Las Vegas Arcade and squints down Brewer Street to check whether the Teeth are outside the old car park. 'Can't see anything.'

Tink-tink-alink. We both jump.

'It's all right,' says Pas after peering inside the dark old casino. 'The slots.' The rusty bells of abandoned slot machines are jangling in the wind.

'Go around the back, I reckon,' Pas breathes, cautious now. 'Peter Street, next left. It's a dead end. Teeth navs won't take them that way. We can climb up the back of Lucien's and get straight into the showroom.'

A minute later we're at a dead end and I'm looking behind me, acutely aware that if a Tooth turns up now, there's nowhere to go. *Apart from up*, I think, as Pas begins to scale the back wall of the car park. Decaying bricks and mortar crumble and fall away, but he moves up and up, carefully placing hands and feet.

'Shit!' He slips.

'Dude!' I run towards him terrified, instinctively holding out my arms.

'I'm – it's – haha, all good,' he says, smiling down at me. 'What, were you gonna catch me? Naaaaaw, thanks bro!'

'I'm not the one hanging on to a drainpipe for dear life, mate.'

'Yeah, well. Don't put your foot in that one, whatever you do.'

Pas swings himself, in one annoyingly slick manoeuvre, across the pipe and onto a ledge, pulling himself up to the level of Lucien's showroom.

My turn. Thankfully, I've seen roughly where to put my feet – and where not to. Eventually, I'm hauling at the final ledge with all my might, tarpaulin slapping me in the face repeatedly, until Pas reaches out and drags me the rest of the way.

'Arrrrrrgh!' I graze my arm and topple over into the dark echoing chamber. 'Steady on, Superman.'

'Barely a scratch, you wimp,' Pas sneers, but helps me to my feet.

'You're unbelievable.' I brush myself off, eyes acclimatizing to the gloom.

The tarpaulin shielding the enormous space from the elements flaps furiously in the wind. It's so loud in here. It's a wonder it hasn't driven Lucien completely mad.

Loffabond's Emporium, I think, as nervously excited as I am whenever we come here. *We're back.*

'What's on the list?' Pas grunts, hushed and rushed, obviously feeling nervy too. I withdraw a scraggly piece of paper from my back pocket, given to me by Mungo on our way up into the Ghetto.

Before I can read it, Lucien's unmistakable cockney burble wafts from the other end of the showroom. 'Afraid I'm recently parted with my last box of plasters, loves. But I can't for the life of me imagine two swashbucklers such as yourselves ever requiring anything as *wet* as a plaster. Not for a scratch, no . . .'

Lucien's characteristically menacing singsong gives me the creeps. *Guess that's the idea.*

A swinging lightbulb lights up above the old oak desk at the far end of the room, and then the striplights *click-a-click-a-fzzzzzzz* into life. There he is, smoking and smirking like a naughty schoolboy caught in the act. His shock of orange curls looks like a ball of thousand-year-old string so brittle it would crumble at a touch.

'Love an entrance, don't you Lucien?' I say, acting more at ease than I really am. You don't want to put a foot wrong in here.

'Appears we have that in common, Mr Jones.' He flashes his orange gnashers, ant-baccy around his gums. 'We were supposed to be meeting at Neasden Railway Works' – he means five o'clock by the *A–Z* code – 'and it's already half-past. Bitten by the midges were we?' he continues.

'Midge' is Lucien-speak for Mig. I'm suddenly nervous, my voice quick and quiet. 'How do you know we saw the Teeth?'

'The patrol was headed this way,' Pas adds, stepping towards Lucien's desk, squaring up.

'What, my boys? So quick to be quarrelsome?' Lucien cackles. 'Realllllly! Teeth, here, in my place of business?' He roars an unnatural, affected laugh, his throat croaking. It sounds like he's being suffocated. 'Don't be so ridiculous.' He smiles a sickening smile with his decomposing fangs, then looks down to rifle around in a drawer.

I'm not reassured. 'How do you know we saw the Teeth? Are they here?'

Lucien whips his head out of the drawer and fixes us with a terrifying glower under his maniacally twisted mono-brow. Then he stands up, tall and thin and casting a huge shadow in his enormous, nineteenth-century policeman's swallowtail coat.

'Now now, we'll not have that. None of that *slander-ousnesssss*.' It's a petrifying hiss, carrying the acrid smell of ant-smoke. 'We'll not have no excitement from you today, loves.' His eyes flit towards one side of the showroom and back. I look around but nothing moves; no one's there.

Then he sits back down, and smiles generously, like nothing happened.

'We saw a patrol,' I say, sounding more timid than I want. 'They went up Windmill. We . . . Have you . . . ?'

But the truth is, as far as most matters of the Ghetto are concerned, Lucien holds the cards. We're on his patch. We need what he's got.

Forget it, I think.

'Have I,' he says, pulling a bag from the drawer, 'got Miss Lovethorne's penicillin? He waggles the bag to show the small vials of clear liquid inside. Then, menacingly, with ants congealed around his rancid gums, 'That what you wanted to know, son?'

Sensing Pas's body tense and twitch, I grab my friend's arm and whisper, 'Don't.'

Lucien slowly puts the bag back and closes the drawer, then plants both elbows on the desk, interlocks his hands and loudly cracks his spindled, hairy fingers. 'Or would you prefer to talk Teeth?'

'No, Lucien. We wouldn't,' I say, handing him the list. *There you go, pig.*

He snatches it and leans back, examining the note so closely it's like he's trying to smell it. His eyes dart up and down it and then peep over the top at us but dart away quickly as if to avoid eye contact, as if he's nervous.

I clear my throat. 'Have you got—'

'What is *up* with you, man?' Pas asks Lucien loudly, angrily.

Lucien ignores the question, jumping to his feet eagerly. 'Of *course* I've got what you need!' Then, 'Come, one of my chappies will make up your order, and in the meantime we'll have a drink.'

'What? *Drink?*' Why is Lucien suddenly offering us the kind of gold-star service usually reserved for people paying in Gnotes?

'Thanks. But we're good,' Pas says suspiciously as Lucien beckons us to follow.

'I insist, my dear boys. You've been very good customers. Dear, regular, very good indeed.'

He begins walking towards the other end of the car

park. We don't move. Realizing we aren't following him, he prompts, 'Well come along, come along!' We stay where we are. I've never seen him like this before. Soho's most powerful crook, suddenly inferior, humble – yet simultaneously agitated. 'All right, *all right*! We haven't the *time*!' he says, his voice nearly hitting top C.

The time for what?

He throws up his hands, stops and turns back to us, frowning and gulping like he can't get the words out, 'Perhaps – I suppose – perhaps, well, yes, perhaps I've overlooked your loyalty and good custom for too long now.' Stops. Then: 'Perhaps I owe you an apology.'

An apology, I think, bamboozled. *From Lucien Loffabond?*

'Times are hard in the Ghetto, boys. They're harder than they've ever been, and it's for us – all us that's chosen to stay – to work together, band together, to be good neighbours, else we'll not make it through, dear loves.' Lucien joins his palms together like he's praying; bows his head solemnly. 'Sorry if I've ever made life less than easy for you.' He looks up again, kindly. 'You're grown now. Older and wiser and . . . ready. Time we Colonised you.'

At this, Lucien gestures to the car park staircase, the way he's been trying to lead us all this time. Finally, bemused, we fall into step behind him, trooping into the echoing stairwell as one of his lackeys scuttles out of another door to begin collecting the items on our scavving list.

Two levels down, we reach the small iron door, painted red. The floor isn't throbbing today – *must be a quiet one*, I think; a spot of jazz, maybe. Lucien claps his hands together three times and, for the first time in all the years I've been coming here, I watch the smooth, twisted glass of the neon lights above the door fill up with gas, glowing red and yellow . . .

MURIŁL'S

Then,

CØMŁ IN

And finally, after a few seconds of flickering,

DO

CHAPTER 58

MURIEL'S

The reality of it finally sinks in. *Us? Allowed in there? Not just allowed, but invited – by Lucien?*

'Wait, *M-M-Muriel's*?' I stutter at Lucien like an idiot. 'Me and Pascale – you're inviting us *inside* Muriel's?'

He only nods, turns, and puts his hand on the little red door.

I look at Pas. Pas looks at me. No matter how pissed off

he is, no matter how confused I am, this is an offer we can't refuse.

I look back to Lucien as the red door opens.

That's why you've been being weird? You wanted to show us Muriel's? And with that all the tension of the previous moment seems to evaporate.

Muriel's is completely out of bounds to youngers. Even the elders aren't exactly encouraged to drink there: those who do inevitably return to the Cell too drunk to stand, or bereft of some prized possession, or black and blue from a barroom fight. Sometimes all three. Now and again, they don't come back at all. So if we go in there now we're not just breaking Cell rules, we're probably putting ourselves in danger. But that's the thing, that's why it's too much to resist. Plus the fact that all Soho's fabulous history of nightlife has ended up reduced to – distilled into – this single mystery, Muriel's. Whatever's on the other side of that little red door has always been too tantalizing for words.

Without saying anything we follow Lucien through the door. I still can't hear the music, but every story I've ever heard about Muriel's swarms into my memory, whilst I simultaneously run through the Rolodex of nights Pas, Lizy and I have sat up discussing which of the 'Muriel myths' are true and which just have to be false. I look over at Pas, and I can tell he's going over them all again too.

The bartender Alberto Metti has worked every day since it opened and hasn't been sober once. Never pays for a drop, but if any of the customers try and skip a bill he knocks them unconscious on the spot. They accept the punishment gallantly – club code.

We're in a corridor lined with flock wallpaper and old playbills – *Wicked, The Phantom of the Opera, Jeffrey Bernard Is Unwell, The Mousetrap* . . . Finally I think I can hear the music, though I can't quite pick out what it is yet.

I heard Petrina Bones and Freudelle Fraser have a thumb war every night at ten. The loser can't leave before completing a thousand-piece jigsaw puzzle made of bits of mosaic from St Peter's in Rome.

We've been waiting for this since we started scavving, aged twelve. This is how it must have felt during the Dusk when you reached eighteen. When you could go out and drink for the first time, become an adult.

I want to say something to Pas but can't find the words.

They say Quentin de Vere Milne's written a short story for every single night that the club's been open.

Now we're close enough to hear glasses clinking and laughter rippling. Close enough to hear that it's not jazz playing inside, but 'Sunny' by Bobby Hepp.

Is it true they have a giant African land snail called Diny Fats Morrison? Apparently she lives in the club and serves drinks on a tray balanced on top of her shell?

And did you hear that in '68 Paloma d'Ertagnan (FRCS) performed gender reassignment surgery inside the club on Sir Aitchison Auerbach (KBE) with only absinthe for anaesthetic? And that Dame Jean Goodman (DBE), who Aitchison became, holds a yearly bridge tournament, which she calls Lourdes on account of how many people travel from overseas to attend?

We're only a few feet away from the end of the corridor now.

What about the night that . . .

He reaches the door, turns the crystal handle.

. . . don't forget the story of . . .

Inside, neon lights flicker and flash. Fast. Hypnotic. I wish Eliza were here so we could all share this moment together.

. . . imagine how it'll feel, the day they let us into Muriel's?

I watch as Lucien steps inside. Bright, swirling, primary colours swallow him up. Pas follows, pushing aside a thick red velvet portière curtain and disappearing into rainbow smoke. The door closes behind me, I nudge the velvet aside, and I'm in.

Muriel's Bar.

I gasp.

'Right?' Pas says, reverently.

The room, hazy with exotic fumes and shaped like a rugby ball, is arranged around a small, gold-rimmed bar, an art deco horseshoe. Behind it a veined and scratched antique mirror, etched with the words *The Ivy*, is bordered by multi-coloured lightbulbs that scintillate off an island of bottles, every shape, size, colour and variety you can imagine. I never dreamt there was so much whisky in the world. Above, more bottles and twinkling glasses form a kind of alcoholic proscenium arch. Dainty mushroom-shaped lights illuminate the faces of the ten or so punters propping up the tiny bar, chatting, quaffing, but mostly just scrabbling for their next drink.

I can't describe what it's like, this pearl in the shell of a ruined car park. Parisian bistro crossed with old English pub maybe. Ropes and pulleys and trapezes recall seedy Soho strip clubs. Lights, music and shimmering disco ball make me itch to dance like I'm in 1970s New York. Undulating outwards from the mirror ball in huge folds of fabric, the ceiling makes me feel like I'm in a Moroccan bell tent. It's a melange of memories of good times. A clash of styles, cultures and periods, brought together out of bars, restaurants, cafés and clubs that throve in the Golden Dusk all over Soho. Mismatched tables and chairs, inscribed *Barrafina, Quo Vadis, Bar Termini, El Camion,* are scattered haphazardly around the paint-spattered, tyre-marked concrete floor.

The clientele sitting at them don't quite live up to the diverse and eclectic decor. Whatever it was like in the Dusk, when things seem to have been pretty tribal, at Muriel's there is obviously no set way to act or dress, no rank, no status quo. Most of the clothes are fairly plain, but with a few flourishes, the kind of thing easily bagged up for discreetly carrying through the Ghetto: a silk scarf here, a floral necktie here, a pair of heels there. Looks like the sole fixed requirement is to be a customer of Lucien. *And,* I think, looking more closely at the crowd, *to look like hell* – though whether it's from lack of Roxi or from years of alcohol abuse, I can't guess.

I *can* guess, however, that those three sitting at that table, dark coats covering their white jumpsuits, are Spectas, their Plugs hidden away somewhere. Five plain black metal briefcases are daisy-chained to the wrist of one of the Spectas, and most of the people in here can't stop staring at them. You wouldn't have to be a Mig to work out what was inside. Roxi. Which would suggest that the two women sitting opposite them – twins maybe, in black overalls with an e-Colt holstered on each hip – are Roxi Runners. Watching them lean in *tête-à-tête* with the Spectas, I don't know what

I feel. Everyone's got to make a living, and without them no Offliner would have any Roxi whatsoever. But they're rarely charitable and they make their money preying on the desperate and the vulnerable.

'Make yourselves at home, my boys,' Lucien barks. 'Back in a jiffy.' After seeing him mostly behind his trader's desk, it's a revelation to see him sidle through the begrimed room greeting the motley crew. Glad-handing the bandits and racketeers, he's a tough gangster; whispering a confidential *bon mot* to his more refined patrons, he's an urbane and witty gentleman; air-kissing the artistically-inclined, he's a theatrical lovey. The consummate chameleon, Lucien is circus ringmaster and veteran diplomat rolled into one.

We watch him disappear back-first through a saloon door beside the shimmering horseshoe, then Pas ventures, 'Shall we—'

'Get a drink?'

'I mean, I guess that's what you do in a place like this. Right?'

'What do I know?' I squawk. Bright-eyed and eager, standing on the threshold totally out of place, we must look a right pair of lemons.

'Okay.' Pas makes to walk down the steps, but I don't move. He turns back. 'Bar's this way, buddy.'

I'm overcome with a strange queasiness, but I can't put my finger on why.

'What if they don't serve us?' I reply, simply for something to say. 'What if they ask for, like, proof or whatever?'

'Proof of *what*?' He screws up his face like he's talking to an idiot.

I'm embarrassed now. 'You know – age?'

'Age? This is Muriel's. We've wanted to come here for . . .' But Pas knows me too well. He comes close and whispers, 'What is *actually* wrong?'

'I just – I've got a weird feeling about it. Don't you think it's odd Lucien inviting us in here?'

'Yes.' Pas says. 'But well, I mean, do you want to leave?'

Now he puts it like that, I feel all those years of curiosity about Muriel's welling up to drown my doubts. After a deep breath, I force the sick feeling back into the pit of my stomach, smile and say, 'What's the worst that could happen?'

We make our way down the stairs. The burgundy walls are covered, floor to ceiling, with photographs of famous and influential people from diverse decades, most of them signed. *They can't all have been to Muriel's*, I think. *Half of them were dead before it even opened.* One black-and-white photo shows a beautiful young man – mass of dark foppish hair, powerful jawline – and in felt-tip: 'To Bernie, the Prince of Soho, turns out you were right: nothing good ever *does* come of staying out later than 4 a.m. Love George Michael.' *Pfffft!* I think. *Don't know much, but George Michael was definitely dead when this place opened.* I wonder who Bernie was; and I smile at the thought of Lucien putting the picture up hoping no one would notice it wasn't addressed to him.

Pas nudges me as we approach the bar. '*You're* worried about looking underage.' He points at a Seeker boy in a booth, hunched over a pewter tankard. An enormous Alsatian sleeps at his feet. 'How'd he get in here?!'

'He can't be more than twelve,' I reply with a snigger as we reach the bar.

'What d'you call me?' The boy withdraws his nose from his beer and shouts across the room.

Shit. Don't look.

'I said – what did you say about me?'

I turn to look at the boy, but he isn't a boy. Now standing on the bench in the booth is a woman. She's short anyway, but also seems to be prematurely bent – battered by life mostly spent in the cruel outdoors. Still, she looks more than keen to establish that she's no victim. Her glowering face is scarred with a long line from ear to chin, like an old battle wound. In her right hand she holds an old policeman's truncheon and in her left a dog lead.

Pas and I stand frozen and momentarily dumbstruck, not knowing whether to feel sympathy or terror. Soon enough, the woman settles that question.

'What did you call me?' she says again, her voice sharp as a knife. This time she cracks the lead like a whip.

The music stops. The whole place goes silent. All eyes are on Pas and me.

She sways and slurs.

Great. Not only is she angry, she's also out-of-her-mind drunk.

Wait a second, I think with sudden fear. *Where's the dog?*

'Whatever you do, don't move.' Pas says, very slowly. I hear a growling noise from below and – *eurggh!* – my feet suddenly feel warm and soggy. I cast a nervous glance downwards. The Alsatian that had been sleeping at the woman's feet is now at mine, very awake and very slobbery.

'Repeat your words, *boy*,' she says, menacingly. 'Every single one.'

'I—'

But the Alsatian starts barking. It's terrifying.

'Don't remember hearing "I". Do you, Lola?' The dog growls, its lips curling back to reveal a terrifying set of fangs. 'Lola doesn't like liars.'

'Look, we're really sorry, we're new here – friends of—' Pas tries to explain, but he's cut off by more barking. I'm deafened, paralysed with fear.

The woman's voice gets louder, her face redder. 'Doesn't like *boys*!' she screams above the dog's racket. 'They make her *hungry!*'

The dog scratches at the floor, preparing to leap . . .

'Oh *do* be *quiet,* Daphne,' a well-spoken voice interjects from the other side of the bar, unfussed and unhurried through the unbearable tension in the room. The woman looks over, eyes on fire. I'm too scared to take my eyes off the dog.

'You and that godforsaken hound are being perfectly pestiferous today,' the voice continues. 'I've a dreadful hangover. A predicament I daresay I share with most of the assemblage here present. Please mute your mutterings and master your mutt. If not, kindly sling yer 'ook.'

I stay still, one eye on the woman and one on her dog. Her expression says she's barely got started. *Thwack!* She cracks the lead once more, then cries, '*Heel!*'

The dog leaves me, leaps up onto a table and bounds across two more to rejoin its owner, then turns to glare in the direction of the voice, fangs dripping.

'What you gonna do about it, hack?' the woman spits.

Who's crazy enough to take this woman on? I turn to search the darkest corner of the club and see a tall, slim black man in his middle age wearing a morning suit – the kind gentlemen used to wear to horse races in the olden days. Beneath it are a waistcoat, a white shirt and a canary-yellow tie. He sucks gently on an old-fashioned cigarette holder, exactly like Leo's. *Maybe his is a disp as well,* I think, marvelling at his cool. It's like he's walked straight out of an old Hollywood movie. Or like we've walked into one.

'What the hell is going on?' says Pas, eyes agog.

'Who *is* he?' I say.

'Who is *she*?' Pas says.

'How you gonna stop me?' The quarrel continues. 'Throw me out y'self, will you? Pansy. Petal. Hack!'

The dog starts barking again.

The man merely rolls a dramatic eye and blows a smoke ring. 'Do tell the pooch to pipe down, Daphne. No one else in here speaks *dog.*'

'You calling me a dog?'

'No. I'm calling you illiterate.'

'Illy *what*?'

'Precisely, dear. Precisely.' Then he takes a long, deep drag of his cigarette and says, 'The dog, Daphne. Or perhaps you'd prefer a write-up?'

Suddenly the woman looks scared. Even the dog stops barking and begins to whimper. A ripple of whispers runs through the club.

'What *will* your friends in Whitechapel think,' the man continues, 'when they hear you spent half their profits pissed as a fart in this receptacle of ruffians, talking to your puppy.'

'You wouldn't—'

'My East End readers simply love a good exposé.' The man's cigarette holder hangs louchely from his lip as he takes out a gold fountain pen. 'Out of interest,' he says, opening a notepad, 'what was your story going to be this time? Short-changed by mean old Uncle Lucien? Jumped by Seekers in the Farringdon Strait? How *were* you going to explain where the money went?'

'I–I–You can't—' she stutters, then, 'Lola, Lola? Lola, come back here!'

The dog is heading for the exit.

'Such intelligent animals,' the man continues suavely. 'Pity about the people who hold the leads.'

The woman looks at him with disgust, spits on the floor and rushes out through the portière after her Alsatian.

Closing his notepad, the man returns to his Martini. Kanye West crackles into song again on the sound system. The chatter resumes, the ambience is restored. *Must happen the whole time*, I think, staring at the man, fascinated.

'Let's go,' Pas breaks in after a moment. 'This isn't a good vibe.'

'We can't just follow her out. The dog. I don't want to be dinner.'

'She's gone. Let's get the stuff and bounce.'

I shrug in resignation and we turn for the exit.

CHAPTER 59

SNARE

'Going so soon?' The man's voice again.

We swivel towards him and I feel my face turning red. *Caught running away by the king of cool.*

But he's smiling a broad, friendly smile. 'Liquid repayment's customary, is it not, when a man saves you from a werewolf *and* her dog? And oh look – there are two of you. Make it a double.' He raises his glass amicably and beckons us over.

No getting out of this one. Pas obviously thinks the same, and we make our way over. In the dark corner he stands up and shakes our hands. 'Augustus Craxton-Burra,' he says. 'Enormously pleased to meet you both. Won't you sit down?'

'Mr – Burra –' I stumble over my words.

'Please, call me Augie,' he smiles. '*I* don't bite.'

Pas and I sit.

'Well,' I begin, 'thank you, for, you know—'

'Oh gosh, you're awfully kind but I'm afraid it is I who ought to be thanking you. Nothing gives me greater pleasure than upsetting the out-of-towners.' He takes an enormous slurp of Martini, finishing it, then holds it up and shouts in the direction of the bar: 'Albie, dear, three more of your finest would be heaven on a stick.' An imposing olive-skinned man behind the bar grunts, '*Va bene*,' and carries on holding court. *Alberto Metti*, I think, amazed.

'Tell you a joke,' Augie chirrups. 'Two Offliners walk into a bar—'

'How do you know we're Offliners?' Pas asks.

'You don't make it particularly difficult, darling.'

Realizing his floppy-disk tattoo is showing, Pas looks shiftily around and quickly rolls down his sleeve.

'And to be in the know is sort of the job.' Augie pats his notepad.

'Oh – yeah,' says Pas. 'If you don't mind me asking – and thank you for helping us—'

I nod in agreement.

'—But *how* did you do it?' asks Pas.

Augie smiles his warmest smile yet.

'Well, I'm a writer. Forgive me, a journalist. "Writer"

would be giving myself too much credit. I edit a humble little rag called the *Gazette*.'

'The *Greek Street Gazette*?' I enquire eagerly.

'The very same.'

'Wow, that's – just – I—'

'Isn't it sort of . . . a myth?' Pas comes to my rescue.

'It's less of a newspaper, more a subscription-based newsletter.' Augie leans in. 'I know a lot about a lot and a lot of people want the information I've got . . . for which they're willing to pay rather a handsome pot.' He pauses. 'Rhymes! What fun!'

Alberto, looking completely wasted, deposits three glass goblets and stumbles back to the bar without a word.

'Daphne is a courier, you see,' Augie continues.

Pas sips his vodka casually like it's his accustomed tipple. I try my very best to keep the petrol-like liquid down. I've never tried it before – barely had alcohol – and it tastes disgusting.

'She works for a small operation called Shackleton's of Shadwell,' Augie says. 'Don't be fooled; it sounds much more venerable than it is. The Shackleton brothers are just a couple of Seeker lads who'd rather be in the Roxi-running game but have neither the intelligence nor the ingenuity. Instead they make their money manufacturing moderately ineffectual respiratory aids, which they sell on to people like Lucien, who sells them on to, well, anyone boneheaded enough to bite.'

'And it's Daphne's job to deliver the resps?' I ask.

'And return with the readies. And there's the rub. Daphne arrived with her shipment this morning; Lucien bought the lot straight away. She could have been back within the sound of Bow bells in time for tea.' He takes a sip, a mischievous look in his eyes. 'But Daphne likes a drink, or twelve. And for someone with her predilection for hooch, time of day matters not.'

'She spent the money she made from the respirators in here,' Pas says.

'Always does. And she's always got a story. And, because they haven't a brain cell between them, the Shackletons *always* believe her.'

'But you were going to tell them in your newsletter,' says Pas.

'I *wasn't*. But Daphne didn't know that, and she couldn't afford to stick around to find out.' He picks up his golden fountain pen and waves it around in front of us. 'You don't need a gun when you've got a pen.' Augie leans back. 'It's all Lucien's fault of course. The whole reason Muriel's was started was so that the mooncalfs he does business with would spend the money he's just paid them in here, rather than taking it home for tea. "Exit through the gift shop," as it were.'

Augie taps his cigarette-holder, depositing one spent butt, then fixes a fresh cigarette in the end. Instead of lighting it, he puts the other end to his mouth and the cigarette begins smoking unaided. *Just like Leo!*

With a pang of guilt that I haven't see my godmother in three weeks, all of a sudden I'm desperate to talk about her.

'Mr—'

'Augie,' he purrs.

'Augie,' I continue, 'do you by any chance know someone called Leonora Skull?'

'Why?' His eyes suddenly sparkle keenly.

'She's my godmother. I just – I thought you might be friends, that's all.'

'Gosh, how extraordinary! How—' He pauses, seemingly lost in reverie for a moment. 'Yes, I did know Leo. Knew her rather well actually.'

Hearing it makes my heart sing. *Someone else, outside the Cell, outside my family, outside my head, is friends with Leo!*

'Started my career as a theatre critic,' Augie goes on, 'not that there was much theatre to criticize by then. Leo had a marvellous habit of writing terrifying letters to any reviewer who didn't mention her costumes. Hilarious! I was the only one brave enough to reply, and so we became friends.'

'I can't believe it, I . . . What happened?' I say, fascinated to hear more about my godmother and their friendship.

'What happened?'

'You said you "did" know Leo. Did you lose touch? I mean – have you seen her recently?'

For the first time Augie seems taken aback.

'Dear boy,' he says. 'She's dead.'

Furrowing his brow, he places his cigarette holder in the ashtray. 'She—' He falters. 'She died years ago. But of course, well, you know that.'

My heart seems to stop. I know she's alive – of course Leo's alive. But I'm also sure this man isn't lying. *It's impossible*, I think, my mind suddenly a soup of hysteria.

'Leo isn't—'

Before I can tell Augie he's just being ludicrous, the slow, intoxicated lull of the barroom is suddenly broken by a flurry of activity beyond the saloon doors on the other side of the bar. Manic shouts. Quick, darting movements.

What now? My mind is like scrambled eggs; I can't focus on anything. But suddenly people are surging to their feet. Pas jumps up on his chair. Someone switches the music off.

Quickly, whatever's happening has my full attention, but I can't see what the hell is going on.

Then a momentary gap opens in the crowd and there's Lucien. He's carrying something with another man. My view's obstructed by the bar.

'Out of the way, out of the *way*!' he cries.

'What's happening?' I shout up to Pas. 'What's going on?!'

Even as I shout, I see Pas suddenly jerk his head forward, jaw dropping, eyes wide with astonishment. Then he looks down at me and there's horror written on his face.

'It's Rosie Rogers! She's – they're carrying her – she's hurt!'

The name alone is enough to send me over the edge. *But hurt too? Here? How?!* My mind is in overdrive.

Pas jumps down from his chair. 'Badly hurt!'

We struggle and push our way through the crowd, out into the middle of the room. And there she is: Rosie, bruises blackening on her cheekbones and jawline.

'What the hell did you do to her?' I scream out in Lucien's direction. I'm boiling hot, rivers of sweat tumbling down across my forehead. He looks over and sees me, but carries on making for the door that leads out into the show-room. 'Lucien! Stop! Now! What did you do?!'

'I didn't do *nothing*!' he shouts, pushing and shoving his way through the flood of spectators, his big hands under her arms. 'Dumped she was! On the steps of the NCP!'

Finally I get to Rosie. I'm horrified by what I see. Dark clots mat her hair, getting thicker by the second. Her eyes are closed. She's losing blood.

'Put her down!' I shout, looking daggers at him. 'Now!'

To my surprise and consternation, Lucien and the man who has her feet both immediately let Rosie's battered body drop with a thud in the middle of the room.

'Well? What boy? What?!' Lucien says, looking at me with an expression I don't recognize. His eyes dart erratically around, lizard-like, under his furrowed monobrow of red hair. I can't work out whether he's terrified or excited. 'It's the Rogers girl, you know? The Rogers girl.' He just keeps repeating it, over and over, like a madman. 'Rosie Rogers, Rogers's girl—'

'I know!' I explode, trying to shut him up so I can think. 'And we have to *do* something. I don't . . . Get more bandages – antiseptic, you must have that – *Lucien!*'

Lucien looks at Rosie on the floor and then across at me, his eyes as blank as a shark's. 'We can't do nothing for her here,' he says, emotionlessly. 'We'll have to get rid of her.'

I lunge forward, not knowing what Lucien means or what I'm going to do when I get to him. Pas grabs me and suddenly he's trying to drag me towards the door. 'Dude, we can't, we've gotta go!' he hisses in my ear. 'We can't be here. Not with her.'

'I'm not leaving her here!' I push him off me, catching him off guard, sending him stumbling backwards into an elderly man wearing a bright-green shell suit. Pas quickly stoops and helps the man to his feet apologetically. Then he turns back to me, his face half desperation, half indignation.

'That's it then!' Lucien erupts, like he's had a brilliant idea. 'You take her – *take her*. That's it. That's what we'll do. If you won't leave her here, then take her with you.' He's getting hysterical now. 'She's putting us all in danger!'

'You were the one that brought her in here, you idiot!' I say, surprised by my own bravery as I barrel through the crowd towards him. No one ever speaks to Lucien like this. I feel like I'm in the middle of a terrible, terrifying nightmare, playing out in quadruple time and where nothing makes any sense.

'What was I supposed to do?' he yells, though I'm now just feet from him and closing. 'Can't have the most famous Specta in the world lying there on Lexington Street, dumped on my doorstep, bringing shame and trouble into my place of work!'

As I reach him, a steely, focused expression comes over Lucien's face. He says, very slowly and clearly, looking only at me: 'We'll have to kill her.'

I'm suddenly aware the room has gone dead silent around us, and around Rosie, her perfect face turning purple, her exquisite features pulped.

'You're not going to touch her,' I say without hesitation. I feel like my voice and my sense of justice are all I need to make Lucien fold.

He doesn't.

'What you gonna do about it, kiddo? Eh?' he responds. The menace in him is palpable. Then he looks down at Rosie. 'Nothing else for it.' Lucien rolls up his sleeves to reveal arms of sinewy strength, then stalks back through the saloon doors purposefully as if to select his weapon of execution.

'Kid,' Pas barks right behind me. 'We have to go. *Now!*'

'We'll take her to the Cell!' The words just burst out of me. I spin round to look at Pas. 'We'll take her to Yottam!'

'Have you gone completely crazy?' Pas shouts, freaking out like I've never seen before. Then he takes me by the shoulders and fixes me with dark, intense eyes. 'You want to take Hamilton Rogers' daughter into an Offliner Cell? Do you want us *all* to die?'

I can't leave her here, I can't leave Rosie, I think, *no matter what.*

Grabbing Pas back, I pull him close. My voice is hushed. 'He'll kill her if we leave her.'

'Are you out of your—' he hisses back. 'He's not going to kill her, you *idiot*. That would be a death sentence for *him*! You know how he works. He's a trader. Rosie's gold dust to him.'

'No, listen to me, Pas! That's what I'm trying to say. Gnosys don't care about her. She's worthless to them, worthless to Lucien. I saw her with her father. She embarrassed him in front of everyone, and he'll make sure she suffers for it. This is punishment, I *know* it. And I don't think Hamilton Rogers knows any limits when he's angry.'

Lucien walks back through the swing door, a big holdall in one hand and in the other a meat cleaver. He's got a couple of heavies behind him who I've never seen before.

I look at all this aghast, then back to Pas. 'We leave her here, she's dead. Lucien's not going to be able to use her as a bargaining tool with the Spectas because they're the ones who did this. They don't want her back.'

Pas says nothing. Just looks at me, breathing heavily and gritting his teeth. Then he runs his hands through his hair, frustration and indecision in his eyes. 'And how are we supposed to carry her?' he says, acidly. 'And what if there's another patrol out there? I'm with Lucien on one thing. She's a bit of a liability is Rosie Rogers.'

'Far be it from me to stick my oar in.' Augie's honeyed words cut through the terror and panic in the room as sweetly as they did before. Turning, I see he hasn't moved since Lucien brought Rosie in here; he's still just sitting there, smoking. 'But if your problem is covert transportation, I could well be of some assistance.'

CHAPTER 60

LADY
PENELOPE

We're on Brewer Street, leaving the old NCP car park. Rosie is laid out on an old bit of curtain stretched between Pas and me, the only thing Lucien's 'chappies' could find, apparently. *This is going to rip any minute*, I think. Her limp head, even bloodier now, lolls from side to side as we go.

Outside, the streets are in shadow. As expected, the winds have brought roiling cloud back over London, making it seem like twilight already, even though sunset's still an hour away. *Should have been back in the Cell long ago*, I think, anxiously going over everything that's just happened. It's all such a blur: the shock of Rosie being brought in, the argument with Lucien, then the struggle to persuade the selfish, crooked punters in the bar to give us enough Roxi to protect her on the short journey outside. Even though it was a relatively clear day earlier on, the Ghetto air is always loaded with toxins, which she would have been breathing in the whole time she was lying, dumped in the street. *How long were you out here?* I wonder, as Pas and I struggle to keep her steady on the curtain. In the barroom we couldn't get Rosie to come round enough to huff the stuff back, so in desperation I finally took it myself then gave it to her mouth-to-mouth, pinching her nose and pumping her chest. One of the earliest counsels I can remember was Yottam giving us a demonstration of how to resuscitate a patient on the edge of death. I feel like Rosie might well be right on the brink now herself.

Standing with my back to the road, I watch as Lucien lurks, muttering to himself, in the dark entrance to the old car park.

Coward. You bloody coward, I think, scowling. He wouldn't even show himself in the street while we edged out and checked every direction for Teeth. I'm still shaken from seeing the patrol earlier, so close to here. Everything about this day has felt strange, wrong almost, and seeing the Migs was where it started. Somehow it's like all of it is part of the same strangeness – Rosie in this stretcher; the Teeth; Lucien's bizarre pendulum swings from hostility to hospitality and back. I look up, catch his eyes, see a glimmer of yellow at the corner of his mouth. *Are you smiling?*

'Here you are,' I hear Augie say, his hushed tones warm and briefly reassuring. 'I mean, really, you can't go trooping down the street with Miss Rogers laid out in a bit of old curtain. Besides, brocade hasn't been in since the Fifties.' He raises an eyebrow mordantly. 'That's the 1550s, incidentally. No, no, a princess must have her carriage.'

He pats the canopy of an old bicycle-rickshaw, lovingly painted in pink and parked proudly on the street like a last relic of a long-lost era of light-hearted pleasures. 'This is Lady Penelope. She's been down every street in London in her time, and up it twice – thrice! – her primary function being the delivery of *Gazettes*, but this will be her first time bearing royalty.' Pas and I turn the curtain-stretcher so that we're parallel with Augie's pride and joy.

'Miss Rogers can go in the back,' hums Augie, unzipping the rickshaw's canopy to reveal a covered compartment with a fluffy, sofa-like seat big enough for three. He flicks a switch and a border of fairy lights comes twinkling to life around the seat. In other circumstances, I would have laughed.

As carefully as we know how, Pas and I ease Rosie off the makeshift stretcher and settle her in the big seat.

Pas says, 'You get in the back too. Make sure she's okay. I'll cycle.'

'Okay.' I say. 'If you're sure.'

'Now, look here,' says Augie with half a glance back at Lucien, still watching silently. 'On our way out one of the attendants here, obviously feeling in unusually philanthropic spirits, shared a little morsel that his boss has somehow failed to mention to you, even though there isn't a scuttle or a screech in Soho that he doesn't know about.' Augie lowers his voice even more, now turning his back to Lucien completely. 'It seems that some of our Mig friends sauntered past not long before we came outside. They went down Great Windmill Street.'

Lucien's stands at a crossroads: east–west runs Brewer Street, northward is Lexington Street and going south Great Windmill Street. Via Windmill, it would be no more than three minutes to the Circus in this contraption – but we can't go that way.

'So my advice,' says Augie, in a velveteen whisper, 'is to make the most of Lady Penelope and go the long way round; take in the sights!'

'Brewer will work,' says Pas. 'Almost as fast anyway.'

'Keep your eyes and ears peeled and you'll be fine,' says Augie. 'Tuck Penelope out of sight under the arches near the Cell entrance, and no one will know you've passed by.'

Pas nods, then looks at me.

But one question is tugging at my heart; I can't let Augie go without saying something. 'Leo's not dead,' I blurt. 'Why did you tell me she was dead?'

'Kid,' Pas says quietly but firmly. 'Get in. Now.'

Augie just looks at me, huge sadness in his eyes. I wait a second more for him to tell me something.

'Be safe.' It's all he says.

'But you're . . . You can't be—'

'Kid!' Pas says sharply.

'Okay!' I snap back at him. Then I bite my lip, close my eyes and say resignedly, 'All right. Okay.' Defeated and depleted, I turn and get in the back of the rickshaw to sit beside Rosie. Never in my wildest dreams have I pictured getting up close with her quite like this. I don't know what to do with my arms – feeling I should cradle her injured form but also, ridiculously, feeling like that would be an imposition.

Pas begins to pedal. As he cranks the wheels up to speed, I crane my head round to look back at Augie, hoping he'll shout out after us with an answer, a clue, anything. He just stares mournfully and I stare back, like I might see inside his head and find Leo there.

Just seconds later I hear Pas swear under his breath and the rickshaw veers suddenly rightwards, juddering over bits of debris. Rosie flops into my lap and I clamp one arm around her, then venture, 'Bro?'

'Spooked, mate,' says Pas over his shoulder. 'There was something up ahead. Could've been Seekers, anything; just didn't want to risk it being Teeth. Augie's magical mystery tour it is.'

It's eerily quiet, with only the creak, creak, creak of pedalling, the noise of a few stones skittering away from the tyres, and my heart thumping against my chest. It feels like it's counting the seconds in double time. Lying now half across me, Rosie looks like she's listening to it.

'Check for a Plug,' calls Pas, sounding breathless already. Lifting her wet, matted hair with my free hand, I look at one ear and then feel for the other, checking whether she's still logged in.

'No Plug.'

'Good,' he says. But he sounds nervous. This detour

north will double or triple the distance home, and with both me and Rosie in the back the going is slower than we could jog.

Illuminated in the gloom by the twinkling fairy lights, he's struggling to get the ungainly old rickshaw moving forward steadily over the crumbled tarmac. His head turns from side to side, scanning our surroundings, squinting through cracked windows into the dank darkness of the derelict buildings lining the street. *Come on Pas*, I think. *You can do it. Just get us home . . .*

We take another corner. A sudden loud rush of noise just ahead sends him ducking his head down and cursing under his breath.

But it's only pigeons, startling up in a flurry of panic from the back of an abandoned, rusting van. Rosie stirs but doesn't wake up. *I can't believe you're here. I can't believe you're here with me*, goes my head, in sync with my heart.

'Beak Street,' says Pas. Now all the noises of Soho crowd in on us. A door bangs. A rusty window flaps in the wind. There's a burst of noise from high up above us. *Chariot!* I think, but then the noise modulates into a keening sound, like a mourner at a funeral, and I realize it's just the wind funnelling through the narrow gaps between upper storeys.

Pas looks like an insect, his head darting around madly as he scans the sky and what's in front and behind us, trying to make sure we're not being tracked. He looks ahead again, down the narrow, sunless street. *Not far now*, I tell myself. But the seconds stretch out unbearably.

The thought of Leo spikes again as I realize our detour has brought us halfway to Skull's. I can't get what Augie said out of my head. *Is he just wrong, or was he lying to me? And if he was lying to me – why? I have to see Leo, I've got to be sure!*

The rickshaw jerks violently. Rosie's eyes spring open, glazed. *Maybe the Roxi's bringing her around.*

'Sorry,' calls Pas. 'Loose manhole cover.'

Rosie heaves herself upright. Gingerly, she rubs her head and then looks at her fingers, sees the blood that's come away. Sitting there with this almost total stranger, this wounded girl, this idol of the holo-pops, I have no idea what to say or do. Bringing her eyes into focus, she sees me; grabs my arm, squeezes it tight.

'Kid?' she says. 'I-I know you.' Her voice is weak, cracking. She looks around, confused. 'Where are we? Where's my dad?'

'We're taking you to a safe place,' I gulp. 'Where you can recover. You've been – you're badly hurt.'

Rosie squeezes her eyes open and closed, then asks with rising panic, 'We're not in the Universe?'

'Perspecta?'

'Perspecta, yes, of course Perspecta!'

I glance at the dereliction all round us. 'No, this is real. We're going—'

My voice is drowned out by an eruption of crunching and coughing and crackling as Beak Street becomes a chasm of bright white.

Craaack! Chips of masonry burst from the wall to our right.

'Where the hell did that come from?' Pas cries.

'Behind!' Through the little plastic rear window I can see figures in shooting posture less than a hundred paces behind us.

The rickshaw veers left at speed, rocking Rosie back onto me.

'Golden Square,' barks Pas.

'Where?' gasps Rosie as we jangle past the desolate brambles and rusted railings of a sad old garden square. The more alert she gets, the more she seems to panic. 'Where are we – where are you taking me?'

'The Offliner Cell,' I say. 'Piccadilly Circus.'

Her eyes fill with alarm. 'No!' She squeezes my arm even tighter, tries to pull herself up. 'No! No, you can't!'

'Will you *please* shut up!' shouts Pas. 'We're almost there, but we'll never make it if you keep—'

'You can't take me!' Rosie protests. 'It's a trap! You have to turn back!'

Pas's voice comes back shaking with anger. 'Are you totally out of your—'

Then he slews to a halt, throwing Rosie and me forward against the canopy fabric.

Before I know it, Pas is unzipping the compartment and leaning in, finger to his lips. Grabbing my arm, he steers me silently from the rickshaw. Rosie seems dazed. She says nothing as he hauls her out and corrals us both back towards the derelict garden square, Rosie tottering as unsteadily as the newborn fawn in the old Disney cartoon.

'In here.' Pas ushers us through the gaping doorway of a crumbling building on the corner of Golden Square, then, 'Couldn't cross Brewer. Another patrol up there. Streets around Lucien's seem to be crawling with them. And they're damn trigger-happy today.'

'Some rescue,' comes Rosie's voice, faint in the shadows.

'Right?' says Pas, like they're sharing a joke. But then he adds acidly, 'From now on, sweetheart, you're on your own with Indiana Jones here.'

'You're—?' I gawp.

'Gonna draw them off.' He takes a blast of Roxi, shudders, then fixes me with sad eyes. 'All good, bro. Just gonna get them off your scent, then shimmy up a wall and vanish.'

As he outlines his plan, I feel Rosie tensing beside me, and when he's done she bursts out, 'You don't understand what you're doing, either of you. I keep trying to tell you, you're heading into a trap. You don't—'

'Wait!' Pas butts in. 'Streets are full of Teeth. You want to turn back and join them? Be my guest.'

Whatever she was going to say, she bites it off.

'Rosie,' I say as gently as I can. 'I – it's – they wouldn't be kind to you. You're already injured. Let Pas do his thing, and I'll get you where our doctor can fix you up.'

'And look,' Pas adds. 'I'll leg it over to our neighbours – Kid's mates who got him out of Westminster – and tell them to be on alert, just in case. Happy?'

I hear her draw in a quavering breath. Her face looks frighteningly pale as she gives a half-nod.

We emerge onto Golden Square again, Pas in front, Rosie leaning on me. The wild, stabbing wind, gusting dust around us, reveals it's almost sunset.

From where we stand, two roads lead across Brewer Street towards the Circus: James and John. I feel a pang for Augie as Pas walks down James Street past the abandoned rickshaw, swinging a length of railing in his hands. He stops at the corner of Brewer.

I turn to Rosie and ask, 'Can you really walk?' She nods, but it seems an age before we've limped round to our own position where John Street meets Brewer.

Peering out gingerly, I give a low pigeon coo that's swallowed by the wind; then another, louder. Pas steps into Brewer and pivots away from us towards Lucien's. Suddenly he's bashing hell out of an old metal garage door with his bit of broken railing.

The clanging echoes give way to the sound of boots running. Through the swirling murk, I see silhouetted forms spill into Brewer Street a hundred paces beyond Pas. Flashing lights glint on four shiny white respirator masks.

'All right lads! Toothache is it? You need to see the dentist!' Pas yells, then immediately dodges out of sight.

Krrraaghgh! The Migs let rip their cannons. I daren't look, but seconds later there comes a metallic rattling, and I know Pas is back in Golden Square running his pole along the old garden railings.

'What time is it, Migs?' comes Pas's voice above the wind. 'Tooth-hurty?'

Military boots thud their way towards us but then – exactly as Pas predicted – turn off towards the square.

'This is it,' I whisper to Rosie and grab her hand. We're across Brewer in a flash and make it the few yards to the corner of Glasshouse Street before she stumbles and sinks to her knees.

'Rosie!'

She slumps against the wall

'You can't do this,' I gasp. 'You can't walk, you have to let me help you.'

'No, no, no . . .' She repeats the word more and more faintly, trying in vain to push herself back up the wall and onto her feet.

I stoop and give her a hit of Roxi, but I can see it's not going to work fast enough. Injuries and stress have drained her, and now the rotten air is attacking her lungs. Crouching down, I pull Rosie into my arms and brace my feet.

'Let . . . go . . .' she mumbles, thumping my back with weak fists.

I can't do this, I think. Then, realizing I'm echoing what I just said to her, I tell myself, *But one of us has to*. With a groan, pushing upwards with everything I've got, I straighten up and heave her off the ground in a fireman's lift.

Round the corner, it's almost a straight line to the Cell. *Two hundred steps*, I tell myself. *Three minutes*. To my surprise Rosie now feels light as a feather, a rag doll over my shoulder. I begin walking as fast as I can, breath loud in my own ears.

'Kid,' moans Rosie, rallying fractionally. 'Put me down . . . This . . . mistake . . .'

Terrified she's going to revive fully before I've got her to safety, I begin to lengthen my stride. Heart thudding, mouth parched, lungs heaving in the vile air, I push myself into a near-run, head down for balance.

The sound of my own steps suddenly tells me that the street has opened out into a wide space. *The Circus!*

Raising my head to peer through the dervish dust, I breathe to Rosie, 'Just a tiny bit furth—'

I skid to a halt as the dust turns blue-silver. Like a leviathan opening its eyes in the darkest depths of the ocean, a Chariot turns its lights on us.

Rosie was right. This is a trap. And I've carried her full-tilt straight into it.

CHAPTER 61

CIRCUS ACT

We're going to die.

We're in the middle of a waiting half-circle of Migs, their guns all pointing directly at us. Revealed in the sudden light, the white smiles on their black visors look murderous. Bright beams are trained on us, like we're on stage.

Trapped.

The old London Underground sign shines above the

Cell entrance about fifty metres away, but it might as well be a hundred miles.

Behind the Teeth, the MantaRay Chariot stands in the middle of the corona of dust and debris where it landed. Beyond the Chariot lies my own Podd, propped up on an open door, stabilizers disengaged, nose buried in the cracked concrete. Unreachable, it looks like a marble left behind by some vastly outsized child.

Game over. They're here to kill us.

But nothing happens. No cannon-fire, no charging, no violence, no carnage. It's like they're waiting for us to make the first move.

'Why aren't they firing?' I mutter, gazing at the circle.

I hear the Teeth charge their e-cannons, but still nothing happens. Around us they're like a noose waiting for the hangman to arrive.

'Kid,' says a voice. It's Rosie's. In the madness of the moment I've virtually forgotten that I'm still holding her, one arm pinning her to me so she doesn't fall. By now I'm so tense my grip must feel like a vice.

She doesn't seem to notice. Her vision is fixed on something ahead. I try to follow her gaze but can't figure out what she's looking at. Not the Teeth, for sure. Her eyes and head are now moving gently, like she's following a feather floating through the air.

She's still dazed, I think, and say out loud, 'We've got to get past—'

'No,' she says, sounding hopeless now. Then, obscurely, she adds, 'Flies.'

Flies . . . What the hell?

'Swat. The. Fly.' She says it almost under her breath, but with unmistakable emphasis. Her body feels rigid with fear and her eyes are wide as saucers.

Swat the fly? I don't . . . I squint into the dusty air, still trying to see what it is she's fixing on. Then I hear a faint, high-pitched hum. Sure enough, there is a fly buzzing a little way from our heads. But all I can think about is the Migs around us, and their e-cannons.

A fly? So what? I think. *Is she concussed?*

'What's wrong? Rosie, it's just a—'

She is looking at the fly like she is staring down the barrel of one of the Mig guns. Then she tears an arm loose from my grip and makes a lunge, thrashing wildly as if to swat the thing out of the air. I watch, transfixed, as it deftly avoids her swipes.

Now that my brain has begun to register its peculiarly angular movements, I spot another fly, then another. We're in the midst of a swarm of insects. They all move in zigzags, loop around our heads in perfect circles, hypnotically.

Rosie's shout snaps me out of my reverie. 'I have to go. I can't be here!'

'What? Why? Don't be—'

'This is a trap. I'm the bait, Kid. You've taken the bait.' She struggles in my grip, twists round, and looks me full in the face. I can't read her expression, it's such an intense mix of sadness and anger and shock. 'I'm sorry,' she says, angrily.

Then she tears herself free from my grip and makes to walk towards the Teeth.

Without a second's thought I grab Rosie and yank her back to me.

'Don't!' she protests. 'Get your hands off me, you bloody *idiot*!'

I don't let go. I can't. There's no time to work out why she's doing what she's doing; sheer frustrated rage leaves space in my head for only one thought.

We didn't just go through all this so you could walk back to the bastards that beat you up in the first place!

Then I realize I'm not just thinking it; I'm yelling it right in her face.

Suddenly I have a creepy feeling that the flies are watching all this as closely as the immobile Migs around us.

Still she's struggling. 'Rosie!' I shake her. 'Look at me! You have to focus!'

But she's looking straight through me, and her face is suddenly bathed in coloured light.

'You're the one who needs to focus,' she says, eyes bright with coldly controlled fury. 'Look behind you.'

I wheel around.

The Circus is ablaze with light. Me. Us. Everywhere. Gigantic images of us, projected on the facades of the old buildings in garish, pulsing colours like the old electrical billboards of the Dusk. But what they show is a Streem of our standoff with the Migs here and now.

How on earth are they . . . ? Up there on the walls, my giant face is shown in close-up, like it's being filmed by an invisible camera almost directly in front of me.

A tiny blurred movement crosses my line of sight and hovers motionless for a second. *God, these flies!* I raise a hand to bat at it, but then the fly comes into focus.

Its eyes. Incongruously large, they glint like glass.

Finally it hits me. *Lenses!* The flies buzzing around us are drones, and they're filming us. They've been filming us ever since I hauled Rosie into the Circus. Now the film is being projected live onto the walls.

No, not quite live. There must be a delay of ten, twenty seconds, because what's showing right now is Rosie struggling out of my grip. Me grabbing Rosie. Me, pulling her in and shaking her like I'm some kind of savage. Me, bellowing at her like she's a hundred yards off rather than inches away. Flecks of my spittle flying at her like snake's venom.

My gaze flits back to the Teeth, baring their fangs as if in delight. Minutes ago I felt like a hero. Now I feel only shame, pure, penetrating shame washing over me like it's never done before.

Up there, I look like Hamilton Rogers when he was throwing Rosie around in the back room at Westminster. To anyone else, I realize with horror, I just look like I'm holding her by force.

The projections segue to a news logo and headline:

STREEM NETWORKS
BREAKING NEWS

**Rosie Rogers kidnapped by Offliner terrorists.
Gnosys chief's daughter is hostage to terror leader in London standoff.**

Hamilton Rogers:
*'My life has been taken from me, my reason to live.
I will stop at nothing to get Rosie home safely and bring*

swift justice. While Offliner insurgents run amok,
ALL our daughters and sons are in danger'

I, we, the Offliners, have been turned into Public Enemy No. 1.

Furious, I lunge at one of the spy-flies, miss it, and flail at another and another. It's hopeless. Even when I manage to hit one, it just restabilizes itself a second later.

Suddenly the image cuts to another location I recognize immediately: Lexington Street near Lucien's. Rosie lies beaten and bloody on the floor, her Plug crushed and useless next to her. Then the image cuts to me and Pas lugging her into Augie's rickshaw like she's a butcher's carcass. Watching myself, I think: I don't recognize you. I look like a thug, a mugger, a monster . . . a kidnapper. When the Migs appear suddenly in the footage, they look like Rosie's saviours.

'This has to be why they've been holding fire,' I say out loud.

'It must have been the plan all along,' replies Rosie.

My stomach knots itself wildly and for a few seconds I struggle not to vomit. Then I look across at her, an arm's length away, and whisper with a defeated groan, 'You were right. You've got to go with them. Go back to Gnosys. You're safer there than with me.'

Her reply takes me completely by surprise. 'Safe?' she spits. 'I may have been dumb, trying to stand up for you at Westminster. And yeah, you've set yourself up like a total idiot and I really, really have no idea how we're going to get out of this one. But it was my father that had me drugged and beaten.'

Wincing at the insult, I look at her without a clue where she's going with this.

'I was the bait, but the trap's been sprung already,' she says, nodding at the news projections.

'Then . . . ?'

'I guess idiots had better stick together.'

To my astonishment, she reaches a hand out. It's the first signal from her today that hasn't been filled with anger, resentment or contempt at my mistakes. I grab hold and our fingers clench together, our two fists joining as one. The fly-spies are still hovering around us, and none of this is anything like the dreams I've had about me and Rosie. But this human touch is absolutely what I need right now, and I feel a spark of resolve and courage spring into life. Energy fills me until I'm like a coiled spring. I feel it in Rosie too, like we're in tune.

As if on cue, out in the middle of the Circus my Podd roars unexpectedly to life. The Migs spin round and fire wildly as it jerks upward into the air, gleaming in the light from the giant Perspecta picture show before being swallowed up by its own billowing cloud of dust and the canopy of smog.

Ponzo! Hope rushes unexpectedly up inside me. *Pas managed to raise the alarm!* The Terrors must have crept to the Podd while the Teeth had all eyes on us.

Rosie and I are instantly on our feet, propelled by the same instinct. Hands still clasped tightly, we dash for the nearest cover – the derelict shopfronts we'd passed just before we walked into the trap. Behind us in the Circus the roar of the Podd's rotors returns and the Mig cannon fire resumes. I dive into a doorway with Rosie and we turn to watch.

The Podd is dodging and diving over the parked MantaRay Chariot, bucking like a bronco in the broken smog. Cannon bolts are glancing off its carapace, leaving black tracks. Poor Bernard, I just have time to think, when there comes a high-pitched yell of 'This is for Ivan the Terrible!' and a small arm drops a fist-sized projectile onto the MantaRay's hood.

A few heartbeats later, sudden flame erupts from the Gnosys vehicle. The blast from the lobbed grenade smashes three of the Teeth off their feet. The Chariot's beams go out. Around us, glinting motes of obsidian suddenly spin wildly then rain to the ground. *The fly-spies!* I think. *It must have been controlling them!* In the light from the giant projections, the Podd careers away, pursued by a hail of e-cannon fire from the Migs.

Excitement courses through me once more. *Terrors to the rescue! It's Westminster all over again!*

The Teeth are distracted; time to move. 'Where now?' Rosie yells.

'The sign!'

We dash along the pavement towards the London Underground logo shining above the Cell entrance like a bull's-eye.

We haven't gone twenty metres before the e-cannon fire peters out. *The Teeth – they'll be looking for us now!*

'Shit!' I gasp and swerve into the cover of the street corner, Rosie right behind me. The Cell sign is still thirty metres away across Shaftesbury Avenue. There's no way to get to it without being seen.

From the black shadow of a deeply recessed doorway, we turn and peer out.

My brief excitement about Ponzo evaporates and my legs turn to lead. Though the fly cameras have gone, the Streem news footage is still being screened up on the walls. Headlined **Live: Rosie Rogers kidnapped by Offliner terrorists**, it shows the Podd rising, the sudden surge of explosive light from the top side of the Chariot, the Teeth bowled over by the blast.

No! The Terrors have just been playing into the bastards' hands.

Up on the screen the Migs, pumping their e-cannons at the retreating Podd, look like the last guardians of order, of Rosie. The footage cuts out at the point when the fly-spies crashed to the ground – just before she and I run for it – but the damage is obviously done.

'Oh Jesus,' I curse, ducking back into the dark. 'They'll be watching this in the Hab-Belts.'

'They'll be watching it everywhere,' says Rosie. 'All over the world . . . And they're watching it in Westminster too. He convened a special conference, just for this . . .' She sighs bitterly. 'You've seen the shareholders. Picture it! It'll have been like the night of the living dead over there . . . then newsflash! Screens light up with a bit of live violence, adrenalin flows, zombie Spectas suddenly feel more alive than they have for months. And bingo! It probably doesn't matter if we've escaped for the moment. You've just won my father the vote he needs to go ahead and destroy you all.'

She jerks her head round at a thudding tramp of heavy boots.

More Migs! Loads more! It sounds like they're coming up from the south side of the Circus.

Then a deep rumble shakes the air. Great looping

dragons of dust lift from the ground; the smog rips into shreds to reveal Chariots – three, four, five – descending to hover above the Circus. I have no idea where Ponzo has gone with the Podd.

From Haymarket across the plaza from us, Teeth now run at full pelt into the open. Many brandish a handgun and an e-cannon apiece. A few are dressed in dust grey and carry transparent shields that are obviously not just for defence: they're studded with glinting steel spikes. Behind them come Medi-Migs in their red-crossed helmet rigs. Men and machines, they are all silhouetted by the blue strobing lights of a line of Macaws – medical evac Chariots – bringing up the rear.

It looks like they've come equipped for a bloodbath.

Two of the MantaRays touch down at the foot of the Wall to Regent Street. Another settles next to the Anteros pedestal. From it steps a tall figure incongruously dressed in suit and high heels.

'Well, if it isn't Smarmy Sal,' laughs Rosie, suddenly girlish for a moment. 'Should have known she'd be here to watch the fun.'

There's a squeal of feedback worthy of Jimi Hendrix as a loudhailer springs to life. Smee's voice suddenly cuts into the noise.

'Offliners!'

Echoes bounce around the Circus walls. She waits for them to fade.

'You were offered friendship in return for your support. Instead you have chosen to strike at the heart of Gnosys.'

She pauses again.

'This we will not tolerate!'

Krrhouaouh! As if at an unseen signal, a blast like a thunderbolt from one of the still-airborne Chariots sends shards of concrete up from the Piccadilly end of the Circus.

'You cannot escape. You will come out from your hole and from wherever else you are hiding, and you will surrender. If you do not—'

Krrrrrrhouaouhrrr! A stretch of facade on the south of the Circus bursts into fragments of steel and concrete.

'Quite the diplomat, isn't she?' I whisper to Rosie as the loudhailer begins to yowl in accompaniment to Smee's rant.

'You will yield up the girl you are holding against her will. You will come into the open with your hands up. You will do so on the count of sixty.' And Smee begins to count down.

As she reaches fifty, there's another cough of e-cannon fire from the smog above and what sounds like a mass of tiles smashing into Coventry Street just out of sight.

'They'll never come up,' I tell Rosie. 'They can't come out and fight, but they'll never just surrender.'

Smee, barking numbers into her loudhailer, is beginning to sound like a schoolteacher at the end of her tether. 'Forty-two . . . forty-one . . . forty!'

Krrrrrrrhouaouh! The hidden Chariot sends a bolt down that gouges a hole in the old tarmac of Shaftesbury Avenue, not ten metres in front of us.

'Shit,' I gasp. 'Are they trying to kill you?'

'Kid,' says Rosie under her breath. 'I know my father's not my number-one fan, but I'd bet anything that they've been told not to fire directly at me.' She grabs my arm. 'Stick close in case we're seen.'

'That,' I whisper, 'is the best plan I've heard all day.'

I venture another look out from the shadow of the doorway – and instantly jerk back. Migs are starting to work their way along the shopfronts we've just sprinted past, methodically poking their e-cannons into each opening.

'Teeth can see in the dark,' I say.

'They have thermal imaging – night vision,' Rosie confirms.

Head pressed immobile against the brickwork, I hear the sound of my own blood pounding in my ears, and Smee's voice – 'Thirty-one . . . thirty!' – followed by another explosion of masonry.

'Reckon she's going to end with "Coming, ready or not"?' whispers Rosie. Before I know it, we're both giggling and shushing each other in the darkness like schoolchildren hiding in a cupboard.

CHAPTER 62

ORCHESTRAL MANOEUVRES IN THE DARK

Suddenly, smothering Smee's countdown, an almighty groan of metal on metal bursts out from somewhere high up across the Circus.

'What the—?' Without stopping to think, I look out into the night and gape in astonishment.

Beams of light from the airborne Chariots are just swinging onto the top of the stacked buses at the entry to Regent Street. At the topmost brink of the Wall, a Routemaster is shifting this way in uneven lurches, grinding and screeching against the steel bus roofs beneath it.

'What the—?' echoes Rosie, her face peeking out above mine.

The Migs who were coming our way have paused and pivoted round to see what's going on. All across the Circus, Teeth stand like toy soldiers, frozen in mid-action, heads tilted up to watch the top of the Wall. Smee's loudhailer hangs by her side. The MantaRay with the thunderbolts is turning in mid-air towards the stacked buses.

I glance quickly up and down Shaftesbury Avenue, head filled with indecision and the noise of gnashing metal. *The last dash*, I tell myself. *But do we risk it? What if someone's still watching? How do we know?*

Just then I see something that answers my question. Small dark figures are dashing silently across the street and filing swiftly along the wall opposite. Squinting into the gloom I can see a tall figure, dark against the darkness, tapping each child on the shoulder as it passes. *Pas! And he's counting the Terrors in!*

The coast is obviously clear. It's now or never.

'This is it,' I hiss to Rosie. 'Come on!'

Rosie and I pelt out into the exposed mouth of Shaftesbury Avenue, skipping and tripping over rubble. Pas has vanished round the corner in the wake of the Terrors. We follow but as we round the corner building and reach the last doorway before the Cell entrance, a voice hisses from within the building.

'Hey, Spunky!'

I skid to a halt. 'Jemma?'

She's inside, silhouetted along with other forms against a

broken window. All I can see is the glitter of many pairs of eyes.

'It's waltz time,' she says, and the eyes turn away to look out of the window.

Across the Circus, the groan of steel turns into a cacophony of noise.

Rosie and I peer out from our doorway just in time to see the huge Routemaster toppling down from the height of the Wall. Below, Migs run pell mell as tons of metal bounce towards them, like a giant steel crate hurtling down a giant's staircase. With an awesome crash, the Routemaster flattens one of the Chariots parked at the Wall's foot.

High above, two Podds hover in the new gap where the bus had been – one of them obviously mine, the other shark-shaped – before vanishing harum-scarum up Regent Street. A hunting MantaRay zips through the gap in pursuit.

They pushed it off! I think. *Ponzo pushed the damn bus off!*

Jemma steps out into the doorway, each hand holding a shotgun so big she looks tiny. 'We cleared out earlier, Spunky,' she says before I ask. 'Knew the clock was ticking as soon as you told us what Mean Mr Gnosys had said. Then today it was Teeth all over the Ghetto, and then your mate turns up in a muck sweat. Half the lads just went down below with him. Now there's just us left for the final fanfare.'

Rosie turns to her. 'Hang on a second . . . I know you. You're the one who chucked a grenade down the corridor, right?'

'Yes ma'am!' says Jemma, nodding proudly.

Rosie rolls her eyes. 'Thanks a bunch for nearly killing me.'

'Rosie, Jemma, Jemma, Rosie,' I say brightly but awkwardly, like we're at some kind of drinks party.

'And waltz time?' says Rosie. 'What does that mean?'

'Little joke,' says Jemma, unruffled by the sharp tone. 'Three-four time. That was the Number Thirty-Four bus.'

'Ho ho ho,' intones Rosie, dryly.

'So what's the final fanfare?' I ask.

'I'm calling that the 1812 Overture,' says Jemma. 'Come and have a butcher's!' She beckons us to join her and the other Terrors at the window of the corner building, then waves everyone down so we're crouching.

Out in the Circus, the big projections now show just the static news announcement about Rosie's kidnap, with Hamilton's quote about dealing 'swift justice' to the perpetrators. Smee is flexing her loudhailer. The Teeth are regrouping, and Medi-Migs are gathering next to the crushed Chariot at the foot of the Wall.

Abruptly, the blank windows of a dozen stacked Routemasters fizz with light. It's like a hundred old-fashioned camera flashes going off and the Circus fills with a sound like firecrackers. Flash after flash after flash, then smoke begins to billow out of the sides of the buses. Teeth scurry away from the Wall, with Medi-Migs overtaking them.

'Wait for it,' says Jemma, her profile lit demonically by the coruscating light. The Terrors look like children eager for storytime.

The firecracker noise multiplies but the black smoke is now so thick that it hides most of the flashes.

'Waaaaaait for it . . .'

In the blink of an eye, the whole Wall turns to an

inferno. I hear myself swearing, 'Shiiit!' The smaller Terrors squeal with happiness.

'Waaaaaaaaaaaait for it,' drawls Jemma.

There's more?

Gnosys personnel mill around like ants against the multistorey conflagration.

Seconds tick by.

'And?' says Rosie.

The thrill of anticipation on Jemma's face looks like it's fossilizing.

'Is there supposed to be more?' I ask, hesitantly.

'It's not bleedin' worked,' pipes up one of the littler Terrors. Others join in a general wail of disappointment. 'What about the big bang, Jem?' 'What happened, Jem?' 'Where'd Big Red Buster go?'

Jemma draws back from the window and pulls herself upright. Her face is a rigid mask, like she's a general whose secret weapon has turned out to be a dud. But when she speaks, she's obviously doing her best to keep morale up.

'Okay, tigers, looks like the show's over. Grand finale's cancelled. Big Red Buster never woke up. Time to rhumba down under.'

She claps her hands and chivvies the young ones towards the door so that there's only Jemma and four other Terrors left. Then she turns to us.

'Ivan started stockpiling explosives in the Wall from the beginning. After he'd gone we just carried on, trailing the demolition gangs round town, nicking a little bit here, a little bit there. Must be tons down at the bottom by now. Idea was, if we ever had to leave we'd blow the whole thing to kingdom come. Scorched earth and all that. Thought we might knock out a few Teeth too.' She sniffs. ''Spose we'll just have to settle for a pretty bonfire instead.'

I look out of the doorway. Actually the Wall looks like a dense black skeleton, slowly collapsing in on itself as flames shoot and burst from its interior and smoke plumes up into the night.

The projections have gone. With only the erratic light of the fire and the constant flicker of the Medi-Mig strobes, I can't immediately tell what Smee or the Migs are up to, but I can see Chariot lights moving about in the smog above. *Better not hang around*, I think and, with a 'Let's go', I put a foot out of the doorway.

Instantly the world turns to noise and fury and I feel myself yanked back under cover and tumbling to the floor. Rosie pulls me to my feet again and prods me in the ribs. 'Next time you think about jerking me around,' she hisses, 'remember I'll get you back.'

As I bite back my protest, another Hendrix squall announces that Smee is ready again with the loudhailer.

'We have you cornered,' comes her amplified voice. 'There's no escape. Send out Rosie Rogers alone and then I'll tell you how and when you're going to come out yourself. As you can see, your friends down below have abandoned you. You're completely alone.'

So she thinks I'm the only one here with Rosie! I see Jemma's face light up.

'Kid,' says Rosie. 'I'm not going out there without you. Remember what I said about sticking close? They'll never fire at you if you're standing next to me.'

I waver just long enough for Jemma to butt in.

'Go. We'll draw their fire if there's a problem. Vince, Ziggy – you with me? Frosty, Pasha?' The boys all nod enthusiastically.

'You certain, Jem?' I ask. 'These guys aren't playing.'

'Go, before I put a round of lead in your arse!' She looks over at me, like a little island of calm, then gives me a wink before cocking both her shotguns and nodding at her trusty sidekicks. 'We've got this, cap'n.'

She moves to the window and fires off a volley, gives a whoop of 'Two down!', then crouches to reload.

There's no response from outside.

'Girl's right,' says Jemma. 'They're holding off. They know that if anyone hits her, he'll be Spam fritters – and so'll the rest of 'em.'

'Kid, let's go!' says Rosie. 'Make like I'm your hostage!'

'One last thing, Spunky,' says Jemma, holding out one of her shotguns. 'Take this. They'll think it was you firing. Might give us a bit of breathing space in here.' She thrusts the gun into my hand, then laughs. 'Don't worry, cap'n, she's empty. Wouldn't want you shooting your own toes off.'

'You are coming, right?' I ask.

'In a mo,' she says, smiling. 'Well, go on then!'

And so Rosie and I edge out through the doorway, me pinioning her to my chest, looking – apart from the gun – just like we did on the projections earlier.

I glance back at Jemma. It's a sight I find hard to digest. I believe in her strength and her tenacity, but I'm looking at a girl barely on the edge of her teens. *This is what the world's done to us: turned kids into soldiers*, I think, terrified I'm going to lose her and it will have all been my fault.

Out on the street we're immediately bathed in light. I don't have to look up to know there's still at least one MantaRay hovering above us. In the Circus, Teeth are lined up, e-cannons at the ready, like they're about to give a gun salute at a funeral.

'Stop!' Smee's loudhailer voice ricochets around the walls.

We don't stop, but continue edging sideways towards the Cell entrance.

There are only a few paces to go . . . a few deathly paces in the crosshairs of a hundred lethal weapons. *What if one of them gets twitchy?* The seconds seem endless.

There's a hollow boom nearby, somewhere in the street beyond Jemma's building. *A grenade! She's trying to draw their fire to Shaftesbury Avenue.* Rapid bursts of gunfire follow, and the cough of e-cannons responding.

Then Rosie and I are suddenly past the London Underground sign at last and turning to leap down the first steps to the Cell. My last glimpse of the street is the Terrors – all five of them – erupting from the corner building with a cry of 'Ivan the Terrible!'

Then we're below street level and they're gone from sight. In front of us, the yellow concertina gate slides back and I smell a familiar vinegary whiff of ant-tobacco just as a huge volley of bullets echoes from above, followed by an answering cannonade as the Migs let rip.

'Spot of rough weather, what?' says Mungo with a fiercely arched eyebrow as he holds the gate open. 'Splendid to see you, *mon brave*. And' – he nods at Rosie like an aged

Lothario – '*mademoiselle*.'

I don't even notice that for the first time ever Mungo hasn't demanded a password. My mind is half on Rosie and her injuries, half on Jemma and her boys.

'Mungo, you know Ro—.' Like a moron, I begin introducing Rosie to Mungo, then remember we're in the middle of a Mig-battering. 'She's injured. She needs Yottam to—'

A loud boom like the sound of something detonating comes from somewhere up above. *Jem!* I think in sudden panic, and before I know what I'm doing I've spun round towards the upward stairs.

'Kid!' I hear Rosie gasp in horror, and I feel her fingers grab at my arm but slide off as I launch myself upward. 'Not up there!'

But I'm already hammering up the steps, no thought in my head except how to rescue the Terrors still trapped up there before—

Just as I get my head clear of the pavement level, the whole world heaves. Something vast hits me, everything goes white and then black, and then I'm gone.

CHAPTER 63

PILLAR TO POST

Get up. You have to get up. But I can't: arms, legs, body stuck to the floor, held down as if by some invisible magnet. I push and push but still I can't move.

Where am I? I ask myself. *What happened?* I remember stairs, rank London air, and then a sledgehammer to my skull.

No, much bigger than a sledgehammer.

Am I hurt? I can push, flex, tense my muscles . . . No pain. *Then why can't I move?*

You have to get up.

I'm trying!

Try harder.

I'm arguing with myself now! A surge of irritation sets my limbs quivering.

See, you can *move!*

Wait, no. I'm not arguing with myself. I'm arguing with the old voice in my head. The one that's been there since I hit my teens.

Kid, it's time.

Shut up, just shut up. I feel weighed down with exhaustion and want this dialogue in my head to stop. *Leave me alone!*

Kid! The voice barks. *You must get up!* The impatience is palpable – so palpable that I even feel the gust of breath against my cheek.

Then the penny drops.

The voice isn't in my head.

I sit bolt upright with a gasp like a free-diver surfacing and open my eyes. Nothing comes into focus except the man kneeling beside me, his slightly pink hand on my shoulder. Beneath a tangle of reddish-brown hair tinged with grey, his worried brown eyes look into mine.

'Let's get you on your feet,' he says gently.

He springs to his feet and reaches a hand to me, hauling me up from the ground where I've been lying. I feel like I'm emerging from molasses, then in no time I'm light as a feather. And then I'm toppling.

'Woah! Caught you!' he says, easing me back upright. 'You've been hit by the shockwave from a blast. You're going to be feeling . . .'

But suddenly his voice whirls away from me like water down the plughole. Before I can ponder who the man was, I'm spinning in midnight air, all equilibrium gone. When I yell for help, I don't know if the words sound out loud or only in my head.

Then another voice roars out of the maelstrom and fills my consciousness.

Scum. Offliner scum.

I know whose voice this is immediately. Everyone in the world knows it. And this time it's definitely not inviting me on a guided tour of Apeiron.

There's a sound like jagged thunder, like a thousand drummers beating on plate iron. The pit of my stomach turns to ice.

Hamilton's voice comes back at me through the iron storm, modulating in a second from a threatening rumble to a disquieting purr.

Mr Jones? it says. *Take a seat.*

I feel armrests under my arms, cold metal under my wrists and hands. The spinning flecks of obsidian slow their wild gyrations and settle into a new view. White. Everything white and smooth and featureless. I suppose you could call it clinical.

Once again I can't move, but this time it's not for want of trying. My legs are clamped to something I can't see because there's something around my head and neck, pinning me to the chair.

Hamilton's voice continues, soft now. It's a tone I imagine being used on a boardroom junior whose eyes had strayed to the view from the window. Simultaneously warm and chilling.

'No need for any of this upset,' it says, and I realize with horror that the voice is coming from just inches away. Breath against my neck again. This time my hairs stand on end as if electrified.

'Only wanted a quick chat,' says Hamilton.

Then he steps in front of me, in his tailored suit and tie, trouser creases knife-edge sharp, black shoes polished to a shine like slick slate.

The man that killed my father, I whisper to myself in my straitjacketed silence.

I'm filled with a kind of sick wonderment. It's like I see a raging giant contained in six feet of immaculately groomed, perfectly poised businessman. A twitch of that hand, a wag of that little finger, can blot out a life. It can move Migs and Chariots and payloads of e-cannons; can focus fatal firepower to annihilate my loved ones, my Cell. The last moments in the Circus are coming back to me now through the fog in my head. Rosie, the trap, the shattering of masonry. And then his voice calling me *offliner scum*.

Scum? I spit silently. *You're the only scum here.*

Out loud I say, with enormous effort, 'Wh-what do you want from us? What do you want from . . . me?'

Now he's circling me like a shark might circle an abandoned seal pup.

'Want?' he stops and turns his head with a questioning half-smile, like someone trying to catch the punchline of a joke.

Then he pounces, his hands grip my arms like vices and his face fills my vision. With my head immobilized, there's nothing I can do to dodge; I can't even flinch.

'What do I want!?' he bellows, his spit flecking my face.

I feel utterly exposed.

The defiance inside me turns to pure terror, radiating out in waves.

'Ha!' Hamilton laughs aloud. Then I feel his thoughts penetrating my brain.

There you go again. The words slide into my cortex like a lobotomist's blade. *A trapped kitten mewling and puling before the boot comes down. Pathetic!*

Aloud he says, 'Feel that fear, kid. Can't shut it down! Even I can feel it. It's pumping out of you like heat from a burn.'

He steps back and surveys me from a couple of paces off. 'Fear is like a klaxon, boy. Like a beacon. You can muffle it up all right when you're wide awake, even in your dreaming sleep maybe. But when you're knocked out cold? You're leakier than a ruptured uranium reactor.'

He pauses, cocks his ear as if he's heard something I can't. Raises an eyebrow.

'That's how *he* found you,' he goes on. 'But not fast enough to stop us getting there too.'

Kid!

I hear it now too. The first voice. The voice of the man with the grey-red hair, faint and remote like it's coming through walls of triple steel.

. . . not really there . . .

Hamilton's expression clouds over. He glares as if into the middle distance and snaps his fingers impatiently.

Trying not to think about whatever he might have in mind for me, I strain with all my might to listen to the faraway voice.

. . . hurt you if you focus on me . . . Kid, I'm . . .

But I just can't hold the focus long enough. It's like a thread is cut and the voice is lost again. Hamilton smiles a smile of self-satisfied triumph, cracks his knuckles.

I squeeze my eyes shut, bite my lip – just about the only movements I can make – and fight down the fear. What I expect to hear is the crunch of knuckles hitting me. But there's a slight pause, then an odd laugh from Hamilton. I open my eyes.

He's leaning back on his heels, with manicured hands on knees, and bending forward to examine me with intense curiosity. 'You look so much like him, it's uncanny,' he says. 'Shame you didn't inherit his fearlessness.'

He smiles again, taps his Plug. *Though, alas, you do seem to have inherited his stupidity. You have no idea who he is, have you? No idea who you are . . .*

'What do you want?' I say again, feebly now. My brain is so exhausted, I can hardly do anything but repeat myself. 'Why would you come for us, for me?'

Hamilton sneers. 'Don't play the wide-eyed innocent with me! You infiltrated my meeting, you spied on my business, you tried to seduce my daughter from my side, and now you've taken her by force.'

His comment stirs the broken fragments of my memory. Rosie in the rickshaw, frantically protesting as we propel her towards the Circus. I ball up the thought and thrust it at Hamilton. 'She's – she's just bait. Bait to trap us.'

'I knew you had a twisted mind,' he says coldly, 'but I'd no idea you'd totally lost it. A father doesn't just throw away his child, *boy*.' He smiles like a man with toothache, then leans in and breathes heat in my face. 'Let me rephrase that,' he adds with sneering emphasis. 'A *normal* father doesn't throw away his child, *Jones*.'

I bunch my fists. His point is impossible to miss. For a second all I want to do is burst my bonds, slam him against the wall and demand, *How the hell do you know about my father?* Instead I swallow bile, bite my inner cheek till I can taste blood. If I follow that thought, I realize, it'll tear away what little strength I have. With an effort, I manage to claw it back, clamp it down where it can't cause trouble.

Two can play at that game, I think to myself.

'Rosie's just not that important to you, is she?' I say.

He just tilts his head and looks at me as if he pities my stupidity. But I sense that he's getting rattled.

'You've used her all her life. She's just an obstacle to you now. No wonder she loathes you.'

He gives me an oily smile. 'My daughter's business is none of yours. If you want to stay connected to your balls, you'll never say her name to me again.'

It's a veneer, somehow I just know it. A smokescreen, like he's in chairman mode trying to fool his shareholders. Behind it, I can suddenly hear his inner voice.

Rosie has her own lesson to learn. A hard one . . .

His inner voice, directed at himself, not at me. I'm eavesdropping on his mind. Like when we were in that room in Westminster and all of a sudden I could listen in to his thoughts, see the images in his head, feel the feelings. He doesn't even know I can hear, I realize.

. . . *A Rogers is a Rogers is a Rogers* . . . He's telling himself for the thousandth time, wrapped up in the obsessive thought. Looking inwards, but radiating his thoughts outwards without knowing it. Like heat from a burn, I remember him saying.

. . . *Asinine teenager! Needs to earn the name. Needs to earn her place at my boardroom table. Earn her place in my—*

And I know I've hit on the distraction I need. Quicker than the thought itself, behind Hamilton the floor and the walls of this perfectly colourless cube come apart. Then everything – Hamilton, the steel chair, my restraints – it all fractures like glass. Shining pieces float for a fraction of a second like a swarm of bright-winged insects, then fly away in every direction, gone from sight in an instant.

CHAPTER 64

IMPERIAL

Hands catch me as I fall through nothingness.

Easy now.

I never knew I could feel so glad to hear that voice from my inner world, as comforting and warm as buttered toast. I realize I'm lying back, my head and shoulders cradled on a pair of knees, in a pair of arms. A faint scent tugs at the edge of reminiscence.

'Easy, my lad. Let's get you sitting up. Take it a bit more gently this time.'

He slides himself from behind me and eases me upright till I'm leaning forward, elbows on knees.

'Here, drink this,' he says. 'It might help.' He doesn't actually sound very convinced. It's the familiarity of the voice that helps.

I swallow what looks like tea from an old, chipped mug blazoned in big joky letters with the words *Life would be much easier if I had the source code.*

Then I gape at the man kneeling there in his tan corduroy jacket.

'Where . . . Wh-who . . . ?'

He's gazing at me with a look that stirs memories, with an expression I can't pin down.

You're . . .

He looks quizzical. Wistful. Wrily amused, maybe; there's a sparkle in his eyes. *Or are those tears?*

Then it comes to me.

'Dad?'

He nods. Under his hair, parted messily to one side, he looks out at me with eyes the colour of my own.

All of a sudden mine are full of stinging, acidic tears, my brain on fire.

As I think the thought, the floor and the walls begin folding into themselves, the whole room turning bright white. And then he's gone again, spun away into a whirling cloud of flecks like the ones in Eliza's old Tower Bridge snowglobe when it's been shaken up. I flail my arms but can't find the wooden floor I was on a second ago; can't find my father.

'Dad!'

My wail falls into the void.

Terror fills me. *Not back to Hamilton? Please, no!*

But the voice that comes back out of the darkness is my father's. *I won't let you go*, he says. The sentence feels as tangible as a thread: something to grab, something to haul myself back along.

Someone is shaking me.

Kid, Kid! Wake up! There isn't any time.

I feel solid boards beneath me again, hands on my arms.

I open my eyes. My father – Christopher Edward Jones – whose likeness I only recognize from a photograph, is kneeling down beside me, cradling me. I can feel his warmth, his breath. But it is the smell of his hair, somehow so achingly familiar across the years, that breaks me.

I sob like a baby, unable to think and overrun by emotion.

'. . . better eat this,' my father is saying from just beside me. 'Help keep you safe in here.'

When I open my eyes again I see him breaking a bar of chocolate and holding out a chunk to me.

'In where?' I say weakly, as I finally take in my surroundings. The dark rectangle behind my dad resolves itself into a chalkboard. The snowy blur on it becomes a blizzard of mathematical equations. There's a desk strewn with papers, pens, books. I put the chunk in my mouth and swallow it obediently. Like the liquid, it tastes good. But like the liquid, it somehow doesn't seem to hit the spot. 'Where are we?'

'Not where we seem to be. This is my old lab at Imperial

College. Except it's not. It's just a construct, a safe place for you while you're still unconscious.'

'But—'

'Yes, darling boy. I'm afraid you're still lying knocked out in Piccadilly Circus. I can't even say what's happening to you there; I'm just hoping your friends will get you to safety. My concern is to keep you safe while you're here. While you're in Perspecta.'

'But—'

'And we may not have much time. Hamilton Rogers has been looking for you since he saw you at Westminster, since he realized who you are. It became hazardous for you to be in Perspecta, when you still don't know how to use your strengths here. And it was even more hazardous for me to try and reach out to you. That's why I had to stop—'

'Why you had to stop talking in my head,' I finish for him, as a piece of the puzzle suddenly falls into place. 'I haven't heard your voice since then.'

'Right,' he says, looking conscious-stricken. 'I'm so sorry.' There's an awkward silence. Emotions well up inside me and I have a lump in my throat so big that it seems to block most of the questions I want to ask. *Why were you ever just a voice? Why did you go?*

Finally I find something that comes from my brain rather than my heart. 'I've been in Perspecta before,' I croak, 'Why am I in danger now?'

'As soon as you began to shake off the massive physical shock you've just had, even with a tiny fraction of your mind, your survival instincts kicked in. Big time. Naturally, you were in Perspecta, just like you are in your dreams. And the survivor in you made you howl like a baby.' He smiles crookedly. 'Believe me, Kid, you always knew how to howl . . .'

A normal father doesn't throw away his child, Jones. Hamilton's words come back to me like an insidious jab to my core. I struggle to suppress them, to hear out what my father is saying now.

'This time you weren't making any physical noise about it, of course. Just howling inside.'

'What did that do?'

'It was like you'd turned on a *Come and get me* sign. A whopping great beacon for Hamilton's snoopers and hackers to home in on. But I got there first – just! And I knew I had to build this deadroom – this safe room. Not my finest work,' he says, looking around critically at where we are, 'by any stretch of the imagination. Coding end-to-end encryption as thorny as this takes time and careful thought, neither of which I had. Just had to grab what I could work with quickest. Which is why we're here. My old lab at Imperial – still fresh in my mind after all these years. And I suppose I poured my feelings about it into making the deadroom secure. It's still my favourite place in the world; the place I think about when I want to feel happy and secure.'

I feel jab of pain in my heart again. 'Happier than our old home?'

He bows his head, turns his palms upward and studies them as if looking for dirt. But he doesn't answer my question; just resumes his story.

'Like I say, didn't have time to properly build a deadroom. Not well enough to hold off every single one of Gnosys's cybersecurity divisions. Seriously,' he continues, like an excited schoolboy, almost like he's impressed, 'he's got them all on it. New York, Mumbai, Rio. Diverted all of them, to you. I'd only just caught you and then you immediately went to pieces, vanished out of my hands.'

'He had me in some kind of interrogation room or – or torture chamber.' I flinch at the memory.

'Yes, Hamilton got you where he wanted you, got you right inside his own safe place. So it was my turn: I had to hack in to the space – his deadroom – and pull you out.' He shuts his eyes and gives a deep sigh. 'Before he did any harm, I hope.'

The memory of the interrogation chamber tugs at my gut, so I push it down with other thoughts: other things I need to hear, need to know.

'If this isn't real, then how, how, how . . . ?' I can barely get the words out. 'Haptic rigs, Plugs – I don't have any of that stuff the Spectas use. How can I see, feel . . . ?'

'You have it all within you, Kid. Perspecta. The code. It's why you hear what you hear and see what you see; why you exist in both worlds all at once.' He squeezes my hand. 'Why you feel me now, though I'm not . . .'

He stops talking and a tear runs down his cheek.

Even though you're not really here, I say in my head, *and never have been.*

He nods as if hearing my thoughts.

'Why didn't anyone tell me?' I ask weakly. I cast my mind back to Skull's and a conversation with Leo – *Why did my dad log me into Perspecta, Leo?* – but I can't hold onto the thought long enough to hear her answer again. Instead I can feel something building inside, like the tremor at the leading edge of an earthquake.

'Why?' I have so many questions, so many answers I need. *What did Leo know? Is she dead or alive? Why does Hamilton Rogers want to get to me so badly?* But then Dad's words about his old lab come stabbing back at me: *Still my favourite place in the world; the place I think about when I want to feel happy and secure.* And Hamilton's words again: *A normal father . . .*

In an instant, all I can feel is anger – anger rearing up in jagged spikes; deep, throbbing, anger in the marrow of my bones.

'Why did you do this to me, *how* could you do this to me? To my mother?' I shout, getting to my feet, and pushing him – *whatever you are!* – off and away from me.

'Kid,' my father implores, 'you have to stay focused, stay calm. This place won't hold otherwise.'

'No! I need to know! I've been waiting all my life—'

I stumble and grab at a workbench. Suddenly the wooden boards beneath us are pitching and rolling like we're on a boat in a squall. No, not a boat; like we're helpless in the water. At the far end of the room, the boards themselves curve upwards like a wave that rolls towards us.

'Kid!' my father calls from somewhere behind me, warning, imploring. But I can't see him. The workbenches buck, buckle and break apart, and I'm tumbling towards a wall pinned with flapping sheets of graph paper.

The walls fold away, the floor is yanked from beneath me like a rug and I start to fall into nothingness.

Kid! calls my father's voice again. But it's inside my head again now.

Loud as a sonic boom, another voice swallows up all

other noise, snarling and sneering out my name as if he's overheard, as if he's mocking me. *Kid!*

Hamilton's. It hits me like a balled fist in my solar plexus.

Kid! My father's cry breaks through again. *Hold on!*

Faint, like a petrel calling through a hurricane.

Listen! Remember!

Tumbling, tumbling, I catch at his words like a drowning swimmer.

. . . your book.

Half the words are inaudible now.

. . . letter!

I can't hold on to the thread any more. I'm being buffeted side to side. Pulled, pushed. Slapped on the cheeks.

CHAPTER 65

SCAV
SQUAD

Kid!

It's yet another voice now, stern though not sharp.

A girl's voice. Close at hand, as real as the tiles I can suddenly feel beneath me and the whiff of ant-tobacco in the air.

'Time to go,' says Rosie. 'It's not safe here.'

'My father,' I whisper, without opening my eyes. 'I'm talking to my father.'

'There's no one there, Kid,' she says. Her voice quavers between pity and terror.

Gruffly, another much older voice butts in. 'When a lady gives you your marching orders, *mon brave*, it's time to march.'

Mungo! I think, and the web of delirium finally begins to fray and untangle itself from around me.

'You can tell us about it later, Kid,' says Rosie, as I open my eyes to find myself staring up at her bruised face. It's streaked with plaster dust, but even where she's tried to wipe that away she looks unnaturally white underneath, like she's in pain or shock or both. 'Your field-marshal says we've got to get away from the entrance in case there's another blast.'

I crick my neck back and see Mungo. *Mungo!* He looks delighted to have been referred to by his proper rank. I'm on the floor of the tunnel, next to his cubbyhole, plaster chunks scattered around me.

'I gather your friends from the Wall set this off,' says Mungo. To my ringing ears, his voice sounds like it's coming from the far end of a tin tube. 'But munitions are unpredictable beasts if they're not handled right. There may be more to come.' He looks me over. 'Had a narrow squeak, Jones. Out like a light, but only for ten minutes. You were still in one piece when Miss Rogers found you, and you stayed in one piece while we eased you down here.'

'You friend Pas lent a hand,' Rosie chips in. 'He came up straight after the blast to see what was going on. He said there's been some damage down below, but no one's hurt.'

'Young Lovethorne fancied another look up top, by Jove. Sent him packing back to the Ticket with a flea in his ear,' Mungo goes on. 'Can't risk more of you; too much afoot. Though I'd give my gammy leg to know what's going on up there. Been so long since I've seen any *real* action.' I crane my aching neck and see he's still standing holding the gate, looking up the stairs into darkness. 'Strange. Not a peep for ten minutes now. Can't have been anyone left standing up there in the Circus.' He pauses, like he's sniffing the air, then says, gravely, 'Bet my old desert boots it won't be like that for long.'

A surge of chaotic emotions courses through me as I try to clear my head of everything that's just happened in Perspecta, force myself to think about reality again.

No one left standing. Smee, her MIGs, all down . . . Maybe all dead.

But then another realization grabs me like a riptide and I'm struggling to my feet, slipping from Rosie's grip, making for the gap beside Mungo so I can get up the stairs.

'Jem! The Terrors! They'll all have been—'

Whack! The air is knocked out of me and I only just manage to stay standing.

'Blimey, cap'n,' says Jemma, who I've just run into. 'First Westminster, now this. D'you never look where yer going?'

She's swaying on her feet at the foot of the stairs, rubbing her head. Around her is a huddle of Terrors.

They look in an even more dreadful state than us: blackened hair standing on end, faces full of dust and soot, groaning and limping. Jemma has one of the boys, Vince I think, leaning on her as he hauls a bloodied leg. Pasha and Frosty are dragging Ziggy between them like he's barely conscious; one side of his head is a mass of red. Frosty is also lugging some tubular gizmo in khaki colours; but as if to signal his total exhaustion he simply drops it to the floor with a loud clatter.

'We have a doctor down below!' I say, sounding tinny in my own ears and much less authoritative than I'd hoped. Still jangling all over from the blast that knocked me out, I feel a pang of selfish regret that I don't have Yottam to myself. But the Terrors' obvious need galvanizes me to push my own pains aside.

With a hand from Rosie, I heave myself up again and we're all heading down the tunnel. Behind us, Mungo draws the yellow gate closed, and – faintly through the buzz in my ears – there's the slam of the steel inner door.

'It was bonkers out there, shrapnel flying all over the shop,' comes Jemma's breathless voice beside me as we shuffle along as fast as we can – a motley crew, all bruised, some bloody. 'We were all still stuck in that gaff up there – thought we'd never get down. And then Big Red Buster finally went off, kerboom! Right on cue – well, nearly! And more like boom-kerboom actually. First bang weren't so bad. Second one though – blimey! Blew Christ knows what through the window – rocks, bits of bus, the odd arm and leg.' She grins with relish. 'Knocked us for six too. Vince was already hit. After the Wall blew, we couldn't move Ziggy at all. 'S why it took so long getting ourselves out the door and down here. Wall's gone, but so are the Chariots, and those Teeth ain't gonna be out partying tonight.'

Hauling ourselves down the shallow steps along the candlelit tunnel, we turn the corner and finally the walls open out to show what's happened to the Ticket.

It looks like a china shop has exploded in a chalk quarry.

White plaster dust coats everything, but amid the white are hundreds of gleaming bits of red, blue, orange, green, yellow, black.

I look up at the high dome and groan. Stars and planets and galaxies have been blasted out of Rory Stillspeare's wondrous mosaic night sky, raining in shattered fragments to the floor. Ominous cracks riddle the dome.

But the huge two-tiered room is an electric whir of activity. I was afraid the blast must have left elders and youngers lying in twitching heaps among the rubble, but the dome seems to have absorbed most of the shock, and instead they're running hither and thither, emptying the Ticket.

It's already half empty. Under the upper, outer perimeter, the doors of the various Offices are wide open and youngers are hauling out filing cabinets, chests of drawers, rolled-up charts, even chairs and tables, and marching them down-ramp towards the top of the Chute. A few elders are helping with the Chute harnesses and ropes or, scarves wrapped around their mouths and noses, dusting off the various bits of Ticket to be sent down below. Two weeks' practice has worked wonders with the newly incorporated Scav Squad. Soon our Seats of Cell government will be vacant shells.

Heads turn as we come down the stairs, gawping at me, gaping at the Terrors, gasping at Rosie. But I have no time to think about that before a yell comes from the top of the ramp. *Pas!* Despite the destruction all round him, he beams broadly as he bounds across the Ticket and gives me a bear hug.

'Never thought I'd be so happy to see you!' he laughs. 'Especially not in one piece.'

'Feeling's mutual, mate. Was sure I'd seen the last of you when you ran off with Teeth snapping at your backside.'

'Nah,' he shakes his head, picking Ziggy up in his arms and starting back towards the Chute. 'Migs don't know the Ghetto like we do. Got myself out of sight, made it up a rusty drainpipe, then did a bit of rooftop athletics and got myself to the Wall.'

I look around at all the activity. 'Suzannah told me we needn't expect any trouble from Gnosys for weeks, but it looks like the evac plan's halfway done already.'

'Yeah, amazing, eh?' says Pas. 'Apparently Lizy got them started as soon as word came that we were in trouble at Loffabond's.'

'Word?'

'Suzannah. Don't know how, but looks like she knew we were heading here with Rosie Rogers almost before we did.'

I eye him in astonishment.

'Right?' he says. 'Suzannah Key, super spy. Wonders never cease. Anyway, Lizy got the Scav Squad busy emptying out the Offices and everything up here. They even lugged Anteros down the Chute somehow. Like they had nothing better to do than rescue his shiny arse.'

'So we're leaving the Circus?'

'Definitely. COOs were convinced this was it.'

With a look at Jemma as we reach the top of the Chute, I ask him, 'We saw you herding some of the Terrors to the Cell. Where'd they go?'

'Where everything else is going. Westbound Piccadilly Line.'

I look at him askance. 'The San? They're not injured?'

'No, they're right as rain.' He turns to Jemma as he lifts Ziggy into the harness and directs her to go down the Chute with him. 'Except they're moaning about missing all the fireworks.'

'Moaning again? Blimey,' she says as she disappears from view. 'I'll give 'em fireworks all right.'

I see Vince and Pasha are already in another harness. 'Wow, quick learner!' says Pas to Rosie. Oblivious to the ongoing stares and whispers from Offliners who recognize her face, she must have watched him buckling in Ziggy and copied it exactly. A few seconds later Rosie's sent Frosty downchute with a consignment from the Office of Education and then turned to help the group of youngers sending more stuff down towards the platform levels.

She's only just logged out, I marvel as I watch how she's already throwing herself into the task at hand. *And a couple of hours ago she was dead to the world.* I wonder where she gets her energy from, because this can't all be down to that dose of Roxi at Lucien's. And I wonder what the hell her father must have done to her to make her jump so fully, so willingly, from one side to another. Everyone around us is at action stations. But I can't take my eyes off her.

I've got to talk to her, I think. *She and I have a few things to straighten out.*

CHAPTER 66

ANY ANSWERS?

'I know we don't have long, but we need to talk,' I say when Rosie and I are alone.

Mungo, who's now officially left his post at the Cell entrance and walked stiffly down to the Ticket, has taken Rosie's place helping at the head of the Chute. She and I are now sitting in his old Office of Defence. It's been efficiently stripped of everything except a last, torn old wartime poster commanding *Dig for Victory NOW* and the dud Second World War bomb that Mungo's so fond of. *Absolute essentials only*, I remember from the evacuation brief. *Everything else stays.*

'We do need to talk, you're right,' she says with a surprising degree of certainty. Her head is still bruised and now looks bloodier than before. 'Hold on,' she adds, ripping off a portion of her cotton T-shirt and wrapping it around her forehead like a bandana.

Wow, I think, *you're seriously incredible*. 'Are you OK?' I ask.

'I'm fine. Still a little light-headed, but fine.'

I'm not exactly convinced. There's a haunted look behind her eyes. 'We should go find Yottam,' I say.

'Your doctor? He'll have plenty to do without me bothering him. Really, I'm fine.' She looks down at herself and her mouth gives an odd quirk. 'Apart from feeling like I've been kicked in the ribs, bashed around the head, knocked out, and then hauled through the streets to be delivered straight into the arms of the people who did it to me.'

Giving me an unreadable look, she ties off the knot she's made with her tee at the back of head.

'What exactly happened?' I ask. 'Do you remember? Last I saw you before today, your father was laying into you for trying to help me. And for sticking up for the Offliners.'

'Westminster? Yes, fun evening. What a laugh that was.' She's not smiling. 'Look, like you say, we don't have much time. I can't explain why I've done all this. And anyway I don't really know. Let's just say I'm eighteen and I'm sick and tired of being trotted out on parade for the Corpse.'

'The Corpse? You mean you dad?'

'No! He's definitely alive and kicking. I mean Gnosys. I used to see this word *corps* on all the papers about his businesses – his corporations – and that's how I thought it was pronounced. When I finally realized what an actual corpse was, Gnosys was already using me in its adverts, and the word seemed to fit.'

She laughs bitterly. 'I was about seven at the time. "Never too soon to start learning the ropes," my father used to say.'

'So what happened at Westminster after you tried to save me from being dragged off to the dungeons?'

'You mean after your friend chucked her grenade? A few Migs went down. The rest chased you, I guess. My father stopped jerking me around. Instead he just seemed consumed with you. Kept shaking his head and saying, "He had no Plug, no Plug," and a bunch of other things I didn't understand. Smee came in and told him she knew where you were from, because she'd seen you before when she was on some diplomatic trip—'

'Diplomatic trip!? She very nearly killed my friend Eliza.'

'She knew where you lived, and that's all he cared about. You'd given his Chariots the slip' – she leans in, raising her eyebrows – 'and trust me, that's saying something. He was more furious than I'd ever seen him. But I was so annoyed about the whole day that I just laughed at him.' She pauses. 'Like an idiot.' Then she looks at the *Dig for Victory* poster as if it will help her say what she has to. 'He hit me. Punched me in the stomach.'

I gape at her. 'Your own father?'

'Oh, it's old news, the hitting. Never leaves a bruise

where it can be seen. Our staff know all about it, but what can they do? They just patch me up and give me painkillers. Daddy works out in the gym obsessively, so it always hurts. But this hurt more than usual because he did it in front of Smee. And then they left the room together, leaving me sitting there like a broken doll. Just winded, actually. But kind of broken inside.'

She blows out a long breath and brings her eyes back to mine. Momentarily the clatter and kerfuffle of the Ticket evacuation work penetrates my ears. We should be helping and instead we're still sitting here jawing. I'm starting to wonder if maybe we really are both delirious, but I can't fight back my curiosity.

'I can't believe he –' I begin, but can't bring myself to repeat the horror of what she's just told me. 'I saw him yank you about at Westminster' is all I can muster. 'And – well, I dreamt about you, about him I mean, dragging you into that room in the clouds,' I stutter. 'The deadroom. So no one could hear you talk.'

'Rogers Tower?' It's Rosie's turn to gape.

'You're in my dreams,' I say and immediately go bright red, fumbling for more words.

'This is too weird!' she exclaims, screwing up her face with disbelief.

My tongue unclenches even though I'm afraid I'm going to sound increasingly crazy. 'Yeah. It is. Weird as hell. It's a long story, but you're right: we don't have much time. Somehow I'm logged into Perspecta, just like you were that time.'

'And somehow you could get into my father's deadroom?' She looks at me with sheer bewilderment.

She thinks I've lost it, I realize, and clutch desperately at something that will convince her.

'This was a week or so before Westminster. It was me who opened your old trunk. That's how I got out.'

Her jaw drops. 'Granny Sylvia's trunk.' Then she adds, 'You got out through my grandmother's trunk? I suppose you had some help from a hookah-smoking caterpillar and a Cheshire cat?' I sense that she's not quite as incredulous as she's trying to make out, but also that there's a long way to go.

'Look,' I sigh. 'I could go on all night about this, but it really isn't going to get any easier to swallow. I'm pretty sure I know as little as you do, which, judging by the expression on your face right now, isn't a lot. All I *can* be certain of is that my dad logged me into Perspecta when I was a little kid and now, somehow, he's living inside my head. It's so, ahhh!' I let out a frustrated breath, the expression on her face still one of total confusion. 'I've been hearing this voice all my life but I had no idea whose it was, or if it was anything except some part of my own brain. And apparently no one else knew about it. But now I know. I know what it was – is. *Who* it is.'

At least she hasn't turned and run, I think, looking at her wide-eyed, battered face. I take a breath and steady myself, then plunge on.

'I'll have to tell you later *how* I know. But all along, my dad's been guiding me on some kind of journey to save us from, well, from *your* dad. And the last thing, the craziest thing . . . I've just met them both. In Perspecta. They had a kind of standoff about me. Duelling hackers and deadrooms.'

'Well, this makes my story sound pretty tame,' she laughs uncertainly. 'Think maybe it's you who needs to see the doc.'

'All right,' I say. 'Maybe I do, really. But can we just, erm, park my side of the story for now. I know it's hard to believe – impossible probably – and it doesn't help that I don't really know what's going on myself. But you were about to tell me about what happened after Westminster . . . How you got to Lucien's. What your dad did.'

'From one crazy to another!' She gives a hollow laugh. 'Okay. We'll talk *Alice in Wonderland* another time. So, like, yeah . . . We went home. Went back to normal. Except I keep out of range of his fists for a while, kept myself to myself.'

'Home? Is that in New York?'

'Yes, but I meant our home—'

The door swings wide and Pas steps through.

'Woah! Wait,' I protest. 'We're—'

'Yeah, really sorry to just barge in,' Pas interrupts, 'but things are getting pretty hectic out there. I can see you guys are getting on like a house on fire,' he says, looking at me, an irritating hint of sarcasm in his voice, 'but the clocks's kinda ticking, man. Can you come and help shift some stuff for Pokes? And' – he turns to Rosie – 'you really should go see Yottam, let him take a look at you.'

'He's right, Kid,' says Rosie, getting to her feet. 'About helping. Not about me. I'm fine. And I can help. I want to help. We'll save the story for another time.'

She doesn't look fine, and her smile is so warm that I'm not sure it's genuine. But I follow her and Pas out the door.

CHAPTER 67

THE SKY
FALLS

So we're back in the Ticket rolling up our sleeves to shift and lift when the enemy comes knocking.

Youngers are still coming in and out of two of the Offices. The others must be empty by now. But a dozen youngers, at least, are now busying themselves around Rory Stillspeare's Spider. And there's Eliza beside one of its splayed feet. She doesn't turn to look my way and I don't want to interrupt her work. She's calling out directions and sweeping her arms around like a conductor.

Rosie moves back to help Pas with the harness-work at the top of the Chute while I turn towards Pokes' Office of Education.

'Kid!'

Ruth's voice stops me in my tracks. She's wheeling herself across the Ticket from the open lift that leads down to her Office of Identity.

'All going according to plan?' she smiles as she reaches the Chute.

'I'm so sorry, Ruth, I never meant to—'

'What, bring the massed ranks of Gnosys down on us?' She laughs, though there's a brittle quality to it. 'Something like this was going to happen sooner or later. And let's face it, you were always going to be what started the fire.'

I start to stutter a reply but my words are cut off by a clatter and crash. Floor and walls vibrate and plaster and tiles shower down from the dome. Everyone stops and eyes the cracked dome nervously.

'They're back,' says Ruth.

Pas nods. 'They won't let a few dead Migs deter them. Plenty more where those came from. Sounds like a Zep unloading up there.'

'My father,' says Rosie. 'He's not going to lose face in front of the shareholders. Like I said to you up there' – she looks pointedly at me – 'you and your Terror friends have just given him the excuse he needs to wipe you all off the map.'

'Ah, Miss Rogers,' says Ruth, turning to Rosie and

holding out a hand. 'Welcome to our merry band.'

Rosie accepts the hand like it's a meeting of equals. 'I always dreamed of running away to join the Circus,' she says, 'but this isn't quite how I pictured it.'

There's another cascade of plaster dust.

'Well,' says Ruth, 'I'd love to say you're welcome if you know how to tame lions and muck out elephants. But we don't have any. And in fact we're going to need you for more urgent matters anyway.'

She nods over Rosie's shoulder and there, coming towards us from the Office of Intelligence, is the tiny mouse-like figure of Suzannah between two strapping men. I feel an unaccountable qualm as I recognize the two biggest and strongest of all the elders.

'Jake and Charlie have just been helping Suzannah with the delicate business of shifting her classified materials,' says Ruth. 'Now they're going to take you, Miss Rogers, so you can be . . .'

'Debriefed, ma'am,' says Suzannah, her voice an almost inaudible squeak even though my hearing has returned to normal now.

Rosie looks rapidly from Ruth to Suzannah as the two men move to flank her. Then she turns to me, panic in her eyes. 'Kid! What's going on? What do they want?'

I'm rooted to the spot, mouth suddenly so dry I couldn't get a sound out even if my brain could work out what to say.

'Ma'am.' Mungo straightens his whiskers and steps to Ruth's side. In a loud whisper, 'Would it be insubordinate of me to suggest we take this, ahem, fine young lady at face value?'

Ruth gives him an indulgent smile. 'I fear it would, Mungo,' she says. 'This is a matter for the Office of Intelligence, not Defence.' I've never seen Ruth behave so callously before; so business-like, clinical.

'Kid!' cries Rosie, squirming furiously but ineffectually as big hands clamp her by the shoulders and wrists.

I snap out of my stupor and spin to confront Ruth. 'No! Rosie's with us! You don't know what she's been through to get here! Her own father had her beaten up. What side do you think she's on?!'

The Chief Elder looks up at me with a steely eye. 'Joshua, there are certainly things we don't know, and certainly things you don't know either. We must let Suzannah do her job, and then we can find out *exactly* what side Miss Rogers is on.'

'Goddammit,' yells Rosie, and aims a sharp kick at Jake's shins. He winces, swears, almost lets her slip from his grasp – then I launch myself at him, my only thought to get her free of her captors.

'Kid.' A strong arm wraps itself around my chest as Pas steps up behind to hold me back. 'Leave it, mate. Ruth's right. This has got to be done.'

I struggle but Pas redoubles his grip. Jake and Charlie do the same with Rosie, while stepping slightly further behind her and warily eyeing the tips of her boots.

'Take her away!' says Ruth.

'She needs Yottam, not Suzannah!' I yell. But it's utterly futile. The two men swing Rosie round and haul her sharply towards the Office of Identity. Suzannah follows up the rear without a glance at me. The tirade of insults from Rosie is worthy of a drunken Seeker, echoing under the dome and sounding like it's directed at each and every one of us.

Just as the lift doors begin to close she looks over her shoulder. I feel pinned by her incandescent glare. 'Lions and elephants?' she spits. 'Bunch of clowns more like! You haven't a hope in hell against my father.'

As if in answer, a sudden boom rolls from the tunnel mouth, like a timpani being struck full force. All heads spin back that way. Pas lets me go.

The steel door! I gasp inwardly as another boom follows. *They're going to break it down.*

'Door will be down in two shakes,' says Mungo. 'Time to break camp and head for fresh fields.'

In the silence that follows, Ruth clears her throat.

'Field-Marshal Moore is quite right. And whatever happens' – she looks around at those of us still standing at the top of the Chute – 'thank you all for playing your part.' Then she whips her wheelchair around nimbly, points at the big clock, and calls over her shoulder, 'We meet at the westbound Piccadilly platform in exactly twenty minutes. Anyone not there gets left behind.'

'Ruth,' I call after her as she wheels herself back towards the Office of Identity, 'what happens to Rosie? Please tell me! And how are we getting out of here?'

'Joshua,' she replies, pausing her wheelchair, 'though I know it's not your forte, you'll have to exercise some patience. The problem of Miss Rogers will take time to unpuzzle, if we can solve it at all. But believe me, we won't be leaving her here. And as for the getaway' – her pursed lips suddenly curve into a smile of undiminished pride – 'Dad liked surprises, even at times like these. *Especially* at times like these.' Then she shoots off across the Ticket back to her lift.

Pas finally releases me from his grip, muttering, 'Sorry bro.'

I pull away from him with a silent glare and start stalking stiffly off, just to put some distance between us. Pokes's Office looks like it's been emptied but I see Eliza's now left the Spider and is busy with some of the other youngers at the far end of the zip wire. *I'll go and help*, I decide.

'Jonesy lad.' Mungo's old voice stops me in my tracks. 'This is no time for squabbling in the ranks. Now quick march to my Office, both of you! We have important work to do.'

I swing reluctantly alongside him, torn between feeling like a naughty child who's been told off and a young soldier who's being given the chance to do something vital.

Boom! The steel entrance door reverberates again, the noise barrelling down the long tunnel towards us.

'Is that an e-cannon?' Pas asks Mungo.

'Battering ram. Probably slung from a Chariot at the top of the entry stairs. Must have come prepared.' He shakes his head. 'Blighters don't want to completely wreck the place for their precious Data-Q.'

After the nightmare chase here, and the relief of getting underground, suddenly I'm filled with an awful realization. 'But this really is it for us, isn't it Mungo?'

'It is and it isn't, old son,' he says as we reach the doorway of his Office. 'The Cell is who we are, not where we live.' He's never sounded so thoughtful before. Then he says, suddenly back to his usual bluff military manner, 'Now, you two see that little beauty? We need to get it out to the top of the far ramp, at the double.'

I gawp. He's pointing at the gleaming snub-nosed Luft-waffe bomb that's stood for years in the corner of his office like a harmless piece of decoration. 'B-but . . . Is it—'

'Ask no questions, you'll get no lies. Now stir your stumps and fetch a trolley and a good length of rope while I get the detonator ready.'

Pas goes for rope while I rush off to grab one of the trolleys that's been used for the big clear-out. My thoughts are a blur. I vividly remember Eliza on her fourteenth birthday, whacking the bomb with a huge metal pipe – not once, but repeatedly, as she did a bad rendition of 'Watermelon Sugar' by Harry Styles and bashed out the rhythm. *It's been sitting there ready to blow up all this time! Right next to the Ticket! And now what? Another Big Red Buster?*

A couple of minutes later Pas and I are standing at the head of the ramp, both covered in sweat and plaster dust, next to the bomb. It's off the trolley again, unroped and standing on its black-painted tailfins. With its snub nose pointed at the great dome, it looks like a small rocket set to blast off into the vast, starlit night.

Mungo is at the top of the far ramp with his big deto-nator, a box with a plunger, all painted in camouflage colours.

'Last thing, Jonesy!' he calls. 'Fetch me Yottam's mucker, what's his name? Sir David, what?'

What?! I gape at Pas.

'Reckon he's finally lost it,' says Pas, gaping back at me.

I cast an eye around the Ticket, thinking, *Got to be something more important to do than this*. But Eliza and her gang have gone. Where the zip wire once ran, a heavy chain now runs from the top of the Spider across the gaping void above the Chute to the Ticket perimeter.

'Oh, and Jones, old boy!' Mungo holds up a finger. 'Bring me a dust sheet too.'

Boom! goes another tunnel-amplified blast.

Looking at Pas, I feel a shiver of guilt for giving him the cold shoulder when Rosie was taken away. *My best mate. Even if he's wrong, he's trying to do the right thing. And he's been doing it all day – nearly got himself killed for me already.*

'Pas,' I say quickly, and fling an arm round his shoulder. 'We're good, mate. Sorry.'

Then, still mystified by Mungo's order, I shrug at Pas, but head resignedly for Yottam's almost empty Office. The words from an old poem run through my head: *Theirs not to reason why; theirs but to do and die.*

With a mixture of regret and relief, I see that Yottam's collection of Attenborough books and DVDs has already been carted away in the general clear-out. I guess the cardboard cut-out of Sir David – standing on the little podium concealing a projector, and with sloths dangling from his arms – doesn't quite count as an essential.

Boom! comes the sound of another e-cannon blast at the steel door up the tunnel – instantly followed by a horrifying sound like someone crushing a giant aluminium can.

Shit. I hesitate momentarily, torn between following orders and saving my own skin, but then wheel the cut-out at breakneck speed round the Ticket perimeter to where Mungo is still waiting beside his detonator.

'No dust sheet, Jonesy?'

Desperately hoping he's not going to send me back, I

just wheel the cut-out up to him. Down the tunnel comes the sound of barked orders.

Ckrkc0101110rkrkcrkrkcrssssss! My head fills with the migraine sound of Mig interference.

'Never mind, lad,' says Mungo, looking with concern at my pained expression. 'This'll have to do. I've sent Pas down below. Your turn now.'

'You're staying?!' I gasp, feeling sweat beading on my brow now. 'But—'

'Go on boy. Two ticks and I'll be with you,' he says gruffly. 'Just have a little more business with young Attenborough here. Fine fellow he was, what. One o' the last,' he says pensively, holding the cardboard cut-out by the shoulders for a short moment and looking at it like it's an old friend. Then, in an instant, it's action stations. 'Need you ready by the Chute, Jones.' He barks.

I take one last look around. The huge room looks totally barren now, nothing like the Ticket I've known almost all my life. No youngers swinging on the Spider, no elders swapping nuggets about the old days. Even today's milling crowd of Scav Squadders has gone, their job complete. The space really is just empty space now, like a white-dusted moonscape under Rory's cracked sky.

You've taken everything from us, Rogers, I think. *Everything, even our home.*

'Jones, that was an order,' says Mungo sharply.

I head down the ramp, sick at the thought that I'm leaving the old man to face the Teeth alone.

To my surprise, Eliza is at the top of the Chute, already strapped into a harness. I can't make out why, but she has hold of the end of a chain that's looped around the big iron strut of one of the Chute pulleys. The rest of the chain, I now see, hangs taut across the gap between this strut and the one on the top Ticket level that used to hold the zip wire.

Eliza looks over at me, smiles faintly with a finger to her lips, and winks.

The sound of barked orders in the tunnel sounds perilously close up above.

'Now what?' I whisper. It's just the two of us down here in the lower circle.

'Throw the lights,' she replies, and nods at the master switch that's routinely used to turn off the big Ticket lamps when everyone's gone below to bed.

The dome is plunged into gloom and suddenly, narrow beams of greenish light spring to life, flickering above us in the dusty air.

Then the e-cannons begin, their characteristic coughs sounding twice as cancerous under the echoing dome. Lightning flashes off the high walls; there's the sound of glass shattering – *the Offices!* – and I see a cascade of hot sparks where the big clock has taken a hit.

Where the hell is Mungo? I wonder desperately. Then I see him on the ramp, still busy with something but maybe – I hope against hope – out of the Migs' line of sight.

Another blast hits the lower edge of the dome, or it might be two or three, and more tiles rain down like meteors from Rory's grand mosaic, amid billowing clouds of pulverized plaster.

'*Hold your fire!*' Suddenly a shrill voice shouts from somewhere above, this end of the entry tunnel.

Smee! She's still alive, I realize, the twinge of disappointed annoyance coming almost as a relief from the oppressive fear now pounding in my skull.

The e-cannons immediately sputter into silence.

'Any one of you morons brings the roof down,' Smee's megaphone voice echoes around the dome, 'and Gordonstone will have you all minced up for pig feed. Now, *advance!*'

Mungo . . . A chill runs through me. *Where are you, old campaigner?*

And there he is, silhouetted against the flickering lights as he marches stiffly but swiftly down the ramp at last, cane swinging. I've never seen him move so fast as he gets to the bottom and swings himself into another of the waiting harnesses.

With an adrenalin burst somewhere in my chest, I realize I'm the last man standing.

'Mungo,' I whisper.

'Jonesy. Pass me that and strap yourself in ready to drop.' He nods towards a long metallic object leaning against one of pulleys. I grab it; it's heavy. In the dimness I only just recognize it as the thing Frosty had lugged down the Cell stairs half an hour ago.

I pass it to Mungo then strap myself in.

And then comes the sound I've been dreading. The massed cocking of e-cannons.

The marrow freezes in my bones.

'We have you in our sights,' comes Smee's voice from some-where behind the row of Teeth now lining the inner edge of the Ticket's outer circle, their weapons all seemingly trained on us.

We're sitting ducks. Worse, in our harnesses we're turkeys trussed for a very early Christmas. I see Eliza nod at Mungo and Mungo nod back.

'Corporal Attenborough!' shouts Mungo. His parade-ground bark makes Smee's megaphone sound pathetic in comparison. 'On the count of three!'

'Jesus Christ!' comes Smee's squeal. 'There's a bomb!'

Torch beams converge across the open space above us to light up the steely Luftwaffe device perched on the opposite perimeter from the Teeth. And on the ramp below I see the familiar, friendly face of David Attenborough hovering just above the big plunger of Mungo's detonator.

'—clock is ticking,' Sir David's recorded voice booms out across the Ticket. 'We have only seconds to live. What will you do to stop the clock ticking?'

Suddenly I understand Mungo's masterplan. The bomb's a dud! But he's rigged it to look like it's going to blow. And I realize why he wanted that dust sheet – to disguise the cardboard sloths still dangling from the cardboard zoologist's arms.

But even as I look up at Smee and the line of Migs to check if they've seen through the trick, a heavy metallic click sounds from Mungo's direction. He has Frosty's whatever-it-is poised on his shoulder.

Wait, what the—? A rocket launcher?!

'Sorry, Rory old friend,' Mungo mutters in the direction of the roof. Then he roars, 'Drop!'

Everything happens at once. Eliza lets go of the big chain and unhooks her harness, dropping away downchute. The chain rattles like machinegun fire through the pulley mechanism it's looped around. As I unhook my own harness, fumbling in my panic, I glance over to Mungo just as he lets rip with the launcher.

Above us, in an eye-blink, I see the projectile strike the apex of the high dome. There's a colossal blast, then Mungo lets the launcher clatter away down the Chute and we're both dropping side-by-side in our harnesses.

Even as the top of the Chute recedes from view, I see plaster and dust blooming with pyroclastic speed across the dome, twisting and curling in the shaky beams of Mig e-cannons. I see something huge and angular coming over the top of the Chute – something with huge girders like legs, and I realize at last what the Spider has been meant for all along. But just before its big steel platform seals the Chute top above us, there's a colossal roar like the eruption of a volcano, and the grand ceiling collapses in on itself, crashes down, and swallows up the gargantuan space in one fell swoop.

As it falls, memories engulf me like an avalanche – so many I am powerless to do anything with them. But I grab one image at random from the past – something I've never remembered until now.

Mummy, is this where Santa lives? And a tight squeeze, then her voice, *No, my darling boy, this is our new home.*

CHAPTER 68

THE END OF THE BOOK

My shoes hit the hard concrete with a stinging smack.

It's gonna come down on us any second. This is it.

Fragments of tile or plaster fall all around me like rain. Their clatter and patter are just the top notes in a symphony of noise. Back up above there's a sustained roar and boom. The floor shakes beneath my feet as I tense for the torrent of concrete about to hit.

Instead, the terrible noise and reverberation fade away. The patter of bits peters out. Then there's only a sifting of sand from the air – like we're at the bottom of a huge hour-glass – and a drift of dust that catches in the throat and eyes.

I'm half blinded by tears – each like a little pearl surrounding a piece of grit. I hear Eliza coughing and splut-tering. My hands are cut and bleeding from friction burn.

But we're alive.

'Bravo! Bra-vo!' Mungo shouts, and I raise my head from where I'm struggling with a particularly stubborn buckle. A joyous smile is spread across every wrinkle on his old face. 'We gave them what for!'

He's already out of his harness, moving like a man half his age. Brushing himself off like he's just stepped indoors from a desert sandstorm, he straightens, glances upward and then across at me.

'Hear that, Jones boy?'

'Hear what, Mungo?'

Mungo cups his hand around his ear and tilts it in the direction of the top of the Chute. I look up and see it's now sealed up, a jet-black canopy at the top of the long shaft.

'The sound of silence,' he whispers, gleefully. 'Victory—'

'Hate to break up the party.' Eliza cuts in, having unleashed herself from her own harness and brought her coughing under control. 'Ruth said twenty minutes – ten minutes ago.'

'Right. Let's move!' I exclaim, finally freeing myself from the straps – just before falling flat on my face. I look up. Eliza studies me hopelessly.

'You—' she begins, her white-dusted face creasing up. But then she just says quietly, 'I love you.'

'Right you are, Miss Lovethorne,' Mungo chips in, grabbing me by the scruff of my jacket and pulling me up, like an old dog hauling a puppy to its feet.

'Still got to do a final inventory check,' says Eliza. 'Westbound Piccadilly soon as, yeah?' Then she turns to go without waiting for a response.

'On the double!' Mungo replies, following Eliza down the tunnel. Then they're gone, swallowed up by the haze of dust before they even reach the first corner.

I don't move. I'm still steadying myself from the aftershock of the landing pulsating up through my legs. Everything seems to be racing by at a thousand miles an hour. What just happened, what's happening now, what's going to happen: all a total blur. I don't know whether I can figure it out now or if I'm just going to have to shove it to the back of my mind. *Until I can really focus*, I think. *If I ever get the chance. If we ever stop running, now we've started.*

It's Mungo's comment, drifting back through the tunnel, that finally clears my head. 'And may I say, Miss Lovethorne,' he says, 'you've carried this out to the letter! To the *letter*! We'll make a general of you yet!'

The letter? In my head I suddenly hear again my dad's last words in his Imperial College lab – in Perspecta. I'd forgotten already. It hits me in the pit of my stomach like a football kicked at close range: the realization that I could have left the Cell today without remembering Dad's last words. *Listen! Remember!* he said. *Your book.* Something about a *letter*.

The book and the letter. But what book? What letter?

'I'll be right behind you!' I call out after Eliza and Mungo, but my voice seems to die feebly in the muffling dust. And then I'm right back into the surging sea inside my head, grabbing wildly at the fragments of thought and memory that churn around.

Books . . .

My things!

In all the build-up to evacuation and the whirlwind of today, I haven't given a single thought to my own stuff and what might happen to it.

My dorm . . .

I turn and begin running like a cheetah in the opposite direction to where I'm supposed to be going. *I have to get the bag, at the very least. My blanket. My music. The Scav Squad. Mum.*

When I reach the dormitories, I have to battle the urge to slow down, to walk along it leaden-footed and soak up the memories like a child savouring the last drops of a milkshake. I've spent my entire childhood running up and down the youngers' passageway, playing corridor cricket, running the gauntlet, sitting, gossiping, laughing hysterically. Now I run full-tilt down the long, dark hallway, empty room after empty room flitting past, wondering if anyone's had time to grab things of their own or if the flotsam of all our old lives is going to be left behind here like so much debris.

I rush into my dorm – third from the end, sandwiched between Pascale's and Eliza's – and stand for a moment to catch my breath. I feel like I'm all of a sudden inside a photograph I once saw, one that Pokes showed me moons and moons ago.

A child's bedroom in a city in Russia . . . Or no, Ukraine. The city had been completely evacuated after some terrible, terrifying nuclear disaster that happened back in the Dusk. The bedroom had been abandoned; the child's books, her coloured building blocks, her doll's house and even her teddy bear all left behind.

You could read the titles on the spines of the books standing on their sturdy wooden bookshelf. The coloured blocks were bright and distinct. The teddy bear was sitting upright and the dolls in the doll's house still wore expressions of blissful happiness, as if oblivious to the catastrophe that had taken place outside. That photo was taken immediately after the disaster.

But then there was another photo of the same bedroom, taken ten or fifteen years later.

All the text on the spines of the books had disappeared, their stories lost forever, and the bookshelf that had once been their home was buckled and crumbling. The pigment in the coloured building blocks had evaporated entirely; the doll's house had become a haunted house, the dolls nowhere to be seen. And the teddy bear had vanished into thin air.

Still panting and frantic, I take in the room that has been *my* bedroom for the last fourteen years – virtually my whole life, almost the only life I've ever known. This will be the very last time. I feel the wet itch of a tear rolling down my cheek.

What will all this look like in fifteen years time? Will it have been bulldozed and whitewashed, I wonder, to make way for the shiny future? Or will it all still be here, left entombed, a mausoleum for the music and the memories of vanished life? What's going to happen to this place? To my posters from gigs and exhibitions I never saw; to my old Persian rug; to my CDs?

My CDs! Some scavved, some traded, some won, and all played half to death: the soundtracks of my life. I have to force myself not to go and grab them by the handful.

I don't have the power to resist my piano. I pull out my stool and sit down one last time, my fingers fanning over the black and white keys. They've brought me more joy over the years than anything else I've ever owned. The single tear becomes two and then three and very soon I'm shuddering with sobs.

But then a thought strikes me and I stop crying almost immediately.

Mum. This is it, I think, looking around me again. *All this. Mum did it for me.*

And how I feel now is how she must have felt when we left Primrose Hill all those years ago. She was brave enough to do it. A smile begins creeping across my face as I remember my mother's courage.

She left everything behind for us; for me. She didn't know where she was going, what was in store. But she had faith. She believed there was a better way and she gave everything up for it. To stand up for what she believed in. To fight for the future.

That's what this is all about, I think as I jump up from the stool, go over to my bed and scrabble around underneath it hastily, grabbing at the darkness.

'There you are,' I say aloud, pulling out the old tarpaulin bag with the Roses chocolate tin in it, holding all my most cherished belongings.

Not much time left now. I quickly open the box and check everything's inside. *No iPhone,* I think. Thoughts of Izzy surge up but I fight them down. *Forget the past. Fight for the future.*

Then I make a quick inventory. It's all there. *Manuscript paper. Blanket . . . Book of legends.*

That's got to be what Dad meant! I realize with a surge of relief. *His old book of legends!*

But the letter? What goddamn letter? There is none!

I clench my fingers in my hair with frustration and quickly try to pierce every cranny of my dorm with the sweep of my gaze. But my pulse is pounding like a clock ticking at double speed . . . I'm all out of time.

Heaving a sigh of bitter resignation, I turn to leave.

'Bye old friend,' I say to the piano as I go. 'Thank you.'

When I skid onto the westbound Piccadilly platform, the old San is abuzz with activity. My eyes take in the people swarming around like bees under the vaulted roof, lifting, lugging, hustling, passing items from hand to hand or over each others heads. My skin tingles with the frenetic energy in the air; everyone is alive with the mission at hand. For a moment I can't even see along the platform; surely it's even busier than rush hour must have been in the old Dusk. Looking up along the wall, I glimpse Babar the Elephant, Zephir the Monkey and their friends gazing down quizzically on it all from the huge mural – the only faces not intensely focused on getting something done fast.

There's a wild babble, courtesies and curses, laughter and sobs, and then – cutting through it all – the ringing voice of Eliza: 'Mind the gap! Two minutes, people! Scav Squad, one last effort now! What we can't get on now, we leave behind!'

All those bustling people carrying bedding, baskets, backpacks, boxes, pots and pans seem to turn with one accord like dancers taking the final steps in a huge dance. They turn towards where the old railway line was before half of it was boarded over to accommodate the San's overflow of beds and equipment.

No way! My jaw drops and I lower my tarpaulin bag to the floor as the moving bodies clear and I see what's happened to our old hospital. Where there were boards and beds, now there is the train.

The train that's always been the heart of our hospital, that's always been parked half in and half out of the long hallway, now stretches the whole length of the platform. Actually it looks like it stretches even further, because the extra carriages that were suspended on winches above it are gone. Looks like they've been lowered and attached to the back of the train to make extra room for everything we have to evacuate. And the train is heaving with people, filled to bursting with every Offliner from the Piccadilly Circus Cell and everything they could carry on board. Vital necessities or prized possession scavved from the Ghetto are clutched in white-knuckled hands. Babies are hugged to chests, some of them wailing, some sound asleep. Children hang on hips, gazing around them wide-eyed in fear and wonder. Elders' eyes glisten with tears, or stare blankly into space, filled with anticipation, exhaustion and anxiety. Youngers exchange glances, whispers, kisses and wisecracks. The irrepressible spirit of the Offliners. *My people.*

As the last of the luggers and lifters pile onto the train,

I pick up my tarpaulin bag and start hurrying along the platform peering through doors and windows to see where Rosie and Pas and Eliza are. *Nope, nope, nope*, I check off the carriages. In one, though, I glimpse Jemma trying to keep the Terrors in check. Some are yelling 'Tickets please! Tickets please!' Several are busy scratching graffiti on the pristine walls of Yottam's train. Others have spotted the looped strap handles that hang from the carriage ceiling – meant for standing passengers to hold – and are competing to swing from one to the next. Just as I pass, a whippet-thin boy jumps up, grabs two handles and attempts to do a flip, but instead gets a leg caught inside a loop and lapses into a head-downwards spin, screeching like a monkey.

That makes me realize suddenly that apart from the hum and bustle of noise from the train, there's a peculiar, unaccustomed hush in the long hall. When the platform finally clears in front of me, I see why.

What! Where—?

Yottam's big glass animal house stands empty. I realize I feel tears prickling again. The soul has gone out of the San.

Smearing a sleeve across my eyes, I look back to the train, towards the furthest carriages.

There they are! A couple of carriages are stacked with baskets and cages, bright eyes and wet snouts glinting in the darkness inside. Another carriage is a flutter of wings among lush plants, flowers and saplings. In yet another – divided into barred sections – big beasts prowl and growl. All the animals are here that Yottam has managed to save from extinction. It's like Noah's Ark. All right, Noah's ark in miniature. And on rails. But still . . .

As I turn back to scan the length of the train again, I see a small figure at the far end of the platform – *Pokes!* – raise one hand high in the air and another to her lips to give a shrill blast on a whistle.

'Doors closing,' comes an amplified and distorted voice from the loudspeakers inside each carriage.

Pokes stands looking at me from afar, hands on hips, head tilted askance, like I'm back at Counsel and I've just muddled the word *naturalist* with *naturist*. She blows her whistle again and spins on her heel to climb aboard.

Staring frantically along the train, I'm just about to leap on the nearest carriage when I catch a glimpse of an arm waving furiously at me from one of the doorways—

'Kid!' It's Eliza, her face a classic mixture of impatience and amusement. 'What time d'you call this?'

Pas pops his head out from behind her. 'I voted to leave you behind,' he yells. 'But she was feeling nice for a change.'

'Doors closing,' says the loudspeaker announcement again, then adds, 'Joshua Jones, that means you.'

I burst into a run and jump into Pas and Eliza's carriage, among the crush of people strap-hanging or squeezed onto seats or huddled on the floor. The doors slide closed behind me and the three of us embrace – more tightly, I think, than we ever have before.

'Where'd you go, slowcoach?' asks Eliza.

'My dorm,' I mumble. 'Had to grab something and say bye to my piano.'

She bites her lip. 'I know. I'm sorry; there was so much to bring and so little time and space, we've had to leave stacks of stuff behind. Lots of broken hearts today.'

Pas scowls. 'Yeah, you know how long it took me to get my drum kit together? I might never find another Zildjian hi-hat again. But hey' – he digs his sister in the ribs – 'Lizy's brought her guitar, so all's right with the world.'

Eliza blushes and begins to protest but Pas grabs her in a bear hug and kisses her. 'You're okay, sis. Guitars are made to travel. You can keep us entertained on the road. Maybe we can switch to three-part harmony.'

Three? I think. *But what about—?*

'Where is she?' I break in.

They know who I mean. 'Next carriage along,' Pas nods over my shoulder. 'But I wouldn't—'

He trails off with an air of futility as I spin round and elbow my way through the throng towards the connecting door between carriages, ignoring the glares and affronted mutterings of 'Excuse me?!' and 'Watch where you're treading, mate!' Over the loudspeaker I vaguely hear a voice saying, 'Sorry for the short delay, folks. Slight hitch with getting the power running but we'll be off in a mo.'

When I reach the connecting door, I find a gaggle of smaller youngers is gawping through the window into the next carriage. Impatiently, I clear them aside and try the handle. The door is locked. Peering through, I see that the carriage beyond isn't jammed with Offliners or Terrors or animals, but mostly stacked high with an astonishing jumble of bric-à-brac, like a mobile warehouse. The near end is largely filing cabinets from the Offices; but a little space has been kept clear for a bench and a swivel chair. It's this little scene that the young teenagers in our carriage have been eyeballing.

it again, I run my fingers over the endpapers to test whether some slip of paper is glued underneath them. *Nothing! This is getting ludicrous.* I run my fingers over the covers to feel if anything is stitched beneath the cloth binding. I hold the book to my eye, endlong, and try to look between the spine and the stitched back edge of the pages. *Goddammit!* I curse inwardly at last, spreadeagling the book by its covers and shaking it again in sheer frustrated fury as I feel the train begin to judder forward on the rails.

Something pale blue slips part way out from the spine, dislodged by my violent flexing of the pages.

The train gathers speed.

Gaping in disbelief, I stop waving the book around, then gently grasp the object and carefully pull it free from the spine. A piece of paper, folded multiple times into a long slim rectangle.

A letter . . .

'All aboard, what!' As I start carefully to unfold the sheet, a clipped military voice suddenly erupts over the train's PA system.

'This is your driver, Field-Marshal Mungo Moore, speaking! This train is ready to depart! Next stop . . .'

EPILOGUE

Dear Christopher,

I think I'm going to die.

Today the doctors told me that if you were to be born premature there'd be a 50-50 chance of me dying while giving birth to you. They also told me there is a strong chance that you will be stillborn. Apparently, I have a condition called placenta previa which means my placenta, the thing that's giving you your food and oxygen right now, is covering my cervix when it shouldn't be. It's covering the exit.

But I know better than the doctors. I know you're not going to be stillborn. If it was just the doctors warning me, I'd be clinging onto the idea that I'd be in the lucky 50%. That I was going to survive. I'm pretty sure now that that isn't going to be the case. But I'll come to that later.

I know you're going to be born and you're going to live to be an adult and meet a wonderful woman and fall in love. I know because I've spoken to your son. He's in the future, and his name is Joshua Jones. But you'll call him 'Kid'.

When I first saw his name I thought it was just a coincidence. Now I know it means you're going to be raised by your real father, Stephen Jones. It's not what I'd imagined happening when I first realised I'd have to pass you on to someone else to look after and cherish you. To be honest, there are people I love much more than your father. But now I figure he must be set to do some serious growing up, and I have to give him that chance. I hope you come to bring each other joy and love.

As a grown-up, life will not be easy for you. You're going to be forced to run and hide and give up everything you love – including your beautiful wife and your son, your pride and joy. I can't tell you yet why you're going to be forced to abandon your family – I don't know why – but I know you'll be doing it to protect them. I'm sure that, in running, you will be doing the only thing you can.

And I know that when you do run, you'll remember this crazy old note from your mum and it will all finally make sense to you. The past and the future will come together and your destiny – and the destiny of your son – will be laid out in front of you, however painful, however difficult. Your son is going to change the world, with your help and your knowledge and your brilliance. Because he is the only one that can.

I'm giving you something to remember me by whenever I'm not there. I know Sylvia and James will be around to help make sure you have everything you need to grow up to be the brilliant man I know you'll be. I already know they'll give you the science books I've been reading like crazy even while you've been growing inside me (though they'll probably be a bit out of date by the time you're old enough to read them!)

But I've also asked Sylvia to give you a phone – it's mine, it has my initials on the back: iP (izzyParry's iPhone, see?) I guess you'll probably think it's an old piece of junk. But you must never let it go.

Thing is, as hard as it may be to understand, as impossible as it may be to believe, this phone is how I know you're going to live on and that I'm going to die. I know because of the iP on the back, though I only saw it after everything had already happened and I wanted to watch your beautiful son – my beautiful grandson – singing again one last time. There he was filming himself in a mirror, and this time I spotted what was on the back of the phone.

It was through this phone that I first saw him singing and then spoke to him. It was through this phone that he told me you had never known your mother. It was through this phone that I saw the future. I didn't believe at first, and even when I did believe, I didn't want to. There was something important I was asked to do, and I refused. But somehow I know – not in my head but in my heart – that I have done something right, and that the story doesn't end there. You CAN change the future by revisiting the past.

Keep the phone safe, keep it with you always, and when the time comes for you to leave behind those who you love most in the world, do what I'm doing for you and pass it on. Give it to him, to Joshua. I don't know exactly how, but I do know it will all make sense to you when it is supposed to make sense.

Don't be sorry for me. I've never felt more alive than this past year, first because of Kid, then of Sylvia and James, then because of you. And my mind is just exploding with ideas. I wish I could have longer to chase them down, to work them all out, but I feel sure my mind's running just as fast as it is now precisely because I have so little time. Sylvia will carry on the chase. My ideas won't die with me, any more than you will. And I know you, of all people, won't mind me mentioning you in the same breath as science and ideas.

*I love you Christopher Edward Jones. I love you forever:
in the past, in the present and in the future.*

This is a history of your future,

With all my love my darling boy.

Isabel Parry, your mother

LYCEUM THEATRE

Every Evening at 8:15
Matinées : Wednesdays and Thursdays at 2.15

SEBASTIAN DE SOUZA

presents

" KID "

List of Characters

Ceccarelli, Stefano: Founder of the Offliner Movement.

Craxton-Burra, Augustus (Augie): Editor of the *Greek Street Gazette*.

d'Achon, Michel: Leo Skull's assistant.

Horrocks, Hecate: UK prime minister at the time of the Upload.

Jones, Christopher Edward: Joshua Jones's father; married El Kellis.

Jones, Joshua: Kid, born St Mary's Hospital, Paddington, 19 April 2060.

Key, Suzannah: COO of Intelligence.

Loffabond, Lucien: Soho trader; 'the Mogul of Marshall Street'.

Lovethorne, Eliza: Scav Squad guitarist, twin to Pascale.

Lovethorne, Pascale (Pas): Scav Squad drummer, twin to Eliza.

Manning, Gregory F.: executive Assistant of Hamilton Rogers in 2064.

Metti, Alberto: barman at Muriel's.

Moore, Mungo: gatekeeper and COO of Defence.

Parry, Isabel (Izzy): schoolgirl from Kentish Town, London; 16 at the start of 2021.

Pokeman, Poppy (Pokes): COO of Education

Potman, Gregory: boss of Potman Percutaneous; multi-billionaire from the North of England; a major shareholder in Gnosys.

Rogers, Hamilton: CEO of Gnosys.

Rogers, Rosie: daughter of Hamilton Rogers.

Rogers, Sylvia: founder of Gnosys; mother of Hamilton Rogers.

Skull, Leonora (Leo): Kid's godmother.

Smee, Sally: a representative of the United Nations Cyber Council and Minister for Offliner Liaison.

Stillspeare, Rory: Founder, first Chief Elder and Head of the Cell; designed the Spider; married Ursula; father of Ruth; died 2076.

Stillspeare, Ruth: COO of Identity and Chief Elder of the London Cell.

Stillspeare, Ursula: runs the Cell Galley; married Rory; mother of Ruth.

Thompson, Ivan: Ivan the Terrible, founder of Terrors.

Yellowfinch, Yottam: COO of Sustainability; also runs the San.

Bernard: Podd personality.

Denis: Perspecta Companion.

Jemma (Jem): leader of the Terrors

Lilly: the Jones's dog.

Pasha, Ziggy, Vince, Frosty, Ponzo: Terrors.

Stephen: boyfriend of Izzy Parry in 2021.

GLOSSARY
OF THE FUTURE

Anteros: statue of a winged boy shooting a bow, on the pedestal in the middle of Piccadilly Circus, still standing in 2078.

Apeiron: Virtual city in top-level Perspecta.

Asian Federation: Dusk-era political and economic grouping of nations.

Banksy: Offliner Cell near the site of old St Paul's Cathedral.

the Bec: Offliner Cell at Tooting, south London.

British Government: defunct organization taken over by the UNCC at the time of the Pittsburgh Pact.

burbs: suburbs around London and other cities, now deserted.

the Bush: Offliner Cell at Shepherd's Bush, west London.

Cell: here, usually refers to the Offliner Cell under Piccadilly Circus, with about 500 members; the largest and oldest of fourteen Cells in London, and the second Cell to be founded, in the 2060s.

Chariot: airborne vehicle larger than a Podd and exclusively used by Gnosys; produced in different varieties such as the MantaRay, Macaw or Zep.

Chief Elder: the Head of the Cell and COO of Identity; at Piccadilly Circus, Ruth Stillspeare.

Chute: the diagonal shaft linking levels of the Piccadilly

Circus Cell, with rope-and-pulley hoist in place of the old escalators.

Circus: Piccadilly Circus.

Coldharbour: Offliner Cell at Brixton, south London.

COO: Chief Offliner Officer, title given to each of six members of the Cell's governing body; *see* Office of Defence, etc.

Counsel: Offliner school, sited at the old southbound Bakerloo Line of Piccadilly Circus Tube station.

Data-Qs: massive facilities housing the hard drives and employees running Perspecta. Data Q-1 is in Manhattan, New York City.

deadroom: surveillance-proof space within Perspecta.

Dewey: Dusk-era classification system for library books.

disp: dispenser for Roxi.

docking station: a station on the Podd Way network.

the Dogs: Offliner Cell on an island in the River Thames.

dorm: a Cell bedroom.

Dusk: *see* Golden Dusk.

e-cannon: hand weapon used by Migs.

e-Colt: laser handgun.

Ecovo: 'green' shopping chain of the pre-Upload decades.

elders: members of Offliner Cells older than 25.

eminent domain: a legal power instituted by the 2060 Pittsburgh Pact allowing the UNCC to seize private property in the public interest.

European Union: Dusk-era political and economic grouping of nations.

Farringdon Strait: east London bottleneck haunted by Seeker gangs.

Flood: Inundation of the Soho area when the Thames rose during early spring floods and high tides in 2060.

Flood Defence Wall: installed along much of the Thames in London in the 2050s; known as the Toaster because of its huge hydraulic pop-up barriers.

Foyle's: once Britain's biggest bookshop, by 2078 a derelict hulk picked over by Seekers and scavvers.

Galley: communal kitchen at the Piccadilly Circus Cell.

Gas: Social media platform of the 2040s, taken over by Slanda.

ghetto: the old Soho area of London (usually 'the Ghetto'), or any other urban area outside full Gnosys control.

Gnome: short for Gnosys Messenger, a proprietary form of email.

Gnosys: the world's most successful company in terms of power, wealth and control; originally Gnosys Virtual.

Gnosys Paramilitary Recruitment Surrogacy (GPRS): the organisation that supplies personnel for the White Teeth; *see* Guard-class Migs.

Gnotes: digital currency developed by Gnosys and now used universally by Spectas.

Golden Dusk: the time before the Upload, from the 1950s to 2060.

***Greek Street Gazette*:** samizdat newspaper rumoured to circulate secretly in Soho.

Guard-class Migs: the Gnosys paramilitary security force. Guards are commonly dubbed the (White) Teeth because of their breathing apparatus.

Hab-Belt: Vast residential structures built by Gnosys around the old cities, optimized for the Perspecta lifestyle. London's

Hab-Belt runs along the line of the old M25 motorway.

Hamleys: former toy shop.

haptic rig: hardware that works in tandem with the Perspecta Plug so users can not only see but also feel that they are inside the Perspecta Universe. The first rigs simulated touch and G-force effects. Now rigs provide smell and taste data too, making them fully immersive. The XoGno2000 rig, standard in the Hab-Belts, has an integrated lavatory facility.

Head of the Cell: *see* Chief Elder

holo-pop: a hologram, often used in advertising; often shortened to pop.

International Institute of Technology: Formerly the Houses of Parliament in Westminster, now a UNCC facility.

iPhone: Apple's proprietary mobile communication device from the Dusk.

iVerse: A former VR universe from tech corporation Apple.

Legend: (1) a status associated with certain Perspecta IDs; (2) an early Gnosys computer game in which players take on the roles of mythological heroes, accruing goodness points.

Level 80: the entry level and lowest level of the Perspecta Universe.

Liberty's: fashionable store built in the 1920s and abandoned in the 2040s.

the Lock: Offliner Cell at Camden, north London.

Loffabond's Emporium: hub of ghetto commerce, at the old Brewer Street NCP car park; home to Muriel's.

Lourdes: annual bridge tournament said to take place at Muriel's.

Macaw: medical evac Chariot

Main Street: commercial artery of Apeiron, leading to

Oakland.

MantaRay Chariot or Manta: multipurpose craft used by Migs, generally for transportation, but equipped for air-to-air combat and bombing.

Medi-Mig: robotic medic.

Migs (MIGS): Mobile Intelligence General Service personnel, including robotic drones such as Medi-Migs and human workers such as T-Class Migs. The term Migs is most often used, however, for White Teeth; *see* Guard-class Migs.

Migbots: Virtual Gnosys security force inside Perspecta.

Muriel's: Soho's last bar in operation, run by Lucien Loffabond behind an iron door in the old Brewer Street NCP car park.

Mynd: *see* Synapps.

Oakland: prestige neighbourhood for the Perspecta elite in Apeiron.

Offices: Offliner Cell departments; *see* Offliner Seats.

Offliners: people refusing to use Perspecta; members of the Offliner Movement founded in March 2063 by Stefano Ceccarelli.

Offliner Cell: any one of the world's hundred or so communities of Offliners, all of them situated in areas abandoned by Gnosys and the Spectas.

Offliner Seats: the five governing organisations of the Piccadilly Circus Cell, consisting of the Offices of Defence run by Mungo Moore, Intelligence run by Suzanna Key, Sustainability run by Yottam Yellowfinch, Education run by 'Pokes' Pokeman, and Identity run by Chief Elder Ruth Stillspeare.

Paperless Post Act: 2061 U.S. law allowing designated corporations, government bodies and high-ranking Perspecta users to ignore paper correspondence, effectively killing off the private letter and letter post.

Percutaneous Endoscopic Gastrostomy System: *see* Potman Percutaneous.

Perspecta: Virtual reality computer application. Perspecta 1.0 was created in 2022 by Sylvia Rogers as an educational tool.

Perspecta Companion: A virtual aide or assistant for certain high-status Perspecta users.

Perspecta ID: unique to every Perspecta user.

Perspecta Plug: earplug that projects a 360-degree visual and audio bubble around the Perspecta user's head; introduced with Perspecta 2.0.

Perspecta suit: all-white, full-body outfit made with microfibres that connect the Perspecta user – when sitting in a rig – with the Universe.

Perpecta 3.0: long-awaited next-generation VR suite from Gnosys.

Perspecta Universe: In full, the Perspecta Virtual Reality Universe.

Peter's: the last music and cabaret club to survive the Upload, run by former theatrical producer Peter Pember; now closed.

Pittsburgh Pact: Security arrangement of 2060 under which the UN paid Gnosys to log the citizens of 193 member states into the Perspecta Universe.

Plug: *see* Perspecta Plug

Podd: Perspecta Operated Desginated Driver. Vehicle for up to eight Spectas, propelled above maglev boosters on the Podd Way. Latterly, wealthy Spectas have fitted their own

Podds with rotors and jets to allow travel beyond the Way. Podd seats double as haptic rigs so users can experience real journeys as if they were virtual.

Podd Way: the Gnosys transport network, built as part of the SmartCity programme and used solely by Spectas, though now in dwindling numbers. London's first stretch of the Podd Way opened in 2054 on the Euston Road.

pop: *see* holo-pop.

Potman Percutaneous: the company that supplies the Percutaneous Endoscopic Gastrostomy System used for human waste disposal in the Hab-Belts; headed by Gregory Potman.

resp: respirator for filtering the heavily polluted air of 2078.

Rogers Tower: VR construct overlooking Oakland, Apeiron.

Ronnie Scott's: Dusk-era jazz club, Frith Street, Soho.

Routemaster: classic London bus design of the Dusk.

Roxi: Retinal Oxygenating Xanthic Isopentyl, produced in pellets and inhaled using dispensers (disps) to give protection against atmospheric pollutants.

Roxi Runner: one of the smugglers – go-betweens to the Specta world – who supply the ghetto with vital Roxi.

San: the sanatorium at the Cell, on the old westbound Piccadilly Line platform, run by Yottam Yellowfinch.

Scav Squad: name adopted by Kid and his friends when they go scavving and for their band when they play music together.

scav: to 'scavenge' for supplies. Scavvers for the Piccadilly Circus Cell find most of what they need in the Ghetto or barter for it from others.

the Scrubs: Offliner Cell at Wormwood Scrubs, west London.

Seekers: people who rejected the Upload but are not affiliated with any group; many live on the streets and in the more ruinous buildings of Soho.

Shackleton's of Shadwell: east London respirator factory run by the Shackleton brothers.

Skull's: Soho emporium opened in 2048 on the site of Liberty's by Leonora Skull (now retired).

Slanda: Social media platform of the 2050s.

SmartCity programme: A deal between city government and Gnosys whereby the tech giant built hi-tech urban infrastructure in return for the right to build Data-Qs without hindrance. The first SmartCity initiative, in London, led to the Podd Way and the Flood Defence Wall.

Specta: a Perspecta user.

Specta suit: *see* Perspecta suit.

Spider: frame above the Chute in the Piccadilly Circus Ticket, designed by Rory Stillspeare and used for recreational climbing.

Spoot: pre-Upload business.

Streem: Gnosys' digital content service.

Synapps: Mid-century tech giant behind Mynd, a competitor for Perspecta.

T-Class Mig: A robotic Gnosys engineer or technician.

Teeth: *see* Migs.

Terrors: Soho child gang founded by a renegade Mig.

Ticket: the old Piccadilly Circus tube station ticket hall.

Toaster: *see* Flood Defence Wall.

tobacco: unobtainable in its genuine form; the chief alternative is made from ground-up ants.

UN: the United Nations, organisation founded during the

Golden Dusk to promote international peace and coopera-
tion. Since the 2060 Pittsburgh Pact, effectively subservient
to Gnosys.

UNCC: the United Nations Cyber Council.

Universe: *see* Perspecta Universe.

Upload: worldwide mass migration into the Hab-Belts and
into the Perspecta Universe, carried out in the wake of the
Pittsburgh Pact.

VEA: *see* Virtual Education Academy.

Virtual Diocese: ecclesiastical district operating in Perspecta,
introduced shortly before the Upload. In the Hab-Belt era,
worship via Perspecta has almost completely replaced physical church attendance.

Virtual Education Academy (VEA): Perspecta Universe
substitute for school, inspired by innovations begun during
the first great pandemic in the early 2020s.

Walkman: a Dusk-era portable player for music compact
discs (CDs).

Wall: barrier made of stacked double-decker buses, erected
by Soho Offliners at strategic points in the ghetto including
at the Piccadilly and Regent Street exits of Piccadilly Circus.

White Teeth: *see* Migs.

youngers: members of Offliner Cells between 12 and 24
years old.

YuVu: A VR universe produced by Microsoft, now defunct.

Zep or E-Zeppelin: a huge commercial Chariot used by
Gnosys for transportation of large payloads of people, cargo
or smaller vehicles; or as mobile Data-Qs in places where it is
impossible to build permanent Data-Q

ACKNOWLEDGEMENTS

This is the first novel I've ever written.

If I told you that writing it had been an enjoyable experience I would be lying. It's taken five years, four drafts and more *noes* than I can bear to recall to get to this point and I have had many more moments of doubt and despair during its creation than I have had confident, jubilant ones.

Yet it has also been the most fulfilling experience of my life to meet Kid and discover the Offliners; to connect the past and the future with the help of wonderful, wise Isabel Parry; and to assemble the Scav Squad as they begin the fight against Gnosys. It has challenged and stimulated me in a way that nothing else ever has before. I have learnt a little bit about how stories are told and how books are written and about the process of publishing them. And I have developed a prodigious desire to learn even more.

Thinking about the Offliners and the universe they belong to has led me to new and previously undiscovered places in my own world and in my own head. Threading the tale together has introduced me to hundreds of new people, both on the page and off. Many of them have become my friends and I hope some of them will want to remain in my life – and have me in theirs – forever.

Without these people, and all the people who were there

before I began, there would be no book.

First, I'd like to thank my mum and dad, who decided to bring me up in a cottage in the middle of the countryside, with a garden surrounded by lots of fields, in which the only other people to talk to were cows; and for allowing my older brother to go to boarding school when I was six; and for refusing to let me watch telly until I was ten or get a PlayStation, ever; and for reading me lots of stories every night before I went to bed. If they hadn't done all of these very unkind things, I wouldn't have been forced to spend a blissfully contented childhood all alone in my very own dreamworld full of wonderful characters and their exciting stories.

In many ways, *Kid: A History of the Future* is a love letter to London. When I was a little boy my parents would occasionally take me to the capital to visit one of its many grand museums or dazzling theatres. Before I'd even set foot in the city itself, I always remember being totally and utterly beguiled by the busyness and griminess and smokiness of Paddington Station. Even to this day getting off the train in London has always given me a huge adrenaline rush: a kind of 'I've arrived!' feeling. If my parents hadn't brought me up in the countryside, I often wonder whether the city would hold such fascination for me.

Second, I must thank Beth Miller, who was the first to suggest that I turn my idea into a book. Without her passion for these characters and her dogged determination to see them come to life, it is very unlikely that they'd ever have been at all.

Third, I must say a huge thankyou to my dear friend (and surrogate older brother) Bert V. Royal, who was kind enough to house, feed and water me when I began writing the story. It is thanks to Bert that Gnosys isn't called 'World Corp' and Perspecta isn't called 'World Talk'. Indeed, had it not been for Bert I don't think I'd ever have written beyond the prologue.

Fourth, enormous thanks must go to Abigail Berstrom and Megan Staunton of Gleam Titles, who took a huge chance on me and my book when every other agent in town had turned me down, and who expended huge amounts of time and energy getting it to the point at which we could take it to publishers. With this in mind, a very special thankyou ought to go to all the publishers who read that draft of *Kid: A History of the Future* – and who all turned it down. Without you I would never have been inspired to start my own publishing company and create the Offliner universe.

Fifth, I want to say thank you to my brother Tristan, who is my greatest ally and biggest supporter. Tristan was also generous, patient and mad enough to undertake the arduous task of proofreading the first draft of this book. He's so saintly that he even pretended to enjoy the book back when it was a soupy, scrambled-egg-like story, full of holes and typos.

Sixth, gargantuan thanks must go to John Garth who took that bowl of literary scrambled eggs and – as editor, brainstormer, and occasional co-writer – turned it into the three-course meal that you have just devoured. Without John's wisdom and intelligence, his tireless work with me on the plot and his almost extraterrestrial attention to detail, it is unlikely that we would have published this book and, even if we had, it would have been a completely different story and nowhere near as good a read.

Seventh, thanks must go to all my brilliantly supportive, long-suffering friends who were compassionate enough to listen to me banging on about this for five whole years without ever losing faith in me or dumping me for being so incredibly annoying. Most notably Kiki Hopkins, for her unwavering support since the very beginning. In fact I was with Kiki, sitting opposite her at a rickety little desk in a sweltering little office on Lexington Street, when Kid and the Offliners first walked into my life.

I'd like to thank Hugo Riley for his tolerance, diligence and astonishing creativity, but most of all for believing in me and Kid after everyone else had given up hope. Without Nico Bannister's illustrations I wonder whether anyone would ever have batted an eyelid at my words. If it hadn't been for the hard work of Talie Delamere and Felix Gibbons and everyone at Offliner Press, I'm almost certain that you wouldn't be reading this now.

As you can see, it takes an army, so last but not least thank you. Welcome to the ranks. This is the first novel I've ever written. Because of all of you, who have inspired, helped create, or read *Kid: A History of the Future*, it won't be my last.